SIMPLY
VORACIOUS

Books by Kate Pearce

The House of Pleasure Series

SIMPLY SEXUAL

SIMPLY SINFUL

SIMPLY SHAMELESS

SIMPLY WICKED

SIMPLY INSATISABLE

SIMPLY FORBIDDEN

SIMPLY CARNAL

SIMPLY VORACIOUS

Single Titles

RAW DESIRE

Anthologies

SOME LIKE IT ROUGH

LORDS OF PASSION

Published by Kensington Publishing Corporation

SIMPLY VORACIOUS

KATE PEARCE

APHRODISIA

KENSINGTON PUBLISHING CORP.

www.kensingtonbooks.com

1

1826, London, England

"Are you all right, ma'am? May I help you?"

Lady Lucinda Haymore flinched as the tall soldier came toward her, his hand outstretched and his voice full of concern. She clutched the torn muslin of her bodice against her bosom, and wondered desperately how much he could see of her in the dark shadows of the garden.

"I'm fine, sir, please ..." She struggled to force any more words out and stared blindly at the elaborate gold buttons of his dress uniform. "I'm afraid I slipped and fell on the steps and have ripped my gown."

He paused, and she realized that he had positioned his body to shield her from the bright lights of the house and the other guests at the ball.

"If you do not require my help, may I fetch someone for you, then?"

His question was softly spoken, as if he feared she might flee.

"Could you find Miss Emily Ross for me?"

"Indeed I can. I have a slight acquaintance with her." He

hesitated. "But first, may I suggest you sit down? You look as if you might swoon."

Even as he spoke, the ground tilted alarmingly, and Lucinda started to sway. Before her knees gave way, the soldier caught her by the elbows and deftly maneuvered her backward to a stone bench framed by climbing roses. Even as she shrank from his direct gaze, she managed to get a fleeting impression of his face. His eyes were deep set and a very light gray, his cheekbones impossibly high, and his hair quite white, despite his apparent youth.

She could only pray he didn't recognize her. No unmarried lady should be loitering in the gardens without a chaperone. Somehow she doubted he was a gossip. He just didn't seem to be the type; all his concern was centered on her, rather than making a grand fuss and alerting others to her plight. He released her and moved back, as if he sensed his presence made her uneasy.

"I'll fetch Miss Ross for you."

"Thank you," Lucinda whispered, and he was gone, disappearing toward the lights of the ballroom and the sounds of the orchestra playing a waltz. She licked her lips and tasted her own blood, and the brutal sting of rejection. How could she have been so foolish as to believe Jeremy loved her? He'd hurt her and called her a tease. Had she encouraged him as he had claimed? Did she really deserve what he had done to her?

Panic engulfed her and she started to shiver. It became increasingly difficult to breathe and she struggled to pull in air. Suddenly the white-haired stranger was there again, crouched down in front of her. He took her clenched fist in his hand and slowly stroked her fingers. She noticed his accent was slightly foreign.

"It's all right. Miss Ross is coming. I took the liberty of hiring a hackney cab, which will be waiting for you at the bottom of the garden."

"Thank you,"

"I'm glad I was able to be of service."

With that, he moved away, and Lucinda saw Emily behind him and reached blindly for her hand.

"I told my aunt I was coming home with you, and I told your mother the opposite, so I think we are safe to leave," Emily murmured.

"Good."

Emily's grip tightened. "Lucinda, what happened?"

She shook her head. "I can't accompany you home, Emily. Where else can we go?"

Emily frowned. "I'll take you to my stepmother's. You'll be safe there. Can you walk?"

"I'll have to." Lucinda struggled to her feet.

"Oh, my goodness, Lucinda," Emily whispered. "There is blood on your gown."

"I fell. Just help me leave this place." Lucinda grabbed hold of Emily's arm and started toward the bottom of the garden. She could only hope that Jeremy had returned to the ball and would not see how low he had brought her. She would never let him see that, *never*. With Emily's help, she managed to climb into the cab and leaned heavily against the side. Her whole body hurt, especially between her legs, where he had . . . She pushed that thought away and forced her eyes open.

It seemed only a moment before Emily was opening the door of the cab and calling for someone named Ambrose to help her. Lucinda gasped as an unknown man carefully picked her up and carried her into the large mansion. Emily ran ahead, issuing instructions as she led the way up the stairs to a large, well-appointed bedchamber. The man gently deposited Lucinda on the bed and went to light some of the candles and the fire.

Lucinda curled up into a tight ball and closed her eyes, shutting out Emily and everything that had happened to her. It was impossible not to remember. She started to shake again.

A cool hand touched her forehead, and she reluctantly focused on her unknown visitor.

"I'm Helene, Emily's stepmother. Everyone else has left, including Emily. Will you let me help you?"

Lucinda stared into the beautiful face of Madame Helene Delornay, one of London's most notorious women, and saw only compassion and understanding in her clear blue eyes.

Helene smiled. "I know this is difficult for you, my dear, but I need to see how badly he hurt you."

"No one hurt me. I slipped on the steps and . . ."

Helene gently placed her finger over Lucinda's mouth. "You can tell everyone else whatever tale you want, but I know what has happened to you, and I want to help you."

"How do you know?" Lucinda whispered.

"Because it happened to me." Helene sat back. "Now, let's get you out of that gown and into bed."

She talked gently to Lucinda while she helped her remove her torn gown and undergarments, brought her warm water to wash with, and ignored the flow of tears Lucinda seemed unable to stop.

When she was finally tucked in under the covers, Helene sat next to her on the bed.

"Thank you," Lucinda whispered.

Helene took her hand. "It was the least I could do." She paused. "Now, do you want to tell me what happened?"

"All I know is that I am quite ruined."

"I'm not so sure about that."

Lucinda blinked. "I'm no longer a virgin. What man would have me now?"

"A man who loves you and understands that what happened was not your fault."

"But it *was* my fault. I went into the gardens with him *alone*, I let him *kiss* me, I *begged* him to kiss me."

"You also asked him to force himself on you?"

"*No*, I couldn't stop him, he was stronger than me and . . ."

"Exactly, so you can hardly take the blame for what happened, can you?" Helene patted her hand. "The fault is his. I assume he imagines you will be forced to marry him now."

Lucinda stared at Helene. "I didn't think of that." She swallowed hard. "He said we needed to keep our love secret because my family would never consider him good enough."

Helene snorted. "He sounds like a dyed-in-the-wool fortune hunter to me. What is his name?"

Lucinda pulled her hand away. "I can't tell you that. I don't want to have to see him ever again."

"Well, that is unfortunate, because I suspect he'll be trying to blackmail his way into marrying you fairly shortly."

Lucinda sat up. "But I wouldn't marry him if he was the last man on earth!"

"I'm glad to hear you say that." Helene hesitated. "But it might not be as easy to avoid his trap as you think. You might be carrying his child. Does that change your opinion as to the necessity of marrying him?"

Lucinda gulped as an even more nightmarish vision of her future unrolled before her. "Surely not?"

"I'm sorry, my dear, but sometimes it takes only a second for a man to impregnate a woman," Helene continued carefully.

"I will *not* marry him."

"Then let us pray that you have not conceived. The consequences for a woman who bears an illegitimate child are harsh." Helene's smile was forced. "I know from Emily that you are much loved by your parents. I'm sure they would do their best to conceal your condition and reintroduce you into society after the event."

Lucinda wrapped her arms around her knees and buried her

face in the covers. Her despair was now edged with anger. If she refused to marry her seducer, she alone would bear the disgust of society, while Jeremy wouldn't suffer at all. It simply wasn't fair.

Eventually she looked up at Madame Helene, who waited quietly beside her.

"Thank you for everything."

Helene shrugged. "I have done very little. I wish I could do more. If you would just tell me the name of this vile man, I could have him banned from good society in a trice."

"That is very kind of you, Madame, but I'd rather not add to the scandal. I doubt he would relinquish his position easily, and my name and my family's reputation would be damaged forever."

"And, as your father is now the Duke of Ashmolton, I understand you all too well, my dear." Helene stood up. "But, if you change your mind, please let me know. I have more influence than you might imagine."

"I'd prefer to deal with this myself." Lucinda took a deep, steadying breath. "I need to think about what I want to do."

Helene hesitated by the door. "Are you sure there isn't another nice young man who might marry you instead?"

Lucinda felt close to tears again. "How could I marry anyone without telling him the truth? And what kind of man would agree to take me on those terms?"

"A man who loves you," Helene said gently. "But you are right to take your time. Don't rush into anything unless you absolutely have no choice. In my experience, an unhappy marriage is a far more terrible prison than an illegitimate child."

Lucinda looked at Helene. "Emily told me you were a remarkable woman, and now I understand why. I'm so glad she brought me here tonight."

"Emily is a treasure," Helene replied. "I only tried to offer you what was not offered to me—a chance to realize that you were not at fault, and a place to rest before you have to make some difficult decisions. Now go to sleep. I will send Emily to you in the morning, and I promise I will not tell her anything."

Lucinda slid down between the sheets and closed her eyes. Sleep seemed impossible, but she found herself drifting off anyway. Would any of her partners have noticed that she hadn't turned up for her dances with them? Would Paul be worried about her? She swallowed down a sudden wash of panic. If anyone could understand her plight, surely it would be Paul. . . .

Paul St. Clare prowled the edge of the ballroom, avoiding the bright smiles and come-hither looks of the latest crop of debutantes. Where on earth had Lucky gone? She was supposed to be dancing the waltz with him, and then he was taking her into supper. It was the only reason he was attending this benighted event after all.

Unfortunately, since the death of the sixth Duke of Ashmolton, speculation as to the new duke's potential successor had alighted on Paul, hence the sudden interest of the ladies of the *ton*. He'd grown up with the vague knowledge that he was in the line of succession, but hadn't paid his mother's fervent interest in the subject much heed until the other male heirs had started to die off in increasing numbers.

And now, here he was, the heir apparent to a dukedom he neither wanted nor felt fit to assume. It was always possible that the duke would produce another child, although unlikely, because of his wife's age. But Paul knew that even beloved wives died, and dukes had been known to make ridiculous second marriages in order to secure the succession. Paul's own father, the current duke's second cousin, had only produced one child before he died in penury, leaving his family dependent on the generosity of the Haymores for a home. In truth, Paul considered Lucky's parents his own, and was very grateful for the care they had given him.

Paul nodded at an army acquaintance, but didn't stop to chat. All his friends seemed to have acquired younger sisters who were just dying to meet him. In truth, he felt hunted. If he had his way, he'd escape this gossip-ridden, perfumed hell and ride up north to the clear skies and bracing company of his best friend, Gabriel Swanfield. But he couldn't even do that, could he? Gabriel belonged, heart and soul, to another.

Paul stopped at the end of the ballroom that led out on to the terrace, and wondered if Lucky had gone out into the gardens. He could do with a breath of fresh air himself. He was about to pass through the open windows when he noticed a familiar figure standing on the balcony staring out into the night.

Paul's stomach gave a peculiar flip. The sight of his commanding officer, Lieutenant Colonel Constantine Delinsky, always stirred his most visceral appetites. Of Russian descent, Delinsky was tall and silver-eyed with prematurely white hair that in no way diminished his beauty. Paul always felt like a stuttering idiot around the man.

Delinsky was looking out into the gardens of the Mallorys' house with a preoccupied frown. Paul briefly debated whether to disturb him, but the opportunity to speak to someone who wouldn't care about his newly elevated status was too appealing to resist.

"Good evening, sir."

Constantine turned and half smiled. "Good evening, Lieutenant St. Clare. I didn't realize you were here tonight. Are you enjoying yourself?"

"Not particularly," Paul said. "I find all these people crammed into one space vaguely repellant."

Again, that slight smile that made Paul want to do whatever he was told. "I can understand why. As a soldier, I always fear an ambush myself."

"Are you waiting for someone, sir?" Paul asked.

"No, I was just contemplating the coolness of the air outside, and deciding whether I wished to stay for supper or leave before the crush." Delinsky's contemplative gaze swept over Paul. "Did you come with Swanfield?"

"Alas, no, sir. Gabriel and his wife are currently up north taking possession of his ancestral home."

Constantine raised his eyebrows. "Ah, that's right, I'd forgotten Swanfield had married."

"I'd like to forget it, but unfortunately the man is so damned content that I find I cannot begrudge him his happiness."

"Even despite your loss?"

"*My* loss?" Paul straightened and stared straight into Delinsky's all-too-knowing eyes.

Delinsky winced. "I beg your pardon, that was damned insensitive of me."

"Not insensitive at all. What do you mean?"

Delinsky lowered his voice. "I always believed you and Swanfield were connected on an intimate level."

Paul forced a smile. "There's no need for delicacy, sir. Gabriel was happy to fuck me when there was no other alternative. He soon realized the error of his ways, or more to the point, I realized the error of mine."

Delinsky continued to study him and Paul found he couldn't look away. "Perhaps you had a lucky escape, St. Clare."

"You think so?"

"Or perhaps the luck is all mine."

A slow burn of excitement grew in Paul's gut. "What exactly are you suggesting, sir?"

Constantine straightened. "Would you care to share a brandy with me at my lodgings? I find the party has grown quite tedious."

Paul wanted to groan. "Unfortunately I accompanied my family to the ball. I feel honor bound to escort them home as well."

"As you should." Constantine shrugged, his smile dying. "It is of no matter."

Paul glanced back at the ballroom and then at the man in front of him. Despite Delinsky's easy acceptance of Paul's reason for not leaving with him, Paul desperately wanted to consign his family to hell and follow this man anywhere. Gabriel was lost to him. He needed to move past that hurt and explore new pastures. And when it came down to it, he had always lusted after Constantine Delinsky.

"Perhaps you might furnish me with your address, sir, and I can join you after I've dispensed with my duties."

"It really isn't that important, St. Clare."

"Perhaps it isn't to you, but it is to me," Paul said softly. "Give me your direction."

2

"Lucinda, dear, whatever is the matter? You jump like a scalded cat every time the door knocker goes. Are you expecting anyone in particular?"

Lucky glanced at her mother and managed a smile. She didn't really expect Jeremy to breach the forbidding walls of Haymore House, the Ashmolton mansion on Portland Square. But, if he really expected to marry her, he would have to confront her father at some point.

"I'm sorry, Mama, I didn't mean to disturb you."

The new Duchess of Ashmolton put her sewing aside and stared at her daughter with a worried frown. "You don't look as if you are sleeping. Is it the move to the new house?" She glanced around the palatial drawing room and gave a palpable shudder. "I must admit that these new ducal surroundings are rather too grand for me too."

"It is rather strange, Mama," Lucky hastened to agree. "I am finding it difficult to sleep, and poor Milly keeps getting lost when she goes from the kitchens to my room."

"She's not the only one who gets lost," the new duchess said gloomily. "If it wasn't for Parsons, I think I'd never find my way anywhere. But we'll get used to it. It's far harder on your father, you know. The previous duke was very secretive about his affairs, and as he lived to such an advanced age, it appears he had a lot to be secretive about."

"So I understand. I certainly feel sorry for poor Papa." Lucky's stomach gave an uncomfortable jolt as Parsons appeared at the door with a gentleman behind him. "Mama, it appears we have a guest."

She let out her breath as Paul St. Clare entered the room and greeted her mother with his usual affection. His blond hair was damp from the rain and his top boots scuffed. He never seemed to care about his appearance as much as most of the soldiers she knew, and he was always getting into trouble for it with his commanding officers.

Despite his easy airs and manners, he'd changed considerably since his capture and long imprisonment in Spain. Beneath his charm was an impenetrable layer of steel that had deflected any concern or interest his family had wished to bestow on him since his return. There was a restlessness about him now that both attracted and repelled Lucky. It was as if he was no longer quite civilized and hated the restraints society placed on him. She wasn't sure if she wished she had his courage, or hated that he made her feel so boring and ordinary.

"Good afternoon, Aunt. I came to see how you are doing in your new home." Paul glanced up at the gloomy portrait of the fourth duke killing a stag. "I suspect you might need to do some redecorating before you really begin to feel at home."

The new duchess laughed. "Indeed. I fear it will take me quite a while to change anything. I'm still convinced my father-in-law will pop out and start scolding me."

Paul grinned, his teeth white against his slightly tanned skin. "He was something of an ogre, wasn't he? I know he reduced my poor mama to tears on many happy occasions."

After accepting the offer of tea, Paul came to sit by Lucky, his searching gaze roaming her face, his hands capturing hers in one easy motion.

"What happened to you at the ball the other night?" he murmured so that her mother couldn't hear. "You abandoned me to the matchmaking mamas and their obnoxious daughters."

"I . . ." To her horror, Lucky found that she couldn't speak. Paul's brown eyes narrowed and he drew her to her feet.

"Aunt, Lucinda promised to show me a book she found in the library. May we go and fetch it? We'll be back in a trice."

He took Lucky's hand and whisked her out of the drawing room, down the stairs, and into the grand library below. As Paul was considered part of the family, Lucky knew her mother wouldn't object in the slightest to them being alone together. He shut the door and leaned against it, his arms folded over his chest.

"Out with it, Lucky. What's wrong?"

Lucinda turned her back on Paul and walked away from him. For the first time in her life, she realized that she didn't want to blurt out her troubles to him. Other people might think Paul too sweet to hurt a fly, but she knew differently. She had a horrible suspicion that he'd immediately demand the name of her seducer, challenge Jeremy to a duel, and be halfway to depriving her father of his last remaining heir if she let him.

She glanced at him over her shoulder. "I'm sorry I left you at the ball. I slipped in the garden and ripped a huge hole in my skirt. I had to ask someone to fetch Emily so that I could gather up my torn petticoats and escape through the garden before anyone saw me."

He didn't answer her, and after a moment she turned to face him.

"I'm sorry you ripped your gown." He angled his head to one side, his expression still courteous, but far too determined for Lucinda's comfort. "Now tell me what really happened."

"Nothing happened."

"Are you sure about that?"

She managed to hold his gaze. "I'm quite sure, Paul."

"I don't believe you."

"Ask Emily. She was with me on the ride home."

"And she'd lie about anything for you." He sighed. "Are you sure you don't want to tell me all about it?"

She spun away from him again, her arms wrapped around herself. "I'm not a child anymore, Paul. Please don't talk to me like that."

He leaned back against the door, blocking her exit. "You are a beautiful woman, Lucky. Even I have noticed that."

"Even you?" She raised her chin at him. "I thought I'd always be your annoying little sister."

His smile was wry. "Not my sister, no, never that, but I must admit that your growing into a beauty did surprise me."

She felt tears threaten. "I'm no beauty."

He considered her as if she were a piece of fine art he had never seen before. "Yes, you are. I'm not surprised you've taken so well with the *ton*."

"Not that well."

Goodness, she wanted to get away from his searching gaze before she forgot herself and cried out her fear and shame into the comfort of his shoulder as she'd always done before. But she couldn't do that. She was beyond cuddles and reassurances now. The choices she faced now were far more painful than even he could protect her from.

"Lucky? Whatever is wrong? Let me help you."

She looked up at his darling face, his brown eyes dark with concern, his whole body angled toward her. He would do anything for her. She'd always loved him, and now it was her turn to protect him. She had a horrible suspicion that if she begged for his help, he'd offer it unreservedly, and it wouldn't be fair to involve him when he wasn't in love with her, had never been in love with her.

"We should be getting back. Mama will be worried and you'll be wanting your tea, I'm sure."

She marched purposefully toward the door.

"Damn it, Lucky." He caught her elbow in a firm grip and yanked her against his side. She couldn't help flinching away from his suddenly intimidating male strength. Her breathing shortened. Could he hurt her, hold her down like Jeremy had? She'd never thought about it before, never considered how weak she was. . . .

"Let me go." Her voice wobbled and she hated it, hated what Jeremy had done to her anew.

"Lucky . . ."

He released her immediately, and opened the door wide for her to pass by him. She picked up her pale blue muslin skirts and made a very undignified run for the stairs.

Paul watched Lucky go with a frown. What the hell was wrong with her? When he'd caught her arm she'd stared at him as if he were a stranger intent on harming her. His suspicions intensified. What had changed to make her regard him as dangerous? Had some other man hurt her? *Touched* her?

He started after her and then slowed at the bottom of the stairs. He certainly couldn't storm into her mother's drawing room and demand answers she was obviously unwilling to give him. He could only hope she'd confide in him eventually. She always had before. He gripped the banister rail tightly. She *loved* him. His own arrogance alarmed him and he shook his head. Perhaps she didn't love him anymore and another had claimed her heart. He should be relieved about that, as he had very little to offer her.

He started slowly up the stairs. Then why wasn't he pleased

for her? Was he truly such a spoilsport that he wanted her to love only him? Disgusted at himself, he resolved to offer her his support and wait patiently for Lucky to reveal whatever was distressing her in her own good time.

After a pleasant half hour, Paul took his farewell and made his way to Lieutenant Colonel Delinsky's lodgings on Half Moon Street. Delinsky had invited him for an early supper and a visit to the theater. For the first time in a long while, Paul was aware of excitement coursing through his veins. On the night after the ball, Delinsky had proved a perfect companion, and Paul had forgotten his former nerves and actually enjoyed himself.

He knocked on Delinsky's door and was admitted by a manservant who ushered him through into the large sitting room, where his host sat reading by the fire. Delinsky immediately put his book aside and rose to his feet. He was dressed in his waistcoat and shirtsleeves, his coat discarded over the back of the chair.

"St. Clare, how kind of you to come." He gestured to the seat opposite him. "Gregor will serve our supper and then he'll be off for the night. I hope you don't mind."

"Not at all. I'm sure we can manage." Paul took the offered seat. "Thank you, sir."

Was the fact that the manservant was leaving for the night significant, or was Delinsky merely being polite? Sometimes Paul hated the subterfuge that came with his sexual preferences. Working out whether another man was interested in going to bed with him often seemed as complex and deadly as negotiating a peace treaty. It wasn't surprising when the punishments for sodomy were painful, humiliating, and in some cases terminal.

After the meal, Delinsky waited until the manservant cleared the small table between them and left before he poured them both glasses of red wine. He raised his glass. "I understand you are to be congratulated."

Paul groaned. "Have I been offered a military promotion I didn't know about? Not that that is likely to happen in the current climate. In truth, I'm thinking of selling out."

"A military promotion does seem unlikely," Delinsky conceded, "but I can see why you might be considering selling out. I expect you will be taking on new and far more onerous duties."

"You're talking about this Ashmolton business, aren't you?" Paul sighed. "Unfortunately it is true. Apparently I'm the heir presumptive of the new Duke of Ashmolton."

"As I said, you are to be congratulated."

"I'm not so sure about that." Paul took a gulp of his excellent wine. "I never thought to succeed to the title. There always seemed a satisfyingly large group of males ahead of me on various branches of the family tree. The war and the climate of India haven't worked in my favor."

"Most men would be delighted to succeed to a dukedom."

"I'm sure they would, but me?" Paul flicked a glance at Delinsky and found he was watching him intently. "You are my commanding officer. You know how well I respond to authority and protocol and everything else the blasted aristocracy stands for."

Delinsky's smile was wry. "You don't take orders worth a damn, but you are still one of the best officers I've ever had under my command, and one of the bravest."

Paul shrugged. "That is very kind of you, but I've done nothing that any man in my shoes would not have done."

"Not so. Swanfield said he couldn't have gotten all the prisoners out of that hellhole without your help."

"He's lying, of course," Paul said flippantly. "He simply didn't want to take all the glory for himself."

Delinsky sat back and studied him, one long-fingered hand wrapped around his wineglass. "You and Swanfield do have something in common. Neither of you can accept a compliment."

"We're not taught to accept praise. It is beaten out of us in school."

"So I've heard, although I understand that Swanfield didn't go to school."

Paul sipped at his wine. "You seem very well informed about Major Lord Gabriel Swanfield."

"I'm well informed about all the men I command. I find it useful to understand them."

"And why is that? Surely all you need to know is that they will die on your order?"

Delinsky went still. "You truly hold such a poor opinion of me?"

"Not of you, particularly, just of the English army in general."

"I'm not even English."

"Then why do you fight for us?"

A muscle flicked in Delinsky's jaw and his eyes narrowed. "You might have forgotten that my original regiment was decimated by Napoléon's forces, as was my entire country."

Paul let out his breath. "I apologize, sir. That was uncalled for. I have never doubted either your courage or your commitment to the cause." He put down his glass and rose to his feet. "Do you wish me to leave?"

Delinsky leaned his head back and looked up at him. "I don't want you to go anywhere. I find your honesty refreshing."

"Are you sure about that?"

"Quite sure. Now please, sit down and tell me about Swanfield. I understand he married Lisette Delornay-Ross."

Paul sank back down into his seat. "You know her?"

"From both the pleasure house and from society. She is a very interesting woman. I think she will do very well with Swanfield."

"I forget that you occasionally frequent the pleasure house."

"I'm not there as much as you are. Christian Delornay says that you are practically a member of the staff."

"Gabriel gave me his membership when he became part of the family." Paul grimaced. "He thought it might console me for his loss, and offer me other avenues of sexual delight."

"You haven't exactly lost him, have you? He only got married. I would imagine that Lisette Delornay is more accommodating than most wives would be of her husband's little peccadilloes."

"But I don't want to take advantage of their particular circumstances."

"Why not?"

"Because I think I deserve more."

Delinsky nodded. "So do I. Is that why you are almost always with a woman at the pleasure house?"

"You've watched me?" Paul looked straight into the other man's eyes and tried to suppress his excitement. "I was attempting to broaden my horizons."

"For what purpose?"

"Because I am a fool."

Delinsky frowned. "I do not understand."

"I promised Gabriel that I would at least learn how to bed a woman. And, to my surprise, I found that it was quite easy to do so and even quite enjoyable."

"Is it also because you wish to marry one day?"

"That would hardly be fair to my poor wife, would it? Marrying someone, knowing that you could never give them what they needed from you? Your whole self?"

"But you can bed a woman."

"That's not enough, though. I'm not sure I would be able to keep my vows and not always yearn for the forbidden."

"I understand." Delinsky nodded and rose to his feet. "I have to dress for the theater; would you mind continuing our conversation while I change?"

Paul felt a ridiculous rush of disappointment and barely managed to keep from voicing his objections to the sudden end of their conversation. Had Delinsky decided he was no longer interested? Did he see Paul's vacillating as a sign of weakness? He followed Delinsky into the other room, noting the newly brushed blue-and-gray uniform laid out on the bed and the shining black boots on the rug in front of the fire.

"Damnation," Delinsky muttered. "This button seems reluctant to open." He held out his wrist to Paul. "Is there a thread caught somewhere?"

Paul cupped Delinsky's elbow and bent his head over the proffered shirt cuff. The scent of warm man and washed linen breathed over him and made it hard to concentrate. It didn't help when Delinsky leaned in and spoke close to his ear.

"Can you work it free?"

Blindly, Paul fumbled with the buttonhole, untangling the reluctant thread. At last he succeeded in freeing the button and looked straight into Delinsky's silver eyes.

"I think I got it." His throat dried as the other man brought his thumb up to caress Paul's lower lip.

"Thank you."

Paul swallowed hard, the motion drawing the tip of Delinsky's thumb between his lips. He couldn't help flicking his tongue over the callused pad, felt the answering response in his cock as it thickened and sprang to life. Delinsky pushed his thumb deeper, and Paul sucked on it as if there was nothing else in the world he needed more.

When Delinsky slowly withdrew his thumb, Paul was pant-

SIMPLY VORACIOUS / 21

ing and already aroused. He watched as Delinsky unbuttoned the placket of his breeches and pulled his shirt over his head to display the taut muscles of his stomach and his battle-scarred chest. His hair there was pale and almost impossible to see. The lieutenant was also both taller and broader than Paul was.

Paul's gaze dropped to the opening of Delinsky's breeches, where an impressive bulge pressed against the constraints of his linen. With all his much-vaunted experience, the sight of Constantine Delinsky's cock made Paul feel like a shy virgin again. He wanted to fall to his knees and use his mouth on the man, to suck him until he came hard and fast.

He shuddered as Delinsky slid a hand under his chin and turned his face up.

"I want you, St. Clare. I have always wanted you."

"Then why didn't you tell me so before?"

"Because there was only ever one man for you—Gabriel Swanfield." He paused. "I will not compete for your affections. I would rather do without."

Paul held his gaze. "Gabriel doesn't want me anymore, and I don't want him."

"I'm not sure I believe you. You love the man."

"And because I love him, I had to let him go. Can you understand that?" Paul touched Delinsky's cheek. "I want this. I want you."

Delinsky's smile was slow and serious. "Then perhaps I'll wait before I put on my new clothes. I wouldn't want to spoil them."

He carried on stripping, his movements assured, as the long beautiful lines of his body emerged into the flickering candlelight. When he was completely naked, he turned to Paul, his cock jutting upward toward his flat belly, and gestured toward Paul's clothes.

"May I help you undress, or would you prefer to have me like this, fully clothed, with just your cock freed to fuck?"

Paul licked his lips and Delinsky's gaze followed the motion. "I'd like to touch you."

"Touch me, then."

Delinsky stepped closer until they were only a few inches apart, and the crown of his cock nudged against Paul's waistcoat. Paul brought his hands up to Delinsky's broad shoulders and felt him shiver. He spread his fingers wide and ran his palms over the other man's chest, tracing every scar, the tight buds of his nipples, and the lush curve of tense muscle.

"Ah," Delinsky sighed. "It's been a long time for me."

"You haven't indulged at the pleasure house?"

Delinsky opened his eyes. "Like you, I've had only women there."

Paul halted his explorations and stared back. "Which do you prefer?"

"I like both, but I prefer women." He hesitated. "Does that offend you? Would you rather I preferred men? Perhaps I should have made myself clear before we started this."

Paul closed his fingers around Delinsky's nipple and squeezed hard. "I can scarcely judge you, can I?"

A smile flickered over Delinsky's face, followed by a hiss as Paul twisted his flesh. "I'm not like Gabriel. I don't have to choose one sex or the other. I'll take you just as you are, if you'll do the same for me."

Paul slid one hand down toward Delinsky's cock and halted his fingers just above the now wet crown. He felt Delinsky's stomach tighten and saw the slight inclination of his hips, as if he couldn't help but strain toward Paul's touch. Being fully clothed while the more powerfully built Delinsky was naked was strangely erotic.

He sat on the edge of the bed and stared up at Delinsky. "Will you make yourself come for me?"

"Is that what you wish?" Delinsky's smile was wild. "I'm so

damned hard, it won't take me but a moment." He wrapped one hand around the base of his shaft, gripping himself tightly. Paul leaned forward and slid his arm around the other man's hips, bringing him closer.

"Come for me."

Delinsky began to move his hand up and down his shaft, his movements unhurried and graceful, only the intent expression on his face giving away his need. Paul inhaled the scent of the slick wetness now pouring from the slit of Delinsky's cock and sighed. He couldn't stop himself from sliding his forefinger around the crown, spreading the pearly wetness and lubricating the straining shaft.

"Oh, God," Delinsky groaned and he started to jerk his cock faster through his clenched fist, the slick sounds loud along with his panting breaths. He started to climax, and Paul watched every jet of come seep through Delinsky's fingers and drip down over his tight balls and thighs.

When Delinsky finished coming, Paul bent his head and carefully licked at his partner's shaft. He kept licking until Delinsky groaned and started to grow again. Paul looked up. "Undo my breeches, release my cock."

Delinsky obliged, and Paul stifled a moan as his cock and balls were carefully drawn away from his soaked underthings and cupped in Delinsky's broad palm.

"Kneel down."

Delinsky knelt between Paul's outstretched thighs; his superior height meant his cock was now level with Paul's. Paul reached forward and gripped the other man's shaft, bringing it against his own. Delinsky sighed as Paul rubbed their cocks together and shifted his grip to surround both of their thrusting shafts.

"Together, then," Paul murmured. "Let's come together." He slid his other hand into Delinsky's hair and brought his lush mouth down to meet his. "Kiss me." Delinsky obliged, his tongue delving deep, thrusting in the same intimate rhythm as their working cocks. Paul closed his eyes and simply enjoyed all the sensations: the feel of Delinsky's skin, the textures of his mouth, and the ferocious yearning behind his kisses. Heat and wet and thrusting flesh, tension building until he groaned into Delinsky's mouth and climaxed.

"Ah, God."

Con murmured a curse in his native language and tore his mouth away from Paul's only to bury his head in the crook of his shoulder as his come flooded all over their joined hands. It had been a long time since he'd allowed a man to touch him like this. He'd forgotten how good it felt. The sensation of his skin against the roughness of St. Clare's clothing made him feel raw and exposed.

He shuddered as St. Clare continued to touch him, his hands skimming over the curve of his arse, making his cock twitch in response. He hadn't lied when he'd told St. Clare that he'd always wanted him. St. Clare's soft brown eyes and blond hair concealed a man of great courage and worth, a true warrior. He'd always admired the man's stubborn loyalty to those he loved, a trait he'd found sadly lacking in his previous relationships.

Constantine raised his head and found St. Clare looking gravely at him. "May we dispense with your clothes now? I would like to see you."

St. Clare's mouth quirked up at the corner. It was one of the things Constantine liked most about him, his ability to joke about the absurdities of life. "I'm not quite as beautiful as you are."

Constantine smoothed a hand over the ragged sword scar at his hip. "I'm hardly perfect." He waited as St. Clare shrugged out of his coat and waistcoat and started on the buttons of his shirt. "May I help you?"

"Of course. Can you undo the cuffs of my shirt? I don't think you'll have any problems with them."

Constantine obliged, and St. Clare pulled the shirt over his head, emerging with his hair sticking up like a blond brush. He sat on the bed and braced his booted foot against the bedpost to remove his footwear and stockings. All that remained were his breeches, which he shed quickly and tossed toward the nearest chair. He was finely built, all slight grace and hard muscle, a sharp contrast to Constantine's broader frame.

Constantine reached out and touched St. Clare's back. "Did this happen to you when you were imprisoned? The scars from a flogging always take a long time to heal."

"I doubt they'll ever disappear," St. Clare answered. "And with my disrespect for authority, I'm quite used to being beaten."

"Your school system is barbaric," Constantine murmured as he joined St. Clare on the bed. "I'm surprised any of you survived it."

"At least surviving it meant we were well prepared for the horrors of war. My uncle once told me that the system was based on the Spartan *agoge*."

Constantine traced a line down St. Clare's sternum. "With your shield, or on it, eh? That makes a terrible kind of sense." He bent to press a kiss over St. Clare's heart. "By the way, you may call me Constantine, or Con, if you prefer."

"And you may call me Paul." St. Clare's quiet chuckle resonated through his chest. "I'm not sure I dare call you by your given name. You will always be Lieutenant Colonel to me."

Constantine cupped the other man's balls. "Not if you sell out. I think I'd prefer it if you did."

Paul sighed. "I might have no choice. My uncle has already suggested it, and with the current peace, I'm hardly likely to be needed unless I go to India or those damned ex-colonies."

Constantine stroked his thumb along the soft skin on the

underside of Paul's thickening cock. "I'd prefer you to stay here."

"Still giving me orders, sir?"

Constantine raised himself up on one elbow and licked delicately at the tip of Paul's cock. "I believe I am. Now perhaps you should lie back and do exactly what you are told."

3

Lucky didn't want to go to the theater, but her mother had refused to listen to her excuses and practically ordered her into the carriage. Sometimes it was easier to obey than to think up another pathetic reason for not wanting to leave the house. At least she might meet with Emily and share her worries without her mother overhearing.

Emily, her brother Richard, and their father were already awaiting them in their box. Lucinda curtsied as Richard bent over her gloved hand and kissed it. He was a pleasant man with a distinct look of Emily and their father, Lord Philip Knowles. She suspected little ruffled Richard's calm composure, and wondered anew how he felt stuck in the middle of the colorful and often scandalous Delornay-Ross clan.

"Lady Lucinda, such a pleasure." He pulled out a chair for her. "Are you looking forward to the performance? I understand from Emily that Shakespeare is a favorite of yours."

"Indeed he is," Lucinda replied as she sat down and opened her fan. "And I particularly enjoy *As You Like It*."

"So do I," Richard replied. "I believe Emily is most enamored of *Romeo and Juliet.*"

Emily took the seat on Lucinda's other side. "And what's wrong with that?"

"Nothing, my dear sister, if your idea of true love is a double suicide."

Emily fixed him with a quelling stare. "It is *romantic,* Richard. Don't you understand anything?" She nudged Lucinda. "Isn't it, Lucky. Tell him."

In the throes of dealing with her own destroyed romance, and realizing that in reality the drama of suicide would only destroy her family further, Lucinda hesitated.

"Lucky!" Emily exclaimed. "How can you not agree with me?"

Richard reached across and patted his sister's gloved hand. "Mayhap Lady Lucinda has a little more common sense than you do, Emily."

Emily was staring at Lucinda. "Maybe she has. . . ."

Lucinda avoided her friend's gaze and stared out over the glittering theater. Almost a week had passed since the unfortunate incident at the ball, and she still hadn't decided what to do about Jeremy. Of course, she'd stayed home like the coward she was, so he'd had no opportunity to accost her anyway. Her gaze scanned the crowds. Was he out there somewhere, just waiting for the opportunity to talk to her?

A loud clashing sound made her jump and look toward the orchestra pit, where the conductor had just taken his place on the podium. The small orchestra started playing and the lights in the theater were extinguished as the curtain rose on an all-too-familiar scene.

Lucinda forced herself to relax. Even if Jeremy was here, there was nothing he could do to spoil her enjoyment of the play—at least until the interval. She snapped her fan shut and placed it in her lap. In truth, she was tired of feeling powerless and hiding from him. Perhaps it was time to be brave and face him after all.

When the curtains shut after the first act, she turned to Emily, who was enthusiastically applauding.

"Will you walk out with me? I'm feeling a little restless."

"If you wish." Emily raised her voice in the direction of her father, who was deep in conversation with the duchess. "Papa, Lucinda and I are going for a stroll. We'll be back shortly."

Before her mother could object, Lucinda headed for the door. The narrow corridor between the boxes was jammed tightly with people either exiting or visiting other playgoers. Lucinda managed to fight her way through the throng to the slightly less crowded landing and turned to look for Emily.

Before she could spot Emily, someone cupped her elbow, and Lucinda had to fight the impulse to shriek and pull away. She looked up into the pleasant face of her rescuer from the ball on the previous week.

"I thought it was you, ma'am. Have you recovered from your ordeal?"

Lucinda could detect no hint of sarcasm or condescension either in his question or in his expression, only a genuine desire to see if she was all right. In the brilliant light from the chandeliers, she could now see how handsome her rescuer truly was, and how young despite the whiteness of his hair. When had his hair turned that color? Why couldn't she have met him before she met Jeremy? One direct look from this man made her realize how mistaken she'd been in thinking Jeremy was either strong or honest.

"I'm quite well, sir," Lucinda murmured. "And thank you again for your assistance."

"It was nothing, ma'am." He smiled and kissed her gloved hand. "I'm just pleased to see that you are well." His attention drifted over her shoulder. "Ah, here comes your good friend,

Miss Ross. At least I know I am leaving you in good hands again."

"Lieutenant Colonel," Emily said cheerfully. "Are you enjoying the play?"

When her soldier turned to Emily, Lucinda was all too conscious of the loss of his warm grip on her hand. How strange that his touch didn't frighten her, while she dreaded even breathing the same air as Jeremy again.

"Indeed I am, Miss Ross." He bowed and briefly held Emily's hand. "How is your family? I understand that your sister has recently married one of my past officers."

"That is correct, sir. Lisette is currently up in Cheshire being introduced to the Swanfield family estates."

"Then I wish her and Swanfield much happiness."

Lucinda watched him smile and envied Emily both her ease of address and her large acquaintance. Before her fall from grace, Lucinda would've barely waited until the lieutenant colonel walked away before bombarding Emily with demands for all the salient details about his marital state and prospects. Now it was too late. What would a man like him ever see in her?

He turned back as if he'd sensed her distress. "Well, it was a pleasure to see you again, and in such improved spirits, ma'am."

"It's 'my lady,'" Lucinda murmured. "I'm not married." As soon as she spoke, she blushed at the absurdity of even mentioning such a stupid detail.

He brought her hand to his lips again. "My lady, then, but still a pleasure." He nodded at Emily. "Good-bye, Miss Ross."

He turned and walked back into the crowd, leaving Lucinda staring after him. Emily drew her arm through Lucky's and walked them over to one of the long windows.

"Constantine Delinsky is a lovely man, isn't he? I've no idea why he hasn't married. He must be past thirty now."

Constantine . . . Lucinda sighed. "He is indeed lovely."

"And not married."

"Have you set your cap at him then, Emily?"

"Unfortunately, I've known him for several years, and he's never so much as glanced my way." She paused. "He seemed far more interested in you."

"Only because he sees himself as my knight in shining armor."

"I think it is more than that. Would you like me to introduce you to him properly next time we meet? I wasn't sure if you wished to reveal your true identity."

"I don't. It's better if he forgets all about me."

Emily touched her cheek. "Oh, Lucky, just because you were kissed at the bottom of the garden and ripped your dress running away doesn't mean you are sunk below reproach. I've done far worse than that."

But it was easy for Emily to say that. With her eclectic family, she wasn't subject to the same strict rules Lucinda had to abide by. The conduct of the daughter of a duke must be above reproach, and so far she had failed miserably at that.

Emily's gaze narrowed. "That *was* all that happened, wasn't it, Lucky? Helene wouldn't tell me anything."

Lucinda went to reply and then saw Jeremy gesticulating at her over Emily's shoulder. Her smile faltered and panic warred with anger at his casual belief that she would come when he called her. But if she didn't face him now, would he think he had won? She had to deal with him at some point, and now that she knew what his handsome exterior concealed she would be on her guard.

Lucinda patted her best friend's hand. "We should be getting back. I'll need to visit the necessary, so I'll meet you at the box."

"I can wait for you, if you like," Emily offered.

"No, I'll be fine." Lucinda gathered her skirts and headed for the staircase Jeremy had already descended.

He caught her midway down the stairs and drew her onto a

narrow landing behind a curtain that concealed a locked exit door. She had no desire to be alone with him for even a second, but it seemed she had no choice.

"Lucinda, my dear."

"Good evening, Mr. Roland."

Lucinda stared up at his familiar face and it was as if the scales had fallen from her eyes. He looked older, anxious, and far less pleasant. Why hadn't she noticed the tension running through him before, the lack of openness and the calculation in his stare?

"Lucinda, my *darling*." He reached for her and she took a hasty step backward.

"Don't touch me."

He smiled at the sharpness of her tone. "You didn't say that last time we met. In fact, I seem to remember you begging me to kiss you."

"I was a fool."

His smile widened and contained a mixture of triumph and pity that made Lucinda want to slap him. "I understand that you might be feeling a little guilty for throwing yourself at me like that, my love. But there is no need for remorse. I am quite willing to marry you and cover up your indiscretion."

"*My* indiscretion?" Lucinda gathered all her courage and forced herself to look into his eyes. She was so glad she'd spoken to Madame Helene. "I'm not willing to marry you at all. In fact, the very thought of it makes me want to puke."

He studied her for a long moment and then smiled. "I don't see that you have a choice. Do you want me to broadcast your shame to the *ton,* to your family, to your *father?*"

"The only thing I am ashamed of is being taken in by you."

"You love me."

"I do not." She steadied her voice. "My father will never force me to marry you."

"Are you so sure of that? He's just assumed his new title. I doubt he'll immediately want to deal with a scandal concerning his only child. It will affect the way he is seen by the elite forever."

"My father will never force me to marry you." Lucinda repeated her statement as calmly as she could with a confidence she was far from feeling. "He trusts me."

"More fool him." Jeremy gave a harsh laugh, all pretense of civility now gone. "I'll give you another couple of days to consider your position, and then I'll meet you again."

"My position will not change, sir. I can assure you of that."

"Brave words, my dear, but I'm not convinced you mean them," he sneered. "I know how much your family means to you, and that you would rather die than besmirch your father's honor." He shoved his face close to hers. "And believe me, I'll ruin you all if you don't see sense and marry me."

Even as Lucinda recoiled from the violence in his eyes, he spun on his heel, shoved the curtain aside, and stormed away. Lucinda leaned back against the wall, wiped his spittle from her face, and waited until her knees stopped trembling. The bell sounded, announcing the beginning of the second act, and she took a deep, steadying breath. If she was a true lady, shouldn't she be swooning at her despoiler's feet instead of thinking up ways of killing him? In truth, her lack of sensibility seemed a blessing at this moment.

If she didn't return to the box, her mother would become anxious, and that was to be avoided at all costs.

She started to walk back up the stairs. Jeremy was right about one thing: She would do anything to avoid upsetting her parents, particularly her father. He had so much to deal with at the moment. His new ducal responsibilities and his government appointments made for a heavy burden she had no wish to add to.

But was she willing to sacrifice herself to a life with Jeremy by assuring her parents that she wanted to marry him? Wouldn't those lies be equally as cruel as not telling them the truth? She stood for a moment at the top of the stairs and stared at nothing. She couldn't tell them the truth.

A couple of uniformed men came down the stairs on the opposite side of the landing, and Lucinda ducked out of sight. She might not be able to talk to her parents, but perhaps she could talk to Paul. It seemed she had little choice. If she made him swear not to ask her exactly who had dishonored her, he might at least have a fresh perspective on her dilemma.

The thought of his knowing what she had done made her heart clench, and she brought her hand to her bodice. She could only hope he would still speak to her afterward and would be able to think of a way out of her horrible plight.

Paul glanced up as Constantine reclaimed his seat beside him. "Where did you go? I lost you in the crush."

"I met with an acquaintance of mine, and stopped to ask her how she did."

"An old acquaintance?"

Constantine squeezed Paul's knee. "Not that kind of friend." He hesitated. "In truth, I'm not even sure exactly who she is."

"Cinderella, perhaps? Did you retrieve her glass slipper for her at a ball?"

"Nothing quite so romantic. I merely assisted her when she needed a way to escape an uncomfortable situation." He frowned. "Not that she would accept much in the way of help from me."

Paul studied the other man's face. "You seem concerned about her."

Constantine sighed. "You know how it is when one of your young soldiers faces his first enemy fire, or makes his first kill? That terrible look of shock—as if the whole world has suddenly become a far more brutal and uncaring place?"

Paul shuddered. "Unfortunately I do."

Constantine shook his head. "This will sound ridiculous, but you do not expect to see that look on the face of a young woman at a ball."

Paul put his hand over Constantine's clenched fist. "It sounds as though you did the best you could for her."

"I did, but you know yourself that once that comfortable screen has been ripped from your eyes, the world is never the same again. I wish I could restore it to her, but I have no idea how to do it."

Paul waited until Constantine looked back at him, and could only admire his lover's character even more. "I don't know about you, sir, but I'd rather be back in bed than here with all these people."

"Indeed. Shall we go?"

Paul rose to his feet. "I would be delighted."

4

"Paul, I'm so glad you could come."

"It is always a pleasure to see you; you know that. Now what is the dark mystery that made me have to skulk around the house until your mother left?"

Paul squeezed Lucky's hands and then gave her a hug. Her whole body tensed, and she immediately shied away from him and returned to pacing the rug in front of the fire. She looked as if she hadn't been sleeping well, with dark circles under her eyes and her mouth pinched and drawn. He took a seat by the fire and continued to watch her carefully.

"There is something I want to ask you."

"Then go ahead." He gestured at the seat opposite him. She didn't seem to notice and continued to walk, this time with her back to him.

"A friend of mine finds herself in a difficult situation, and as I have no useful advice to give her, I thought of you."

"A friend."

"Yes, she . . . behaved quite indiscreetly at a ball recently, and now the man with whom she . . . dallied is insisting that they must marry to save her reputation."

Paul frowned and rapidly tried to work out exactly what Lucinda was really saying. "When you say 'dallied,' what do you mean?"

"What do you think I mean? She was alone with this man without a chaperone. That alone is enough to force an offer of marriage—you know that."

"But does she want to marry the man?"

An almost imperceptible shiver shook through Lucinda, and Paul tensed. "No, I don't believe she does."

"Then surely all she has to do is tell him she doesn't wish to wed him. If he is a gentleman, he'll accept her decision and withdraw his suit."

She slowly faced him, her expression blank. "And what if he won't?"

"Then he is a complete and utter scoundrel, and she should inform her parents and ask them to deliver the news for her."

"And what if she doesn't want to tell her parents?"

Up until then, he'd quite decided they were talking about her, but that didn't fit at all. Lucky's parents adored her and would never hesitate to set any man about his business who had offended their daughter.

"Why wouldn't she tell her parents?"

She turned away from him again. "Perhaps she dreads upsetting them, or they are already burdened with great responsibilities she fears to add to."

Paul considered everything she had told him anew. "I would still counsel her to talk to her parents. I doubt they would reject her entirely." Her sudden, brittle laugh was unexpected. "What exactly did I say to amuse you?"

"Nothing in particular. It's just that your advice is exactly the same as the advice I thought to give her."

"What else did you expect me to say?"

She stared down at the floor. "I'm not quite sure. I just hoped . . ."

Paul sighed. "Lucky, will you please sit down and talk to me? None of this is making much sense." She didn't move, and he got out of his chair and went over to her. "Lucky . . ." When she finally raised her head, her eyes were full of tears, and he instinctively took her into his arms. "What is it, love? Surely you know you can tell me anything?"

"Not this," she whispered against the lapel of his coat.

He smoothed a curl back from her pale forehead and tucked it behind her ear. He couldn't have his Lucky in tears, and whatever had happened, he was sure he could fix it. If some young fool had tried to compromise her over a stolen kiss, he'd soon sort that out. He gave her his handkerchief.

"Nonsense, you can tell me anything." He paused. "What will it take to make you confide in me? Must I swear not to tell another soul under pain of death?"

She finished dabbing at her face with the handkerchief and raised her head to look at him. "You would promise that?"

He hadn't really expected her to believe his melodramatic statement, but the desperate hope in her blue eyes undid him. Mentally he berated himself. How bad could it be? He was sure he would be able to persuade her to confide in her parents anyway. He traced a cross over his heart.

"I promise I will not tell a soul."

She sighed and fixed her gaze on his waistcoat. "I wasn't talking about a friend."

"I gathered that," Paul said gravely. "Are you saying that some man is pestering you to marry him?"

"He's not pestering me. He's insisting."

"Because you let him steal a kiss?"

She pulled out of his arms. "No, because I let him steal *everything*." She raised her chin, her gaze defiant. "Do you understand now why I don't want to tell my parents? Their only daughter, ruined for the marriage mart."

Paul heard her through a gathering cloud of disbelief and rage. "Who was it?" She shook her head, but he took a step toward her. "Who in *damnation* was it?"

She swallowed hard and flinched away from him. "I'm not telling you."

His rage cooled to a deadly white heat and his hand came to rest on the hilt of his sword. "I'll kill him."

"And create exactly the kind of scandal I am trying to avoid?" Her voice was shaking, but he had to give her credit for standing her ground. "I will not marry him. I just need to find a way to avoid the scandal."

"When I've lopped off his head you'll be able to avoid him permanently."

She touched his arm. "And have you facing a murder charge for me? I don't think I could live with myself if that happened. *I'd* rather kill him."

"Lucinda, we can have him disposed of quietly. I have friends who could arrange it, I swear it."

"I can't condone another human being's murder. I just can't."

"You won't have to. I'll take care of it for you. You'll never even have to know," Paul said urgently.

"All I care about is protecting my parents from the folly of my actions," Lucinda said. "My father has recently become a *duke*. I *cannot* let him down now."

Paul had taken up pacing now. "Lucky, he won't care. His first priority will always be you and his family. If you won't let me kill the bastard, tell your father and leave him to sort it out. Mayhap the fool will allow himself to be bought off."

"I don't think he will. I truly believe he wants to marry me." She sighed. "He thinks to influence my father and gain a substantial part of his fortune, supposedly on my behalf."

"He *told* you this?"

"Well, he has no reason to lie to me anymore, does he? I met with him yesterday, and he laid out his plans quite plainly. He thinks the dukedom can be milked for his entire lifetime."

There was a bitter weariness in her tone that he'd never heard before. "Lucky, you have to tell your father."

"And what will he do, Paul?" She faced him, her hands clasped tightly at her waist. "Have you thought this through?"

Paul slowly shook his head.

"He'll either face the scandal head-on and we'll all be ruined, or he'll try and solve it in a different way."

"Exactly. He'll find a way to avoid a scandal."

Her gaze softened. "Yes, he'll try and make you marry me. You know that is his fondest wish, and he'll have the perfect opportunity to push for it."

Paul stared at her for a long moment, as all the air in his chest seemed to explode outward. There was a terrifying sense of inevitability to this moment that made him want to howl and rage at the Fates. Instead, he took a deep, steadying breath.

"Then we'll have to marry."

Lucinda stared at Paul. "*What?*"

He straightened like a man ready to walk out to his death. In other, less personal circumstances, she might have laughed at his resolute face.

"We'll have to marry." He nodded jerkily. "There is no other solution."

"No! That's not what you are supposed to say!"

He raised his eyebrows at her. "What the hell does that mean?"

"You're supposed to offer to take me away for a few months until the scandal dies down, or *something*. You're not supposed to offer yourself up as a willing sacrifice!"

He looked at her steadily. "But I am willing. Didn't I just tell you that I'd do anything for you?"

"But I can't let you do that." Lucinda gathered herself and practically galloped toward the door. "I'll think of another way."

"Lucky, don't you dare run away from me again," Paul said quietly and started after her. "We haven't decided what to do!"

She glanced at him over her shoulder. "I can't drag everyone down with me, Paul. I'll just have to marry him."

He marched toward her, his expression furious. "You will do no such thing!"

She didn't dare wait to see if he would try and catch her but sprinted for the relative safety of her bedchamber, leaving her confused Sir Galahad behind. Talking to him had only made her even more aware of her folly and her stupid belief that someone else would come along to make everything right for her. She now knew that the price for that help was far too high. She alone could make this right, and she would have to find a way to do so.

After ascertaining that his uncle wasn't home, Paul made his way to the pleasure house, his thoughts in a daze. He was supposed to be meeting Constantine there anyway, and somehow it seemed the most natural place to go to deal with his suddenly upended life.

Ambrose was sitting at the kitchen table, drinking from a tankard of ale and reading a newspaper. He looked up as Paul entered the kitchen and nodded an absent greeting. Paul took the seat opposite and poured himself a pint of ale. He drank it down in one swallow and poured another.

"Are you feeling all right, St. Clare?" Ambrose inquired. "You look a little green around the gills."

Paul sighed. "Is it that obvious? I've had something of a shock."

Ambrose lowered the paper. "Are your family all well? The duke and duchess? Lady Lucinda?"

"They are all well, thank you," Paul replied.

"And yourself?"

"I'm fine too." He groaned and buried his face in his hands. "I'm just grappling with an impossible dilemma."

"Is this about your relationship with Constantine Delinsky?"

Paul peered at Ambrose through his fingers. "You are full of questions today. How is it that you know everything that goes on in society without appearing to move from this kitchen? What *about* Constantine Delinsky?"

"He is your commanding officer. Has that led to any official inquiries as to your relationship?"

"Not at all." Paul glared at Ambrose. "Don't add to my list of potential worries. Actually, I'd already decided to sell out."

Ambrose nodded. "If you intend to pursue a relationship with the lieutenant colonel, then that would probably be the wisest thing for both of you."

"I'm not selling out because of him." Paul rested his chin on his hand and stared at the scarred pine table. "There is little hope of advancement unless I choose to go overseas. I'm not exactly a favorite among the top brass. And my uncle wants me to sell out."

"As you are the heir to a dukedom, I suppose that's fair enough."

Paul fixed Ambrose with his most quelling stare. "It isn't fair. It isn't fair at all. I'll make a bloody awful duke and you know it." *A bloody awful husband as well, but that seemed almost inevitable too. . . .*

Ambrose opened his mouth, and Paul held up his hand. "And don't tell me how lucky I am."

"I wasn't going to." Ambrose patted his hand. "I wouldn't want that responsibility either."

"Thank you," Paul said. "I'm sorry. I'm not in the best of humors."

Ambrose laughed, his teeth white against his dark skin. "*I'm* surprised you haven't slit your throat."

Despite his worries, Paul found himself grinning back at his old friend and sometime lover. "Perhaps you'd like that honor?"

"No thanks, my friend. I detest the sight of blood. Ask Delinsky. He's a true military hero."

Gloom crashed over Paul again. "He's supposed to be coming here to see me this evening."

"Isn't that a good thing?" Ambrose asked gently. "I know you've always liked him."

"And as usual the Fates are working against me. I'm going to have to tell him good-bye tonight."

"Why? Does he object to your work here? You can always stop doing that. You aren't actually employed here. In truth, Delinsky looks happier than I've ever seen him."

"Don't say that," Paul groused. "I'm happy, too, and I'm going to have to spoil everything."

Ambrose sat back. "You are dying, aren't you? Tell me the truth."

"I might as well be." Paul rose to his feet. "Is Madame Helene here by any chance?"

"I believe she is. She had a meeting with Christian earlier and stayed to finish up some paperwork."

"Excellent." Paul blew Ambrose a kiss. "Thank you, my friend."

"Will you be coming back to the kitchen before you see Delinsky? I'll ask Madame Durand to save you some dinner."

"That would be most welcome." Paul wasn't sure if he'd ever feel like eating again, but he had to be polite. "Now let me go and find Madame."

He found her in her old office, sitting behind her desk, a pair of spectacles perched on the end of her pert nose as she studied a crumpled letter. She wore a faded muslin gown that did nothing to diminish her considerable beauty. He knocked softly on the open door, and she glanced up at him and smiled.

"Paul, I was just thinking about you today. How is your family?"

He came in and shut the door behind him, noticing the piles of boxes strewn around the floor and an unusual sense of emptiness.

Helene made a wide gesture encompassing all the disorder. "I'm cleaning out my office so that my daughter-in-law, Elizabeth, can use it. I can't believe how much I have accumulated over the past twenty or so years. Can you find a seat?"

Paul removed a box of ledgers from a chair and sat. Madame put down her work and studied him.

"Now what can I do for you?"

"I would appreciate your advice."

"Of course. How can I help you?"

"I asked Lady Lucinda to marry me, and she refused."

Helene went still. "What on earth made you do that?"

He sighed. "She needs to marry, and it will make her family happy if she marries me. That's all I am going to say about the matter."

"I'm sure that isn't all there is to it."

He met her gaze. "You are correct, but I don't wish to betray a confidence."

"And what if I told you that I already know why Lady Lucinda might need to marry?"

Paul blinked at her. "You *know*?"

"Emily brought her to me after the event."

"That was very astute of her." Paul let out his breath. "Did Lucky tell you who the bastard was?"

"No, she didn't, and even if she had, I wouldn't tell you."

"But you would take steps to deal with the man."

Madame's smile was cold. "Naturally. I would have ruined him."

"I appreciate that. If you do manage to find out who he is, I'd appreciate being informed of his demise."

"You wish him dead?"

"He hurt Lucky. She is . . ." He struggled to find the words. "She is the sweetest girl I have ever known."

"She's far more than that, Paul. She is also very brave," Helene said quietly. "Faced with similar circumstances, most women of her class would have gone running to their parents, screaming for help. She told me she doesn't want to worry them."

"She said the same to me."

Helene watched him closely, nodding as he explained Lucky's somewhat flawed reasoning about worrying her parents and her belief that there had to be another way out of her dilemma.

"She can't marry the man. I won't allow it."

Helene studied him. "Even at the expense of your own freedom?"

He sighed. "Madame, you know me. I am no more suited to be a woman's husband than I am to be a duke, but Lucky is . . . she is the most important thing in the world to me. I can't allow her to suffer."

"Would she not suffer being tied to you?"

"I thought I would tell her the truth about myself, the whole truth. Then she can make an honest decision about whether she really wants to be tied to a man like me."

"You don't think she will be too naive to understand what you are saying to her, and grasp at any opportunity to avoid disgrace?"

"I'll make sure she understands me," Paul said firmly. "And as she has already turned me down once, I don't think she is grasping at straws."

Helene studied her clasped hands. "This other man might be able to give her children."

Paul raised his head as the hollow sensation in his gut increased. "If she wants children, she can have them, either with me or a man of her choosing. I'd never stand in the way of her happiness."

Helene sighed. "But what about your happiness?"

Paul fleetingly thought of Constantine Delinsky and swallowed down his unexpected grief that something so promising was doomed to a quick death. He met Madame's worried gaze head-on.

"My uncle and aunt brought me up, and they have asked very little of me. If marrying Lucky makes them happy, secures her future, and keeps this fool away from her, I'll be happy, I swear it."

Madame's face softened. "You are a good man, Paul."

"Not according to the Bible and the laws of this land."

Madame snapped her fingers. "As if we care about that here." She hesitated. "May I make a suggestion?"

"Of course."

"Lady Lucinda is still very young, but she isn't stupid. When you tell her about your sexual tastes, don't be coy. Tell her the whole truth. It is only fair."

Paul stood up and bowed. "I agree, and thank you for your help." He glanced around the room. "Are you leaving us for good?"

"It appears that I am." She swallowed hard. "Philip is determined to whisk me away on what he calls a much belated wedding trip, and Christian is perfectly capable of running the place, as you know."

"You'll still be missed."

"Nonsense." Her smile was a little uncertain. "You won't even notice that I'm gone."

Paul walked toward her and bent to kiss her hand. "We'll notice. But have a wonderful trip."

Tears glinted in her beautiful blue eyes. For a moment, Paul wondered whether he had the nerve to put his arm around the formidable founder of the pleasure house. Before he could act on the notion, she drew away from him and busied herself with the books on the desk.

"Well, I mustn't keep you, Paul. I'm sure you have a lot to discuss with Constantine Delinsky."

Paul groaned. "Does everyone know about that?"

"Everyone who cares about you. I'm sorry that you have finally found each other just as your path is so unsure."

"You don't need to worry. I won't bed anyone if I marry."

Helene smiled. "That remains to be seen. Perhaps you should also talk about that with your potential wife." She held his stare. "I did say that you should be completely honest with her, didn't I? Just because you are tied together doesn't mean that neither of you can ever have a lover."

"I hadn't thought of that. It seems . . . deceitful somehow."

Madame shrugged. "Only if one of you is lying to the other, surely? If you are both happy about it, and let's be honest, there are many married couples in the *ton* who have similar arrangements, then why shouldn't you?"

Paul simply stared at her as a thousand new possibilities flooded his thoughts. "Thank you."

"Don't thank me, thank the fact that you might be marrying a woman who sees exactly who you are and still loves you anyway. Don't you think you might do the same for her?"

Paul nodded and walked out into the hallway. Madame had a way of seeing through conventional problems that sometimes astounded him. He liked to consider himself unconventional, but when it came down to it, it seemed he was too worried about exposing Lucky and her family to the scorn and ridicule of society.

He paused to look down the stairway at the now busy first level. Was Constantine already here? He couldn't think about that. He had no idea how his lover was going to react to his abrupt withdrawal from their relationship. But did he really know Lucky at all either? If she had been forced . . . His hand tightened on the banister. She might not even know what she wanted physically, or her view of what was normal might be scarred for good. He could help her with that. At least he could do that. . . .

Paul set off along the corridor to the servants' door and used his passkey to access the dimly lit narrow stairs that went down to the kitchen. He'd force down some food, and prepare Christian Delornay, the new owner of the pleasure house, for the fact that he might not be offering his sexual services any longer. He couldn't decide if Christian would be pleased to be rid of him or annoyed at his loss. But that wasn't his problem. He had far more important things to worry about after all.

5

Constantine sat quietly drinking a glass of brandy in one of the second-floor salons and watched the erotic tableau unfolding in front of him. Two men and two women were entangled on the low bed in the center of the room, and all of them were engaged in some kind of sexual congress with at least one of the others. He angled his head to try and work out which appendage belonged to which of the writhing bodies but it still wasn't clear.

As always, his gaze was drawn more to the women than the men, but he appreciated all of the erotic sights. One of the men was blond and slim and reminded him of Paul St. Clare. Constantine found himself smiling as he thought of his new lover's remarkable skill in bed. He'd never met a man like Paul before, or felt quite so sexually aroused since his days in Russia. Just thinking about the things Paul could do with his mouth made Constantine's cock twitch.

"All alone, sir?"

"Not anymore."

He looked up into Paul's smiling face and rose to his feet.

Paul had his back to the center of the room. Constantine stepped close and deliberately palmed the other man's cock. "I was just thinking about you."

Paul's pupils dilated and he pushed himself into Constantine's hand. "And I wanted to talk to you."

"Can I fuck you first?" Con asked. "I'm desperate." He nuzzled Paul's ear and bit down on the lobe. "I'll be quick, I swear it."

"Here?"

Con almost came in his breeches at that salacious thought. He could just see Paul bent over the back of the couch while he pumped himself deep and hard into the other man's arse. . . . He knew Paul had no qualms about being publicly fucked, but he wasn't quite so open. "No, somewhere more private."

Without another word, Paul turned and headed out of the room to the discreet line of doorways that shielded the more intimate chambers. He opened a door, and Con followed him inside, spun Paul around, and kissed him full on the mouth.

"I haven't felt like this with another man for years. I woke up last night hard and aching for you."

Paul kissed him back, and Con shoved his hand down between their bodies and worked on the buttons of both sets of breeches. Something in Paul's face made him eager to have the other man under him immediately. "I want to be inside you."

"I don't think I have the will to stop you." Paul sounded strained, but Con was too far gone with lust to want to break away now. He freed Paul's cock and worked his fingers around the straining shaft, using the increasing wetness to lubricate his pumping fist.

"Fuck me hard, sir, make me scream for you."

Constantine spun Paul around until he was facing the side of the bed and shoved Paul's breeches down, revealing his muscled buttocks. He sank to his knees and used his tongue to lick and lubricate the tight pucker of Paul's arse and the swell of his balls.

"Oh, God, sir, that's . . ." Paul arched his back, giving Con more access. Con reached around and drew some of the wetness streaming down Paul's cock onto his fingers, swirling it around Paul's arsehole until he could ease a finger inside.

"Give me more, give me all of you," Paul gasped.

"Not yet, you're not ready," Con murmured.

"You said you'd be quick."

Con pushed his finger deep and Paul bucked under his hands. "But I don't want to hurt you."

He flinched when Paul reached back, grabbed his wrist, and squeezed it until his bones ground together. "But I want to feel you rough and hard, feel you owning me, making me come for you."

Con's cock grew even bigger and he stared at Paul's arse. "Just me?"

"Please . . ."

With a harsh groan, Con spread the wetness seeping from his cock over the crown and pressed the head against Paul's arsehole. "Are you sure?"

"Just do it, sir, please."

Con shoved himself inward, ignoring both the unforgiving but exquisite tightness and Paul's gasp. He worked himself gradually deeper, one hand now wrapped around Paul's shaft, rubbing him hard. It took a while, but eventually he was lodged deep, his balls tucked against Paul.

"Do you like that?" he breathed into Paul's ear.

"Yes."

"Like it when I take you hard and raw?"

"*Yes.*"

"You'll like it even more when I start to fuck you and you'll be full of my come."

Paul sighed Con's name and that was enough to make Con

start to thrust himself in and out, in and out, until he was slamming himself deep and hard with every long, deliberate stroke. He reached down and drew Paul's mouth toward him so that he could kiss him.

"You'll still feel me tomorrow, you'll be so sore. Do you like that too?"

"God, *yes.*"

He felt Paul start to come all over his hand, gave one last desperate thrust, and spilled himself inside.

He lay over Paul for a long time, regaining his breath and simply enjoying the texture and scent of the other man's skin. Eventually he kissed Paul's cheek and eased his cock free. When he straightened, his legs were shaking, and it took him a moment to walk over to the table where he could wash himself clean. He rinsed out a washcloth and returned to the bed to administer to Paul, who still lay sprawled against the side of the bed.

"Are you all right?"

Paul rolled over on to his back and shielded his eyes with his forearm.

Con touched his knee. "Paul? Did I hurt you?"

"No, you . . ." Paul bit his lip. "You were perfect."

"Then what is wrong?"

Paul gestured at his disordered clothing. "Let me get dressed and then we can talk."

Something inside Con went still. "You don't want to get undressed and fuck me properly?"

"I want to fuck you more than I want to breathe, but . . ."

Con slowly set himself to rights and rebuttoned his breeches. "But what?"

Paul gestured at the pair of chairs in front of the fire. "Can we sit down?"

Con did as he was asked, and Paul joined him. Paul sat forward, his hands clasped lightly between his knees, and stared at his boots.

"This is one of the most difficult things I have ever had to say to anyone."

Con strove for a neutral expression and sat back in his chair. He didn't say anything, and waited for Paul to look up at him. The anguish in the other man's face made his gut tighten.

"What's wrong?"

"I can't see you anymore."

Con allowed the words to settle over him like a drift of snow and then slowly stood up. "Then you'll understand if I wish to be excused."

Paul grabbed his hand and rose too. "Please, don't go. Will you at least allow me to explain?"

"I'm not sure there is anything else to say, is there? You have obviously found me not to your liking. There is no crime in that. I'll find someone else."

Paul winced, and Con was suddenly glad. It wasn't like him to be petty, but after just having the best and roughest sex of his life, he was more shaken than perhaps he would like to admit.

"It's not like that. Please sit down and hear me out."

Con reluctantly sat and Paul did as well.

"I wish to God this hadn't happened now, but . . ." He visibly inhaled. "I'm getting married."

"*Married?*" Con asked.

"I know, it's ridiculous, isn't it?" Paul managed a smile that looked more like a grimace. "But if I have to marry, I'd at least like to try and be faithful to my wife."

"I see," Con said.

Paul laughed. "No, you don't, and I'm not sure that I do either. All I can tell you is that it is a matter of honor and urgency. Otherwise, I would not be doing it." He hesitated. "Especially now, when I have you."

"So you haven't found another man."

Paul looked into Con's eyes. "How could I?"

Despite Paul's words, the pain in the region of Con's heart redoubled. "If I might be so bold, do you think you will be satisfied married to a woman?"

Paul sighed. "I'll have to be, won't I?"

"But she won't understand your needs."

"I'm not going to lie to her. I've already decided that if she marries me, it will be with the full knowledge of who and what I am."

"Then you are very brave." Con hesitated. "I didn't tell my wife about my particular sexual tastes, and it caused all sorts of problems in our marriage." Not the kind that Paul was probably envisioning, but bad enough.

"You're married?" Paul asked.

"I was married at eighteen, when I still lived in Russia and was serving in the Tsar's army." He took a steadying breath. "Apparently my wife refused to leave Moscow when the French army were advancing. When I finally reached the charred remnants of our home, there was no sign of her or anything living."

"I'm sorry, Constantine. I had no idea."

"It was a long time ago." Con smiled. "I have all but forgotten about it." Another lie, but one he'd repeated so often that he almost believed it.

"But you haven't married again."

"No."

Paul reached for his hand. "I wish things were different. I wish I could have you both."

"That would be my ideal situation as well." Con brought Paul's hand to his lips and kissed it.

"Or even better, I wish she was in love with you, and we could find a way to all be together."

Con found himself smiling at Paul. "And now you are being

ridiculous. You cannot arrange the love lives of your friends simply to suit yourself."

"I suppose not." Paul sighed. "I just hate having to lose you."

Con stroked his cheek. "But we must say good-bye. I can scarcely interfere with an honorable man's duty."

"I don't feel very honorable." Paul swallowed hard. "After everything I've said, would you stay with me tonight? I have to go and talk to Lucky's father tomorrow, and I'll be married by special license within the month."

"Of course I'll stay, and I'll also wish you much happiness."

Paul met his gaze. "She deserves to be happy. I at least know that."

Con leaned forward and slid his hand around Paul's neck. "So do you. May I help you out of your clothes?"

6

—————————

"His Grace requires your presence in the library, my lady," Parsons murmured.

Lucinda looked up from her unhappy perusal of a book of sermons at the hovering butler. "Thank you, Parsons, I'll go down at once."

Her heart started to thump, and she nervously smoothed her hands over the creased skirts of her pink muslin morning dress. Any unexpected summons from her father was a cause for alarm these days. Would Jeremy follow through with his threat to speak to her father before she came up with a solution to her dilemma? In truth, she was no closer to an answer than she had been three days ago.

She walked down the wide spiral staircase and noticed a gentleman's hat and gloves on the marble-inlay hall table. Her father obviously had a visitor, as it was too early for social calls to her mother. She paused for a moment and stared at the imposing double doors of her father's study. If Jeremy was in there, this was her perfect opportunity to accept his marriage proposal before he told her father everything. She swallowed down a sensation of nausea. As her father was fond of reminding her, she was a Haymore, and Haymores did their duty regardless of their personal emotions.

She raised her chin and went toward the doors, tapping lightly on the wood before letting herself inside. Her smile disappeared as the two men rose to greet her and she realized it wasn't Jeremy sitting with her father after all.

"Ah, Lucinda," her father said. "I'm glad you could join us." There was a peculiar look on his face she couldn't quite decipher. "Paul has something he wishes to ask you."

"Paul does?" Lucky turned to Paul and found he shared her father's strained expression. She also noticed that he was dressed very smartly in civilian clothes that not only fit him but also looked brand-new. She took the chair in front of her father's desk and finally remembered to smile. "Whatever can it be?"

Her father came out from behind his desk and clapped Paul on the shoulder. "I've just realized that I have an urgent message for my wife. I'll be back in a moment."

Lucky watched him leave and then looked at Paul. "What on earth is going on? My father looks quite odd. What did you say to him?"

He faced her and took an obvious breath. "I asked for permission to marry you."

"You did what?" Lucky was only aware that her voice was quite shrill because Paul winced.

"I offered for your hand, and he told me to ask you, so here I am."

"Haven't we already discussed this?"

He came down on one knee in front of her chair and took both her hands in his.

"You told me you had some harebrained scheme to marry the very man who ruined you. I think you can do better than that. I think you should marry me."

She stared down into his familiar brown eyes and temptation swirled around her.

"Why?"

"Because you have always loved me?"

She felt herself blushing. "Which is meaningless if you do not love me back."

He sighed. "I love you, surely you know that?" He squeezed her fingers. "I want to do this for you."

"For me or for my father?"

"That's a fair question," Paul conceded, "but I'll already inherit everything whether I'm married to you or not. I'd much rather you got to share it with me."

"I don't know what to say."

"Then say yes. If you won't tell me this blaggard's name and let me kill him, at least let me keep you safe in the only other way I can."

Lucky stood up and pushed past him. "But it seems so unfair."

Paul sat in her vacated chair. "In what way?"

She presented him with her back. "If I marry you, I gain everything I've ever wanted."

"And what's wrong with that?" There was a hint of loving amusement in his voice that made her want to cry.

"I don't deserve it. I've ruined myself."

She flinched as he came up behind her and grasped her shoulders. "You have not ruined yourself. You were taken advantage of."

"And now I can't bear it when a man touches me. What kind of wife would I be to you?"

He gave an odd laugh and spun her around to look at him. "The kind I want? Listen, if you agree to this betrothal, it will keep your seducer at bay for a few more days while we discuss how we mean to go on, and whether we both truly wish to go through with the marriage."

She shivered. "Or it will draw him out in the open and he'll ruin me anyway."

"I almost hope he tries it." The cool determination in Paul's voice made Lucky stare at him anew. "I could finish him off for good, and then you wouldn't have to marry me after all." His cold smile died. "We've always been the best of friends, and I want us to continue to be honest with each other. Will you at least try and see if we will suit?"

"And what if we don't?"

He bent to kiss her forehead. "I'd never force you to do anything. You know that, don't you? We're *friends*."

Lucky took a deep breath and felt her resolve weakening. "I'm still not sure if this is the right thing to do."

He sighed. "Neither am I, but at least we can explore the possibilities. Shall we go and find your parents?"

She clutched at his coat lapels. "Right now?"

"Indeed." He looked down at her. "I know you'd prefer to keep the news in the family until we make up our minds, but if we wish to discourage your seducer, we'll need to make it public. I'm sorry, Lucky."

Whatever way she turned there were obstacles in her path, so surely all she could do was pick the best way forward? It seemed she was too weak to stand completely alone. At least with Paul she could be honest.

"If I want to break the engagement, you'll let me?"

"I've already told you I will. I give you my word."

He waited quietly in front of her, his gaze sympathetic but full of resolution.

She took a deep breath and reached for his hand. "Then let's go and find my parents."

Constantine saw the sealed note on the silver platter when he walked into his lodgings and picked up the heavy parchment. He recognized Paul's signet ring in the wax and carefully opened the letter. The message was short and to the point.

Lady Lucinda Haymore has accepted my hand in marriage.
Yours, Paul St. Clare.

Con studied the words for a long moment and then crumpled the parchment in his hand. If he remembered correctly, Lady Lucinda was the new Duke of Ashmolton's only child. How convenient for the Haymore family that the male heir to the title had offered to marry their daughter. Despite knowing that this would probably be the outcome, and understanding Paul's decision even more clearly now, Con turned toward the fire, threw the note into the center of the red heat, and poured himself a large brandy.

"Good evening, sir, may I serve your dinner?"

Con looked up to see Gregor hovering by the door and drew himself up.

"Yes indeed, and then pack my bags. I'm almost certainly leaving for the countryside tomorrow."

"Very good, sir. Do you wish me to accompany you?"

"Not this time, Gregor." He couldn't bear the thought of his longtime batman worrying and fussing over him. "I'm sure Major Thomas Wesley has someone who can take care of my needs at his hunting lodge."

"If you are certain, sir."

"I am. Now please bring me my dinner. I'm famished."

It was definitely time to accept a long-standing invitation from Thomas Wesley to his country house. He'd sally forth to his club tonight and see if Wesley was there and willing to put up with him for a few weeks. At least in the countryside he could legally murder a few things without anyone realizing how fraught his temper was, or fearing for their own lives.

He sat down by the fire and stared into its glowing depths. Although they'd been aware of each other for years, it wasn't as if he and Paul had been lovers for long. Con wished he'd spoken up sooner, taken Paul away from Gabriel when it had become clear to everyone that Gabriel no longer wanted Paul. They might have had years of happiness together. He had no intention of marrying again, so a relationship with Paul would have suited him quite nicely, until Paul had decided to wed . . .

Not that he could fault Paul. Honor was an important element of every man's life and much undervalued in Con's book. Honor prevented him from marrying again, despite the interest of the *ton*'s females. Con sat back as Gregor arranged a table in front of him and placed a covered tray on it.

"Enjoy your dinner, sir. Will you require anything else this evening, sir?"

"Just a bottle of the burgundy. I'll be going out. Don't wait up for me."

"As you wish, sir." Gregor paused. "Should I be expecting any visitors tonight?"

"No, Gregor. Not tonight."

Gregor brought the wine and then withdrew, leaving Con staring down at his suddenly unappetizing plate of food. Paul had taken to dropping in at all times of the day to snatch a moment with Con. His lodgings were going to seem unbearably empty now. Con's gut twisted, and he pushed the tray of food away. He needed to get out of London until Paul was married and unavailable.

"Mama, I know that you are excited about the prospect of my marrying Paul, but could you please listen to me?" Lucinda said loudly.

After their celebratory family dinner, her mother had bidden Paul a fond farewell and followed her daughter upstairs to her bedroom. Lucky already had a headache, and her mother's happy exuberance was not making her feel any better. Every time she opened her mouth she felt like she was deceiving her parents and Paul anew.

Paul had been magnificent during dinner, holding her hand and smiling down at her as if she truly were the woman he adored and wanted to marry. He'd also deflected most of her mother's questions as to the progress of their romance, suggesting adroitly that his regard for Lucky had simply grown through the years until he had been unable to deny his feelings for her.

"Lucinda." Her mother sat down on the bed and patted the space beside her, her smile disappearing. "I am listening to you. I don't understand why you have agreed to marry Paul at all."

Lucky stared at her mother. "What?"

"I'm not stupid, my dear. Did you think to please your father?"

Lucky shook her head. "No, it wasn't like that at all. I . . ."

"Then why?" Her mother frowned. "Paul is a lovely man, and I know he will take good care of you and the estate, but why have you settled for him? I always thought you more adventurous than that."

Lucky sat down next to her mother and took her hand. She had to see this through. She had to find the strength to convince her mother that she was happy with her choice, for all their sakes.

"I don't think I'm settling, Mama. Paul is wonderful."

Something flickered in her mother's eyes. "Paul is not as sweet and uncomplicated as he might seem."

"What man is?" Lucky answered. "At least we are good friends and intend to discuss all these potential problems before we go ahead with the marriage."

Her mother sighed. "Make sure you do. I would hate for you to be miserable in your marriage."

Lucky forced a laugh. "I don't think Paul would ever want to make me miserable. He's always been so kind to me."

"That is true. I just hope you make the right decision, my love."

Lucky kissed her mother's scented cheek. "I know I have. Carry on being happy for me, please?"

"Of course I will. There will be no prouder mother around than I am. I'll boast about your conquest at every social event for years!"

Lucky wrapped her arms around her mother and hugged her tight. "Thank you, Mama. I love you so much," she whispered.

"And I love you too. Now go to sleep and be prepared for your whole life to change tomorrow. We'll need to start on that trousseau right away."

Lucky raised her head. "I won't have to have a big wedding, will I?"

"You can't have a big wedding. We're still in mourning for the last duke, remember?"

"Oh good," Lucky said thankfully. "I mean, that's right. I don't think either of us would relish a huge fashionable crush. Maybe we can have something small and private instead."

"If we organized a huge society wedding, Paul would probably run away." Her mother kissed her nose. "However, we still have plenty of time to make you look beautiful; don't worry about that."

Lucinda got off the bed and allowed her mother to loosen the back of her gown and her stays. There was at least one memory she could share with her mother that was quite sincere.

"I know you won't believe me, Mama, but ever since I was a little girl, whenever I pictured my wedding day, Paul was standing beside me."

Her mother headed for the door. "Then perhaps you have

made the right choice after all." She paused to look back at Lucky. "If, perhaps, for all the wrong reasons. Good night, my love."

Lucky waited until her mother had left before sinking down into the nearest chair and covering her face with her hands.

7

From the moment he saw Lucky being greeted by the hostess at the ball, Paul guessed she was already quite close to reneging on their arrangement. He wasn't even surprised. Expecting her to keep deceiving those she loved under such difficult circumstances would be hard for anyone, let alone a sheltered twenty-one-year-old who had probably never lied to her parents about anything before.

Before he went to claim her hand for the first waltz, Paul took the opportunity to study her from afar. She wore a light blue silk gown with blond lace trimming, which only accentuated the paleness of her complexion. Her dark hair fell in a cascade of ringlets from the crown of her head, and her blue eyes looked enormous. She stood tall though, her bearing suitable to her high rank and her manner daring anyone to contradict her about anything. A sense of pride consumed Paul. She was indeed much stronger than she looked, and he was certain that she would grow into a remarkable woman.

Despite the fact that there had been no formal announcement of the upcoming engagement, Paul could already sense the undercurrent of interest that swirled around him as he approached the Haymores. He wasn't known for regular appearances at social gatherings, and it was possible that the duchess had already whispered the news to a few chosen friends.

His aunt held out her hand and he kissed it. "How lovely to see you, Paul. Have you come to dance with Lucinda?"

"Indeed I have, Aunt." He turned to Lucky, who was still looking rather apprehensive. "If she is willing."

She gave him her gloved hand and he tucked it into the crook of his arm and walked her toward the dance floor. The orchestra struck a chord, and he took her into his arms, amazed at how fragile she felt and how light she was on her feet.

"Are you well, Lucky?"

She looked up at him. "I'm not sure."

He kept his social smile pinned in place. "Do you want to stop dancing? I can take you back to your mother."

"No, I'd rather dance."

She returned her gaze to his shirtfront and refused to look up again, replying to all his efforts at conversation with the smallest of smiles and the shortest of replies.

After a while he tried again. "Lucky, what is going on?"

"I'm not sure what you mean."

"If you wish people to think that we are so attracted to each other that we intend to marry posthaste, you might want to smile at me a little more."

She sighed. "I'm sorry, Paul. I'm not feeling too well tonight."

"Then let me take you back to your mother." He stopped dancing and began to lead her back across the dance floor until she pulled at his hand.

"Can you take me somewhere not quite so unbearably hot?"

Paul glanced around and changed direction, bringing her toward the open floor-length windows that looked out on to the balcony. He found Lucky a chair and sat opposite her.

"Is that better?" He took the ivory fan out of her unresisting fingers, opened it, and started fanning her.

"Much." She glanced back through the window at the dancing couples. "Are we all right being out here?"

"As we're going to be married, I would hope so."

"As to that . . ."

Paul tensed as she stared at him. "You wish to break it off already?"

"No. It's just that everything is far more complicated that I realized. By trying to avoid my fate, I've simply exchanged one set of problems for another."

Paul stopped fanning her. "Not quite. I'm not a money-grubbing bastard who forced himself on you to get his hands on your father's fortune."

She gaped at him. "I wasn't comparing you to him at all!"

"Well, that's what it sounded like." He realized he was glaring at her in a most unlover-like way. "Has he approached you again since we last spoke?"

"No, he hasn't, thank goodness."

"Is he here?"

She hesitated. "I doubt he has the necessary pedigree to enter this particular gathering. To be honest, I didn't even think about him being here. I was waiting for you."

He felt himself relax. "A wise decision, but let me know if you see him and I'll get rid of him for you. Is that really what is worrying you?"

"*Everything* is worrying me. Even my mother is suspicious of my choice."

"The duchess?" Paul blinked. "She's always been one of my greatest champions."

"But I'm her only surviving daughter. She wants me to be as happy in my marriage as she is in hers."

"And she doesn't think I'll make you happy?"

Lucky reached out and patted his knee. "I told her that you would never want to hurt me."

"Then why was she concerned?"

Lucky shrugged. "Oh, she thought I might be marrying you to please my father. She has no idea that I'm marrying you to prevent him from hearing the worst of me."

Not deceived by her light tone, Paul regarded her for a long moment. He'd always wondered exactly what the duke and duchess had heard about his wild past and his current sexual activities. "You can still tell him the truth, Lucky. That really would be the simplest thing to do."

She set her mouth in an obstinate line that he was coming to know very well. "But I'm not a child anymore. I can't expect everyone to solve my problems for me. It's bad enough that I have to involve you."

Paul held her gaze. "Lucky, involving me was the most intelligent thing you've done so far."

"I know that." She smiled at him. "I think I'm all right now. Shall we go back in? I suspect we've given the gossips plenty to talk about for the rest of the night."

Paul stood and took her hand. "I'll come and take you out tomorrow so that we can converse more comfortably."

"That would be lovely."

He took both her hands in his. "Just remember there is no right or wrong way here. There is only what we choose to do and how we choose to do it. No one can make us feel bad about that except ourselves."

She pulled out of his grasp and patted his cheek. "I never knew you were quite so profound, Paul."

Neither had Paul until he started wanting to make everything right for her. It was a strange feeling, being the responsible one, the one everyone was depending on. He'd avoided that all his life, but now it seemed he had no choice but to see this most important matter through.

He walked back with Lucky to her mother and spent a pleasant few minutes conversing with the duke and duchess before heading off to the card room. There was no sign of Constantine, and Paul wasn't sure if that made things better or worse. Earlier he'd heard someone mention that Con had been seen in the company of Major Thomas Wesley, another patron of the pleasure house and a particular friend of Lord and Lady Blaize Minshom. He tried to be glad that Con would have a sympathetic ear, but the thought of Wesley offering anything of a more tender nature to his lover made him furious.

He stopped at the entrance of the card room so abruptly that several men ran into him. Con wasn't his anymore. After apologizing, Paul turned back toward the ballroom and the doors that led back to the hallway below. He'd only come for Lucky's sake, and, as it seemed that her despoiler was not present, perhaps he might go and drown his sorrows at his lodging house in the company of Captain David Grey and his lover, Robert. They at least might be able to stop him from falling into a pit of self-made despair.

When Milly drew the curtains the next morning to the sound of rain hammering on the panes, Lucky's first reaction was to huddle back under the sheets and stay there for the remainder of the day. But she was a duke's daughter, and she had to accompany her mother to several establishments that morning that dealt with clothes for her trousseau. If society hadn't guessed that she and Paul were now engaged, the gossip from the various shops would probably convince them.

Lucky yawned and sat up, swinging her legs over the side of the high bed. A wave of black giddiness swept over her, and she had to clutch on to the bedpost for support.

"Are you all right, miss?"

Lucky breathed through her nose until the nausea subsided and the world stopped spinning cartwheels, and then carefully let go of the bedpost. She knew enough about what happened to women who were breeding to be afraid. She could not swoon now; her maid would almost certainly run for the duchess, and Lucky had no desire to speak to her mother at this moment at all.

Milly was already moving around the room, assembling Lucky's shift, stays, and petticoats. She turned to point out the stockings that hung over the back of a chair.

"Sit down and put those on, miss."

Lucky was quite glad to take the chair and bend to her task. By the time she straightened, she felt far more the thing and was able to finish dressing in a warm gown and make her way down to breakfast.

Her mother greeted her with a bright smile and a list of errands that seemed to stretch for longer than a week. Lucky ate some toast and drank her tea while her mother talked and planned and asked questions she didn't really require the answers for.

By the time they were ready to leave the house, it was still raining, and Parsons protected their bonneted heads with a large umbrella. Lucky stared out of the small window as the ducal coach made its slow way through the always crowded streets of central London.

The duchess consulted her list. "I think we'll start at the lending library first, as it is closest, and it will be less busy at this time in the morning."

"Of course, Mama," Lucky replied.

"You are being remarkably biddable this morning, my dear, and you look remarkably cheerful. Can it be that you are looking forward to marrying Paul after all?"

"Of *course* I am looking forward to it." Lucky smiled at her mother. "I could scarcely sleep last night thinking about all the arrangements that need to be made."

Her mother chuckled. "Well, don't worry about that. Your father and I will take care of the details. All you have to do is choose your new dresses and all the other things a young bride needs." She hesitated. "I must confess that the thought of you being comfortably settled with Paul does stop me from worrying about all the fortune hunters circling around you."

Lucky kept smiling. There was no point in telling her mother that she'd already been caught and ruined by one of those very vultures. "I'm sure there is much more for me to help you with than that, Mama," Lucky said. "I'm quite capable."

"I know that, and I'll be asking your opinion on everything. Do not worry."

The carriage came to a stop and they waited until the coachman came around to open the door for them. It wasn't far to the shop entrance, but despite her best efforts, Lucky still got wet and her half boots were covered in mud. Inside the lending library, the smell of old books, ink, and wet wool made for an unpleasant combination.

While a clerk attended her mother, Lucky wandered off down one of the rows of shelves, hardly glancing at the imposing row of titles. The damp smells were likely to upset her stomach again. She refused to even consider the fact that she might be breeding and pushed it away to the back of her mind. She had to try harder to convince her mother that she wanted the marriage with Paul. That was the least she could do for him when he'd given up so much. . . .

"My lady."

She was brought out of her reverie when the aisle behind her was blocked by an all-too-familiar figure. She took a quick glance over her shoulder and realized she had inadvertently trapped herself in a dead end.

"Jeremy," Lucky said. "What do you want?"

He leaned against the bookshelf and stared down at her, his face half in shadows. "You know what I want, my love, but it appears that you have been playing me for a fool. The gossip all over London is that you intend to marry your father's heir."

"I am neither your love nor interested in playing games with you." Lucky took a defiant step toward him. "Now if you will please excuse me, my mother is waiting for me."

He held up his hand. "This conversation isn't finished until I say so. I told you to think about what you intended to do. Are you saying that you have decided to cast me aside for that cowardly imbecile, St. Clare? I'd advise you to think again."

"Lieutenant St. Clare is no coward. He has been awarded the highest military honors for bravery."

"And yet you would deceive him by marrying him in your soiled state?"

Lucky bit her lip. "That is none of your business."

Jeremy laughed. "He might be a fool, but even he will know that you aren't a virgin." He considered her. "Perhaps I should go and speak to St. Clare as well as your parents."

"If you seek him out, he will kill you."

"And cause yet more scandal?"

Lucky forced a smile. "But then at least you will be dead."

A wave of something that looked like fear crossed Jeremy's face and quickly vanished. "Then I won't go to St. Clare. I'll go to your father as I originally planned."

"My father will not believe you." Desperately Lucky considered her options. Being this close to him, fearing he might reach out and actually touch her, was making her feel physically ill. "I have nothing further to say to you, Mr. Roland, and I no longer consider you a friend. I insist that you let me pass."

She tried to move by, but he grabbed her arm and tightened his grip.

"You have to marry me!"

"I do not!" she hissed through her clenched teeth. "Now unhand me, or else I'll puke all over your shoes."

She brought her hand to her mouth and he hurriedly released her, allowing her to stumble back into the more populated sections of the lending library, where her mother was still talking to the clerk.

"Mama, I have to leave. I'll meet you in the carriage."

"What's wrong, my dear?"

Lucky shook her head and kept moving. If she was going to disgrace herself, she'd rather it wasn't in front of the entire shop; outside in the rain was bad enough. She pushed open the front door, ignoring the jolly jangle of the bell, and launched herself on to the pavement. Thankfully, the carriage was still outside. She steadied herself against the panel portraying the ducal crest and gulped in some much needed air.

After a moment, she managed to reassure the concerned coachman that she was quite well and climbed inside the dry interior of the coach. It took only a second before she started shivering.

Things just kept getting worse. Now Jeremy knew about Paul and was convinced that she was lying to her potential fiancé as well. She wanted to laugh hysterically. The plot was worthy of a Drury Lane farce, and she'd almost vomited all over the villain. She needed to calm down before her sharp-eyed mother appeared and demanded an explanation.

Lucky took a deep breath and the nausea started to settle. All she could do at this point was move forward. As Paul had reminded her, none of her choices were perfect; they were just the best she could manage at this point. Somehow that calmed her, and she was able to greet her mother with not only a reasonable explanation as to why she'd fled the shop, but a bright anticipation for the remaining tasks on her list, which seemed to fool her mother remarkably well.

8

"Well, thank God the weather has cooperated for once, and we can have our walk without fear of being soaked."

Paul drew Lucky's arm through his and walked her off the main path, down to the more secluded trails closer to the edge of the lake. It was still quite early in the morning, and very few people were about to observe their progress around the Serpentine. Lucky's maid followed at a decorous distance but would be unable to hear their conversation, which suited Paul perfectly.

"It probably won't last," Lucky muttered.

Paul glanced down at her averted face. "My, you are in an optimistic frame of mind this morning, my dear. I'm always pleased to see the sun myself."

"Probably because you were locked away from it for so long."

"That's true. How kind of you to remember that."

She stopped to look up at him. "I remember how debilitated you were when you returned to England. You could barely walk."

He shrugged. "There were many in a far worse state than I was."

"So Major Lord Swanfield said. He also told us that he couldn't have gotten everyone out if you hadn't been there to help him."

"Gabriel said that to you?" Paul raised his eyebrows. "When?"

Lucky squeezed his arm and they started walking again. "You probably don't remember, but he was the person who brought you home to us. He was in a terrible state himself, but he refused our offer to stay."

"Did he, by God? I have no recollection of that at all."

"I'm not surprised you don't recall your arrival. You were unconscious, filthy, and emaciated. You were in such a state that Mama nursed you by herself for a week before she let anyone else near you." Lucky poked at a pile of weeds with the tip of her parasol. "Do you remember much about that first month?"

"Not really, although I do remember you being there with me a lot."

She smiled. "I had the least to do, so I was often sent to keep you company."

"And I was very glad about that."

"Eventually you were, but not at first." She paused. "You didn't really want me there. You cried out for someone else."

Paul spotted a conveniently placed stone bench and headed toward it. He sat next to Lucky and looked into her guileless blue eyes.

"For whom did I call out?"

"For Gabriel Swanfield." She held his gaze, hers quite steady. "You cared for him a lot, didn't you?"

Paul took a deep breath. "Yes, I did."

She nodded as though unsurprised. "In fact, you loved him."

"Yes." Paul let go of her hands. "Which is why I thought I would never make a conventional marriage."

She considered him for a long moment. "Because you were in love with Gabriel? But didn't he just get married to Emily's half sister?"

"He did. And I'm sure he will be very happy."

"If you think he will be happy being married, why are you convinced that you will not? And more to the point, why on earth are you considering marrying me?"

He struggled to think of what to say, and for a moment he simply stared at her.

She reached forward and smacked his upper arm. "Paul, we are best friends. I thought we could tell each other everything. I *thought* that was the whole purpose of this masquerade."

"It is a little complicated to explain. I'm trying to think of the right way to put it."

She smacked him again, this time with more force. "Just tell me."

He raised his gaze to her determined chin. "When I said I loved Gabriel, I didn't just mean from afar or as a friend. I meant in every possible way."

Her mouth opened. "You mean, physically?" She frowned. "I didn't even know that was possible."

"When a group of men are incarcerated together for a long period of time, sometimes they turn to each other for . . . physical release."

"And that is what happened between you and Gabriel?"

"Yes, although I was the instigator. He merely went along with me."

Lucky wrinkled her brow. "Is it even allowed?"

"It certainly isn't allowed. Being found with another man can lead to the stocks, imprisonment, and a harsh, possibly life-ending, sentence."

"Oh. And you like to . . ." She flapped her gloved hand in the general direction of his body.

"Yes, I do like to do that with Gabriel."

She jumped up to her feet and started pacing the path in front of the bench. "Then you won't want to . . . do that with me?"

"That depends on what you want." He waited until she turned to look at him. "I'm quite capable of bedding you, if that is what you mean."

She was already blushing, but he persevered. He'd promised her his honesty. "Are you horrified?"

"By what?"

"That I like to bed men?"

She studied him slowly. "I'm not exactly surprised, Paul. When you were delirious, I heard you beg and plead for Gabriel to touch you. That's one of the reasons why I stayed with you so often. I didn't want you to betray yourself to anyone else."

He felt like the one who should have his mouth open now. His young bride-to-be had shown remarkably good sense all those years ago.

She continued talking. "I still don't quite understand what you 'do,' but I understand that you loved Gabriel."

Paul gathered his wits. "I have a solution for that."

"Whatever do you mean?"

"Emily took you to Madame Helene's."

Lucky came and sat down beside him again. She looked remarkably pretty in her blue wool pelisse and matching bonnet. "Yes, she did. Madame Helene was very kind and gave me some excellent advice."

"Madame is an astonishing woman, and she thought very highly of you. Did you know that she and her family run a pleasure house?"

"I don't even know what that means, although I might hazard a guess."

"It's a place where men and women go to indulge in carnal games."

"Carnal, as in physical?"

"As in sexual," Paul said bluntly.

"Do you go there?"

He met her fascinated gaze. "Yes, I do. I mean I did, until I offered to marry you."

"Married people can't go there?"

He fought a smile. "One would assume they wouldn't *need* to go there, but some do, and some married couples go together."

"And what does this have to do with us?"

It was Paul's turn to stand and pace the edge of the lake. "I would like to take you there again, so that you can see what kind of a man I am, to see what kind of a man you would be marrying."

"And mayhap change my mind?"

He loved that about her, her clear-eyed perception. Despite her age she was no shrinking flower. There was a tough resilience in her that he almost envied.

"I want to give you that chance. I also want you to understand that you would not be the only one to benefit greatly from this marriage."

"I don't understand."

"My sexual tastes are not unknown within the *ton.* By marrying you, I would silence a lot of the gossips and protect myself from the fear of disclosure."

"I hadn't thought of that."

"Which is why I want you to be absolutely certain about marrying me." He held her hands in his. "You do not have to give me your answer right away, but if you want to visit the pleasure house and see exactly what a man like me might get up to, let me know."

She gently released her hands from his grasp. "I'd like to think about it. May I do that?"

"Of course. I'm just relieved that you haven't run away screaming already."

She cupped his cheek with her gloved hand. "We agreed to be honest with each other, did we not? I'm glad you told me about Gabriel. I wondered if you were ever going to mention it."

"Thank you for being so understanding."

Her smile was wistful. "I know how it feels to be in love with someone who doesn't love you back."

"That fool didn't love you, he used you." Paul stood and drew Lucky to her feet too.

She started to walk and then looked back at him over her shoulder. "I wasn't talking about him, Paul. I was talking about myself."

"So Paul is set to marry Lady Lucinda Haymore?" Thomas Wesley stared at Constantine. "Are you quite certain about that? I hadn't heard a thing."

Con sighed. "It is a secret at the moment, so keep it to yourself." He groaned. "I probably shouldn't have said anything, but I suspect by the time I return to Town they will be married."

"That quickly?"

Thomas sipped his brandy and so did Con. They had shared an excellent dinner and the servants had already withdrawn, leaving the two men to themselves. They'd left town on the previous day for Wesley's hunting box in the county of Leicestershire, which was a decent few miles from London, and suited Con quite nicely. He had started to relax in his host's genial, undemanding company and had ended up confiding probably more than he should.

"Paul has never struck me as an ideal candidate for marriage," Thomas continued. "But I suppose this is more of a dynastic issue than a love match. By marrying Lady Lucinda, he unites both branches of the Haymore family, and makes sure that the current duke's daughter is provided for in the best way possible."

"I suppose that's it," Con agreed, trying his hardest to forget Paul's anguished face.

Thomas filled up both their glasses. "You and Paul are lovers?"

"Were lovers," Con corrected. "He intends to be faithful to his wife."

"Oh, God." Thomas chuckled gently. "I've heard that before."

Con frowned. "Paul is an honorable man. I think he means what he says. I am not going to hang around like some lovesick maiden hoping he will change his mind."

"I apologize, Delinsky. I didn't mean to suggest either of you would act in a less than honorable way. Your situation just reminds me a little of my own."

"Your own?" Con asked.

"I came back from military service in India to inherit a title I didn't want, and to settle some old hurts with a former lover of mine. When I approached my old lover, he wanted nothing to do with me or my attempts to show him how much I cared about him."

"Ah, I believe I've heard some of this story. Are you talking about the infamous Lord Minshom?"

"Yes, I am. When Blaize turned me down, I thought my life was over." Thomas smiled. "But, in truth, things turned out very differently."

"How so?" Con found himself leaning forward. "Did Minshom change his mind?"

"Not exactly. His wife changed it for him."

"His wife?"

"She put Minshom in a position where he was able to have us both."

"And she didn't object?"

Thomas shrugged. "She loves him."

"But . . . how?"

Thomas's smile was wicked. "We all fuck each other."

"And Minshom doesn't mind?"

"Why would he? He loves his wife."

Con shook his head. "Don't you feel . . . jealous of each other? Jealous that she gets to share her life with him?"

Thomas gave a little shudder. "Minshom is an extremely difficult man to live with. I wouldn't be in Jane's shoes for anything. I just appreciate sharing their bed every so often."

"And that is truly enough for you?"

"Yes." Thomas grinned. "I have other lovers as well, but the Minshoms hold a very special place in my affections. I don't intend to marry or settle down, so they are the closest I will ever come to having a family."

"Why not marry? You are an earl."

Thomas's smile died. "And I have no desire to continue my father's line. I hate everything the man stood for."

Con nodded. "I don't intend to marry again either. My wife died in the occupation of Moscow by the French."

"My condolences, Delinsky." Thomas opened a box of cigarillos and offered one to Constantine, who accepted. He used the nearest candle flame to light the tip and blew a cloud of smoke.

"Thank you, but it was a long time ago."

"Obviously not long enough if you can't contemplate replacing her."

"It's not quite that simple. I have no proof of my wife's death. I'm not sure I want to stir up all that grief for myself or her family again by trying to make things official."

"I can understand that, and I might even be able to help. I have some acquaintances at the Russian embassy who might be able to make some discreet inquiries as to what needs to be done."

"That's very kind of you, but I'm still not sure I need to sort anything out. I really don't intend to marry again."

"You prefer men, then?"

Con smiled. "Not really. I've only fucked three men in my life, compared with countless women."

"Is that because you really prefer women, or because you choose to conform to what society expects of you?"

Con tapped the ash of his cigarillo on to the plate. "I chose my lovers because I desire them. It is as simple as that. My first lovers were a married couple. I suppose they dictated my tastes and I appreciate variety."

Thomas reached across the table and put his hand over Con's. "I'm sure you've already worked out that I would be quite willing to compensate you for Paul's loss, and that I wouldn't object to being used in the slightest."

Con turned his hand over and squeezed Thomas's fingers. "I appreciate the offer, and I wish I could accept it. It would be much easier if I could simply fuck my way out of this."

"You care for him, don't you?"

"It seems that I do." Con raised his eyes to meet Thomas's all-too-understanding gaze. "But I will come about. I promise you that." He took a deep breath. "I appreciate your companionship more than I can tell you."

"Not enough to fuck me, though," Thomas joked. He ground out the remains of his cigarillo and finished his brandy. "Are you ready for bed, my friend? Your own bed, obviously."

"I think I am." Con rose to his feet. "I expect we'll see a notice in the paper soon to announce their official betrothal and wedding."

"I wonder why there is all this urgency?" Thomas mused. He walked to the door and held it open for Con. He patted his shoulder. "You're welcome to stay until the whole matter is settled."

"Thank you," Con said. "I think that would be for the best. Good night, Wesley."

He took a candle from the hall table and headed up the oak staircase, his shadow dancing along the paneled walls. He hadn't wanted to tell Wesley that he didn't particularly care to find out the details of his wife's death. He'd heard a few unkind rumors about her behavior after the French had occupied the city, and he didn't really want to find out if they were true. Surely it was better for her to rest in peace?

He was so damn sick of gossip and rumor; it seemed to follow him around like a ball and chain. He couldn't bear to return to London and hear all the talk about Paul and his bride-to-be and pretend he didn't care. He simply couldn't bear it.

He walked past Thomas's suite and almost wanted to stop and change his mind. He could easily go inside and wait for Thomas to come to bed. He could lose himself in the oblivion of fucking, the feel of another body, the most basic of needs both shared and expressed in the most basic and ancient of ways.

But it wouldn't be Paul. Con couldn't quite believe that the man had affected him so completely, but it appeared that he had. At least Con knew that he'd move on. Even gossip eventually died. He'd survived a scandal before and he'd damn well do it again.

Lucky sat at her desk and looked out of her bedroom window that faced the front of the square. It was dark now and still raining, and she'd already had to light extra candles to illuminate the room. She nibbled on her pen as she contemplated yet again the letter she was trying to write to Jeremy.

It was hard to concentrate because her mind kept going back to her earlier conversation with Paul and his startling offer. She hadn't been that surprised by his revelation about his love for Gabriel; in fact, she'd been expecting it. But she had been surprised that he wanted to *show* her what he meant as well.

Did she want to know? Her only experience of the physical side of love hadn't exactly inspired her to seek out more. The thought that Paul wouldn't want that from her was strangely liberating, although he'd said he would bed her if she wanted it. . . . She shuddered at the very thought.

She considered her letter to Jeremy again. Could she put him off until she had made a decision about Paul? Her hand slid over her stomach. She hadn't bled for over a month now, which wasn't unusual for her. After what Madame Helene had told her about how quickly a man could give a woman a child, she was a little concerned. In truth, she was terrified.

She'd asked Emily to pass a note to Madame about when a pregnancy would become visible, and Helene had replied that it might take months. Lucky glanced down at her flat stomach. It was almost four weeks since Jeremy had forced himself on her, and far too early to know anything yet. Unfortunately Helene had also cautioned her that the gossips would notice if she waited too long and delivered a baby five months after the wedding.

She'd decided to allow herself another two weeks. Two weeks to take Paul up on his scandalous offer to visit a notorious pleasure house, and two weeks to placate Jeremy or agree to marry him. She stared down at her letter again. Perhaps that was all she needed to say, that she would give him her answer in a fortnight. She'd sweeten the blow by stuffing the envelope with her newly received quarterly allowance. Jeremy was always short of ready cash. She was certain that would both mollify him and persuade him to leave her alone, at least until he ran out of money.

She finished her letter and set it aside for Milly, her maid, to secretly deliver the next day. Her second letter, to Paul, was far easier to write and just as short. All she needed to do was agree to his shocking suggestion and wait to see exactly what he would do.

9

"Miss Ross." Paul stopped abruptly at the entrance to the kitchen of the pleasure house and stared at the unexpected visitor. "I didn't expect to see you here tonight." He also hadn't expected to find her nose-to-nose with Ambrose, arguing over what looked like a novel.

"Good evening, Paul. I was just asking Ambrose for his opinion about this book I was reading." Emily jumped up so quickly that Ambrose had to reach up and steady her. "Is it late? I think I'm supposed to be going to a ball or something."

"It's almost nine," Ambrose said quietly. "Would you like me to escort you home, Miss Emily?"

Emily smiled at Ambrose, her color high, and briefly touched his cheek. "Oh, no, you are far too busy, and Seamus Kelly is waiting for me outside."

Ambrose bowed. "As you wish, Miss Ross. I hope you have a pleasant evening."

"I'm sure I won't," Emily groaned before switching her attention to Paul. "Aren't you supposed to be escorting Lucky to the same ball?" Her eyes narrowed. "And by the way, I'm still not sure what is going on with this engagement, but I will find out."

Paul smiled innocently at her. "Lucky is indisposed this evening, so I came to see my old friend Ambrose. I don't see him much now that I no longer participate in the games upstairs."

For a moment, Emily looked mutinous. "I wish I was allowed to participate in those games."

"You aren't old enough, Miss Ross," Ambrose said.

"Why not? Lisette was allowed up there when she was my age."

"Lisette was brought up quite differently from you."

"That's not an excuse." Emily pouted. "Sometimes I wish Helene had brought me up instead of my own mother. *She* was afraid of her own shadow."

Ambrose didn't say anything to that, and Paul decided to hold his tongue too.

"All right, I'll go." Emily picked up her gloves and Ambrose draped her cloak around her shoulders. She looked up into his face. "You can keep the book. We can discuss it next time I'm here."

"You're not supposed to be here, Miss Ross," Ambrose replied. "You know that."

"And I don't care what my father says. I have as much right to be here as everyone else in the family. Richard has even been allowed to become a member!"

Paul walked over to the back door and opened it. The large bulk of Seamus Kelly leaned against the back wall, and Paul winked at him. "The lady is ready to be escorted home, Mr. Kelly."

Seamus straightened up. "At your service, Miss Ross."

Emily swept out of the kitchen, ignoring both Ambrose and Paul, and smiled up at Seamus. "Thank you."

Paul shut the door and turned to face Ambrose, who stood

by the table looking down at the book. There was an expression on his face that Paul found hard to interpret.

"Emily Ross is a handful," Paul remarked as he took a seat and waited for Ambrose to join him.

"She has a point though, doesn't she? Everyone else in her family gets to do what they want here, except her."

"Would you like to see her up in the pleasure house, Ambrose?"

"I would like . . ." Ambrose met Paul's gaze and stopped speaking. "What I would like is immaterial. It is not my place to judge the Delornay-Ross family."

Paul studied Ambrose intently. "Are you fond of Emily, my friend?"

"Of course I'm fond of her." Ambrose fidgeted with the cover of the book. "I've known her for years, and her family has been very good to me."

"When I said 'fond,' perhaps I should have been more specific. You're in love with the girl, aren't you?"

Ambrose's gaze flew to Paul's. "Don't be absurd."

"I don't think I am being absurd." Paul searched his friend's face. "But all's well, as it appears that she is quite 'fond' of you too."

Ambrose abruptly rose. "As I said, she has known me for years. She sees me as some kind of brother."

"No, I don't think she does. I think she comes here to see you." Paul shook his head. "Why didn't I notice it before?"

"Because it is complete nonsense!" Ambrose snapped. "Now, why *are* you here tonight?"

Paul opened his eyes wide. He'd never seen Ambrose close to losing his temper before. Was it worth pursuing a subject that his friend obviously found so uncomfortable? He of all people knew that unrequited love was a delicate subject at the best of times, even between good friends. He decided that in this case discretion was the better part of valor.

"I'm here to see my affianced bride."

Ambrose stared at him. "Lady Lucinda Haymore, the person you just told Miss Emily was unwell tonight?"

Paul shrugged. "That is the story Lucky has told her mother, so I wanted to be consistent."

"Why are you bringing her *here* of all places, and does Mr. Delornay know?"

"He does. I can't say he was happy about it, but he agreed with my reasoning eventually." Paul gestured at the nearest seat. "Will you sit down? I'm getting a crick in my neck with you towering over me like that."

Ambrose complied with unusually ill grace.

"Thank you. I'm bringing Lucky here because I want her to see me as I really am."

"Naked and fucking anyone who asks you?"

Paul winced. "That's a little harsh, my friend."

"But that's my point. That isn't all there is to you. You are so much more than that." Ambrose hesitated. "Are you trying to drive her away?"

"No!"

"Then why focus on showing her this part of you?"

"Because she deserves to know what she is marrying. I want her to understand about sex in all its many facets so that she can make an informed decision."

Ambrose sighed. "That's the most ridiculous thing I've ever heard you say. In fact, it doesn't even *sound* like something you would say. Have you been talking to Madame Helene?"

"She helped me come to a decision, yes, but I do want to be honest with Lucky."

"With all due respect, Paul, I was here when your future wife was brought in. And despite what Emily thinks, I don't believe Lady Lucinda was simply kissed in the garden and tore her dress."

"And your point is?"

"If she was . . . forced, then bringing her here to such a blatantly sexual place might not be the best idea. She might panic."

Paul shoved a hand through his hair. "I've thought of that, but you don't know her as well as I do, Ambrose. She is very strong, and she is also determined that I show her my true nature before she commits herself totally to this marriage. She insisted that I be honest"

"Is she pregnant? Is that why she is willing to agree to try anything?"

Paul felt as if someone had punched him in the stomach. He fought for control before rising slowly to his feet. "She will be here in a moment. I'm going up to the main hall to meet her."

"Be careful, Paul," Ambrose said.

"I'll do my best." Paul nodded and went toward the door, his thoughts in a whirl. He hadn't considered all the possible consequences of Lucky's ordeal. Was Lucky even aware that she might have conceived? If she was, Ambrose might be right, and all her protestations of honesty might mean nothing. She had been protected all her life, so the thought of having a child out of wedlock would devastate her and thus her family.

More to the point, would he be able to welcome another man's child into his life? At least he might give the dukedom an heir. Would Lucky be happy about that too?

By the time he reached the main hallway, he was no closer to knowing the answers. He intercepted one of the footmen who dealt with incoming guests and verified their membership.

"Jarvis, I'm expecting a lady. She will be wearing a dark brown cloak edged with fur, and she will ask for me by name. Send her into the first waiting room, will you? I'll meet her there."

"Certainly, sir."

Paul went into the already warm room and took a couple of masks out of one of the drawers. It would be hard to conceal his identity when he was so well known at the pleasure house, but it was imperative that they concealed Lucky's. The clock on the mantelpiece chimed nine times, and he started to pace the carpet.

He couldn't ask Lucky if she was breeding. She might not even know herself. If he married her, he had to take on everything about her, even her child. It was little to ask in return for a dukedom and a life free of gossip and innuendo. He stared into the red heart of the fire. Sometimes he felt like he was being slowly smothered and that no one could hear his screams.

The door opened and Jarvis stepped inside, ushering a well-concealed figure.

"Your guest, sir."

"Thank you, Jarvis."

Paul waited until Jarvis retired before moving toward Lucky. She took down her hood and stared around the room.

"This wasn't quite what I expected."

He kissed her cheek. "What did you expect?"

She blushed and took off her gloves. "Something a little less like my mother's morning room."

"But you have been here before, haven't you?"

"Only to the private part of the house on Barrington Square." Her gaze strayed to the painting over the mantelpiece. "This is quite different."

Paul grabbed her hands. "Are you sure you want to go through with this?"

"Yes, I am."

"You will see things that might shock you."

She smiled. "After what that rogue did to me, I fear I won't be shocked."

Paul didn't say anything to that. "If you want to leave at any time, just tell me and we will go."

"Thank you, Paul, but I am quite determined to see this through."

For a moment, she looked just as resolute as her father, and

Paul wanted to laugh. Instead, he showed her the blue velvet mask he held in his hand.

"You need to be incognito. Turn around so that I can tie this in place for you."

She obediently turned, and he carefully positioned the mask on her nose and secured the ties at the back of her head. "How's that?"

"Perfect." She swung around. "Should I keep my cloak on as well?"

"That is up to you. It might get a bit warm in the various rooms."

She took off her cloak and laid it over the back of a chair. "I borrowed this dress from my mother's closet. But I don't think anyone will associate it with her or me. She wears it when she does her charity visiting back at our country estate."

The dress was cut almost like a riding habit, with buttons up the front to a high collar and tight long sleeves. The clean lines suited Lucky, and for the first time he could see how much she took after her mother. She'd eschewed her usual curls, and braided her hair on the top of her head in a coronet.

"You look lovely."

She wrinkled her nose at him. "I look quite unlike myself, which is the purpose, yes?"

"Exactly." He put on his own mask and offered her his arm. "Are you ready, then?"

"Indeed I am."

He opened the door for her and headed toward the grand staircase. "This evening I thought I'd give you an overview of the pleasure house and point out the places where I like to . . . enjoy myself."

Her fingers dug into his arm. Beneath her smiling exterior she wasn't as calm as she wanted to appear. "You won't go off and leave me to fend for myself?"

"Of course not."

"Then how am I to see you 'enjoying' yourself?"

"That will have to wait for another evening," he muttered. "If we survive this one."

Lucky glanced around as they ascended the staircase and came out on to a large landing dominated by a portrait of an almost naked blond beauty. She nudged Paul in the ribs.

"Is that Madame Helene?"

"Yes, it is. I believe it was painted about twenty years ago by an admirer."

"She is so beautiful." Lucky sighed.

"Indeed, and as I'm sure she's told you, beauty brings both great rewards and great trouble."

Lucky remembered Helene's sympathetic gaze and slowly nodded. "Indeed. I don't think her life has been easy."

Paul drew her farther along the landing toward a set of double doors. "Here we have the first of the main salons on this level. It is where most of the guests congregate to meet their friends and decide what particular type of entertainment they desire for the evening."

Lucky peered around Paul's shoulder and studied the large gold-and-scarlet room. At one end there was a buffet table, and footmen moved through the throng offering various beverages. After that, all similarity to one of her mother's parties ended. Some of the guests were already naked and sprawled with others on the many couches and cushions spread around the space.

"I don't have to take my clothes off, do I?" she whispered to Paul.

"Not unless you want to," he replied, his expression serious. "But I don't think I have ever survived a whole evening here without losing at least one article of clothing."

"Oh," Lucky said. "What else is there to do here other than . . . this?"

"I'll show you. Just keep walking through the salon, Lucky.

Don't let anyone stop you, and don't speak to anyone or let on that you know who they are."

Before she could question him further, he tucked her hand into the crook of his arm and moved forward, steering a fast and direct path to the other set of double doors that led out of the salon on the opposite wall. It was difficult for Lucky to keep her mouth closed. She'd already spotted two of her mother's friends, and several of her father's acquaintances from the House of Lords, in among the melee. And none of them had been behaving in an appropriate manner.

She let out her breath as they reached the other side of the room and again looked up at Paul, who seemed totally unperturbed by what he'd seen. She supposed that for him it was commonplace. Doubt crashed over her. Would she ever understand her enigmatic betrothed, or was she forever doomed to suffer from her own ignorance?

She swallowed hard. "These people look as if they are enjoying themselves."

"I think they are. They pay a lot of money to belong to this particular club and have the freedom to explore their sexual desires."

She met his gaze. "*I* didn't enjoy it."

His brown eyes hardened. "That's because the man who touched you was a complete bastard, who used your body against your will. When two people come together willingly, the result is far more pleasant. I hope to show you that."

She leaned back against the wall. "Sometimes I feel that my whole life became *fantastical* from the moment he forced himself on me." She gestured at the salon. "And all this? Seems no less fantastical to me either. I know I should be shocked, but I'm not. If this is another, better form of physical pleasure, I can only be glad of it."

Paul smiled at her and she frowned.

"What is wrong?"

"Nothing is wrong. I'm just impressed by your ability to think these things through."

"But I'm not. I'm simply allowing myself to experience this without judging anyone."

"Ambrose thought bringing you here might be a mistake."

"But he was wrong." She shook her head. "I can't explain it, but this is far less frightening and shocking than what happened to me in that garden."

"Perhaps it feels like that because you are not actually involved."

"That's true, but I'm not scared, Paul. I can assure you of that."

He held her gaze for a long moment and then nodded.

"Then we will carry on with our tour." He pointed down a long carpeted corridor with doors on either side. "The house is deceptive. It is actually quite deep and extends into the mansion in the square behind."

"What are all the doors for?" Lucky asked.

"Each one conceals a particular scenario that guests enjoy watching."

"Such as?"

He smiled down at her. "Let me put it another way. When you can't sleep at night, what do you dream about? Who comes to your bed?"

"I'm not sure what you mean."

He cupped her chin so that she had no choice but to look into his brown eyes. "You must have dreamed of, say, a prince taking you away on his stallion, or a pirate king, or *something?* I know the books you like to read, Lucky; you must have pictured yourself as the heroine of at least one of them."

She gazed into his eyes. She could hardly tell him that most of her romantic dreams had featured him. But maybe there *was* a way to do so after all.

"I dreamed of saving the life of a wounded warrior. Of

watching him wake up and fall in love with me," she said breathlessly.

His eyes narrowed as he considered her. "I think there might be something to your taste here, after all. Would you like to try it?"

"I will if you are with me." She hesitated. "Or will you be in it?"

"Not this time. I don't want to leave you by yourself tonight. If you enjoy the experience, perhaps we could find something we could appear in together on another night."

"Together?"

"Why not?"

Lucky took his hand and he led her down the long corridor, pausing at every door to read the handwritten card in the brass holder. Eventually he stopped near the end of the hallway and nodded.

"This should do it. Are you game?"

Lucky took a deep breath. "Yes, I am."

"Remember, if you want to leave at any point, just do so, and I'll follow you out."

He carefully opened the door and ushered her inside. To her surprise, there were already a few people sitting in the chairs that surrounded a central stage-like area. It was too dark to see anyone else's faces, and Lucky didn't really try. She sat down where Paul indicated, and he kept hold of her hand.

In the center of the stage was a narrow pallet occupied by a man who looked like a rather battered Roman soldier. Armor was piled up beside the bed, and a small earthenware oil lamp flickered, throwing light on to the man's face. His head was heavily bandaged, and he moved restlessly on the sheets, moaning some garbled form of Latin.

A woman approached him from the darkness wearing a dark green tunic and a plaid shawl, and carrying a pottery bowl. Her hair was red and worn in two long braids, and crowned by a bronze circlet. Lucky found herself holding her breath as the woman knelt down beside the man and started to wash the exposed parts of his skin.

He groaned more loudly and suddenly grabbed her wrist. His eyes opened and he stared at the woman.

"Who are you?"

"I'm Lady Carys."

"And why are you caring for me? From your speech you are my enemy."

The woman resumed washing the man's face. "Because I could not let any man die."

Lucky watched, transfixed, as Carys pulled aside the thin blanket and undid the ties of his tunic, exposing the man's muscled chest. She found herself sitting forward as the woman continued to wash her way down the man's body. She wondered what that felt like, the warmth of his skin, the crisp hair on his chest, and the way his muscles flexed as the woman touched him.

Jeremy hadn't undressed at all. All she remembered was the roughness of his coat pressed against her face, almost suffocating her, and his knee forcing her legs apart. . . . She shivered, and Paul squeezed her hand.

"Are you all right?"

She nodded and looked back at the man and woman in the center of the room. Carys was untying the man's belt now, pulling his tunic completely off to reveal a scrap of cloth covering his loins. A cloth that wasn't lying completely flat.

"What is your name, sir?" Carys asked softly.

"Flavian," the man replied. "When you've made me well, will your menfolk drag me out and kill me?"

"Not if I can prevent it," Carys murmured and dropped her head to kiss the soldier's battered face. Lucky found she was holding her breath as the kiss went on and on. Flavian brought his hand up and undid the woman's braids, burying his fingers in the woman's beautiful red hair.

Carys dropped the washcloth and removed the linen covering Flavian's groin. Lucky swallowed a gasp as his *protuberance* sprang free. . . .

She nudged Paul. "What is it called?"

"His cock?" he whispered. "His shaft, his rod?"

She stopped listening to him as Carys wrapped a hand around Flavian's "cock" and began to rub it. The man groaned and kissed her harder, urging her closer, tearing at her clothes in an effort to reach her skin. Not that Carys seemed to mind. Lucky had minded her dress being torn, but even she could see that this was very different.

Suddenly Flavian flipped Carys over on to her back and covered her with his body, pushing up her skirts as he continued to kiss her. Lucky found herself tensing, waiting for Carys to realize that the pleasantness of the kissing was about to be replaced by the pain of penetration.

"I want you, my lady."

Carys gazed up at the Roman, her breathing ragged, her nipples hard against the thin muslin of her shift. He curved a hand around her hip and then went lower to the place between her legs. Lucky felt her own body tighten in response, but Flavian didn't drive himself inside Carys; he slid two fingers in and out in a slow, deliberate rhythm.

"Do you want me?"

Carys was moaning now and lifting her hips into each stroke of Flavian's fingers. In the quietness of the room, Lucky could even hear the slick wet sounds he made. He shifted again, and Lucky gasped along with the woman when he lowered his mouth between Carys's legs and started to kiss and lick her there.

Lucky wanted to squirm on her seat. What they were seeing was far too intimate, yet she couldn't help but imagine herself in Carys's place, her body well prepared and willing to accept a man.

Carys screamed and the man rose over her, one hand on his cock, and plunged himself deep inside her. Beside her, Paul hissed a curse and jumped, and Lucky realized that she had dug her nails into his skin.

Without his tunic, Lucky could see the taut muscles of Flavian's arse as he pumped into Carys. He seemed to be taking a long time about it too—much longer than Jeremy had taken. . . .

As Flavian let out a final groan and collapsed over Carys, Lucky relaxed her grip on Paul's hand and let out a very shaky breath. Paul touched her shoulder and motioned toward the door, and she gladly followed him out.

10

Paul took Lucky to a smaller salon that appeared to be unoc-
cupied and sat opposite her. He took off his mask, and she removed hers as well. He fixed his attention on her face.

"Well?"

Lucky shook her head. "It was nothing like I expected it to
be. Are those people employed here, or are they actors from the
theater?"

"No, they are just guests who sign up to try out a particular
fantasy of theirs."

"Do they even know each other?"

"Sometimes they do, and sometimes they are strangers."

Lucky looked down at her tightly clasped hands. "But they
seemed to like what they were doing."

"Some people like sex, Lucky," he said gently.

She raised her head to look at him. "I don't."

"And I told you why." He paused. "I'm sure I can help you
enjoy it too."

She studied his brown coat, cream waistcoat, and buckskin

breeches. What did he look like under his clothes? Did he have muscles like Flavian and dark hair drifting down to a narrow point over his stomach?

"Why are you staring at me like that?"

"I'm trying to picture you without your clothing." She slapped a hand over her mouth and wished the words might disappear. "I'm so sorry, Paul. I don't know why I said that. This place is having a very strange effect on me."

He smiled at her and went to the door and locked it. "We're quite private in here. I'm quite happy to undress for you."

Lucky sat frozen in her seat as he tugged at his simply tied cravat. Did she really want him to strip for her, and what if she didn't like what she saw?

As usual, it was as if Paul could read her thoughts. "You might as well see what you'll be sharing your bed with. If you find me too off-putting it might stop you from making a terrible mistake." His tone was light, but she knew he understood her fears and was giving her yet another opportunity to change her mind.

He continued taking off his coat and unbuttoning his waistcoat. Lucky couldn't look away, her gaze now fixed to the placket of his breeches, which, like Flavian's, was not lying entirely flat either. He undid the top button of his shirt and then his hands dropped to his waist.

"I have to warn you that I am already aroused. Are you sure you want to see me like this?"

Lucky managed to nod. She might as well go through with it. A man had already ruined her. If she was too scared to even look at Paul, at least by finding out now, she'd avoid having to run away on her wedding night.

He slowly released the placket and stopped to pull his shirt over his head. She'd seen his scars before, so they didn't bother her. But her mother had made certain that during his convalescence, Lucky never saw Paul naked below the waist. He bent to step out of his breeches and boots, and Lucky held her breath when he finally straightened.

His cock was large and stiff, and pointing upward toward his flat stomach. It was purple at the crown and a dark red on the shaft that seemed to quiver with life. Lucky stared hard at it. No wonder it hurt when it went inside a woman.

"Would you like to touch me?" Paul asked.

Lucky jerked her gaze back to his face and found he looked remarkably calm, considering he was naked and she was probably about to bolt. What would he do if she ran? He could hardly follow her in his present state, although in the pleasure house, perhaps no one would notice.

"Touch you where?" Her voice came out a little breathlessly.

His smile was beautiful. "Anywhere. I promise I won't do anything except stand here."

Almost against her will, Lucky found herself walking toward him. His hands were by his sides and he appeared quite relaxed. She reached out her hand and placed it squarely on his chest, surprised at the warmth of his skin and the way he exhaled at her touch. She traced one of the longer scars that curled around his rib cage from a lash on his back.

"I remember when these scars were fresh."

He shrugged, making his muscles gleam and flex in the candlelight. He was finely drawn, his frame elegant rather than bulky like Jeremy's, yet she could still feel his strength. "The guards liked to beat us."

She concentrated on the feel of the ragged scar under the softness of her fingertip, and his heartbeat accelerated. She knew that if she looked down she would see the thrust of his cock perilously close to the silk of her dress. She hadn't seen Jeremy's cock, just felt it pushing at her and hurting her.

With all the courage she could muster, she reached down and touched the tip of him and almost pulled away when she realized he was wet. She wrapped two fingers around the first inch of his shaft and slowly squeezed. The softness covered a rigid interior that felt as solid as an iron railing.

"It's hard."

"Yes." With a muttered groan, Paul pushed against her tight grip, making her fingers even wetter.

"Why?"

"Because I'm standing here naked in front of you and you're touching my cock."

"That excites you?"

"Lucky, I'm not a saint. Of course it excites me."

"Would it matter who was touching you?"

He sighed. "It matters to me now."

She tried to recall what Carys had done to Flavian's cock and moved her fingers up and down Paul's shaft. "But you also said that complete strangers come together and do this."

"But we are not strangers, are we?"

The wetness made moving her fingers over him easier and faster. The rhythm of it absorbed her and made her whole body seem to hold its breath.

"I thought I knew the man who forced me. I thought I loved him." She kept her gaze on his cock. Faster now, and Paul was angling his hips into each pull of her hand, his breathing as erratic as her own. "How do I know that you won't be the same?"

"Did he let you do this?" Paul murmured. "Did he let you take control of him?"

"No." Lucky squeezed him hard and suddenly he clamped his fingers around her working wrist. "Are you going to stop me, now? Are you going to hurt me like he hurt me?"

"God, no, I'm going to come. I'm going to . . ."

He went rigid and then his cock pulsed hard once, then twice, in her hand, and then her palm was awash with his seed. She watched it flood between her fingers and drip down toward the carpet. His cock went soft, and she slowly released her grip on him.

"Let me help you."

Before she could even move, Paul produced a handkerchief, which he used to wipe her fingers and the rest of her hand. Despite his efforts she could still feel him there against her skin. She wanted to put her finger in her mouth and taste him. . . .

"God, *Lucky* . . ."

He turned back just as she was doing just that, his gaze fixed on her mouth.

She stared at him. "You taste like a mixture of the sea and the starch Milly puts on my petticoats."

"I know." He sat down in one of the chairs, still completely naked, and looked up at her. "Are you all right?"

"I feel quite odd," Lucky admitted. "As if I have been pulled into a completely different world from the one I thought I lived in."

"And do you like this world?"

She considered him for a long while. She didn't yet know how she felt about having a man "come" for her. "I'm not sure. But I can't change what happened to me, so I might as well move forward."

Paul smiled. "That's the spirit. Now, would you like me to pleasure you with my mouth, or do you want to complete the rest of your tour of the pleasure house?"

Lucky thought she had misheard his casually posed question. Perhaps he did know how she'd feel about what she'd done to him after all. It wasn't really surprising. He was probably used to his effect on women.

"You want to touch me?"

He shrugged. "If you want to be touched."

For a moment, Lucky actually considered the shocking idea, and then she headed for the door. "I'm not sure I'm ready for that yet. Shall we go?"

"Do you want to wait until I put my clothes on?"

She looked back at him over her shoulder and saw that he was grinning at her.

"I'm quite happy to follow you around naked, Lucky, but that will create a lot of interest, and you might have to stop and wait for me to fuck someone."

Lucky felt her cheeks grow warm. He'd said "fuck" to her, a word she'd only heard once before in her life when she'd inadvertently come across one of the stable hands and a maid copulating in the hayloft.

"I'd rather you were clothed," she said primly.

Actually that was a lie. She'd like to stay in that room and touch him for hours, but it was probably best that she didn't mention it, because he'd probably let her. She tried not to stare as he pulled his shirt over his head and stepped into his breeches and boots.

It would be difficult enough to look at him now, knowing what he concealed beneath his clothes, wondering whether he was aroused as they walked around the pleasure house and why. Difficult to see him as just her friend anymore as well.

"You liked it, didn't you?" Paul said.

"Liked what?" Lucky knew she was blushing.

"Touching me, making me come."

She raised her chin. "Yes, I did."

His smile was slow and full of warmth and admiration. "I'm glad."

He picked up his waistcoat and then dropped it back on to the chair. "I don't think I'll bother with that. I'll pick them up later. Shall we go?"

Being seen with a man in his shirtsleeves was tantamount to seeing him in his nightshirt, but Lucky was determined not to say anything. She'd voluntarily entered Paul's world and now she had to accept it. It was also possible that he was testing her again.

"Yes, indeed." They replaced their masks, and she unlocked and opened the door. He moved past her into the hallway and took her hand again. "What else is there to see?"

He guided her back on to the main landing again and pointed up the stairs. "There are three levels to the pleasure house. On the second level, things become a little more risqué."

"*More* risqué?" Lucky murmured.

"Yes." Paul took her arm and drew her out of the way of a group of men who were heading up the stairs. "Men are able to find other men up there to fuck. Others with very distinct sexual tastes can find partners who share them, and pair off for the evening."

"And on the third floor?" Lucky asked.

"The third floor is for those with a taste for pain and domination in their sexual play. You do not need to worry yourself about that level. I have no intention of taking you up there."

"Do you go there yourself?"

"I used to, but I found myself growing bored with it." His smile grew pensive. "I realized I liked to be fucked without being hurt or humiliated."

"Are you sure that it isn't the level for me?"

He raised an eyebrow. "You enjoyed being hurt and humiliated?"

"No, I hated it."

"Then it is definitely not the place for you."

"Why would anyone enjoy being hurt?"

"I can't explain that, but trust me, some people do." He looked back up the stairs. "Let's go and inspect the second floor. It *is* where I spend the majority of my time after all."

Paul led Lucky up the stairs and considered what best to show her first. Despite being exposed to some particularly sensual sights, including his own cock, she'd done remarkably well so far. Her composure and ability to understand what she was seeing was mature beyond her years. Yet she'd always been like that. As an only child much in the company of adults, she'd grown up fast.

He spied Marie-Claude, who kept the second floor working in perfect order, and waved her over. She was an older woman in her mid-forties with a pleasant, round face and a voluptuous body that Paul knew many patrons of the house still craved. She was extremely selective of her lovers, and the competition to win her favors was fierce.

"Good evening, Lieutenant," Marie-Claude said. "Ambrose told me you might be bringing a guest through with you tonight." She turned to smile at Lucky. "You are most welcome, ma'am."

"Thank you."

Paul squeezed Lucky's arm. "This is Marie-Claude. She works here and organizes all the activities on this floor."

"Indeed I do." Marie-Claude looked back at Paul. "Is there anything in particular that you wish to show your guest tonight?"

"Nothing in particular, thanks, Marie-Claude. I just wished to give her a general taste for what goes on here."

He grimaced at his choice of words. He'd been semi-erect ever since he'd seen Lucky tasting his come on her fingers.

"Ah, well, I'll just let you be then," Marie-Claude said. "But if there is anything you need, just come and find me, *cheri*."

Lucky watched Marie-Claude until she walked out of the main salon. "She is very nice."

"And she is also extremely knowledgeable. If there is anything you want to know about what goes on between men and women, ask Marie-Claude."

"Does she decide what parts you play, Paul?"

Paul looked down at his masked companion. "Sometimes, if a guest asks for a particular type of lover or a particular look. Usually I make my own choices." He walked her over to a deserted table and chairs and waited until she sat down. There were very few people in the main salon at this early hour, and he was hopeful of remaining undisturbed for a while.

"What do you like doing the most?" Lucky asked.

"Everything," Paul answered with a smile. "I'm quite willing to try anything."

"But what do you like?"

Her simple question made him think rather harder than he usually wanted to. "Do I have to have a preference?"

Her color rose. "I didn't mean to be rude, I . . ."

He reached for her hand. "I'm sorry, my lady. You have a perfect right to ask me whatever you want. When Gabriel bequeathed me his membership in the club, he told me to experience everything the place had to offer, and I've definitely tried to do that."

"Why do you think Gabriel told you to do that?"

"Because he wanted me well occupied and out of his way while he made love to his wife? So that he didn't feel guilty about abandoning me?" Paul shrugged. "Who knows? Perhaps he thought bedding a lot of women would make me become more like him."

"And did it?"

"It taught me that I could fuck a woman," Paul said flatly. "It didn't make me like Gabriel. I still prefer men."

"Then how can you even contemplate marrying me?"

Paul looked up sharply from his inspection of the floorboards into Lucky's eyes and forced a smile. "Let's not go over all that again, shall we? I thought we'd already decided that we both have good reasons for wanting to marry."

Lucky was about to reply when someone came up behind Paul and she quickly looked down.

"Lieutenant St. Clare?"

He turned to find Ambrose standing over him.

Ambrose bowed in Lucky's direction, "Ma'am, a pleasure."

Paul rose to his feet. "What is it?"

"Madame told me to remind you not to forget to visit the room of desires with your guest."

"Madame is here?"

"No, she left a note for you. I forgot about it earlier when we were in the kitchen."

Paul stared at his old friend. Forgetting anything was most unlike Ambrose and indicative of his earlier disquiet about Miss Ross.

"I'll certainly show her that room. Thank you for reminding me, Ambrose." Paul smiled dismissively, but Ambrose refused to budge. "Was there something else?"

"Mr. Carstairs asked me if you were available to join him and his female companion tonight."

"And I assume you told him no?"

Lucky stood and touched his arm. "If you wish to join them, I'm sure Mr. Ambrose would be able to see me safely home."

Paul patted her hand. "No, that won't be necessary." He turned back to Ambrose. He might as well burn all his bridges at once. "You may tell Mr. Carstairs, and anyone else who asks, that I'm no longer available here ever again."

He bowed to Ambrose and walked Lucky away from him. He wasn't quite sure why Ambrose had insisted on forcing the issue of his involvement with the pleasure house right in front of Lucky, but at least she now knew what he'd done.

He kept moving until they reached the last door next to the entrance to the servants' stairs. Lucky stopped and touched his cheek.

"You didn't have to do that."

"I did. If we marry, I don't expect you to have to listen to obscene gossip about what I get up to without you at the pleasure house. I don't want you to have to worry about whether the lord and lady you are entertaining for dinner have both been in my bed."

"That is very noble of you."

"No, it's not. As I said, I gain a lot from this marriage as well." Anxious to change the subject, he took a deep breath and knocked on the door in front of him. "This is the room of desires Ambrose was talking about."

He opened the door and led her into the lobby. "A guest can come here and ask for a secret sexual fantasy to be organized for him. If possible, we will try to arrange it as quickly as possible. Only a few of us participate in the sexual games in here because, obviously, by choosing this option, most of the guests don't want others to know they have these particular desires. We keep their wishes to ourselves."

Lucky walked around the small space and peered into one of the empty rooms. "So is this your favorite thing to do here?"

"One of my favorites. I like the intimacy of it, and to be honest, the things that people ask for can be a bit more interesting than the norm."

She swung around to look at him. "Like what?"

"Are you sure that you want to know?"

"I've come this far with you, surely you can trust me with the rest of it?"

He leaned back against the wall. "If you are sure." At her nod, he continued. "There was one occasion when a widowed woman asked for three men to service her."

"Three?"

"Indeed. She also demanded that the men be leashed and naked, that they only speak when spoken to, and then only say yes or no, mistress."

"And what did she want you all to do? Behave like dogs?"

He smiled. "Well, she certainly wanted to hold our leashes and whip us if we misbehaved, but mainly she wanted all three of us pleasuring her at the same time."

"All three of you," Lucky said slowly. "How . . . ?"

He decided to be blunt. "One in her mouth, one in her cunt, and one in her arse."

"Oh."

"And she wanted us to keep changing position, so that she could experience all of us in every possible way."

"Oh." Lucky looked away from him. "And now I can't stop trying to figure out exactly what such a scenario would look like."

Paul found himself laughing. "Lucky, you are a delight." He took her hand. "If you want to see such a thing, all we have to do is go downstairs."

She squeezed his fingers. "I think I've seen quite enough for one night, don't you?"

"But have I repulsed you?"

She looked into his eyes. "Not at all; I just have a lot to think about."

He held his breath. "Do you think you will want to come back here with me?"

Her smile was calm. "It seems inevitable somehow, doesn't it? And I'm sure there is a lot more of you to be seen here." She sighed. "I suppose I should be shocked, shouldn't I? Part of me wants to curl up in a ball and refuse to go out in society ever again in case someone tries to touch me. But there is another part of me that refuses to let one man destroy who I am." She bit down on her lip. "Does that make any sense at all?"

He kissed her fingers. "It makes perfect sense to me, and I'm glad that you've chosen to be brave. I admire you enormously for it."

At that, she blushed and looked away from him, but he was happy to let her, certain that he'd made his point and more than willing to take her back to the safety of Haymore House.

11

Lucky stared out of her bedroom window and considered everything she had observed at the pleasure house on the previous evening. She'd seen her first fully naked and aroused man and then asked Paul to strip for her so that she could see him too. She rested her hot face against the windowpane. How could she have done that? In the familiar girlish surroundings of her bedchamber it seemed completely out of character.

But she was glad she'd seen him—touched him—even given him pleasure. By offering her a choice, he'd somehow restored some of the confidence she'd lost after Jeremy's assault on her person. And it had been an assault. The more she thought about how well Paul had treated her, the angrier she became at Jeremy.

But there was more to learn both about Paul and herself. Did she want to see him with another man? Did her curiosity really stretch that far? Apparently it did, or she wouldn't be dressed up, ready to leave with Paul when he finally appeared at the ducal mansion on another expedition to the pleasure house.

Milly came into the room, her face ablaze with anticipation, and hissed, "He's here, my lady!"

Lucky smiled at her excited maid. "Thank you, Milly."

"Should I tell him to hide in the morning room?"

"There is no need. My parents know that he is escorting me this evening. We plan to meet up with them later." Milly's face fell, and Lucky hastened to add, "We're just not going to exactly the place that we told them we were going to."

"Ooh, my lady," Milly breathed. "You will be careful now, won't you?"

Milly didn't need to know it was far too late to worry about that. "Of course I will." Lucky picked up her evening cloak and tied the ribbons at her throat. "I'm sure Lieutenant St. Clare will take excellent care of me."

Milly held the door open, and Lucky slipped past her. She paused to look down on Paul, who stood in the large entrance hall, apparently observing a bust depicting Hades dragging Persephone down into the underworld. He was dressed in his uniform and his blond hair touched the back of his collar. He looked older and uncharacteristically serious. Lucky experienced a pang of doubt. Would he really let her out of the engagement that easily? He was proving remarkably more stubborn than she had expected. In truth, he was proving far more complex all around.

He turned as she came down the stairs and smiled at her. "Good evening, Lucky. You look beautiful. Are you ready for another adventure?"

"Indeed I am." She placed her hand in his, and he brought it to his lips. "I told my mother we would meet them at the Lakeland ball by midnight."

"Then I shall endeavor to ensure that you are taken there safely and don't turn into a pumpkin."

She chuckled as he led her toward the door. He was the only person who could make her laugh even at the worst of times.

She would hate to lose his friendship. That unsettling thought made her glance up at him as he helped her into the hired coach.

He slammed the door and took the seat next to her. "What's wrong, Lucky? Do you not want to go? We can attend that dreadful musicale evening your parents suggested instead, if you prefer."

In the gloom of the single carriage lamp, Lucky studied his familiar, and now *not* so familiar, features. "If I don't choose to marry you, will we still be friends?"

He reclaimed her hand. "I don't see why not."

"Won't you think of me differently?"

He studied her carefully. "I've already begun to think of you differently, but I quite like it."

"Because I touched you?"

"There is that, and because you have displayed the most remarkable common sense throughout all this madness." He bent forward and brushed his mouth over hers. "But mainly because you made me hard and made me come."

"I did nothing of the sort," she whispered almost against his lips.

His tongue flicked out and traced the line of her lower lip. "Yes, you did. You touched me, you held my shaft in your hand, and you stroked me until I had no choice but to climax."

"Yes, I suppose I did," she breathed and opened her mouth to his questing tongue.

She'd always enjoyed the kissing part, and Paul was obviously a master at it. Unlike Jeremy, he didn't seem in a rush to end the kiss either. She'd always thought Jeremy saw kissing as a token that had to be paid in order to venture on to more visceral and uncomfortable pursuits. Paul took his time learning her mouth, what she liked and what made her inch closer and closer to his body until he was supporting most of her weight.

When he eventually pulled away, Lucky realized the carriage was no longer moving, and that the outline of a footman was visible through the mercifully grimy window. She touched her mouth and the kidskin of her glove felt rough against her now swollen lips. Paul's gaze dropped to her questing fingers and he groaned.

"Now all I will be thinking about for the rest of the evening is the sweet taste of your mouth." He hesitated. "Did I scare you?"

"No," she replied. "Not at all."

"Good." He held out his hand. "Then shall we go in?"

She drew her hood over her head and allowed him to help her down from the carriage and into the back entrance of the pleasure house. To her surprise, he led her through into a large, homely kitchen, where the dark-skinned man he'd called Ambrose sat reading a newspaper at the table.

"Evening, Ambrose," Paul said cheerfully.

Ambrose lowered the paper and studied them. "You should use the proper entrance, Lieutenant. You no longer work here, remember?"

Lucky pulled at Paul's hand, but he kept advancing.

"Oh, for goodness' sake, Ambrose. Stop being such a scold. I'm trying to keep my intended's identity a secret. I'm sure Christian won't mind."

"I'm sure he'll give you his opinion on that in his own good time. He's upstairs with Marie-Claude and Madame Elizabeth."

"I know."

Ambrose put the paper down completely. "You do?"

"I asked him to meet me there." Paul grinned at Ambrose and clapped him on the shoulder. "I just need a mask for my lady, and we'll be off."

A few minutes later, Lucky found herself being escorted up the narrow servants' stairs and out into a deserted hallway.

"Where are we?" she whispered.

"At the room of desires." Paul unlocked the door and held it open. There was already light seeping under one of the closed doors and a banked fire in the grate. "I thought you might be more comfortable in a more private environment."

"More comfortable doing what?"

He smiled down at her. "Watching me."

She could think of nothing to say to that, but was acutely aware of a thrill of anticipation shooting through her. Who would've thought she had such a wicked streak? Maybe she was more like Paul's side of the family than she realized.

"What do you want me to do?"

He pulled back a thick velvet curtain and ushered her into a room where two comfortable wing chairs faced a large, draped mirror. "When you hear a knock on the wall, pull back the curtain and just watch. You will be able to see us, but no one will see you, I promise."

Lucky sank down into one of the gold brocade chairs and squeezed her trembling knees together. "You said 'us.' "

He'd already turned toward the entrance. "Indeed I did. I told you that I was going to meet up with Christian, Elizabeth, and Marie-Claude." He hesitated, his smile disappearing. "If you find what you see . . . distasteful, you can leave the way we came and seek out Ambrose in the kitchen. He will see you safely to your parents at the Lakeland ball."

Paul closed the curtain over the exit and headed next door, where he assumed he would find his coconspirators. After a lot of thought, he'd decided it would be better to ask the people he trusted to fuck him rather than some random guest. One never knew quite what would happen with a new partner, and he didn't want to scare Lucky away. When he first came to the pleasure house, he'd loved the unpredictability of a new lover, but now he craved something else. Something he'd thought he'd found with Constantine, a lover who actually seemed to care about him.

"Ah, there you are, Paul," Christian Delornay said. "We

were beginning to wonder whether you had changed your mind."

Paul smiled at Helene's son, the new owner of the pleasure house and a force to be reckoned with. He was blond like his mother, but had the hazel eyes and determined jawline of his father. He was also one of Paul's favorite sexual partners.

Paul turned and bowed at the two women. "Good evening, Elizabeth, Marie-Claude, and thank you for helping me."

Marie-Claude shrugged. "It is a pleasure."

"And ours too." Christian took Elizabeth's hand and kissed it. "Have you thought about what you want us to do?"

Paul sighed. "I was hoping you'd have some ideas. The most important thing is that my lady sees me being fucked by a man."

"*And* sees that you can successfully perform with a woman," Elizabeth added, her hand still entwined with her husband's. "Surely that, too?"

"You're right, my love."

Christian's tender smile at his wife was as unexpected as it was beautiful. He had a reputation as a cold, unemotional man, but there was no evidence of that in his treatment of Elizabeth. Gossip said she had wrought a miracle and must be an angel, but Paul knew better. From personal experience, Paul knew that Christian's lovemaking could become a little rough, something they obviously both enjoyed despite Elizabeth's fragile appearance.

Paul moved to the center of the room where a large, low daybed, big enough to hold all of them, occupied most of the space. "Why don't I stand here and you can start by undressing me?"

The other three nodded and came to stand around him. None of them had bothered to wear a mask, as it was unlikely that Lucky would see any of them at society events. Despite her rank, Elizabeth's shocking behavior had resulted in the entire *ton*'s disapproval. She didn't seem to care, and Christian had always hated society anyway.

Marie-Claude went over and knocked on the large mirror that faced the room, and Paul listened intently for the small scraping sound of the curtain being opened on the other side. He wondered how Lucky was feeling and realized he was already hard at the mere thought of her watching him. His lust was tempered with fear that she'd be so shocked she'd end the engagement, but his cock didn't seem to care.

He took a deep breath and allowed Marie-Claude and Elizabeth to slowly strip him out of his coat. They wore only their shifts and stockings. Christian, who was the only one still fully dressed, took a seat on the daybed and started to direct the women as to what to remove next. It was typical of Christian to have to be in charge, but Paul didn't mind.

When Paul was completely naked, the women turned him fully to face the mirror. Elizabeth played with his nipples while Marie-Claude worked his cock until he was stiff and wet.

"Marie-Claude, kneel in front of him," Christian ordered. Paul looked over his shoulder and found that Christian had already opened the placket of his breeches and was fondling his own cock. "Elizabeth, come and kneel in front of me."

Paul waited until both the women were in position and then stared at Christian. "What next?"

"Isn't it obvious? They'll suck our cocks, but not quite enough to make us come."

Paul groaned as Marie-Claude licked the tip of his cock and then drew him into the warm cavern of her extremely talented mouth. His hips started to rock in time to the pull of her mouth, and he rested one shaking hand in her dark hair. Behind him, he heard the slick sounds of Elizabeth working Christian's cock. What would Lucky make of it? Would she ever think of taking him like this? The thought made him want to come.

Marie-Claude slid her fingers around the base of his shaft and squeezed hard, making him gulp for air.

"Not yet, Lieutenant."

Christian's voice again, this time slightly hoarser. "Change places and lift your skirt, Marie-Claude; let him lick you to a climax."

Paul tried to ignore the insistent throb of his cock and did as he was told. He eagerly lapped at the intriguing swollen folds of his partner, dragging his tongue over her most sensitive bud, drawing her deep into his mouth and then stabbing his tongue deep within her.

She clutched at his hair, and he increased his pace until she was grinding her sex against his mouth, practically drowning him in her wet, wanting flesh. Pain shot through him as she pulled hard on his hair and came against his waiting mouth. He took it all, gentling her down with his tongue and his kisses, imagining it was Lucky and that she was begging him to plunge his cock deep inside her.

When Marie-Claude finally released her grip on his hair, he was panting and covered in her juices. Elizabeth had collapsed on to the divan, and Christian was kissing her still open thighs. Paul's gaze was inexorably drawn back to the mirror. Was Lucky enthralled or horrified by what she'd seen so far? He wished to God he knew, but in his present state, he could hardly pop in there and ask her. And if she was aroused by what she'd seen, he might find it difficult to leave without inviting her to join them.

He realized Christian was speaking and turned to listen.

Lucky gripped the armrests of her chair until her fingernails protested. She hadn't expected to see two couples in the room beyond the mirror. She hadn't expected to feel so *warm* and find it so difficult to sit still without squirming. Since Paul was the only completely naked person in the room, her gaze naturally fell on him the most. Had he liked that woman's mouth on him? He'd looked as if he were in paradise.

The aristocratic blond man seemed to be directing the events. He reminded her of someone. It took her a moment to work out that he must be the infamous Christian Delornay, the son of Madame Helene. She could only assume that the petite, dark-haired woman was his equally scandalous wife, a disgraced French noblewoman.

Lucky pressed her hand to her heart as Paul nodded and climbed up onto the divan next to the other man. They both turned sideways, and Lucky shivered as Christian wrapped his hand around Paul's cock and slid his fingers up and down. Paul's eyes started to close and his hands fisted by his sides. Lucky found herself licking her own lips as Christian leaned in and kissed Paul's mouth.

Another command from Christian, and Paul rolled over on to his hands and knees. Lucky held her breath as Marie-Claude brought over a glass jar and gave it to Christian. He dipped his fingers in the pot and then gently caressed Paul's buttocks, his fingers disappearing between them in a regular rocking motion.

Lucky craned forward, trying to see exactly what he was doing, but it was too difficult. For a moment she considered leaving the safety of her viewing chamber, marching into the other room, and demanding a closer look. She was on her feet before she realized that if she wanted to see Paul like this again, he would probably let her at another, more private date.

She sat back down and watched as Christian slowly removed his clothes and slathered the oily substance over his thick cock. He lay full-length on the divan, one hand on his cock, holding it away from his belly, and beckoned to Paul.

Lucky crept as close to the mirror as she could. Paul faced Christian's feet, straddled the man, and gently lowered himself down on to Christian's thick cock. Both men gasped, and Paul dropped his head to stare at where he was impaled, his own cock still stiff and thrusting upward.

Christian snapped his fingers and Marie-Claude carefully straddled his legs. She moved closer to Paul until he was able to support her enough so that she could take his cock inside her. Lucky let out a gasp, which misted up the mirror so much that she had to rub frantically at the glass. By the time she could see again, the second woman, whom she assumed was Christian's wife, lowered her sex over Christian's face.

They all started to move, Paul providing most of the motion, while the others reacted to him. Lucky couldn't look away, and couldn't help but wonder which of the four she would like to be. This wasn't at all like the horrible encounter she had experienced with Jeremy. Yes, it was brash and crude, but not in a way that humiliated anyone. In truth, they all seemed to be enjoying themselves immensely.

Lucky imagined being the center of such concentrated attention and felt a pulse begin between her legs. She wanted to press her fingers against the ache to ease it, to cup and stroke her breast as Paul was doing to Marie-Claude. Even if her body hadn't enjoyed what Jeremy did to her, it still remembered the primitive rough thrust and withdrawal she was witnessing.

Paul started to move faster, his back arching and his hips rolling. Lucky bit her lip as Marie-Claude bucked once more against him and then they suddenly both froze and clutched each other hard. Marie-Claude's scream was loud enough to penetrate the wall.

Lucky drew the curtain and stumbled backward until she fell into the chair, her breathing unsteady, her whole body shaking. She cast one wild glance at the door. Could she run back to the safety of the life she'd had before? Her sweet, pleasant existence with her parents and her unrequited love for Paul? Did she want *this* with him? This raw, physical union? Her mind still hesitated even as her body trembled with arousal.

Could she have such a physical union with Jeremy? She tried to imagine being naked with him in the same bed and shuddered. Instinct told her no. She leaned back against the solid frame of the chair. Then what should she do? She took a moment to calm her agitated breathing and then slowly stood up and headed for the door.

"*Merci.*" Marie-Claude kissed Paul on the cheek and then bent to retie her stocking. Christian and Elizabeth had already departed in some haste, no doubt to finish their evening in private. "I know you prefer men, *mon cher*, but you are an excellent lover."

"Perhaps you could tell my lady that," Paul said, his gaze anxiously focused on the mirror. "I hope she hasn't run away."

Marie-Claude chuckled. "I don't believe she has."

Something in her voice made Paul turn to find Lucky framed in the doorway. Marie-Claude patted his arm.

"I will see you tomorrow, *oui*? Now good night."

Paul nodded as she slipped away, his attention all on Lucky, who had remained just inside the door, her gaze wandering all around the room. He didn't try and hide either his nakedness or the marks on his body where Christian and Marie-Claude had held him. She'd demanded his honesty, and he would give it to her whatever the cost.

He walked over to where a basin of water, soap, and a drying cloth awaited him and busied himself cleaning off. When he turned back, Lucky was still in the same spot, although now she was staring at him. He held her gaze and walked slowly toward her. She didn't back away, which gave him some hope.

"Well?"

She bit down on her lip. "It was terrifying."

He felt as if she'd punched him in the stomach. He tried to think of what to say, but she continued before he had a chance.

She wrapped her arms around herself as if to keep him out. "I kept thinking about how primitive we all are at our cores. We try and cover it up with good manners and clothes and *morals,* but when you strip them away, we're still animals."

He looked around for his shirt and pantaloons, suddenly wanting, needing, something between them. It was obvious that he'd gone too far and reminded her too vividly of her rape. Ambrose had warned him, and he'd decided not to listen. Now it was time to pay the price.

He finally spied his clothes stacked neatly on a chair by the door. Marie-Claude was nothing if not practical. He pulled his shirt over his head and stepped into his satin pantaloons.

"I'll take you to your parents, or would you prefer to go with someone else?"

"What?"

He went to move past her, but she grabbed his arm, her fingernails digging deep.

"You don't understand."

He fixed his gaze on her restraining hand. "It's all right, Lucky. I'll take you home."

"No!"

Startled, he looked up into her eyes. "Whatever you want from me, just tell me," he whispered. "I'll do anything."

Tears filled her eyes. "I wanted to be on that bed with you. I wanted to be touched!"

"You did?"

She brought her hand up to her cheek and dashed away the tears. "I was scared of what I saw, but something inside me still wanted it."

"There's nothing wrong with that," Paul said gently. "As you said, it is the most natural thing in the world."

"But it is raw and messy, and undignified and . . ."

Paul put his fingers over her mouth. "I've fought in battles where my entire focus was on staying alive. I didn't care who or what I killed as long as I survived."

She jerked away from his hand. "What does that have to do with anything?"

"I'm just trying to tell you that instinct will out. I'm not proud of what I've done, but I'm damned glad to be alive."

"But you had no choice. It's not the same as wanting to . . ."

"To make love to someone? Yes, it is." He held her gaze. "It's just as basic an instinct. Sometimes I think that's all we were put on this earth for. It is perfectly natural and acceptable to want to get messy and wet and uncivilized with another person. It can bring you great joy."

"But it didn't, so why do I still want to try it again?"

He smiled. "Because you liked what you saw? Because you liked the idea of me doing those things to you rather than this other man?"

Color rose in her cheeks. "But what if it isn't any different from last time?"

"It will be different because I care about you."

She swallowed hard. "He said that I was a disappointment, that I was a cold and unlovable woman and that it was all my own fault for luring him on."

Paul fought to keep his voice even. If he ever met the bastard who had hurt Lucky he was going to rip off the man's cock and feed it to his dogs.

"Shall we prove him wrong then?" He tugged on her hand until she sat on the edge of the divan and drew her into his arms. "Let me give you pleasure. Let me touch you."

Before she could say another word, he kissed her and her arms came around his neck and held him tight. He could feel her whole body trembling, and he slowly stroked her until she sighed into his mouth and relaxed against him. He'd learned a lot about pleasuring women over the past year, and he intended to make sure that Lucky benefited from every bit of his experience. Perhaps that was what it had all been about, preparing him to help Lucky enjoy sex.

He shifted his hands, running them over her buttocks, hips, and the sides of her breasts. He kept up the slow, drugging kisses until she was kissing him back with a languid ease that made his body tighten. Eventually she turned willingly in his arms and he slid his hand between them to cup her breast. The bodice of her gown was a flimsy, shallow piece of silk that he could easily slide his thumb under. Her stays were another matter entirely.

He dragged his mouth away from hers. "Will you let me take off your gown and stays? I don't want to ruin the silk."

To his relief she nodded, and he worked quickly and efficiently to release her, laying the garments on one of the chairs. It occurred to him that after her past experience, this might even be easier for her than being fully clothed. He kissed her again until she moved sensuously against him, her body wanting more than perhaps her mind was prepared for.

He curved a hand over her hip and buttock and felt her quiver in response. He widened the caress, letting his thumb drift toward her mound, his mouth never leaving hers, his movements as unhurried as he could make them. She moaned and he slid his thumb lower, rubbing against her sex until he felt the swell of her bud beneath the pad of his thumb.

God, she was already wet and open. His cock kicked against his pantaloons and he was glad that he was at least partially clothed. The desire to slam his hard length into her welcoming softness was surprisingly strong. But wasn't that what he'd just been telling her? The instinct to fuck was an incredibly powerful one.

He kept his thumb on her bud and worked the tip of his finger through the wetness and inside her. Her fingernails dug into his shoulder and he went still.

"Let me take care of you, Lucky," he whispered. "Let me inside. I promise I won't hurt you."

He began to move his finger back and forth, deeper with every careful stroke until she was taking all of it. She gasped his name against his lips, and he increased his tempo, flicking and rubbing at her clit with each thrust. She started to tighten around him and he worked her even harder, let her hear the wetness of her desire and the smack of his fingers, the wildness of it.

"Please," she whispered.

"It's all right, I've got you. Let it go, love, take your pleasure."

"I don't know how. . . ."

He glanced down the length of her body to where his finger was embedded in her. "I'll help you." As he continued to finger-fuck her, he kissed his way down her throat, cupped her breast, and sucked hard on her already taut nipple. She gasped his name, but he didn't stop there. He kissed his way down over her flat stomach and set his mouth where he'd wanted to put it, over her sex.

She settled her fingers into his hair, her nails into his scalp, and he didn't care, as he used all his expertise, his mouth, and his fingers to make her climax. She gave in with a strangled scream that made her whole body arch off the divan. Paul smiled against her swollen flesh and gently brought her back down until she was lying pliantly beside him.

Eventually he rose up on one elbow and looked down at her. "Well?"

She returned his gaze, her cheeks flushed, her blue eyes reflecting the new sensual knowledge that he had shared with her.

"It was still terrifying but also extraordinary."

He brushed a curl away from her cheek. "I'm glad."

"But I need to get to the Lakeland ball now."

"Right now?" Paul frowned as she struggled to sit up.

"Yes."

He got off the divan and waited while she righted herself. "Let me help you into your stays and gown. I can also call a maid to attend to your hair."

She smiled at him. "Thank you. She can attend to me while you ready yourself."

He paused in the act of picking up the rest of his clothes. It all seemed far too easy. "You still want me to come with you, then?"

"Of course!"

"Are you absolutely sure?"

She raised her chin and he was suddenly reminded of her father. "I still want to marry you, Paul. What could be clearer than that?"

12

Paul fidgeted as his new valet arranged the intricate folds of his cravat and secured the arrangement with a diamond-headed pin. Paul squinted down to look at it.

"Where did that come from, Jordan? I don't own any jewelry apart from my father's signet ring."

"It is a present from His Grace, sir."

"You mean, from the duchess."

"I believe she might've had a hand in the decision, sir, being as she is the main organizer of the wedding. But I'm loath to comment on my betters."

Paul studied his ornate silver waistcoat in the long mirror that Jordan had insisted on installing in Paul's new apartment in Haymore House. It was only two weeks since he and Lucky had visited the pleasure house together, and they hadn't been alone since. To his surprise, the engagement had been announced formally the next day and preparations for the wedding had started immediately.

Not that he'd been consulted about anything. The ladies seemed to have that well in hand. His fingers strayed to his cravat, and his valet cleared his throat warningly. Paul dropped his hand and resisted the urge to complain that he felt as if he were being hung. Some part of him still felt like a condemned man, but he'd promised Lucky he'd do whatever she wanted, and he was determined to stick to that.

"Let me help you on with your coat now, sir," Jordan murmured.

Paul let Jordan ease him into the tightly fitted black garment and again studied his reflection. After his well-worn uniform, it felt strange to be encased in such fashionable clothing. He looked quite unlike himself, his hair ruthlessly trimmed and his whiskers non-existent. His friends would hardly recognize him.

At that thought, Paul looked at the clock on the mantel-piece. "When am I supposed to leave for the church?"

"You have another few minutes, sir," Jordan replied as he brushed Paul's coat. "I understand that Mr. Delornay and Cap-tain David Grey are already waiting downstairs to accompany you."

"They are already here?" Paul took his pocket watch from Jordan and a purse full of coin, and put them in his coat pocket. He'd asked Ambrose to stand up with him as well, but his old friend had refused, saying he'd be more comfortable and less conspicuous among the congregation. Despite his disappoint-ment, Paul understood his need for privacy and didn't press him.

He wondered how Lucky was, and whether her nerve would hold until they were safely married. On the rare social occasions when he'd been allowed to see her, she'd seemed a lit-tle brittle. She'd refused to change her mind about wanting to marry him as quickly as possible, so he had to be content with that.

"Don't forget your hat and cloak, sir." Absentmindedly, Paul accepted the garments and headed for the door. "And may

I wish you all the best, sir? Lady Lucinda is a remarkable young woman."

Paul paused at the door to smile at his valet, who had previously been employed as an assistant to the duke's valet. "Yes, she is, isn't she? I'm a very lucky man."

Christian Delornay and Captain David Grey awaited him in the circular marble hallway below. Christian looked immaculate in a black coat and white pantaloons; David, far more comfortable in his naval uniform, his tricorn hat tucked under his elbow. For one terrible moment, Paul wondered if he would have gone through with it if Gabriel and Constantine had been down there in their place. But both men were lost to him now, and at last he had the opportunity to make something out of his worthless life.

Paul managed to smile. "Good morning, my friends. Shall we be off?"

"If you are ready, Paul, and if you are quite sure that you are doing the right thing," said Christian.

Paul grimaced. "It's a little bit late for that, isn't it? I've made my choices, and I'll abide by them."

Christian opened the door of the ducal carriage and Paul went by him. "I'm not worried about you. I'm concerned about Lady Lucinda."

"I'm concerned about her too! Why else do you think I'm doing this?" Paul sat down opposite David and struggled to collect himself. "She wants this, and for the first time in my life, I'm trying not to be selfish and to do what is right."

Christian opened his mouth again, but David put his hand on his knee. "Paul is correct. This isn't the time to go into that now, Christian. They have both made a decision and, whether we agree with it or not, we are here to support our friend."

Paul met the other man's calm gaze. "Thank you, David. I appreciate you being here."

"And I apologize." Christian stirred in his seat. "I can't say that you haven't shown your prospective wife exactly what she is getting into by marrying you."

"Damning me with faint praise, eh? I'll take it," Paul replied. "I hope, after all this, that she'll turn up."

David laughed. "I can't see her mother allowing her to do anything else. That woman is magnificent."

Paul found himself smiling. "You'd be surprised. Lucky is her match in many ways."

"So I've heard." David glanced out of the window. "Oh, we're here. Are you ready?"

Paul swallowed hard and stared at the closed doors of Saint George's Church. It was still early, and he could bolt if he wanted. Instead, he followed David and Christian out into the gloomy gray mist and through the side door into the sacristy where the pastor, and his fate, awaited him.

"Oh, my dear, you look absolutely beautiful."

Lucky turned to see her mother dabbing at her eyes.

"Thank you, Mama. I feel quite beautiful too."

Her wedding dress was made of soft lilac silk over an underskirt of gray with silver lace trimmings. It made her eyes look very blue. She felt rather like a dressed-up doll from one of the fashion plates, but that was better than feeling sick and worrying herself half to death that Jeremy was going to turn up and ruin her wedding.

Her wedding . . . and she was marrying her best friend, Paul, just as she had planned all those years ago. Paul, who had male lovers and frequented a pleasure house where anything could happen. At least she would be safe and loved. Surely that was better than she could have expected after her fall from grace?

"Don't forget your bonnet and flowers, my dear."

Her mother handed her a small posy of violets and pansies framed with greenery, and her fan. Lucky took them with a quiet thank you and managed to smile at a weeping Milly. Milly had reported that Paul had already left for the church with some of his supporters, so Lucky had nothing to worry about.

Unless he had escaped to the coast. . . .

Lucky shrugged off that awful thought and walked down the stairs with her mother at her side.

"Marcus, doesn't our daughter look lovely?"

She studied her father, and for once he appeared to be at a loss for words. He simply opened his arms and she flew into them. A sense of certainty enveloped her. Whatever happened between her and Paul, at least she knew she had protected her parents.

"She looks as beautiful as you did on our wedding day," her father said gruffly. "I hope Paul realizes what a lucky man he is."

Lucky rose on tiptoe to kiss his cheek. "I'm sure he does, Papa. Now we must see Mama on her way to the church and be ready to leave ourselves."

She was amazed at the calmness that surrounded her. For the first time in her life, she felt more in control of her destiny than either of her parents were. In theory, she was simply exchanging her father's rule for Paul's, but she would have far more freedom as a married woman than as a young debutante. And after much careful thought, she intended to use that freedom to benefit both her *and* Paul.

The ride to the church passed in a blur, and the next thing she knew, she was being fussed over again by her mother and Emily. From her restricted view at the back of the church, she could just make out the small group of guests in the pews and at least one man at the front. It was cold inside the stone confines of the church, and she found herself shivering. Her father patted her arm, and, after a deep breath, she paced down the aisle at his side, his large hand covering her gloved one.

As they reached the front of the church, Paul stepped up and occupied the space on her other side. She dared to glance up at him and discovered he looked remarkably serious and rather pale. She suspected she must look the same, because he smiled at her encouragingly and suddenly everything was all right again. He was still her best friend and nothing would ever change that.

She made her vows in a steady voice and so did he. Before very long, the ceremony was over, and the vicar pronounced them man and wife.

As they progressed down the narrow aisle, Paul held tightly to Lucky's hand and managed to nod and smile at the guests. His smile faltered when he saw an all-too-familiar dark-haired figure in the back of the church. He paused for a moment and stared into Gabriel Swanfield's dark blue eyes.

"I'm so glad you found the time to grace us with your presence, my lord, although I don't actually remember inviting you."

Gabriel bowed low to Lucky. "May I offer you my felicitations, my lady?" He turned back to Paul. "I was invited by the bride's family. That is, I believe, the more traditional method."

"Of course." Paul nodded. "Then I'm sure you will join us at the wedding breakfast at Haymore House."

Paul kept moving and handed Lucky into the beribboned carriage. She immediately dropped his hand and peered up at him.

"Are you angry because I invited him?"

"Not at all, my love. I have to face him at some point, and now is as good a time as any."

She frowned. "I thought you were friends."

He hastened to reassure her. "We are friends. He just tends to want to mother me a little, a habit I intend to discourage now that I'm a married man."

She sat back and sighed. "We actually did it. We're married."

"Don't tell me that you are regretting it already."

Her smile warmed him. "Not at all. When we Haymores make up our minds, we can be remarkably stubborn."

"I believe I inherited some of those traits from my father as well." He leaned forward to capture her gloved hands. "I won't let Gabriel ruin our day, and I promise I won't elope with him either."

That made her smile again, and he realized he was quite relieved. Seeing Gabriel had shaken him for a moment, and if he knew his blunt-speaking friend, there would be a reckoning to come. And he was almost certain that his answers would not satisfy Gabriel.

"Did I tell you that you look lovely in that gown?"

She smoothed her skirts. "Thank you. I wanted to look nice for you."

"Not for yourself?"

"Well, perhaps a little." She drew her cloak more closely around herself. "It is rather late in the season for such short sleeves though."

The carriage drew up at Haymore House, and Paul realized that the entire staff had lined up to greet them. He supposed he'd have to get used to it. He could only hope that by the time he succeeded Lucky's father to the title, it would feel commonplace. At the moment it felt stifling. Lucky, having been brought up with such grandeur, was unaffected by the display of bonhomie and made her way along the line, smiling and chatting to the staff. All Paul had to do was follow her lead, and the next moment they were in the house being offered a glass of wine.

After a while, he lost sight of his bride in the crowd of guests. Despite the wedding being small on account of the previous duke's recent demise, there were still enough people to make Paul feel trapped. His hand was shaken numerous times and he felt as if his smile was becoming forced. Eventually he found his way over to one of the floor-length windows that faced out over the square and stared out at the trees.

He wasn't surprised when Gabriel joined him. He knew the major suffered similarly in crowds. He looked up into Gabriel's eyes and smiled.

"You might as well say whatever it is you came to say, and then we can both enjoy the rest of the wedding breakfast."

Gabriel didn't smile back at him. "I wish you'd written and told me what you intended to do."

"Why? Do you think you still have the power to change my mind?"

Gabriel stiffened. "You know what I think. I am also aware that this misguided union is entirely my fault."

"I beg your pardon?"

"I abandoned you, and then I encouraged you to explore at the pleasure house."

"I certainly didn't feel abandoned, Gabriel, and you gave me a great blessing by setting me to work at Madame's."

"I didn't expect you to fool yourself into getting married."

"Fool myself?" Paul realized he was getting annoyed. "Are you suggesting that you're in some way better than me? That you can get married, and I can't?"

"We're not alike. Did you do this to emulate me?" The emergence of Gabriel's northern accent was the only indication that he was upset. "We've always had different needs."

"Not always."

Gabriel flushed. "I thought we had forgiven each other and moved on."

"Perhaps our sexual needs are different, but I find it offensive that you imagine I would marry just for that."

"Many men marry to hide their true natures. Perhaps I am concerned that Lady Lucinda is unaware of yours. I'm not saying there is anything wrong with you, but—"

Paul held up his hand. "Gabriel, you have waltzed in here

without bothering to ask for my side of the story and made several assumptions that are not only wrong but *incredibly* insensitive."

"But—"

Paul continued talking over the interruption. "I married Lady Lucinda because *she* needed *me*. I did it for her. That is all there is to it. Any other motives you ascribe to me are completely wrong. And I resent your assumption that I make all my decisions based on sex." He inclined his head a bare inch. "If you wished to find out exactly why I married, you only had to ask. Unlike you, I value our past friendship and assumed you would at least give me the benefit of an unbiased hearing."

"Paul, this is ridiculous. I'm not trying to tell you what to do or condemn you. I'm simply trying to help."

"Maybe I don't need your help anymore, Gabriel." He held the other man's gaze, saw his mingled concern and puzzlement. "I have to go and find my bride. How long are you in town?"

"Only until tomorrow."

"Then I'll wish you a safe journey home." Paul bowed. "Give my regards to your wife."

Paul walked straight back into the center of the crowd and saw Lucky standing by herself near the fireplace. She put her hand on his arm when he drew near.

"I thought you weren't going to argue with Lord Swanfield."

"I wasn't, but he made it impossible to resist."

"Does he not agree with our marriage?"

"Oh, he likes you. He just doesn't think I should ever marry."

Lucky squeezed his arm. "What a dog in the manger."

"What?"

"He doesn't want you himself, but he doesn't want anyone else to have you either."

"Lucky, that's hardly the case."

Before he finished speaking, his new bride was walking determinedly toward his first love. He contemplated stopping her but was reluctant to draw anyone's attention to a potentially disastrous altercation. Somewhere within him, the thought that she was on his side and determined to defend him made him feel warm.

Even though Lucky smiled as she approached Gabriel Swanfield, he still looked as if he might bolt. At the last moment he appeared to collect himself and offered her a slight smile of his own. "My lady."

She turned to face the window and he followed suit. "Lord Swanfield, would you mind if I was a little blunt with you?"

"I'm from the north, my lady. We are famous for our bluntness. Please, be my guest."

Lucky took a deep breath. "Then please don't worry about me. I know everything there is to know about Paul, and I still wanted to marry him."

"Everything?"

She met his skeptical blue gaze. "Indeed. I know that he was in love with you for many years."

Pain flickered behind Lord Swanfield's fine eyes. "I was aware of that."

"And I'm sure you want Paul to be happy, don't you?"

"With all my heart." He hesitated. "I'm just not certain if this is best for either of you."

"If it is what we both want, perhaps you could find it in your heart to be glad for us?"

"My lady, Paul is my best friend. Of course I want him to be happy, but doesn't the mere fact that he loves me, another man, give you pause?"

"You think he can't love me as well?" Lucky swallowed hard. "Don't you think that is rather arrogant of you? If there is anything I know about Paul, it is that he has a great capacity for love."

Lord Swanfield let out his breath, his gaze straying over her shoulder toward Paul. "He does and you are right. I should never have attempted to interfere."

Lucky put her hand on his arm. "I will keep him safe, my lord, I promise you that." She smiled. "At first I thought you might be jealous, but now I realize you speak out of concern for him."

"I do love him, my lady, just not in the way that he wants."

"And I love him, too, also not quite in the way that he wants, but I'll do my very best to make him happy. He probably hasn't mentioned it, but he has sacrificed a great deal by marrying me."

Lord Swanfield brought her hand to his lips and kissed it. "By your leave, I will go and try and make my peace with him."

"I'm sure he'll be delighted. He cherishes your good opinion."

She watched him walk away and approach Paul, who welcomed him with a certain reserve. She was convinced the two men would find a way to overcome their differences. Their relationship ran too deep to be destroyed over this. When Paul smiled up at Lord Swanfield, she fought her own pang of jealousy. Would he ever want her with the intensity that he'd wanted Gabriel? She wasn't sure if it was in his nature, but some part of her still yearned to be needed like that.

She stared hard at the two men and promised herself that she would indeed do all in her power to make Paul happy.

13

Paul paced the rug in front of the fireplace and contemplated the door that connected his bedroom to Lucky's. They had considered going away after the wedding, but the duke and duchess volunteered to leave them in the huge Haymore town house for the first week of their married life. It was an offer Paul gratefully accepted, due to his still-limited funds and lack of his own home.

He hadn't decided if they had made the right decision or not. He was also far more nervous than he had anticipated. The solemnity of his wedding vows was a more binding thing than he had expected.

And seeing Gabriel again . . . Paul sighed. He was glad they'd come to some measure of agreement before Gabriel left. The interesting thing was that he'd been more angry than upset. To his amazement, it seemed that, in the months since Gabriel's marriage, he'd actually achieved a measure of acceptance and independence. He could only wish he felt the same about Constantine Delinsky, who didn't seem to have Gabriel's concerns about loving another man and just *loved*.

But this was no time to be thinking about Con. He had to face his bride and let her decide how she wished to proceed. The way she'd gone straight to Gabriel and spoken up for him still amazed Paul.

That she thought him worth defending was harder to fathom. He was so used to being a disappointment to people that he'd grown into that role and allowed his peers to treat him as if he were of no account. But that would have to end. He had to be there to support Lucky.

He walked across the dressing room that divided their suite and tapped on the door of Lucky's bedchamber. When she bade him enter, he pushed open the door and went in. She was sitting in one of the chairs beside the fire, her feet tucked up underneath her like a little girl. She wore a long white nightgown and her hair was loose around her shoulders.

She didn't look apprehensive or horrified by his appearance, and that made everything a little easier. Despite the dramatic change in their circumstances, she was still a familiar and calming presence.

"Are you tired, Lucky?"

She looked up at him. "I suppose I should be, but my mind is so busy I don't think I will be able to sleep at all."

Her tone was conversational, and he relaxed even further. He took the seat opposite her, and her gaze fastened on his silk dressing gown and bare feet.

"It's certainly been a long, exhausting day."

She rested her chin on her drawn-up knees. "Was it very horrible for you?"

He found himself smiling at her. "What a peculiar thing to say. You would think I'd been forced to marry a dragon instead of a very charming and courageous woman."

"I didn't mean me. I *meant* that it must have been trying to be with all those people. I know that you don't like crowds."

"Neither does Lord Swanfield." He wanted to kick himself for bringing up that particular name at that particular moment.

"I noticed that. He looked almost as uncomfortable as you did." Her gaze dropped to his bare feet. "Did you settle your differences?"

"Indeed we did. Thanks to you."

She shrugged. "It was bound to be difficult for him to see you getting married."

"Why would you think that?"

"Because he still feels responsible for you. He's worried that you will make the wrong choice."

Paul shifted in his seat. "He thinks I have."

"And I told him he was wrong. I'm sure you did the same thing."

"I did. In truth, I told him off for interfering." He smiled slowly at her. "I wrongly assumed you would be more worried about me seeing Lord Swanfield and casting you off than worrying about him being jealous."

"I knew you wouldn't do that."

"I appreciate your confidence in me."

She shrugged and a long curl of brown hair slipped over her shoulder and landed on the soft swell of her bosom. He wanted to reach forward and touch it, see if it felt as soft as it looked. He glanced across at the large four-poster bed and then back at Lucky.

"Do you want to go to bed with me?" he said abruptly. "We don't have to do anything but sleep."

"It *is* our wedding night."

"I know, but I promised you I'd abide by any decision you made about our physical relationship."

She rose to her feet and looked down at him. Her nightgown was long-sleeved and had a high neck. It fell to the floor like a flour sack. "You don't wish to make love to me?"

"If that is what you want, it will be a pleasure, but . . ."

She was already heading for the bed, so he followed her over. "Are you sure, Lucky?"

She looked steadily back at him. "I'm sure that I want you to consummate this marriage, yes."

He couldn't quite determine her mood, but he couldn't deny the interest she aroused in him. This new, grown-up version of Lucky intrigued him far more than any of the women in the pleasure house. If she wanted him, he would be delighted to oblige her. He climbed in beside her and lay on his side facing her. He reached out and cupped her chin. "Thank you for today. You were magnificent and are far more than I deserve."

A faint blush rose on her cheeks. "I was just relieved that everything went off so well."

"Were you worried that your discarded suitor would turn up and ruin the day?"

She shivered. "Yes."

"Well, he can't hurt you now. I will keep you safe, I swear it." He leaned in and kissed her soft, trembling mouth. She sighed his name, and he slid his hand around to the nape of her neck and kissed her until she started to respond, her body softening against his, her arms coming up to hold him.

"I want you, Lucky. Do you want me?"

He waited for her to speak, his emotions embarrassingly close to the surface, and his need for her surprising him. She wasn't just a woman he could give pleasure to; Gabriel had been right: that could indeed be learned. Lucky was his wife, his best friend, and his most loyal supporter.

"Yes, please, Paul."

He let out his breath, slowly rolled her on to her back, and looked down at her. Despite her calm expression, she was still quite nervous.

"I'll make this the best wedding night you could ever have dreamed of. I promise."

Her smile warmed him with its sweetness. "You forget, you always were my dream."

He kissed her nose and then her chin, his fingers working at the ribbon at her neck to open her nightgown. Her hand came up around his neck and held him tightly. Even though they'd been intimate before, he was still careful, still determined not to scare her in any way.

She brought his mouth back to hers and he succumbed to the need in her kiss, his hands wandering over her body, pushing her nightgown out of the way as he rediscovered her soft curves and hollows. He shaped her hip and thigh, his fingers drifting closer to her mound and the delights that awaited him between her thighs. Deepening the kiss, he slid his hand between her legs and cupped her sex.

She pushed against him and his fingers sunk deeper until he was able to slide them back and forth. His thumb centered over her bud as he brought her to a shuddering climax that made his cock ache and throb with need.

"Let me inside you, Lucky."

She sighed his name against his mouth, and he came down over her, his hips aligned with hers, his cock pressing against her most tender, welcoming flesh. He slowly filled her, watching her face, the way her eyes widened as he rocked against her.

He wanted to tell her not to be afraid, but instinct took over and he started to thrust, sliding one hand under her buttocks to bring her closer and open her wider to him. Her hands tightened around his neck, and she shoved his dressing gown aside until it slid off his shoulders. Her nails dug into his skin, but he paid no heed to the tiny irritation; all his focus was on pleasing her, on making his cock last long enough to give her another climax.

She tensed under him, and he set his teeth as she started to tighten around his shaft. He kept thrusting even as his cock wanted to come, kept grinding against her swollen bud until she gave in to the pleasure and screamed it out. He climaxed then, in long, shuddering waves that made him collapse over her.

When he was able to breathe normally again, he rolled on to his back and brought her with him to nestle against his chest. He kissed the top of her head and she laid her palm flat on his chest over his heart.

"Are you all right, Lucky?" he whispered.

In answer, he received a tiny snore and found himself smiling into the darkness. For a man who'd never imagined having a wedding night, this one had turned out to be quite extraordinary after all.

Lucky retrieved her dressing gown, got out of bed, her finger to her lips, and approached Milly, who had just slipped into the room.

"Thank you, Milly. Leave the hot water, and bring up some tea and coffee, will you?" she whispered. "I'll ring when I want you to come back and help me dress."

"Yes, my lady," Milly hissed back. "I have your tray right outside the door."

Lucky wrapped a shawl around her shoulders and waited until Milly poured her a cup of tea and departed. She glanced back at the bed, where Paul still lay sleeping. He was on his front, the covers down at his waist. One hand draped gracefully over the edge of the bed and trailed on the floor. His blond hair caught the strands of sunlight filtering through the curtains and he looked positively angelic.

She couldn't quite believe he was her husband. The mere sight of him made her body throb in already sensitive places. He'd been so careful with her that she'd almost wanted to weep. The intense pleasure had surprised her; the feel of him inside her had been nothing like Jeremy's rough invasion, despite the fact that Paul had felt . . . bigger.

But he was hers now, legally and completely, and she wanted him to be happy more than anything else in the world. She swallowed down an unexpected swell of emotion. It was a shame she hadn't seen Paul with Gabriel Swanfield before she had rushed him into marriage.

Lucky had a quick wash and then curled up on the couch to drink her tea. Paul's gentle lovemaking had only reinforced her decision to do the right thing for both of them. All she had to do was find a way to tell him her thoughts without him growing too angry with her. And he would be angry; she had no doubt of that.

She finished her tea and got up to pour herself another cup. When she turned back, she saw that Paul was awake and regarding her through half-closed eyes.

"I hope you have coffee there as well as some food. I'm famished."

"You are always hungry." She picked up the other silver pot. "I do have some coffee for you. I'll ring for breakfast in a moment."

He sat up, the covers falling away from him, and shoved a hand through his untidy hair. "Why are you up so early, Lucky? I believe you are supposed to languish in bed after your wedding night."

She blushed as she handed him the cup of coffee and resumed her place on the sofa. Sometimes it was uncanny how well he knew her. "I just wanted to talk to you about something."

"Something more important than food?" His smile died and his brown eyes narrowed. "Out with it, Lucky."

She took a deep breath. "First, I want you to swear that our marriage is now completely legal and completely consummated."

"Yes, it is—unless you have the power and the funds to seek

a divorce. It is extremely unlikely that will happen unless you become the mistress of one of the king's sons."

"I don't want a divorce."

"Then for all intents and purposes, we are married until death do us part."

"That is good."

"I'm glad you feel like that. Now what's the matter?"

Lucky took a deep breath. "I don't want you to force yourself to make love to me anymore."

"What?" The shock on his face made Lucky feel as if she'd struck him. He got out of bed and came toward her. "Did I hurt you, frighten you? For God's sake, Lucky, tell me what I did wrong. I swear I'll make it right for you."

"It's not that. You didn't do anything wrong."

He sank down in front of her and looked up. "Then what? What has happened?"

"Madame Helene suggested we didn't need to have a conventional marriage, and I wasn't quite sure what she meant. And then I saw you with Gabriel Swanfield, and I realized that I had been incredibly selfish."

He took her hand. "But I don't want him anymore. I promised I would remain faithful to you."

She looked into his brown eyes. "But it isn't *fair*, Paul."

His grip tightened. "I thought we decided it was *completely* fair right before we were married."

"When I talked to Gabriel, I insisted that you had the capacity to love more than one person, and he agreed with me."

He held her gaze, his brown eyes steady. "I do not love Gabriel Swanfield in the way you imagine. He is nothing more than a good friend to me now. I swear it." He hesitated. "In fact, he offered me the opportunity to join him and his wife in bed occasionally, and I decided against it."

"Why?"

"Because I decided I deserved better. I wanted to be loved wholeheartedly."

"And, instead of finding that person, you married me. Now I feel even worse."

"But you shouldn't." Paul smiled. "You were right about one thing. I do have the capacity to love more than one person, and I love you."

"So what right do I have to stop you from loving where you please?"

"The right of a wife?"

He stood up and walked away from her, presenting her with a fine view of his muscled buttocks. He bent down to retrieve his dressing gown and tied the sash with a savage jerk of his wrist. "I don't understand you, Lucky. I thought we had sorted this out." He raised his head to stare at her. "Are you sure you don't want to get out of this marriage?"

"Of course I'm sure. Why do you think I waited until we had consummated it to set you free?"

He groaned and sank down on to the side of the bed. "But I don't want to be free. I entered this marriage in good faith, and I don't intend to stray."

"I'm not saying that you 'have' to stray. I'm saying that if you find you need another person in your bed, I would quite understand."

He held her gaze, his expression serious. "Lucky, saying it and actually meaning it are two very different things."

"Are you suggesting I'm lying?" She sat forward. "I'm trying to be honest with you. We said we would always do that!"

"I know, and I don't think you are lying. You don't have enough experience of physical relationships to understand how it feels when someone you love makes love to someone else."

She raised her chin at him. "Actually, I do. I saw the way you looked at Gabriel Swanfield." She pressed her hand to her breast. "I know how much that hurts." She waited, her heart thumping so loudly she was certain he would hear it. "And don't you dare tell me I don't know how I feel."

"I wouldn't dream of it." He picked up his coffee cup and sipped slowly and she wanted to scream. "Perhaps we should leave it like this." He inclined his head a formal inch. "Thank you for your generous offer, but I have no intention of actually breaking my word to you."

"Then I have achieved nothing, have I?"

He stood up and put his cup back on the silver tray. "I don't know, Lucky, have you? If you don't want me in your bed, all you had to do was say so."

He bowed and headed for the door that connected their two suites, shutting it gently behind him. Lucky remained on the sofa for a long moment and slowly let out her breath. So much for honesty. All she'd done was make him suspect she didn't want him anymore, that he hadn't been good enough for her after all.

She thought about chasing after him and making him see sense, but knew him well enough to realize he wouldn't be in any mood to listen to her. Beneath that sweet exterior was a very stubborn man. She would simply have to think of another way of putting the matter to him and hope that this time she would achieve success.

14

Paul contemplated his well-dressed reflection in the mirror and mentally thanked his father-in-law for footing the bill for his new wardrobe. The duke had insisted that if Paul was to squire Lucky around town, he needed more than one decent coat and three rather tatty army uniforms. Somehow the new clothes helped Paul fit into his new life; sometimes they made him feel like a complete fraud.

In truth, he felt like a fraud anyway. He'd kept away from Lucky's bed for the past four nights and out of her sight. He wasn't proud of his behavior, but needed to calm down and think carefully about what she'd said. At first he assumed she regretted her decision to marry him and that his lovemaking had been inadequate in some way. That hurt more than he had anticipated and made him doubt himself all over again.

But they were married for life, and he couldn't run away from her forever, nor would he want to. There had to be a way to convince her that he'd meant what he said *and* find a way to keep her happy in bed and out of it.

In pursuit of that return to marital harmony, he was taking

Lucky to the theater, where they would enjoy the privacy of the duke's box and watch some opera the duchess had insisted Lucky would enjoy. He shoved a jet pin at random into his cravat, and his new valet uttered an audible groan.

"Let me, sir, please." He repositioned the pin and fussed around the intricate folds of the cravat. "There. That's much better."

"Thank you, Jordan." Paul couldn't deny that he needed help, but it still felt strange to have a man completely devoted to making him look properly turned out. "Will you inform my wife's maid that I'll meet her ladyship downstairs when she is ready to leave?"

"Of course, sir."

Jordan bowed and silently withdrew, leaving Paul still staring at his reflection like some dandy. He imagined all his army friends laughing at him and that was enough to send him down the stairs to await Lucky in the drawing room.

"So you've decided to speak to me again, have you?" his wife inquired with such great sweetness that Paul winced. They were sitting in the ducal carriage on their way to the theater and unless he fancied throwing himself out and under the horses' feet, he was trapped.

"I know. I've been a cowardly fool. Please don't remind me."

She fixed him with her usual clear gaze. "I do know you, Paul. I also knew you'd come around eventually."

"To your point of view?"

She opened her eyes wide at him. "Naturally. I am always right."

He smiled at her. "I forgot that." He hesitated. "I still don't know what to say to you."

"You don't have to say anything. I obviously misjudged you."

"In what way?"

She looked down at her neatly folded gloved hands in her lap. "I thought you were more honest."

"I am honest."

"Can you swear to me that you don't find men attractive?"

"Of course I can't. But just because I find them attractive doesn't mean I have to bed them."

"Even with my permission?"

He regarded her for a long, cool moment and felt the faint stirring of his temper. There were very few people who even knew he *had* a temper or how to rouse it. Unfortunately Lucky was one of them. She was as tenacious as the duke when he spoke on a pet subject in the House of Lords.

"Actually, as your husband, I don't need your permission to do anything."

"That is true." She nodded as though something he'd said satisfied her. "Does that mean I would need your permission to bed someone else?"

"*What?*"

She shrugged. "I thought the notion might be more palatable for you if we both had the same opportunities. But, as you just reminded me, you have more say in the matter simply because you are a man."

Paul stiffened. "We've been married for less than a week. You've found someone else—*already?*"

"No, of course not, but would you let me if I wanted to?" She raised her gaze to his, and he found himself speechless. She reached across and patted his hand. "Don't worry about it now. Are you looking forward to the opera?"

He pulled his hand away. "Lucky, if you think you can introduce such a topic and then casually discard it, you are very much mistaken."

She turned to the window and looked out. "Oh, look, we are already here. Will you help me down, Paul? I fear the path is quite icy."

Paul assisted Lucky out of the carriage and up the steps to the Covent Garden Opera House, his thoughts in a whirl, his mind simply unable to deal with the idea that his Lucky was contemplating a sexual adventure of her own. As he followed her up the stairs to the Haymore box, he reluctantly remembered that Madame Helene had offered him some advice too. Hadn't she told him that he and Lucky didn't have to have a conventional marriage, just one that suited them both?

Was he really not willing to extend the same liberties to his wife that she was offering to him? The idea was so unfamiliar that he couldn't quite decide how he felt about it. It seemed he was more of a traditionalist than he'd thought. And Lucky was young; it was possible she had no idea what she was agreeing to.

"Paul?"

He started as she gazed up at him and hurriedly drew a chair out for her.

"Are you all right?"

"Not really."

He sat next to her and studied her familiar face. She looked very smart in a blue silk gown that matched her eyes, and a sapphire-and-diamond necklace that he knew had been a gift from her mother. He wished he had the funds to buy her something beautiful, but as an ex-army lieutenant, despite his lofty expectations, he had very little money of his own.

"I'm still reeling from what you said to me in the carriage."

"Did I offend you?"

He took her hand. "Not at all. I was just . . . surprised that you had even thought of such a thing."

"I've always had a practical streak."

"I know that and I'm quite glad of it. In your situation, most women would have had hysterics."

She sighed. "And I have no sensibility at all."

Paul gripped her hand tightly. "Lucky, I don't want you to take a lover just because you want to make things easier for me." She colored slightly and looked out over the packed theater. Paul pressed his point. "Unless there is someone you already care about?"

"If there was someone else, I would have asked him to marry me instead of you, wouldn't I?"

"Ah, good point." He regarded her closely. "Are you sure about that?"

She smiled. "I've only met one other man who treated me with the same care and civility that you do."

"Who is that?"

"That is none of your business," she said severely.

"Don't you want to introduce him to me?"

"Now you are being ridiculous."

"No, I'm not." He took a deep breath. "If you truly wish to grant me my freedom within our marriage, I would insist that you had the same rights."

She raised her gaze to his. "Really?"

"Absolutely. In fact, here is my counteroffer to you. If you find a man who loves you and you want him, *then* I promise I'll find someone else."

She touched his cheek, her expression serious. "But we would still remain married and be best friends?"

"If that was what we both wanted, yes."

He held her gaze and hoped she could read only sincerity in his. By putting the onus back on her to find a true love, he believed he had averted a crisis. If, in the future, she grew dissatisfied with him, at least she knew she could find another man and that he would never hold it against her. In the meantime, they were still married, and he would remain faithful to her.

"There is one more thing," Paul said.

"What is it?"

"Do you want me in your bed or not?" The thought of not being with Lucky was surprisingly unsettling. "I thought you were determined to provide me and the duke with an heir."

She sighed. "I don't want you there if it is distasteful to you."

"Did I appear disgusted?"

"I suppose not."

"Did I hurt you like that other man did?"

"No, you gave me great pleasure."

It was his turn to sigh. "What do I have to do to convince you that I want to share your bed?"

She bit down on her lower lip, and he wanted to draw her into his arms and hold her close. Perhaps she didn't have an answer for him, and he should stop forcing her to make a decision. He'd hated it when Gabriel had insisted on trying to control his love life.

He brought her hand to his lips and kissed it. "If you want me, you know where I am. Now, do you want to attend the Marshalls' ball after this performance or not?"

"It seems that you were right, Delinsky."

"Right about what?"

"Paul St. Clare's marriage."

Constantine looked up from his breakfast as Thomas Wesley tossed the morning newspaper at him. It wasn't the local paper, but one of the London ones that often took a day or two to reach them. He had to squint to read the small print, as the breakfast room was still quite dark. A series of thunderstorms had swept through the countryside overnight, leaving the grounds littered with fallen leaves and debris.

Con opened the paper and scanned the narrow columns until his gaze fell on the small announcement. "Ah, they were married a few days ago in a small private ceremony."

Thomas took the seat opposite him and poured himself

some coffee. He had the wind-blown look of a man who had already been out riding in the blustery autumnal air.

"I suppose they kept it private because of the last duke's recent death."

"I assume so." Con shut the paper and carefully folded it up again. Despite knowing this was the likely outcome, he still felt sick to his stomach. "Well, I wish them joy."

Thomas raised his eyebrows. "You don't sound particularly pleased about it. Did you not expect him to go through with it?"

"He told me he was going to do it, and I believed him."

"Perhaps he'll come around eventually, and you'll see him again."

Con pushed back his chair and rose to his feet, his appetite deserting him. "Unless I want to live permanently in the countryside or abroad, I'll have to see him again."

Thomas looked up at him. "That's not quite what I meant."

Con forced a smile. "I know, but I'm not going to hang around on the off chance that he'll change his mind. It wouldn't be fair to his wife or to me."

"And you'd still be tempted, wouldn't you?"

"Yes." Con met Thomas's sympathetic gaze. "I'm ashamed to say that I would."

"Nothing to be ashamed of, old fellow. You can't help loving someone." Thomas grimaced. "I know all about that."

"But I don't usually fall in love with men, especially not so quickly."

"More's the pity," Thomas said softly. "Are you going to look for the love of a good woman instead? I'm sure there would be many women eager to console you. You are a very handsome man."

Con headed for the door. "You flatter me. With this white hair I look about twice my age."

"And every woman I've ever met has told me how it makes you look so foreign and delicious."

Con paused at the door. "You discuss me with other people?"

Thomas shrugged. "Of course I do. The *ton* thrives on gossip, and you are a prime subject for it."

"When have I ever done anything to merit such attention?"

"As I said, you are young, handsome, apparently unwed, and you have that devilish foreign accent."

"I will never understand English society," Con muttered. "Will you be very surprised if I thank you most kindly for your hospitality and tell you that I need to get back to Town?"

"I suppose you want to get it over with, eh?" Thomas rose to his feet and came to shake Con's hand. "I've enjoyed your visit immensely."

"I cannot thank you enough for offering me this sanctuary in my time of need. If there is ever anything I can do for you in return, please let me know."

Thomas patted his shoulder. "It was nothing. We military men have to support each other."

Con held his gaze. "Then, thank you."

"I hope you find your happiness as I have done with the Minshoms, and I'll be sure to discuss your marital situation with the Russian ambassador."

"There is no need for that, but I appreciate your interest."

Thomas grinned. "You never know what might happen, Delinsky. It's always best to be prepared for anything."

15

Despite the slight drizzle of rain, Constantine put on his cloak and decided to walk from his rooms to the mansion on Great Portland Street where the ball was taking place. Having grown up in Saint Petersburg, he thought the English made far too much fuss about their mildly cold weather. It would take him longer to find a hackney cab than it would to walk, and he liked the feel of the cold air on his face.

The street leading up to the square was already clogged with carriages. He had to cross and re-cross the road several times to avoid shouting coachmen jostling for position and footmen sent out by the big house to help guests alight. He looked up at the mansion, which was ablaze with lights, and wondered if Paul and his unknown bride were already there.

He'd decided to make their meeting as public as possible and on his own terms. At the ball he would hardly be expected to do more than acknowledge the happy couple and move on. No one would require anything more from him, and that suited him perfectly. After the initial meeting, he could only hope things would become easier.

He climbed the steps, and a footman relieved him of his cloak and hat. The vestibule was crowded and the roar of conversation seemed to reverberate around the space, making even the crystals in the chandeliers tremble. Con took a deep breath and started up the stairs to the ballroom from where he could already hear the sound of an orchestra tuning up.

The woman in front of him stopped abruptly, and Con inadvertently trod on her train. Before he could warn her, she started moving again, only to be yanked backward into Con's arms.

"I do apologize, ma'am, my boot . . ." Con stopped talking as he recognized his fair captive. "My lady, what a pleasant surprise. If you will just give me a moment to remove my weight from your train, all will be well again."

"It is of no consequence, sir. I was the one who stopped moving."

He smiled down at her, aware of the press of people around them but content to share the moment with her. Unlike most women, she wasn't lamenting her ripped hem or shrieking at him for being so clumsy. It made for a refreshing change. In truth, even in extremis, he remembered she had behaved remarkably calmly.

"Do you need to fix your dress? May I escort you to the ladies' retiring room?"

"That would be very kind of you." She glanced up at him as the crowd before them eased a little and they moved forward. Her dark hair was braided into a coil on the top of her head with a few ringlets framing her face. "It's Lieutenant Colonel, isn't it?"

He inclined his head. "Indeed, my lady. Lieutenant Colonel Delinsky. I assume our mutual acquaintance Miss Ross told you who I was."

"Yes, she did, although seeing as how you always appear at

just the right moment to save me from embarrassment, I should have asked your name earlier."

"It is of no matter, my lady. I was just pleased to be of service."

They reached the top of the stairs, and Con looked about him for a servant to direct them toward the retiring room. He located a footman, gained the necessary information, and set off again with his lady across the wide landing to a concealed hallway.

"You don't need to wait for me, sir." She gave him a grateful smile. "I'm sure I can find my way back to the ballroom from here."

He bowed. "It would be my pleasure to escort you back to your party, my lady, and perhaps help explain your disappearance."

She nodded and went into the room, leaving him leaning against the wall with the opportunity of observing quite unseen the guests as they arrived. Despite her youth, his companion was an interesting woman. Unlike his late wife, he could well imagine her following the drum without complaint. He sighed. Not that there would be much more of that in his future. With Napoléon beaten, his career was finished, unless he managed to gain a promotion, and that, too, was unlikely without money or influence.

The door opened and he looked up, but it wasn't his lady. It was two young debutantes, who giggled and whispered when they saw him and giggled even more when he nodded a cordial greeting. He recalled Thomas Wesley's words about his mysterious popularity with the ladies and wondered if he should start frowning at everyone instead.

He straightened as the door opened again.

"I'm ready, Lieutenant Colonel." She glanced down at her gown. "It only took a few stitches to reattach the lace."

"I'm glad to hear it. I would hate to have ruined your evening."

"Hardly, sir. I'm not that much of a fashion plate."

He chuckled and placed her hand on his sleeve. "Thank goodness for that. Shall we go and find your parents?"

"I recently married, sir, so I came with my husband." She glanced at his uniform. "He has just sold out from the army. I wonder if you have met him?"

They avoided the receiving line and walked down into the ballroom. Con was conscious of a sense of disappointment. How was it that everyone he was attracted to was already taken? Did he have an uncanny ability to choose the wrong people, or was he avoiding the possibility of actually having a real relationship? The thought didn't sit well with him, and he forced it away.

"Do you see your husband, my lady?"

She scanned the crowd and then pointed toward the row of windows. "I see him talking to Emily Ross."

She moved purposefully through the crowds, bringing Con with her. It wasn't until the last second, when he took his gaze off Miss Ross, that he realized exactly whom she was talking about.

"Paul?" his companion said. "Do you know Lieutenant Colonel Delinsky? He helped me avoid a catastrophe on the stairs when I ripped the lace on my train. Lieutenant Colonel, this is my husband, Lieutenant St. Clare."

Paul turned slowly and stared at Con.

Con held out his hand. "Good evening, Lieutenant."

"Sir . . . I thought you were out of town, or else I would've called on you. . . ."

Con forced a smile. "I only came back yesterday." He turned to include the others in the conversation. "I understand that I should wish you both happy."

Paul swallowed hard and claimed his bride's hand. "Indeed,

I am the luckiest of men. Lady Lucinda is a goddess among women."

"Oh, do you know each other?" Lady Lucinda smiled brightly. "Your uniforms are not similar at all."

Con wondered whether she was worried about what he'd tell Paul about their first meeting. As Paul seemed unable to speak, Con took on the burden of conversation when all he wanted to do was fall to his knees and kiss the other man's feet.

"Indeed we are acquainted. I was St. Clare's commanding officer during the peninsular campaigns. I joined your husband's regiment as an aide after my own regiment was destroyed by Napoléon." He glanced down at his dark blue dress uniform, which had gold facings and a white sash. "As you can see, I retained my original uniform."

"Oh, that's why I didn't recognize you." Lady Lucinda glanced at Paul. "You must ask the lieutenant colonel over for dinner. I'm sure my father would like to meet him as well."

The orchestra played a loud chord that drowned out Paul's reply. Lady Lucinda took Paul's hand.

"I am engaged to dance with my husband for this set, but I hope we will see you afterward?"

Con bowed. "Indeed. May I request the pleasure of a dance with you later, my lady? I will endeavor not to tread on your feet or your train again."

She smiled. "I'd love to dance with you, sir. Perhaps the supper dance?"

"That would be delightful."

Con stepped back and allowed Paul to escort his wife to the dance floor. He resisted the impulse to watch them too closely and instead found himself staring straight at Miss Ross, who was regarding him quizzically.

"Did you not know Paul was getting married?"

"Indeed I did." He manufactured another smile. "He informed me of the happy event some weeks ago."

"Yet you appear quite shocked."

"Perhaps because I was unaware of his choice of bride."

"You find Lady Lucinda in some way objectionable?"

He took Miss Ross's elbow and walked her away to a quieter spot. "Are you certain you wish to have this conversation at a public ball? You might not care about gossip, but I suspect Lady Lucinda and Paul will."

Miss Ross raised her chin. "I'm well aware of that. What *you* might not be aware of is that I am privy to the secrets of the pleasure house."

"I know you are connected to the Delornay family, but I doubt they let you run loose in the pleasure house."

"They don't, more's the pity, but I am allowed in the kitchens, and there is plenty of gossip to be had there." She drew in a breath. "I don't want you to hurt Lucky. Lady Lucinda, I mean."

"I have no intention of hurting either of them."

Miss Ross brought her hand to her mouth. "You were the person who fetched me to Lucky in the garden at the ball."

"I was, but I have never spoken of it to anyone, and I never will."

"Despite your relationship with Paul?"

Constantine held her gaze. "I no longer have a 'relationship' with Lieutenant St. Clare. I swear it."

Miss Ross sighed. "It's all so unfair, isn't it?"

Braced for more outrage, Con could only blink at her. "I beg your pardon?"

"Why can't people just love each other regardless of who or what they are?"

Con relaxed. "I don't know, Miss Ross, but I can only echo your sentiment. Would you care to dance with me?"

Lucky muddled her way through her dance with Paul, glad that for once he seemed as distracted as she was. The shock of finding out that her knight in shining armor was already well acquainted with her new husband was disconcerting to say the least. Would the lieutenant colonel feel obliged to share the circumstances of their first meeting with Paul, or worse, would he feel obligated to warn his comrade-in-arms that her reputation wasn't as pristine as it should be?

She wasn't sure what was for the best. If she didn't tell Paul how his commanding officer had helped her on that fateful night, Paul might feel he had to react unfavorably to any suggestion that his wife's reputation was at fault. She didn't want them facing each other in a duel.

She was still in a quandary when Lieutenant Colonel Delinsky came to claim her for the supper dance. She hadn't realized it was a waltz, and that they would be holding each other closely for the entire dance. It gave him far too many opportunities for intimate conversation.

After the first few minutes, she had relaxed enough to stop minding her steps and managed to look up at him. His smile was quite breathtaking.

"You have nothing to worry about, my lady."

"In what way?"

"I will let you be my guide as to what you want me to reveal about our acquaintance to your husband. I do not want to embarrass you."

"That is very kind of you, sir." She didn't feel at liberty to disclose Paul's knowledge of her ruin to him yet, but she appreciated his quiet offer. "If my husband asks you directly about our relationship, you should tell him the truth."

His grip tightened. "Are you sure about that, my lady?"

"Yes, I'm sure. Paul and I are old friends. We try and be truthful with each other."

Something flickered in her partner's fine gray eyes. "That is admirable, my lady. So few marriages are based on trust."

"I understand you are not married, sir?"

"I'm a widower. My wife died many years ago in Russia."

"You must have loved her very much if you have never thought to replace her."

She heard the wistful note in her own voice as he expertly twirled her around the corner of the dance floor. It seemed Lieutenant Colonel Delinsky was loyal in love too. As she'd mentioned to Paul, her dancing partner was the only man she'd ever met who seemed as honorable as Paul and her father. She doubted he would ever expose her secrets to the world.

The music ended, and she curtsied low and then placed her hand on his sleeve. "We should find Paul and go into supper before it gets too crowded."

Paul watched as Constantine and Lucky approached him, his heart beating fast, his nerves surprisingly on edge. They looked remarkably handsome together, Lucky's darker coloring a lovely foil for Con's silver. How in God's name had they come to know each other, and why hadn't one of them mentioned it to him? It would surely have lessened his shock.

Con's unexpected appearance had taken his breath away and shaken his resolve far more than he'd anticipated. The trouble was, he could claim anything he wanted, but he was still attracted to Delinsky. It didn't mean he had to act on it though. Both of them were honorable men, and he was convinced Con wouldn't beg to be taken back.

"Ah, there you are, Paul," Lucky said. "Are you ready to go in to supper?"

Since being half starved in captivity in a French prison, he rarely passed up an opportunity to eat. He followed them through to the supper room and found a space at a vacant table. Despite his shock, he still managed to eat everything he'd blindly put on his plate.

After a while, Lucky excused herself, leaving him alone with

Con for the first time. Paul kept his gaze on his plate and continued stolidly chewing.

"Are you well, Paul?" Con asked quietly.

Paul considered not answering, but found the need to look up into Con's face too hard to resist.

"I'm very well, thank you. And you?"

"I am much refreshed. I spent a very agreeable few weeks with Thomas Wesley at his country house."

"I'm surprised Lord Minshom allowed that," Paul found himself saying. "Thomas is his pet."

Con's smile was sweet. "So I heard."

Paul stabbed at a piece of ham on his plate. "I'm glad you enjoyed your visit. Did you hunt?"

"We indulged in several gentlemanly pursuits. It was quite refreshing to be out of town."

"I'm sure it was."

Con sighed. "You didn't expect me to stay and watch you get married, did you?"

"Obviously not, especially when you'd already found consolation in Thomas Wesley's bed."

"With all due respect, you are the one who dissolved our relationship."

"Which was obviously of no real meaning to you, seeing as you recovered from it so damned quickly."

Con put down his fork and started to rise. "If you will excuse me, I'll . . ."

Paul put out his hand. "Please, forgive me, I have no right to question you about anything. Your private life is nothing to do with me. I just wasn't expecting to see you here tonight, and now I'm acting like a complete fool."

"You're not the only one."

"What do you mean?"

Con's smile was sad. "I miss you."

"And I miss you." Paul slowly exhaled. "Being honorable is much harder than I thought."

"But you'll continue to do it, won't you? Your wife is a remarkable woman."

"Indeed I will." Paul managed a shaky smile. "I'm sure this will become easier as time goes on."

"I damn well hope so." Con rose to his feet and bowed. "I must go and pay my respects to Miss Ross, and then I'll be leaving." He leaned in closer. "And I didn't fuck Wesley, even though he offered."

Paul had nothing to say to that, and Con turned and walked away.

Moments later, Lucky returned and took her seat, glancing over at Paul, who had focused his attention on his empty glass.

"Are you not hungry?"

He looked down at his plate. "Not particularly."

"That is not like you."

"I know." Paul signaled to one of the footman and asked for more wine. "Do you want anything to drink, my lady?"

"No, thank you." She took an audible breath. "Did Lieutenant Colonel Delinsky say something to upset you?"

Her cautious inquiry made him look at her. "Not at all."

"You seem a little . . . put out."

He forced a smile. "I'm fine. It was just a surprise to see him again. I thought he'd gone abroad." He grimaced. That at least was the truth. "You know how well I deal with my superiors."

"He didn't say anything about me, did he?"

"No, why should he?" Something was definitely wrong and he didn't know quite what to say. Had she heard rumors about him and Delinsky, and if so, from whom? "Did you think he might speak ill of you?"

"No, of course not. He seemed very pleasant." She blushed, and Paul studied her intently.

"What's wrong, Lucky?"

"Nothing at all." She glanced around the room and fanned herself. "Do you think we might leave soon? I'm quite fatigued."

He instantly rose to his feet. "Of course, my dear. We can leave right now. Let me go and fetch your cloak and order the carriage."

Paul waited until Lucky had said her good-byes and then escorted her down to the entrance hall. He made sure she had somewhere to sit while he called for their coach and retrieved her belongings. Even though they were leaving, guests still poured into the house and moved up the stairs, which made maneuvering through the crowds rather difficult.

It was while he waited for the footman to reappear with Lucky's cloak that he saw a man approach her and start up a conversation. Paul frowned as he tried and failed to place the man within their social circle. A second later, he found himself moving purposefully toward the man. The closer he got, the more aware he became of Lucky's horrified expression. Whoever it was, his wife had no wish to talk to the blaggard.

He waited until the man walked away from Lucky and then followed him.

"Excuse me, sir?"

When Paul tapped him peremptorily on the shoulder, the man finally swung around. Something in Paul's expression must have frightened him, because he started to back away. Paul managed to grab his arm and maneuver him toward the rear of the hallway and through the door to the servants' quarters.

"Unhand me, sir!"

Paul shoved him up against the wall and stood over him. When he continued to struggle, Paul brought out the knife he always carried and held it to his opponent's throat. Despite his slight frame, he'd survived almost two years in a French prison and knew some very ungentlemanly fighting skills that he was quite happy to employ.

"You were upsetting my wife. What business did you have with her?"

"I don't know what you mean, sir. I was just giving the lady a message!"

"From whom?"

"A gentleman that told me to give it to her, sir."

"Your employer?"

"No, sir. I work at the bank where this gentleman has his account, sir, and he asked me to deliver this message on my way home."

"And what is your name?"

"Jack Taylor, sir."

Paul studied his captive. Although the man was relatively well dressed, it was obvious from his flat accent that he was a cit rather than a member of the aristocracy.

"Didn't you think it a rather odd request, Mr. Taylor?"

"Not really, sir, not until I saw the lady's face. I didn't mean to worry her, sir. I really didn't."

"What exactly was the message?"

"He said to tell the lady that her account was overdue and that she was to rectify the oversight immediately."

"And what is the name of the man who gave you this message?"

"Mr. Roland, sir."

"And where exactly is your place of employment?"

"At number sixty-five Cornhill, sir."

Paul stepped back and put his knife away. "Well, we can't disappoint Mr. Roland, can we? Tell him my wife will meet him at the bank tomorrow at four."

"But the lady said she would send me a note to confirm the time."

"She doesn't need to worry about this anymore. I'll take

care of it for her. I'll meet you in the main office just before four o'clock."

"Yes, sir."

"And one more thing. You will not disclose my part in this at all. When you communicate with your customer, you will pretend that you spoke only to my wife. Is that clear?"

The man swallowed. "Absolutely, sir."

16

After Milly had undressed her and left for the night, Lucky couldn't even contemplate hopping into bed and sleeping. The evening had turned into a complete disaster. Not only had she found out that Lieutenant Colonel Delinsky knew Paul rather well, but Jeremy had managed to find her too.

She'd naively hoped that when Jeremy heard about her marriage, he would just leave her be. But it seemed that sending him her allowance had done nothing but convince him that she was ready and willing to be blackmailed for the rest of her life. She pressed her hands to her hot cheeks and quietly groaned.

The thing was, she was still such a coward that if she had the money, she would give it to Jeremy for all eternity. But Paul was now her husband, and he controlled their joint finances. They hadn't even discussed the subject of pin money or her monthly allowance and what it was to cover. It hadn't seemed important.

She paused and stared at the door that connected her to Paul's bedchamber. She couldn't just stay here and worry. Better to have it out with Paul right away. She wrapped a long paisley shawl around herself, headed for the door, and unlocked it.

A cloud of steam momentarily blinded her as she entered the dressing room. She waved her hand in front of her face and discovered her husband was lying naked in the bathtub not five feet away from her.

"Could you close the door? I don't want to catch a chill."

She obediently did as he asked and then wondered if he meant her to be on the other side of it. She took another peek at him and discovered he was quite serene as he leisurely washed his chest with a cloth. His blond hair was dripping wet, as if he'd already plunged his head beneath the soapy water.

"I'm sorry, I didn't mean to disturb you."

"It's of no matter. As long as you don't mind me finishing my bath. Jordan has left for the evening." He waved a soapy hand in her direction. "Did you want to talk to me?"

She came across the carpet and searched for something to sit on. There was a jug of water on a stool right next to the bath. She set the jug on the hearth to keep warm and seated herself on the stool. It gave her a fine view of her husband's naked chest. He reclined against the rear of the tub and his knees were slightly drawn up. The washcloth now rested across his groin.

Faced with such male splendor, Lucky struggled to remember what she had wanted to say.

"It's about my allowance."

Paul turned his head slightly toward her and regarded her carefully. "What about it?"

"My father said he had passed all the financial details over to you, and that I should ask you how you wished to proceed."

"Is there something you particularly need to pay for right now?"

"Oh, no," Lucky hastened to reassure him. "It just occurred to me that if I wanted to order a new gown I had no idea who the bill should be sent to."

Paul picked up the washcloth and rubbed it over his muscled stomach. "You can send all the bills you incur to me."

"You do not wish me to have my own allowance?"

She spoke more sharply than she had intended, and he sat up, disturbing the bathwater and making it slosh out onto the floor.

"That's not what I meant. I haven't had time to go through all these matters with your father's secretary yet. He's been rather busy writing speeches for the duke's favorite parliamentary causes to bother with me." He wrung out the cloth and wiped it over his face. "The duke offered me my own secretary, and I intend to meet with him for the first time this week." He paused. "Are you worried I'll run through your fortune?"

"No, of course not!" Lucky tried to laugh.

"Then will you please tell me what the devil is going on?"

"I can't."

"I thought we agreed to be honest with each other?"

"If you wanted money, I would give it to you, no questions asked!"

He stared at her for a long moment. "I'm sure you would. Obviously I'm not as trusting as you are."

She stood up and walked away from him, wrapping the shawl more tightly around her. "And what if I came to you and said I'd done something stupid, and that I needed money to fix the problem. Would you give it to me then?"

He sighed. "And what if I did give it to you? How long would it be before you came back and asked for more?"

"Probably in about a month."

She tensed as she heard him get out of the bath. When she turned around, he was wrapping one of the larger drying cloths around his narrow waist. Water streamed down from his shoulders, catching the candlelight like tears.

"You wish me to stand by and allow you to be blackmailed?" He shook his head, all traces of amiability removed from his face. "If you were my friend, I might help you, but you are my *wife*."

"And thus less capable than your *friend*?" She glared at him. "I thought we *were* friends."

"So did I, but here you are lying to me again." He threw the washcloth to the floor. "Why can't you just tell me the truth?"

"Because I don't want you to have to clean up any more of my messes. You've already sacrificed yourself and who you are to marry me. How do you think I feel having yet another problem to bring to you?" Lucky realized she was shouting, but she didn't care. It was imperative that he understood. "I don't *want* to be a burden to you; I don't *want* you patting me on the head and making things right for me!"

He stared at her for a long moment, his chest rising and falling as though he also struggled with his temper. "You are my wife."

She took a step toward him, and then another, until she was standing right in front of him. He smelled of lavender soap and damp linen, and she wanted to bury her face against his chest and howl. Instead she raised her hand and poked him squarely in the ribs.

"You don't want me as a real wife, so I *am* just your friend."

"I want you." He caught her wrist as she went to poke him again and yanked her against him. "Don't play this game with me, Lucky. You are the one who doubted my desire for you. Don't turn it around to suit your own purposes."

She tried to pull out of his grasp, but he was deceptively strong. She placed her other palm on his chest over his heart and he shuddered. "Don't come to me in anger, Lucky. If you want me, I'm here for you."

She raised her head and stared into his eyes, saw desire there when she had expected only fury. He lowered their joined hands until her fingers were pressed against the cloth around his waist and then lower to where his stiff shaft pushed against the linen.

"Do you want this?" He pushed against her. "Will you at least give me your truth in that?"

God, it was suddenly hard to breathe as her knees turned to water and her body quickened with excitement. Her frustration with him magically transformed into a physical need that she knew only he could ease. He lowered his head and his mouth met hers in a demanding kiss that she had no intention of refusing.

He groaned into her mouth and released her wrist, leaving her free to shape and pet his hardening shaft through the cloth. His hands roamed over her body, pulling away the shawl and untying her nightgown at the neck. He lifted her, and she wrapped her legs around him and clung to him as he took her through to his bedroom. She cried out as he tossed her on to his bed, stripped off her nightgown completely, and came down over her, his body still warm and wet from the bath, his hair damp, his cock a hard, thrusting presence that sought entry between her legs.

He held back though, his fingers searching out her secrets and her needs, until she was as slick and wet as he was, a pulse pounding through her bud, her knees drawn up to receive the heavy, thrusting weight of his body between her thighs. His mouth left hers and she cried out as he sucked on her breast, her nipple trapped between his tongue and the roof of his mouth until she writhed against him and came around his fingers.

He groaned her name as he replaced his fingers with his cock and pressed deep and held himself there until she wanted to beg him to move. Even as she framed the thought, he started to thrust, each long stroke bringing him almost out of her and then back in. He set up a strong, fast rhythm that gave her no

respite, just sent her spiraling ever upward until she was screaming out her pleasure again.

He pulled out, and she grabbed for him, but he only turned
her on to her hands and knees and started again. His hot breath
against her neck, his hands plucking at her breasts and teasing
her bud until she was almost crying with the pleasure of it, with
the need, with *his* need.

His thumb settled on her sex, and he rubbed a fast, wet circle around her clit and down to where his cock thrust deep inside her. She whimpered as his slick thumb slipped lower and
rimmed her arse, bringing a whole new set of sensations that
had her arching her back and demanding more.

He bit her earlobe. "I want you there, too, one day, my cock
filling your arse." He pressed his thumb a little way inside her
and she felt doubly filled. "Do you remember what we saw at
the pleasure house?"

Lucky climaxed at the very thought, and Paul groaned her
name and came with her, his hot seed pumping deep inside her.
She was flattened against the mattress and then he rolled off her,
leaving her feeling cold.

She heard him sigh and felt his hand smooth a path down
between her shoulder blades to the base of her spine.

"If you want money, Lucky, go and ask your father's secretary. I will tell him to give you whatever you want."

She turned her head toward him, but he wasn't even looking
at her. He was staring up at the ceiling.

Paul waited until Lucky's breathing evened out and then
turned on his side to study her. In some strange way he understood her need to do things for herself, her fear that everyone
thought she was incapable and that she would make mistakes.
He'd suffered from that sense of inadequacy his whole life and
allowed others to make decisions for him far too often. But it
was also frustrating that Lucky didn't seem to want to trust

him, as if by marrying her he'd somehow made her position worse than if he'd left well enough alone. But she was his wife, and that did change things whether they liked it or not.

He should have told her about his plans for the morrow, but he feared her response. Perhaps there was a way to make her still feel she had won after all. . . . He shifted restlessly against the sheets. So much for honesty between them. Had seeing Constantine shaken him so badly that he'd taken solace in his wife's arms? That was an ugly thing to contemplate, and he wasn't even sure if he knew the answer. Seeing Con had made him realize how much he missed being touched, how much he liked simply sleeping next to another warm body. Gabriel had never understood that, had shaken Paul off after a fuck like a dog scratching an annoying flea.

Lucky went to sleep beside him without a care in the world, and he liked that. At least she trusted him at some level. He liked the scent of their lovemaking on his skin, her soft breathing, and the way she turned to him in the night. He stroked her tangled hair as a sense of certainty swept over him. No, this wasn't just about Con. This was about Lucky, too.

It was about wanting to be *loved*.

And if he wanted to be loved, he had to try and be honest. Lucky needed to know about his past feelings for Con, and he would have to be the one to tell her before someone else did it with crueler intent.

The next morning, Paul didn't see Lucky because he was closeted with his new man of business. Mr. Walker very patiently explained the financial responsibilities of Paul's new position as a married man who had earned the right to spend his wife's considerable income. The sums of money being casually tossed about were incredible, and Paul felt terribly guilty.

It didn't seem right that just because she was a woman Lucky had to give up everything. Paul spent a fair bit of time insisting that most of her money was placed in trust either for her or for their potential offspring. As his new secretary was a longtime employee of the duke's, his actions were met with considerable surprise and increasing respect.

They worked on through luncheon and eventually Paul signed the last of the papers Mr. Walker offered him. He sat back with a relieved sigh. "Are we finally done?"

Mr. Walker smiled. "Indeed we are, Lieutenant. It has been a pleasure to discover that you are a man of great common sense and even greater understanding."

Paul groaned. "You flatter me."

"No, sir, I do not. I must admit to some qualms when I heard that Lady Lucinda was to be married. But you have removed all my doubts. You definitely have her best interests at heart."

"I should damn well hope so, seeing as she and her family are the source of everything I now apparently control."

"I'm glad you saw reason and went with my suggested amount for your allowance, sir, although it is still quite modest by most men's standards." Mr. Walker pressed the seal from Paul's signet ring into the still-warm wax on the bottom of the letter. "We have also discussed Lady Lucinda's requirements."

"Indeed we have, and I have also given you my instructions as to her having complete access to any extra funds that she needs without question."

"Indeed, sir." Mr. Walker continued to put the papers away in his case. "I will use this room as my office whenever I come to call on you. I will also maintain a cash box here for your convenience. Sometimes gold is the only thing that will solve a problem."

"So I've heard."

Mr. Walker paused. "There is one more thing I would like to touch on as well, sir, if you have the time?"

Paul rubbed his aching temples. "Yes, of course, Mr. Walker."

"I refer to your ongoing residence."

"My residence?"

"I would assume that you and Lady Lucinda might wish to purchase or rent a town house of your own. There are several country properties owned by the Haymore family where you might choose to rusticate, but unfortunately only this house in London."

Paul thought longingly of his old attic rooms and the companionship he'd found there.

"I'll have to speak to my wife about this."

"Of course, sir. But if you do wish to establish your own dwelling, I can make up a list of desirable properties for you to view."

"Thank you, Mr. Walker. You are indeed a treasure. I wasn't even aware that we could afford such a thing."

"Oh, yes, you can, sir." Mr. Walker's smile was broad. "Despite the last duke's longevity, or perhaps because of it, the dukedom is in a very healthy financial state."

"I'm glad to hear it."

"Naturally, sir, seeing as one day all the responsibility for administering it will all be yours."

Paul got the usual hollow feeling in his stomach when he was reminded about that, but managed a smile. Mr. Walker had been exceptionally patient with him, after all. Paul rose to his feet and shook Mr. Walker's hand.

"Thank you, Mr. Walker."

"Thank you, sir. I look forward to calling on you in a week to tell you what progress I have made on all your requests."

Paul patted his shoulder. "Don't wear yourself out on my account."

"I'd be glad to do so, sir. The present duke and his family have been very good to me."

"That makes two of us," Paul replied, and Mr. Walker gathered up his papers and left.

After almost five hours of financial matters, Paul was more than ready to leave the house, meet Mr. Roland, and plant his fist in the man's face. But, he owed it to Lucky to be a little more careful than that. He at least needed a witness.

He downed a quick glass of brandy, and decided to walk around to the pleasure house in Mayfair. It was starting to rain, but he was glad of the fresh air on his face. He splashed through a puddle and grimaced at the old but well-tended leather of his boots. If what Mr. Walker said was true, he could afford to have several new pairs made without even noticing the cost. For a man used to counting every penny, his newfound wealth felt both disquieting and remarkably undeserved.

Aware that his feet were now wet, he resolved to avoid any more puddles until he could order at least one new pair of boots. He walked around to the back entrance of the pleasure house and down the stairs into the kitchens.

Madame Durand looked up from her usual position at the stove and smiled.

"Monsieur Paul."

"Madame." He grinned back at her. She'd always liked him because he adored everything she cooked and ate what was put in front of him without a single complaint. "*Ou est* Ambrose?"

Madame Durand jerked her head in the direction of the cellars.

"*Merci*, Madame." Paul took off his cloak and hat and placed them over a chair near to the fire to dry. As he approached the stairs leading down to the cellars, he heard the unmistakable sound of someone climbing up and waited at the door. Ambrose emerged with several bottles of fine claret in his hands.

"Are those for me?" Paul asked.

"No, they are not. Good afternoon, Lieutenant. Aren't you supposed to be elsewhere?" Ambrose regarded him severely for a second and then walked back into the kitchen and placed the bottles on the table.

"I haven't come here to enjoy myself, Ambrose. I wanted to talk to you."

Ambrose raised an eyebrow and opened one of the bottles. He left it sitting on the table while he collected some glasses.

"It really needs time to settle, but I don't see why we shouldn't sample it."

"I'm always happy to oblige." Paul took a seat next to his friend and held up a glass. "I need your help."

Ambrose paused in the act of pouring out the claret. "What's wrong?"

"I need a witness in case I do something foolish."

Ambrose set the bottle down on the table with great care. "You are intending to kill someone?"

"Not *kill*, precisely, but definitely put the fear of God into them."

Ambrose sipped the claret and frowned. "Of course I'll come with you, but can you be a little more specific?"

Paul lowered his voice. "I think I have found the man who tried to ruin Lady Lucinda. I'm due to meet him at four o'clock today. He thinks he is meeting my wife to drum up more money out of her."

Ambrose finished his glass of claret and wiped his mouth. "Then I shall definitely accompany you. We should take one of the Kelly brothers with us as well. Seamus is here today." He glanced at the clock on the mantelpiece. "We should be on our way. It is almost fifteen minutes to the hour."

Paul caught Ambrose's arm. "If the man needs to be killed, I will do it. I don't want you or Seamus with blood on your hands."

"Let's hope it doesn't come to that," Ambrose replied. "But, in my opinion, any man who behaves so despicably to a woman deserves to be punished."

"You are condoning violence, my friend?" Paul shook out his still-damp cloak and put his hat back on. He'd dressed in his old regimentals in an attempt to remind the weasel he would be facing that he was, in fact, a hardened soldier inured to death.

Ambrose's answering smile was fierce. "I do believe I am. Let me fetch Seamus. Did you bring your coach?"

Paul regarded his sodden boots. "No, I walked."

"Then I'll find us a hackney cab."

Paul had to squeeze in beside Ambrose as Seamus took up a whole seat by himself. The rain continued to pour down and the streets were all but deserted apart from a stalwart few who continued to ply their trade. The small windows steamed up and the scent of damp wool and unhealthy gutters permeated the dank air.

"Did you know that Constantine Delinsky is back in Town?" Ambrose asked quietly.

"Yes, I saw him last night at a ball we attended."

"And how was he?"

"Well enough."

Ambrose lapsed into silence, and Paul hoped he'd remain so for the rest of the journey.

"Did he meet your wife again?"

Paul frowned. "He certainly met her. What do you mean, *again?*"

Ambrose's shoulder went rigid against his. "It is of no matter; I must be mistaken."

"About what?"

Paul turned to stare into the other man's face. His suspicions about Lucky's cautious questions to him about Con suddenly revived.

"Are you sure you want to know?"

"Yes, I'm absolutely sure. Out with it."

Ambrose sighed. "I thought Miss Ross told me that it was

Delinsky who discovered Lady Lucinda in distress at the ball a month or two ago and found help for her."

"Delinsky did?" Paul frowned. "He didn't mention it to me, and neither did Lucky."

"Then I must indeed have been mistaken." Ambrose sat forward. "I believe we are almost at our destination."

While he found the necessary coin to pay the driver Paul had no more time to think about that interesting piece of information. Cornhill was still busy, but for once he didn't have to worry about who would see him. Visiting a bank was a perfectly respectable activity for a gentleman.

It still lacked five minutes to the hour, and Paul beckoned for Ambrose and Seamus to follow him inside the tall stone building. He'd told his informant, Mr. Taylor, to meet him there and discreetly point out which of the gentlemen was Mr. Roland.

Seamus lingered by the front door in case Mr. Roland should decide to make a run for it, while Ambrose followed behind Paul. Mr. Taylor showed them into a small office to the side of the main clerks' hall.

"If you leave the door open a crack, I'll be able to point Mr. Roland out to you."

"And then you can leave the rest to us," Paul said.

Mr. Taylor looked rather worried. "You won't cause a scene now, will you, sir? I don't want to lose my employment over this."

Paul wanted to say something about Mr. Taylor's conduct in carrying such a message and frightening his wife, but he restrained himself. "I promise we'll behave ourselves."

Ambrose leaned against the wall and Paul took up a position behind Mr. Taylor. Just as the clock struck four, Mr. Taylor stiffened.

"He's here, sir. The young gentleman in the long brown coat and the black hat."

"I see him," Paul replied. "Thank you, Mr. Taylor. You may go. Ask Mr. Kelly to bring our visitor in here, will you?"

Mr. Taylor exited through a different door and emerged close to Seamus. He whispered something and pointed in Mr. Roland's direction. Even as he continued to gesticulate, Seamus was already moving through the crowded lobby, his gaze fixed on his prey. Paul fought a smile as Seamus simply caught Mr. Roland up in a whirl of forward motion and herded him toward the door of the office.

"What is going on here? I say!"

Mr. Roland's indignant protest broke off as Seamus shoved him into the office and closed the door.

"Good afternoon, Mr. Roland. So good of you to spare the time to speak to me."

"I have no idea who you are, sir, let alone why you encouraged that oaf to manhandle me. I'll have you both up before a magistrate by morning."

"I don't think you will, Roland. Please sit down."

Roland smoothed a hand over his disordered cravat. "I will not, sir. Who are you to tell me what to do?"

"The husband of the lady you expected to see this afternoon." Roland's sneering smile disappeared. "Now sit down, or I'll ask Seamus to help you."

Roland took a seat in front of the desk Paul sat on, his face suddenly pale. "I still have no idea what you are talking about, sir."

"A liar *and* a blackmailer, as well as a rapist and despoiler of young ladies. What an unpleasant individual you are, Roland." Paul produced his knife and studied the sharp blade. "I'd like to cut off your balls, but I doubt you have any."

Roland tried to rise, but Seamus shoved him back down into the chair.

"Just so that we are clear, Roland, I am Lieutenant Paul St.

Clare. You have been attempting to blackmail my wife, and I don't like to see her upset."

Roland pulled out a handkerchief and patted his face. "Alack, you, too, have been beguiled by her pretty face. She has lied to both of us!"

"Oh, no," Paul said tranquilly. "She has never lied to me."

"Perhaps you do not understand, sir. She threw herself at *me* and then offered me money not to reveal her shame to you."

Paul rose to his feet and approached Roland, and the man shrank back in his chair.

"I'm sorry to bring you such bad tidings of your bride, sir, but surely it is unfair to harm the messenger?"

"You . . ." Paul shook his head as a cold rage engulfed him. He wished he could draw his cavalry sword and shove it right through Roland's guts. "Hold him still, please, Seamus." Instead, he placed the edge of his knife blade on Roland's throat and pressed until a thin line of blood appeared.

"You are less than the filth on the bottom of my boots, Mr. Roland. You preyed upon an innocent and forced her simply to gain her hand in marriage. When she found the strength to refuse you, you decided you'd make her pay in another way by blackmailing her."

"That's a lie!" Roland gasped. "She gave me the money willingly. Ask her!"

Paul pushed the blade a little deeper, and drops of red stained the whiteness of Roland's cravat. "If she gave you *anything* it was to make you leave her alone, and yet here you are, crawling back for more."

Roland groaned. "You can't prove anything. Perhaps I meant to tell her I didn't want her money."

Paul laughed. "I don't need to prove anything. Dead men can't tell tales."

"You can't kill me," whimpered Roland. "I have friends; my second cousin twice removed is a *viscount.* I will be *missed.*"

"Missed maybe, but never found. . . ."

Ambrose came to stand beside Paul. "Lieutenant St. Clare, you can't kill him here. It is too public."

Paul sighed. "I suppose it is." He glanced up at Ambrose. "Then what should we do with him?"

"Seamus and I can kill him and leave his body down by the docks. No one will find him there, and no one will connect you with the death."

Under Paul's hands Roland started to shake and stutter. It pleased Paul immensely. If he could make this worm suffer one-thousandth of Lucky's anguish, it would be worth it.

"I wonder if we should give him one chance to redeem himself?"

Ambrose sighed. "I'd rather we just killed him."

Paul looked down into Roland's terrified eyes. "What do you say, Mr. Roland? One last chance, or a quick and bloody death?"

After a long moment, Roland licked his lips. "What do you want me to do?"

Paul gestured at the desk. "You will write a letter to my wife. In it you will tell her that you have suffered a change of heart and no longer intend to pursue your interest with her."

"All right. I'll do it."

Paul nodded at Seamus to escort Roland to the chair behind the desk, while Ambrose set out a sheet of paper and ink. For a while there was only the sound of the pen scratching on the paper as Paul focused on controlling his anger.

"It is done."

Paul leaned over to read what Roland had written and nodded. "It will suffice."

Roland shot to his feet. "And you will let me go now?"

Paul smiled. "Not quite." He drew back his fist and smashed it squarely into Roland's face and heard the satisfying crunch of cartilage breaking. He hit him again until Roland was sprawled on the floor, his nose bleeding and his eyes terrified.

Paul knelt beside him and grabbed him around the throat. "Now that I know who you are, I will be watching you very carefully, as will my friends. If you so much as glance at my wife again, or attempt to see her, I *will* kill you. And if you mention this matter to anyone, I will make sure that you can never show your face in London again. You might be second cousin to a viscount, but I am the heir of a *duke*. Do you understand me?"

Roland managed a feeble nod, and Paul dropped his hold on him. Roland's head thumped down on the floor, and he appeared to lose consciousness.

"Lieutenant, Seamus and I will take care of Mr. Roland," Ambrose said. "I suggest you take the letter to Mr. Taylor and ask him to deliver it to your wife when she contacts him. Lieutenant?"

Paul swallowed hard. "I want to kill him, Ambrose. I want to beat him to a pulp, rip off his prick, and stuff it in his mouth."

"Quite understandably, sir, but we have to give him at least one chance to make things right."

"Why?" Paul stood up and put his knife away. "He is an abomination and he hurt my wife."

"Because, unfortunately, he is too well born to disappear without an outcry, and neither Seamus nor I wish to be taken up for assisting in a murder. And, if you admit to killing him, you would destroy your wife and her family's reputation, which defeats the whole purpose of this exercise."

"Damn you for being so reasonable, Ambrose."

"Isn't that why you brought me along, sir? To stop you from doing something you'd regret?"

"I suppose that's true." Paul regarded the prostrate form of Mr. Roland. "You'll take care of him, then?"

Ambrose glanced at Seamus, who winked. "Indeed we will, sir. Now why don't you go and deliver that letter to Mr. Taylor."

Paul paused at the door to look back over his shoulder. Seamus was hefting Mr. Roland over his shoulder and wrapping him in his cloak. "You're going to give him the beating he deserves, aren't you?"

"Aye, sir. When we get him somewhere more private." Seamus cracked his knuckles and grinned. "But never fear, sir, we won't let him die."

17

———————————

"We're here, Lieutenant Colonel," Miss Ross announced, and Con came around to help her out of his carriage, leaving his driver to walk the horses. It was already starting to get dark, and the wind held the promise of a frost. A nearby clock struck five times.

"Isn't it a little late to be making a call?"

"Oh, no," Miss Ross said airily. "Lucky told me I could visit her whenever I wanted." She glanced up at the imposing façade. "They are still living at Haymore House. I assume they will be finding a place of their own at some point. The duke and duchess are very nice, but it must be a little difficult living with your in-laws."

"I agree, Miss Ross."

She glanced up at him. "Is there something wrong?"

"Not at all, Miss Ross."

"You didn't want to escort me today, did you?"

He grasped her elbow and steered her up the impressive steps. Of course he hadn't wanted to come. What did she think he was? A man who enjoyed being hurt? Unfortunately he could hardly say that, so he concentrated on knocking on the door and summoning the butler.

"I think it is important for you to see Lucky and Paul together."

"And why is that?"

"Because you will soon become accustomed to it, and then it won't upset you so badly."

He smiled down at her. "I'm hardly upset, Miss Ross. I think you are imagining us as star-crossed lovers when the reality is far different."

She sighed. "I scarcely think it is romantic, sir. Lucky looks at you as if you are the embodiment of all her dreams, and you look at Paul in the same way. That is more tragic than romantic."

When had Lady Lucinda ever looked at him like that? "I see you have a pragmatic streak, Miss Ross."

"Well, somebody in our family has to have *some* common sense. The others are always flying into alt."

"Especially the Delornay side," Con suggested as the butler opened the door and ushered them into the palatial entrance hall. "They are French, after all."

Miss Ross smiled and squeezed his arm. "Exactly."

The butler returned and escorted them up the stairs to what appeared to be a separate wing of the house. He opened a set of double doors and announced them.

"Miss Ross and Lieutenant Colonel Delinsky, my lady."

Lady Lucinda put down her book and rose to her feet, her smile dazzling. She came toward them and held out her hands. She wore a green flowered muslin dress that complemented her eyes and porcelain skin. Her long dark hair was curled and piled on top of her head.

"Such a pleasure to see you both. My book was failing to interest me, and I was almost settling in for a nap."

Constantine stood back and waited until Miss Ross hugged

SIMPLY VORACIOUS / 191

her hostess, and then bent to kiss her hand. As he straightened, he noticed a faint bruise on her throat and immediately pictured her with Paul, wondered whether he'd marked her when he came as he'd done to Con. . . .

"Lady Lucinda, a pleasure."

She blushed when she looked up at him, and he considered Miss Ross's casual remark that Lady Lucinda wasn't indifferent to him. For a moment he wondered what would have happened if he'd not found Miss Ross for her in the garden and had, instead, taken care of her himself. Would they now be heading toward marriage?

He pushed that thought away. With his own marital status still unclear, he had no right to speculate or dream about another man's wife, especially Paul's wife.

"What was the book that failed to keep your interest, my lady?" Con inquired as they took their seats around the fireplace.

"Oh, something about crop rotation, I think. My father is very interested in the newest farming methods, and I was just trying to keep up. It makes for far more interesting dinnertime conversation if one can occasionally ask a relevant question."

"I'm impressed that you even made the attempt, my lady. I must admit to knowing little about farming. I've spent most of my life in the army or in the city."

She gave him a grateful smile. "Paul is the same, Lieutenant Colonel. But, because he is my father's heir, he is having to learn far more than he ever wanted to about the management of a great estate."

Miss Ross chuckled. "I keep forgetting that Paul is your father's heir. I can't imagine him as a pompous old duke. He's always defied authority."

"I should imagine Lieutenant Colonel Delinsky knows that rather well," Lady Lucinda said.

Con nodded. "Indeed, he was not the easiest of officers to

manage. He always had a thousand questions as to why I phrased an order in a particular way. I had to remind him quite frequently that an order was supposed to be instantly obeyed and not questioned in the first place."

Both of the ladies were still laughing when the door opened again and Paul appeared. He halted in the doorway. Con suspected he wanted to bolt, but he mastered the desire and advanced with a smile.

"Miss Ross, Lieutenant Colonel Delinsky, what a delightful surprise." He bent to kiss the top of his wife's head. "I apologize for my absence. I was busy with some correspondence."

He took a seat opposite Con, and matters turned to ordering tea for the ladies and spirits for the gentleman. Con couldn't help but stare covertly at Paul. He seemed different somehow, and it wasn't just that he was out of uniform. His face looked older, and the laughter in his brown eyes was somewhat subdued. Con blinked as those eyes fixed on him, and he hurriedly looked away.

He didn't want to sit here and make polite conversation. He wanted . . . Con took a deep breath. What he wanted wasn't a subject he could air in this setting or anywhere. Perhaps he should have taken Thomas Wesley up on his offer after all. Then Paul would hate him, and the healing process would begin. But he didn't want Paul to hate him, he . . .

He realized Lady Lucinda was asking him a question.

"No, my lady, I own no property here in London. I rent my rooms."

"Do you still have property in Russia?" Miss Ross asked.

Con accepted a glass of brandy from Paul, avoiding his gaze. "There are some family holdings that survived Napoléon and his troops. I receive the occasional letter from my mother. I rely on her excellent guidance for my decisions about the property there."

"Do you receive an income from those properties?"

Paul cleared his throat. "That is scarcely any of your business, Emily."

She shrugged. "I know, I'm just being curious. I'm sure the lieutenant colonel doesn't mind." She turned back to Con. "I hear your family was very high in the Tsar's favor, and that we really should be calling you *Prince* Constantine."

Con smiled. "That title has a different meaning in my country. It is almost as common as a baronet is here."

"Oh." Emily looked quite disappointed. "I was quite looking forward to dancing with a real prince."

Con had to smile at that. "Not quite so pragmatic after all, Miss Ross, if you dream of royalty?"

"A girl can still dream, sir, even a practical one."

The tea arrived, and Lady Lucinda and Miss Ross busied themselves with the cups, leaving Con staring at Paul. To his surprise, Paul rose to his feet.

"Lucky, would you mind if I took Delinsky down to my study for a moment? There is a trifling matter about my military papers that he might be able to settle for me."

Lady Lucinda paused to look around at them. "Of course not. Please go ahead."

Paul bowed and walked toward the door, leaving Con to follow meekly after him. He tried to keep his expression neutral as Paul ushered him into his study and shut the door firmly behind him.

"There really is something I need your signature on, sir, and then I'll be free of the military once and for all." Paul searched on his desk for the relevant paper and then passed it over to Con. "Here you are."

Con signed his name and then his attention shifted to Paul's outstretched hand. "What happened to your knuckles?"

Paul glanced at them and then thrust his hand into his coat pocket. "A minor skirmish."

"You *fought* someone?"

Paul's smile was cold. "Well, I didn't exactly let him fight back."

"That is not like you."

Paul sat on the edge of his desk and looked up at Con. "I always fought well when I had reason. Surely you remember that."

"Then you must have had a very good reason."

"The best." Paul hesitated. "In truth, you might be pleased to hear what I did, seeing as I understand from Ambrose that you were peripherally involved in the whole affair." He raised his gaze to meet Con's. "Of course, anything we speak of here is in the strictest of confidence."

"I'm not generally accounted a gossip."

"I of all men know that." Paul glanced down at his bruised knuckles. "I found the man who accosted my wife at the ball a few weeks ago."

"Did you kill him?"

"God, I wanted to, but wiser counsel prevailed. I merely told him to leave my wife alone or I would ruin him. I left him to the tender mercies of Ambrose and Seamus Kelly."

"Not *entirely* to them, I see." Con gestured at Paul's fist.

"I couldn't resist. He was a nasty, bloodsucking little weasel, but he was also 'gentry,' so I had to be careful."

"I would've killed him for you."

Paul met his gaze. "I know." He sighed. "Con, I had no idea that you already knew my wife. I have to tell Lucky about our relationship."

Constantine stiffened. "We have no relationship."

"I promised to be honest with her. She knows me very well. She knew about Gabriel long before I had the guts to tell her." He hesitated. "If I am in your company, she will guess how I feel—I mean, how I *felt* about you."

Con frowned. "She married you knowing that you had male lovers?"

"Yes. We promised to be honest with each other. I knew about the rape, and she knew about my . . . complicated love life."

"But not about me." Con stood up and headed for the door.

Paul grabbed his arm. "I couldn't tell her about you." Con tried to pull away, but Paul persisted. "If I'd mentioned you, she would never have agreed to marry me. She would have insisted I *stay* with you, and I could not do that to her. She needed me."

"More than I did?"

"Yes."

Con yanked his arm free. "Then tell her whatever you damn well like."

He opened the door and started up the stairs, aware that Paul was following him.

"Will you stop for a moment and listen to me?"

Con kept going. "I think you've made your point, and as I have a great deal of respect for your wife, I'm not going to start a brawl with you in her house."

He reached the top of the stairs and turned left. There was no sign of the butler, but he remembered the drawing room was about three doors down. Before he could reach his target, Paul came up behind him and shoved him through one of the doors into an empty room.

"We had only just begun our association," Paul said, his breathing as irregular as Con's. "I had no idea if you were interested in being with me for more than a few quick fucks."

"Just because Gabriel treated you like that does not mean I would've done so."

"*Most* people treat me like that." Paul glared at him. "I have always been expendable. Lucky had no one else to turn to, and for once in my life, I could do something unselfish and save my friend and her parents from disgrace."

Con gave into the temptation to cup Paul's chin. "I thought

I could love you, Paul. I apologize if I didn't make that clear. I, too, have learned to be cautious about expressing my feelings." He managed a shaky laugh. "And this is neither helping, nor an appropriate place to discuss such an intimate matter."

Paul stepped back and shoved a hand through his hair. "I'm sorry, Con."

"Don't be. You have married a courageous and wonderful woman who obviously loves you for yourself." He hesitated. "Would it help if I asked to be assigned elsewhere?"

"No!" Paul went pale. "Please, don't do that. If I can just see you occasionally, know that things are all right with you, I swear I won't ask for anything more."

Con forced a smile. "We're quite pathetic, aren't we?"

Paul smiled back. "Well, I am. You have always been one of my heroes."

"I think you are the one who has been quite heroic, my friend. I'm not sure I would've had the strength to push you away." He sighed. "It was easier when I wondered if you had married to consolidate your position with the Haymore family."

Paul held his gaze. "That's what most people think, but I wanted you to know the truth." He swallowed hard. "I wanted to be as honest with you as I am with Lucky."

Con took a deep breath. "We should go. I think it might snow tonight, and I need to get my horses back."

Paul held open the door. "Absolutely."

Lucky glanced at Emily, who was enjoying her second cup of tea, and then up at the clock. For some reason she felt ill at ease.

"I wonder what has happened to Paul and the lieutenant colonel?"

Emily gave her a sideways glance. "They probably had a lot to talk about."

"I suppose that is true. They are both from the same regiment, after all, and I know how Papa and his friends like to reminisce." She bit her lip. "Perhaps the matter turned out to be more complicated than Paul thought."

"That might well be true," Emily agreed and started to rise from her chair. "Do you want me to go and look for them?"

"No, it's all right. I'll go myself."

Emily frowned. "Perhaps I had better . . ."

Lucky stared at her. "What are you worried about? Do you think the lieutenant colonel has left without you?" She continued on to the door and opened it slightly, just in time to see Constantine Delinsky and her husband emerge from one of the unused rooms close to the drawing room. She inadvertently took a step back and pulled the bell for the servants.

"I see them coming up the stairs now. I wonder if I should order some fresh tea?"

She hurried back to her seat, picked up her sewing, and tried to appear as though she hadn't moved an inch or worried at all. She smiled as Paul came through the door and approached her.

"I'm sorry, my dear. I kept Delinsky occupied for far longer than I intended."

"It is of no matter," Lucky said graciously. "Would you like some more tea? I have just rung for the butler."

Lieutenant Colonel Delinsky bowed. "I apologize, my lady, but I really need to take Miss Ross safely home before the weather becomes even worse. I believe it might snow tonight."

"Then of course you must be off." She rose from her seat and held out her hand. "Please come and see us again soon. You are welcome at any time."

"Thank you, my lady St. Clare." He kissed her fingers. "Are you ready, Miss Ross?"

"Indeed I am." Emily walked over and hugged Lucky hard. "It will all work out in the end, I swear it," she whispered. "And I will come and see you on Friday."

Lucky stayed behind as Paul escorted their visitors down the stairs, and then sank back into her chair. She frowned down at her hands in her lap and tried to marshal her thoughts into some kind of order. There was obviously some tension between Paul and his commanding officer, but what was the cause? Constantine Delinsky seemed to be a good man; in truth, she liked him excessively.

"Lucky?" She looked up to find Paul standing in front of her. "Are you going upstairs to change for dinner?"

"Yes, I suppose I should." She groaned. "I am such a terrible hostess. It is so late we should have asked them to stay for dinner. But it feels awkward asking them when it is still my mother's house."

He tucked her hand in the crook of his arm, and they walked together up another flight of stairs to their bedroom suite.

"Mr. Walker suggested we rent or buy a house of our own. What do you think of the idea?"

She considered it as they traversed the corridor to their rooms. "I've never lived without my parents before. It would be strange at first, but it would be nice to be able to choose my own furniture and make all the decisions as to what we should eat."

"Then I'll ask Mr. Walker to find us some houses to look at. I must admit I'd rather we had our own home." Paul hesitated. "I've never really had one before. I've always lived with other people."

He paused at her door and let go of her hand. "May I come in with you for a moment?"

"Of course. I'll ring for Milly when we're done."

She wandered over to her dressing table and sat down, eager to find something to do to ease her nervousness. Had Paul seen Mr. Taylor talk to her at the ball the previous night? If he had, why hadn't he mentioned it already? Or had the lieutenant colonel seen her and passed the information on to his friend? Perhaps that explained why they had spent so much time together earlier.

"Lucky . . ." Paul said and then he stopped again. "I know we agreed to be honest with each other, but there is something I didn't tell you before we married."

She blinked at him. "What?"

He sat down on the chaise longue at the bottom of her bed, his gaze directed downward to his dirty boots. "Lieutenant Colonel Delinsky and I were lovers."

"Oh."

He looked up. "Is that all you have to say?"

"Well, it certainly explains why you seem so ill at ease with each other." It also might explain why they had disappeared into an empty room together, but she really didn't want to think about that.

Paul ran a hand through his blond hair. "He is a good and honorable man, and I disappointed him."

"By marrying me?"

"No, not at all. He understands why I did that, and he has nothing but respect for you."

"Then why are you telling me this? Do you think he plans to win you back?"

"He wouldn't do that." Paul looked away from her again. "It's just that I wanted you to know the truth."

"Did the lieutenant colonel tell you he found me in the gardens that night and made certain I got home safely?"

She wasn't sure why, but the thought that Constantine Delinsky had broken his word to her and told Paul made everything worse.

"No, he didn't mention it, but Ambrose inadvertently did." He sighed. "I'm glad it was Con who helped you. He is just the sort of man you can trust."

"He was the perfect gentleman."

He raised his gaze to meet hers. "You approve of him, then?"

Lucky realized her fingernails were digging into her skin. "I have already told you, Paul. If you wish to take a lover, you should do so."

He shot to his feet. "Lucky, do you ever listen to a damned word I say? I told you I would not take a lover."

She stood, too, her hands clenched at her sides. "And I told you to be honest with me."

"Which I have been." He flung the words at her over his shoulder as he paced. "Which is why I told you about Con!"

"*After* we were married, and you knew you had me safe and secure!"

"What the devil is that supposed to mean?" Paul demanded.

She held his gaze. "I know you, Paul. You didn't mention Constantine Delinsky because you care for him."

He swallowed. "You knew I liked men. I took you to the pleasure house. I showed you exactly who I am."

"No, you showed me that you like to have sex with anonymous people. You *knew* that if I thought you were in love again, I'd never agree to marry you whatever my circumstances."

His expression stilled. "And mayhap I still think I made the right decision. We are married now, and that is the end of it."

"And be damned to what you really want?"

"That isn't the point."

Lucky opened her mouth to protest and was interrupted by a knock on the door. Before Paul could issue a denial, Lucky pushed past him and opened the door.

"Come in, Milly. My husband is just leaving."

Milly looked from her to Paul, her expression worried. "I just came to deliver this note to you, my lady. You can ring for me to help you dress later."

"It's all right, Milly. My wife is correct. I am going," Paul said.

Lucky waited until he stalked out of the room and returned to sit at her dressing table, the note clenched in her hand.

"Are you all right, my lady?" Milly inquired.

"I'm fine, Milly," Lucky said to her reflection, and saw Paul's anger reflected in her own eyes. "I don't think I'll bother to dress for dinner after all. I have a headache. Please send my apologies to my parents."

Milly loosened the back of Lucky's dress and unlaced her corset. "Do you want me to brush out your hair, then, my lady? That can sometimes help with a headache."

"It's all right, Milly. I think I'll do it myself. It helps me think. You can retire for the night."

"If you are sure, my lady. I'll send up some supper for you on a tray and leave your nightgown to warm by the fire."

"Thank you." Lucky dredged up another smile. "Good night, Milly."

"Good night, my lady, and don't you worry about the lieutenant. Whatever he did, I'm sure he'll be sorry enough in the morning."

Lucky put her elbows on the dressing table and buried her face in her hands. She wanted to cry, the tears crowded in her throat, her eyes burning, but somehow she just couldn't. She didn't want to think about Paul and Constantine Delinsky being lovers. Of all the men in the world, why did it have to be Delinsky? The man who had guessed what had happened to her, and hadn't taken advantage of her plight or judged her in any way.

She glanced down at the letter in her hand and read the return address. It seemed that Mr. Taylor from the bank on Cornhill had replied to her about arranging a meeting with Jeremy. God, she wanted to see Jeremy so badly, wanted to borrow Paul's pistol and shoot him herself.

She ripped open the covering sheet, and then frowned at the all-too-familiar handwriting. Why was Jeremy writing to her again? Was it another demand for money? She opened the letter with shaking hands and scanned the sparse sentences. Then she had to read it again. Jeremy was relinquishing all claims to her affection, and would not be troubling her again.

She dropped the letter on to her dressing table and stared at it. The expected rush of relief didn't come. What in God's name had happened for him to have such a dramatic change of heart? Or was he simply playing with her? She shook her head as her tears finally started to fall.

18

"I have the morning papers and your mail, sir."

Gregor placed the paper at Constantine's elbow and propped up the mail against the coffeepot.

"Thank you, Gregor."

Con picked up the pile of envelopes and sifted through them. There was a bill from the cobbler, and one from his tailor, both of which were expected. There was also the usual clutch of invitations, which he would consider later. A letter in an unknown feminine hand caught his attention and he opened that one first.

It was a note from Lady Lucinda St. Clare asking him for dinner on the following night. He stared at her neat handwriting and wondered if Paul had told her about their affair. He'd half expected her to cut all communications with him rather than invite him to dinner. Maybe she was as unusual and open-minded as Paul implied. He liked to think that was true, and that his friend had found happiness.

He looked up as Gregor returned with more toast. "Will

you make sure that my dress uniform is presentable? I wish to wear it tomorrow night."

Gregor snorted. "It is always presentable, *podpolkovnik*, because I keep it so."

"Of course, Gregor."

There was also a long overdue letter from his mother in Russia. Con took a piece of toast and rose from the table, bringing his coffee with him. He picked up his mail and took everything across to the small desk where he dealt with his correspondence.

His first task was to write an acceptance note to Lady Lucinda, and then decide which social events he wished to attend. At present, his military duties were almost non-existent, seeing as most of his regiment was overseas. He'd been asked to stay at home and liaise with the war office and the Duke of Wellington's staff. The duke encouraged his officers to socialize, so Con's presence at so many events wouldn't be remarked upon and would actually be expected.

He opened his mother's letter with some trepidation. Despite his remarks to Miss Ross about how much he depended on his mother, he sometimes found her rather overwhelming. She struggled with their reduced circumstances and complained constantly about the things she could no longer afford and the lack of convivial society. In truth, compared with the majority of her countrymen, she had escaped relatively unscathed. But she seemed unable to contemplate that reality, and Con had given up trying to explain it to her.

He sighed and settled down to read her list of complaints, only rousing to make the occasional note or thank Gregor for replacing his coffee. She wanted him to come home and take over the task of running the estates, and he had no wish to do so. Even the thought of returning to his homeland made him want to puke. As an eighteen-year-old soldier retreating before

Napoléon's army, he'd seen such horrors that he still had nightmares.

With a groan he thrust those images away, knowing he'd be facing them in his dreams later. He composed a long reply to his mother, recommending she rely on his cousin Michael, his land agent, for advice, and not to worry so much about him. In his soul he knew he'd have to return to Russia at some point, but not quite yet. Even as he finished his letter, he started another one to Michael, a good, honest soul who would make sure all Con's requests were carried out.

He sat back and stretched, guilt clouding his senses. His mother was right. He was a neglectful landlord and an undutiful son who lived off the income of an estate he never visited. There was no escaping that. But he'd learned to his cost during the war that he had to live his life as he thought fit. At least he was almost done with his correspondence for the day and, weather permitting, could take one of his horses out for a ride in the park.

There was a knock on his door, and Gregor appeared again.

"There is a gentleman to see you, sir, a Major Thomas Wesley. Shall I admit him?"

"Of course, Gregor."

Con rose to his feet and put on his discarded coat, which Gregor held out to him. When Thomas appeared, Con walked forward to shake his hand.

"Major Wesley, a pleasure."

"Likewise." Thomas took a seat by the fire and rubbed his hands together. "It is damned chilly out there today. I miss the warmer climate of India."

"Would you prefer something hot to drink?" Con inquired. "Some punch or a hot toddy, perhaps?"

"That would be delightful."

Con instructed Gregor, and then took the seat opposite

Thomas and waited for his visitor to get comfortable enough to disclose his errand. It occurred to him that Thomas Wesley was a very handsome man. Con almost wished he could convince himself to take him to bed, but it wouldn't be fair. In Con's mind there was only the slim strength and fair skin of Paul St. Clare.

"I hope you don't mind me bothering you, Delinsky, but I wanted to give you the news as soon as I could."

"What news would that be?" Con asked.

"Well, after our last conversation when you told me about your missing wife, I had occasion to visit the Russian embassy. I put your problem, quite anonymously of course, to the ambassador, and asked him what a man could do in such circumstances."

"That was very kind of you, my friend."

Thomas smiled. "He said he would look into the matter for me, and I'm awaiting his reply. He did say that after the terrible events of the war, your situation was not as uncommon as you might think. Thousands of people have disappeared or been misplaced, and it is the devil's own job finding out what has happened to them."

"I'm sure, which is why I haven't instigated such a search before. My needs are far less pressing than many."

"Because you don't want to marry again anyway, eh? And being married gives you some protection from the matchmakers of the *ton*."

"Exactly, sir."

Gregor appeared with two steaming glasses, which smelled strongly of whiskey, ginger, and cloves, and handed one to each man.

Thomas inhaled deeply. "Ah, that smells wonderful. The reason why I called in person is because I'm off to the Russian embassy this afternoon. I thought you might wish to accompany me there to see if there is any news."

"I was about to go out riding myself, so I suppose I could accompany you."

"You don't sound too keen on the idea, old chap." Thomas finished off his punch. "If it bothers you, I can call off my hounds, and tell the ambassador the matter has been resolved to your satisfaction."

Con thought about that and then glanced down at the letter addressed to his mother. Shame rose over him at his continued aversion to all things Russian. He could at least do this for his family. It was one matter he could set to rest, which would benefit them all.

He finished off his punch in one swallow. "I'll come with you. Just let me find my hat and my gloves."

Con looked warily around the entrance hall of the embassy and marveled at the sound of Russian voices echoing around him. He only spoke Russian to Gregor these days, but it was still so ingrained in him that he understood every word. Of course, the Russian nobility spoke mostly French, but as a child he'd heard nothing but Russian from the servants and serfs at his family home.

"You may come up, sirs. Count Lieven will receive you in his office."

For a moment, the English was jarring before Con collected himself and followed Thomas up the stairs. The Russian ambassador rose as they entered the room and bowed.

"Major Wesley, it is a pleasure to see you again."

Thomas saluted. "Indeed it is, sir. May I introduce Lieutenant Colonel Constantine Delinsky?"

Count Lieven came around his desk and held out his hand to Con. He lapsed into Russian. "There is no need for such formality between us, Delinsky. I believe my aunt is related to one of your second cousins."

Con shook the proffered hand, and then found himself

being embraced and kissed in the more traditional Russian style. From habit he returned the salutation and mumbled something appropriate in Russian before stepping back. The ambassador resumed his seat behind the desk, and Con and Thomas sat down.

"I hope you don't mind me bringing Delinsky along with me this afternoon, but he was particularly interested in your response to the problem I put to you a few days ago."

"In truth, ambassador"—as Thomas drew breath, Con spoke over him—"I am the one who needs to find out what happened to my wife."

"Ah." Count Lieven looked thoughtful.

Thomas half rose from his seat. "Do you want me to leave you in peace, Delinsky?"

"No, I'd rather you stayed. Your advice is always useful."

Thomas subsided, and Con turned back to the ambassador.

"My wife was residing in Moscow, and she refused to leave despite being told of the French advance. As far as I understand it, she was still there when the French arrived. By the time I got back to Moscow after the French abandoned it, there was nothing left of our house but a smoking ruin."

"Do you believe she died in the fire?"

Con exhaled. "That would be the easiest explanation, but I fear the truth is not that simple. There were rumors that Natasha had found herself a lover among the French officers, and that she might have left with the French army."

"She might have left with the army, Delinsky, but precious few of the French survived the retreat; you know that."

"I do, ambassador. I was sent on many a scouting party to count the bodies of our enemies." Con sighed. "I never found Natasha though, or discovered any further word of her."

Count Lieven folded his hands in front of him on the desk. "A sad tale, Delinsky, but not that uncommon. It's a long time since Moscow was occupied. Considering your wife might have betrayed you with a Frenchman, why didn't you simply assume she was dead and carry on?"

"She was very young, sir. I bear her no ill will. For her family's sake, I'd prefer some kind of legal settlement of the matter for all concerned."

"Quite understandable, Delinsky. I will share with you the information I intended to give Major Wesley. We will ask the Russian community here in London and our new allies at the French court to see if we can discover any trace of your wife. If we cannot, we can set about the legal process of declaring her dead. Once that is achieved, you will be a free man again."

"Thank you, sir." Con bowed his head. At least he could sort out this one thing, and please his mother. Although he had vowed never to marry again, it would also bring him peace.

Thomas rose to his feet, and Con followed suit. "Thank you, ambassador. You have been all that is gracious."

Count Lieven spread his hands wide. "I am honored to help a countryman, especially one who has fought for his homeland and suffered great loss." He smiled. "I will contact you by the end of the month with the results of my preliminary investigation."

"Thank you." Con bowed deeply again, and he and Thomas were shown out into the hallway. It wasn't until they were out of the residence that Thomas turned to speak to him.

"Delinsky, you look quite white around the gills. Let's stop at my club and have something to drink."

Con allowed Thomas to lead him where he wanted. For a so-called man of action, Con realized he dreaded change. Was that why he'd been so slow to deal with the complications of Natasha's death? Or was Thomas right, and he'd preferred to keep his marital status to ward off other women?

He handed his hat and gloves to the footman at the door of

the club and followed Thomas into the warm, smoke-filled depths of the building. Waiting for news from the ambassador would be difficult, but he'd waited for over a decade to settle this. A few more weeks would hardly make a difference.

"Still no sign of your monthly, my lady," Milly said brightly. She winked at Lucky. "Maybe you are already carrying another heir to the dukedom."

Lucky managed a weak smile and unconsciously rubbed her stomach. Her cycle had never been very regular, but there was no denying that she hadn't bled since the night Jeremy had forced her. And that was almost two months ago. The notion that she might be carrying his child made her feel nauseous.

Lucky sat down as Milly began to pin up her hair. But what if it was Paul's child? It was a possibility. She should have waited to make certain before she had insisted on Paul sharing her bed. Her gaze dropped to the strange letter she had received from Jeremy. She still couldn't believe he would let her be so easily.

She sighed and stared at her wan reflection. There were so many things that weren't right in her world, and she wasn't sure if she could fix any of them. Paul had confessed to an attachment to Lieutenant Colonel Delinsky and then refused to do anything about it, Jeremy had stopped threatening her, and she might be carrying a child whose father was unknown.

"Cheer up, my lady, it is a beautiful day," Milly said as she deftly pinned Lucky's curls in place. "You should go out for a walk and get some color into your cheeks."

"Perhaps I will do that," Lucky replied.

One of the things her father had always taught her was to break problems down into smaller pieces and conquer them individually. She'd already invited Lieutenant Colonel Delinsky for dinner and would endeavor to find out how he felt about Paul. She hoped he might be willing to be honest with her, but even just seeing the two men together would give her a better idea of how to deal with the situation.

She could do nothing about the possibility of being pregnant, but she could write a note to Jeremy and ask him to confirm what he'd said in his last letter. She needed to be sure that he'd meant what he'd said. She was suspicious that he'd been coerced into writing that note and wouldn't abide by its dictates for long.

She smiled into the mirror and Milly smiled back at her. "Feeling better, my lady?"

"Indeed I am, Milly. I need to write a letter, and then I'm going to see if my mother has any errands for me, so go and put your bonnet on."

19

"I know. I'm late, Gregor."

Con went straight into his bedchamber and started to unbutton his coat and waistcoat. He'd spent most of the day with the Duke of Wellington's staff, and had barely managed to escape in time to dress for dinner with the St. Clares. He stripped off his shirt and breeches and turned to find Gregor offering him a bowl of hot water, soap, and a drying cloth.

"Thank you." Con busied himself washing as much of his skin as he could manage. Being so fair, he rarely had to shave, which in this instance was a blessing.

Gregor had already laid out his best dress uniform on the bed, and Con hurried to put it on. At least wearing a uniform meant he avoided spending two hours folding his cravat like some men.

"I've already hired you a hackney, sir. I assumed you wouldn't wish to take your own horses out in this weather."

"You are indeed a treasure, Gregor. Please, don't wait up for me." Con snatched up his hat, cloak, and gloves and headed for the door. On the silver tray he noticed a sealed letter, and he took it with him to read. He gave the driver his direction and settled back on the cracked leather seat.

It was already dark and most of the streetlamps had been lit, spreading meager pools of light among the gloom. It wasn't far to Haymore House, but as the cold crept over him, Con wished he'd brought a scarf.

He opened the letter, scanned the sentences, and frowned. *What the devil?*

"Haymore House, guv," the driver called down.

Con searched for some coins, paid the driver, and found himself standing in front of the towering mansion. He ascended the steps, his thoughts still caught up in his mysterious letter. The door opened as he approached, and the Haymore butler welcomed him by name.

"Please come in, Lieutenant Colonel. Her ladyship is awaiting you in the small drawing room."

It didn't occur to Con that he might be the only guest until he was ushered into the room and discovered his hostess sitting alone by the fireside. She rose to her feet, her expression apprehensive, and held out her hand.

"It's so kind of you to come, Lieutenant Colonel. I'm afraid Paul has been delayed."

Con realized he was still holding the offending letter in his hand and hastily stuffed it into his pocket.

"Good evening, my lady." He brought her fingers to his lips and kissed them. "If this is inconvenient, do you wish me to leave?"

"Oh, no, not unless you have to, sir. I'd be happy to share my evening with you until Paul arrives."

"Then I'll stay. It will be an honor."

Lady Lucinda smiled up at him, and he was struck again by the calm openness of her face and the directness of her gaze. She might appear quite young, but he sensed a maturity in her blue eyes that spoke to him. She was charmingly attired in a yellow silk gown with blond lace that suited her perfectly. He wasn't surprised that Paul had wanted to help her. After all, he'd had the same desire when he'd encountered her at the ball.

"Are you sure that everything is all right, Lieutenant Colonel?"

"I apologize if I seem a little distracted. I just received a rather strange letter."

"Strange in what way?"

"The person who wrote it didn't sign it."

She shivered. "That is horrible. Do you have any idea who it was from?"

He forced a smile. "My problems can hardly be of interest to you, my lady. Shall we talk about something else?"

"If you wish, sir, but I'm quite happy to help you puzzle out who sent you the note."

His smile now was genuine. "Paul said you had an inquiring mind. Are you sure I'm not boring you?"

A footman appeared at the door and announced that dinner was being served. Con took Lady Lucinda's arm and walked through into a small paneled dining room lit by two branches of candelabra. The upper walls were covered in faded red silk and the lower level paneled in oak. The embroidery on the chairs matched the walls and gave the room a lovely, homely feel.

Lady Lucinda glanced up at him as he pulled out a chair and waited for her to sit. "What did your peculiar note say?"

"I'd let you read it, but it is written in Russian."

She held out her hand. "I speak Russian and French. My father thought it was important for me to be able to talk to anyone."

He delved in his coat pocket and brought out the note. It was strange how well they got on. There was no sense of awkwardness between them at all.

She read the sparse sentences; her brow furrowed and translated them into English. " 'Leave the past alone, or you will be sorry. A friend.' " She raised her gaze to his. "A friend? That seems a little overdramatic and rather general. What exactly did you do to provoke such a letter?"

He took the letter back and folded it up. "As it suggests, I delved into the past."

"Ah." She waited as the footmen placed several covered dishes on the table. "Thank you, you may leave. We will serve ourselves."

Con waited until the door closed behind the last servant. "It is rather a long story."

"And we have the whole evening to fill." She smiled encouragingly at him. "I know we are newly acquainted, but I'd love to help you and I'll keep your confidences. I'm sure Paul will, too, when he returns."

"It is a story that doesn't reflect very well on me."

She shrugged. "I'm quite relieved to hear that. You seem so perfect to me." She blushed, and Con was aware yet again of a strong pull of attraction. He concentrated on his story.

"My wife, Natasha, and I moved to Moscow during the first year of our marriage. I was already heavily engaged in the army and not there to attend to her needs."

"Well, obviously." Lady Lucinda nodded. "She could scare have expected anything different."

Con wanted to smile. There spoke a true soldier's wife.

"We were very young when we married. She was seventeen and I was eighteen. It was an arranged marriage, but we liked to imagine we were in love. I wrote to her urging her to leave Moscow before the French descended on the city, but she refused. She said she was afraid and that she wanted me to come and get her. She didn't seem to understand that I was unable to desert my post."

"As you said, you were both very young."

He sighed. "I know she was there when the French arrived, because I had several letters from well-meaning friends telling me that she was disporting herself with the French officers and was a disgrace to my name." He looked across the table at Lady Lucinda. "She liked to be happy and be admired. In truth, she thrived on it."

"Was she very beautiful?"

"Most men seemed to think so. She was blond, with blue eyes and a petite figure. Men likened her to a china figurine or a Madonna." He grimaced. "By the time I was able to fight my way back to Moscow, the place was a horrific empty shell filled with the dead. Our house was burned to the ground, and my wife was gone. I tried to find her, but it was quite impossible."

"I'm sure it was. My father has told me about Napoléon's tactics in Russia and the thousands of men he left behind to die in the snow and the ice."

"After a while, I left Russia to fight with the British cavalry, and I tried to forget what had happened. It was easy enough during the remaining years of the war, as I had much to occupy my time. But since the peace, I've had time to think and wonder about what happened to my wife."

"And you decided to do something about it."

"Exactly. I visited the Russian ambassador yesterday and asked for his help in finding my wife, or legally declaring her dead."

"Hence the note."

"One has to assume so. The Russian community is very close-knit."

"You mustn't let it stop you."

"I don't intend to. If someone has something against me, they'll have to show themselves. Vague anonymous threats are not going to rattle my resolve."

Lady Lucinda smiled at him. "Thank you for telling me about your wife and your current efforts to bring your uncertainties to a close. You will let me know what happens, won't you?"

"Absolutely, my lady." He picked up his fork. "Now perhaps we should eat this beautifully prepared dinner and turn the conversation to happier topics."

"Would you care for something to drink, Lieutenant Colonel?"

Lady Lucinda walked back with Con into the cozy sitting room to the side of the dining room. There was still no sign of Paul, and Con was beginning to wonder if he was even aware that his wife was dining with his old lover.

"A glass of brandy would be much appreciated, my lady. It is cold out there tonight."

"Yet you grew up in Russia, sir. I should imagine it is much colder than this."

After the footman got him his drink, Con followed Lady Lucinda toward the comfortable wing chairs drawn up to the fire and waited until she took a seat.

"Indeed it is, my lady. I fear I have grown soft living here."

"How long is it since you have been back to Russia?"

"Many years, my lady."

"Yet you have family there."

He sighed. "Yes, I do, but I still have no wish to return."

"From what you have told me, I can understand why." Her expression was one of sympathy. "The place must hold many tragic memories for you."

"It is rather more complicated than that."

"Do your family not approve of you, then?"

"In what way?" Con took a generous sip of his brandy.

"Because you like . . ." His hostess turned an unbecoming shade of red. "I do beg your pardon, that was an awful thing to say, what was I thinking? I . . ."

Con waited until the servant left. "If you are referring to my liking to bed men, then you are correct. My mother does not approve of that at all. One of the reasons why I was forced to marry so young was to avoid just such a scandal."

She met his gaze. "I'm sorry, Lieutenant Colonel. That was very rude of me. It is none of my business."

Con sat back and studied her. Over dinner they'd gotten on so well that he'd felt like they were old friends. "If I might be equally indiscreet, it is your business though, isn't it? I suspect you asked me here tonight because Paul told you he and I were lovers."

She sagged into her chair. "He did tell me that."

"I'm sure he also told you that our affair ended before your marriage."

She nodded. "Paul tries to be honest with me, but he didn't tell me how he felt about you until after we'd married."

Pain coalesced around Con's heart. "I know. He didn't consider it important. I understand that."

"Please, Lieutenant Colonel, don't be ridiculous. If you know Paul as well as I do, you must realize he didn't mention you because he didn't want me to guess he was in love with you." She sat forward, her hands clasped together. "If I had known that, I wouldn't have gone through with the marriage."

Con stared at her, his thoughts in turmoil. Paul had said that his wife knew everything about him, but Con hadn't believed he'd meant it.

"If you think I intend to encourage your husband to be unfaithful, telling me that he is in love with me is hardly beneficial to your cause."

"But it's true." She winced. "I'm not as naïve as I look, Lieutenant Colonel. I want Paul to be happy, and if you make him happy, that is all I care about."

Con contemplated his options for so long that his hostess began to look anxious.

"Have I offended you, sir?"

"Not at all, and by the way, would you like to call me Constantine? It only seems fair." She nodded and he went on. "As we are being so honest with each other, I also know that Paul is committed to you and your marriage."

Her smile was almost sad. "He has been all that is honorable." She sighed. "It is ironic. I always wanted him to marry me, but I never really expected it to happen."

"You love him, don't you?" Con said softly.

She looked away from him. "That isn't really the point, is it?"

The door opened and the subject of their conversation came in and went straight across to his wife.

"Lucky, I'm so terribly sorry I'm late."

She took his proffered hand and squeezed it. "It is of no matter. Lieutenant Colonel Delinsky was an excellent dinner companion."

Paul swung around, his expression startled as if he hadn't realized that Con was there. "Good evening, sir. I can only apologize again for my tardiness. My horse went lame, and I had to walk three miles to the nearest inn to seek a replacement."

The clock on the mantelpiece struck eleven times and Con rose. "I'm glad you returned safely, St. Clare." He bowed to Lady Lucinda. "Thank you for your charming hospitality. I will keep you informed about any developments."

"It was a pleasure, sir." She smiled at him, and then at Paul. "Perhaps Paul can show you out rather than rousing the butler."

Con had only a moment to wonder if she was deliberately putting him and Paul together before he was descending the staircase into the quiet, cool dignity of the marble hall below.

"Did you come to see me, Delinsky?" Paul asked.

"Why would you think that?"

Paul shrugged. "Because you are a soldier and well used to judging your enemy."

"Lady Lucinda is scarcely that."

Paul faced him. "Exactly. She is not part of this . . . issue between us."

Con raised an eyebrow. "Is she not? Before you make such statements, you might wish to talk to your wife. *She* invited *me* for dinner. I didn't presume." He turned to pick up his hat and gloves. "Good night, St. Clare."

He opened the heavy door himself and headed into the street, aware of a sense of injustice. Did Paul think he meant to intimidate Lady Lucinda into giving him up? If so, he was badly mistaken. Lady Lucinda loved Paul and that, as far as he was concerned, trumped everything.

Paul walked slowly back up the stairs, his thoughts in turmoil. Why had Lucky invited Con to dinner on an evening when she knew he had business out of town and was bound to be home late? It seemed that he had underestimated his wife's determination to involve herself in his affairs. But devil take it, she was his wife. Didn't she have a perfect right to interfere?

The small drawing room was empty, and the fire was dying in the grate. Paul stood at the door and surveyed the deserted space. He inhaled a hint of Lucky's perfume mingled with Con's soap in the air. They'd spent a whole evening together in apparent amity. Shouldn't he be pleased?

He went on up the stairs to the suite he shared with Lucky, and allowed Jordan to help him out of his mud-stained clothes. He declined a bath and dismissed his valet, his gaze fixed on the door that connected him to his wife's bedchamber, his questions refusing to die. Lucky was one of the very few people in the world who knew he had a temper and how to rouse it.

With a curse, he put on his dressing gown and let himself in through the unlocked door. Lucky was already in bed, her hair neatly braided down her back and a pair of reading glasses perched on her nose. She looked remarkably young and unthreatening, which Paul knew was a disguise. She closed the book as he approached and looked inquiringly at him.

"Was there something you wished to ask me?"

"Did you invite Constantine Delinsky for dinner?"

"Yes, I did."

"Did you deliberately ask him on an evening when I was likely to be delayed?"

"Yes."

"Why?"

"Because I wanted to talk to him."

"About what?"

"That is hardly your business."

He advanced a step closer. "Everything you do is my business. You are my wife."

"I didn't realize that meant I had to report every conversation I have to you or allow you to choose my friends."

"Actually I could order you to do all those things, and no man would consider me unfair."

"I would," she snapped.

"And you're not a man." He paused to gather his temper. "What did you and Delinsky talk about?"

"Paul, you can hardly expect me to repeat everything we said."

"Just the main topics will suffice."

She pressed her lips together as if she were considering never speaking to him again. He'd forgotten how stubborn she could be.

She sighed. "You are behaving like one of those horrid tortured heroes in a Gothic novel. We talked mainly about his life in Russia and the disappearance of his wife during the siege of Moscow. Did you know he was married?"

"I knew that his wife was missing."

"He is trying to establish exactly what happened to her. There is some notion that she might have left with a French officer. Apparently the Russian ambassador is going to look into the matter for him."

"I wonder why he wants to delve into that now."

She met his gaze. "Perhaps he wants to marry again."

Pain shot through him. "I doubt it, although he does prefer women in his bed to men."

"We didn't discuss his preferences in bed."

He raised his eyebrows. "Not even his preference for me?"

"He assured me that he has no intention of luring you away from me."

"How very noble of him, when I have absolutely no intention of allowing myself to be 'lured' anyway."

She angled her head to one side. "Then why are you so angry?"

"Perhaps I'm angry with you for meddling."

"I'm not meddling, I—"

He cut through her protest. "I know you, Lucky. You hate to be bested, and you'll do everything you can to try and find out about your enemy and bring him down before he even realizes it."

"Perhaps I don't want to bring Constantine Delinsky down."

"Then why seek his company?"

"Perhaps I *like* him!" She threw back the covers and got out of bed. "Perhaps this isn't about you after all, Paul."

"Unlikely."

She stared at him and slowly shook her head. "You are very arrogant and, in this instance, completely wrong. I'll leave you to your delusions."

He pointed his finger at her. "You are up to something, Lucky. Pretending that you want to be friends with Con and shoving the two of us together at every opportunity won't work. We will not become lovers again."

She turned her back on him and climbed back into bed. "As

I said, arrogant. Good night, Paul. I'll see you in the morning."
She blew out the candles, leaving him stranded and still fuming
in the darkness. After a long moment, he turned around and
fumbled his way back to his own bed.

"Arrogant and stupid and . . ." Lucky ran out of words to
describe to Emily how she felt about her late night encounter
with Paul.

"What *exactly* did he do?"

"He suggested that he had the right to decide who I con-
versed with, and even demanded to know exactly what I said!"

"Perhaps you shouldn't have married him after all." Emily
sat opposite Lucky in the cozy splendor of her bedroom in the
Knowles town house. "I would hate to have a husband like
that. Who would've thought Paul would turn into such a
dragon?"

Lucky glanced at her friend. "The trouble is, there is some
truth in his concerns. I am up to something."

"Of course you are. There's a reason why your father calls
you his little general. You are always plotting something."

"How much do you know about Lieutenant Colonel Delinsky?"

"Why do you ask?"

"Because I suspect you already know that he and Paul were
lovers."

Emily grimaced. "I wasn't sure whether I should tell you or
not."

"Didn't your Ambrose tell you that Paul brought me to the
pleasure house so I could see exactly what kind of a man I was
contemplating marrying?"

Emily blushed. "He isn't *my* Ambrose and no, he didn't. He
is incredibly discreet."

"Paul didn't quite mention his relationship with Constantine until after we were married."

224 / *Kate Pearce*

"Oh, dear." Emily patted Lucky's hand. "That was rather remiss of him."

"He didn't mention it because he knew I wouldn't marry him if I knew."

Emily frowned. "That doesn't make sense. If Paul made sure you knew he liked to bed everyone at the pleasure house, why would he think you likely to balk at one more man?"

"Because *that* man is important to him, and all the others at the pleasure house were not." Lucky found her voice was trembling. "Paul loves him, Emily."

"Oh, Lucky." Emily hugged her hard. "I'm so sorry."

"Paul insists that he isn't going to do anything about it."

"Well, that must be a relief to you."

"*No,* I want him to be happy."

"But why should he be happy if it makes you miserable?"

"Because he married me. He gave up *everything* for me."

Emily grabbed hold of her hand. "He also gained a lot, don't forget that. I think you underestimate your effect on him. He loves you, too."

"I don't know about that." Lucky wiped hastily at a stray tear. "But I intend to make him happy."

"By giving him something he insists he no longer wants?"

"Don't sound so skeptical, Emily." Lucky drew in a deep breath. "I have a plan. I'm going to flirt with Constantine Delinsky until Paul becomes so jealous that he'll take him back."

Emily sat back and studied Lucky's face. "Are you sure about that? It sounds rather risky."

"I'm sure, Emily. It is the least I can do. And to be quite honest, Constantine Delinsky is extremely easy to flirt with."

Con was so engrossed in watching a horse he fancied showing its paces at Tattersall's that he didn't realize Paul had come up behind him until his friend cleared his throat. He glanced over his shoulder and then returned his attention to the horse. It was unlike him to be uncivil, but he was still seething from their encounter the day before.

"Con?" Paul shifted beside him. "I want to apologize."

"For assuming I'd come into your home to spy on your wife and treat her like the enemy?"

"Yes."

"Lady Lucinda confirmed that she invited me to dinner then."

"Indeed she did." Paul hesitated. "Would you mind accompanying me to a less public place where we can talk?"

Con finally turned to look into Paul's anxious face. "Of course, St. Clare. I've finished here for the day, anyway. But are you sure you wish to be seen with me? We can't have your newly minted reputation being damaged by association." As soon as the words came out of his mouth, he realized he must be angrier than he'd thought.

"I didn't mean it like that," Paul said softly, "Although I know I deserve your disdain."

Con started walking, barely remembering to reply to the salutations of his acquaintances as he passed.

Paul pointed down the street. "There is a coffee house on the corner. Shall we adjourn there?"

"Why not?" Con stuck his hands into his pockets as they turned into the chill wind that ran down the narrow street. The sky was overcast, and he hadn't seen the sun for days. It was beginning to feel more like winter than autumn and more like Russia than England.

He found a seat in the corner and settled back into the cozy warmth and thick fug of smoke while Paul spoke to the waiter. His friend looked even more miserable than he did—which should have helped, but didn't.

"What did you want to talk to me about, St. Clare?" Con asked.

"Mainly to apologize for my behavior. I was surprised to see you, and rather annoyed with my wife for not telling me that she had invited you to dinner. Unfortunately some of that irritation spilled over on to you."

"I did wonder if she had told you."

Paul sighed. "I must warn you that my wife seems determined to pursue her acquaintance with you."

"I find her quite charming. Do you object?"

Paul looked even more wretched. "She isn't quite as sweet as she might appear. She has the mind of a Machiavelli prince and the curiosity of a cat."

"Which simply makes her more charming than ever. What are you worried about?"

"I suspect she means to throw us together on every occasion possible."

Con shrugged. "So? We are both gentlemen, and neither of us wish to dishonor your wife."

"Apart from the fact that she wishes to be dishonored," Paul muttered.

Con almost choked on his coffee. "I beg your pardon?"

"She is convinced that the only way I can be happy is if I have you."

For a wild moment, Con allowed himself to enjoy the pleasurable scenarios such a statement aroused in him. Then he shook his head. "She is in love with you, Paul. She will do whatever she thinks will make you happy."

"I know that."

Con held Paul's gaze. "And you love her too."

"Yes."

"Then I repeat. We are both gentlemen, and we will do nothing to harm her or her reputation. She has suffered enough at the hands of untrustworthy men." He reached into his pocket and withdrew an invitation card. "She has invited me to your ball next week. Do you want me to refuse?"

Paul slowly exhaled. "No. I want you to come. I hate it when we are at odds with each other." He smiled, and Con wanted to reach forward and kiss him on the lips.

"Your wife is a truly extraordinary woman, my friend. You should cherish her."

"I know. She is the perfect woman for a man like me. I really don't deserve her."

"If I were a free man, I would be honored to court her."

"Is that so?" Paul's smile was tinged with sorrow. "She rather likes you too." He seemed to make an effort to change the subject. "In truth, she is intrigued by the mystery of your missing wife. Is there any news?"

"None yet, although I did receive another letter telling me to leave well alone."

"How peculiar. Do you have any idea who is sending them?"

"Presumably someone who knows something about my wife. I wish whoever it is would just stop being a coward and come and face me."

"That would be far too simple. Perhaps you could set a man to watch your house and see who is delivering the notes."

"I've already done that. I hope to catch my letter writer soon and wrest some more information out of him."

"Well, good luck." Paul checked his pocket watch and sighed. "I'll have to leave soon. I have an appointment with my new secretary in half an hour. I'm not sure why I ever believed the rich were idle. I am far busier these days than when I was in the army."

"But you *are* far less likely to be killed."

"That indeed is true." Paul's smile faded. "But sometimes I miss those days, don't you?"

"You forget, I'm still employed by the military, I can hardly miss them." Con rose to his feet and clapped Paul on the shoulder. He needed to touch him and was furious that he couldn't embrace him in the way he wanted without drawing curious glances and condemnation. "I'll walk out with you."

After he watched Paul depart in a hackney cab, Con started back toward the center of the city. It would be easier on all of them if he left London, but he couldn't quite bring himself to do it yet. He'd already fled Russia, and he'd be damned if he ran away again. But seeing Paul and his intriguing wife would bring him such heartache.

Con stared up at the iron-gray clouds and shivered as the first drops of rain hit his face. But perhaps that was as it should be, his penance for abandoning his country and his wife in the first place.

20

Lucky settled the lace at the neckline of her white satin ball dress, tied the cherry-red sash, and studied herself critically in the mirror. In the years since she'd come out fashion had gradually changed from airy, high-waisted dresses to more elaborate and heavier fabrics with a natural waistline. Her gaze settled on the row of flounces at the bottom of her skirt, and she did an experimental twirl.

"You look beautiful, my lady."

She stopped twirling and found that Paul had come through from his bedchamber and was smiling at her. He looked very fine in a black coat, a silver-patterned waistcoat, and white trousers. As the weight of Paul's responsibilities grew, she could barely see her scruffy lieutenant anymore. And she missed him. She missed him quite dreadfully.

She curtsied as if to royalty. "Thank you."

"I particularly like your hair."

Lucky reached up to carefully touch her head. "Milly put real roses and French pearl beads in there. I am half afraid to move."

He kissed her hand. "Don't be, or who am I going to open the ball with?" He put a small box into her hand. "I'm glad you are wearing pearls in your hair. I've been wanting to give you something pretty."

She opened the long, shallow box to find a string of pearls. "Oh, they are quite beautiful! Thank you, may I wear them?"

"I would be offended if you didn't." Paul stood behind her and carefully placed the necklace around her throat. "I'm sure you have a much finer set than this."

Lucky tried not to look over at her dressing table where her mother's splendidly large pearls awaited her. "In truth, I usually borrow my mother's. I don't have a set of my own."

He kissed her collarbone and she shivered. "Well, you do now. I just wish I'd thought to get you something sooner." His laugh was self-deprecating. "I never had the financial resources before, so in fact, I'm only giving you what was already yours."

She reached up to clasp his hand and he went still. "I don't care about the money, you know that. You give me far more than I deserve."

He pulled gently out of her grasp and held out his hand. "Shall we go down then?"

She forced a smile and allowed him to escort her down the stairs to the ballroom, where her parents had insisted on holding a ball to celebrate their marriage. She hoped Constantine Delinsky would attend. Her plan to flirt with him was still much on her mind, and this was the perfect place to do it. Trapped at his own ball, Paul would have no choice but to stay and watch.

Even though Lucky had received no response to her letter to Jeremy, she hoped he wouldn't try and enter the ball and confront her here. She'd already decided that if she didn't hear from him in another week, she would seek him at his lodgings. Paul wouldn't approve, but she had to find out exactly what had happened to him. It had occurred to her that Jeremy might be dead. And, if Paul had been involved in that, she was doubly anxious.

"Ah, there you are, my dears!"

Her mother's cheerful greeting drew Lucky out of her thoughts, and she went to stand beside her parents in the receiving line.

Con paused at the top of the stairway and looked down into the crowded ballroom. Despite the cold outside, it was already hot in the elegant space, and Con began to perspire beneath his dress uniform. He'd deliberately arrived late so that he would avoid having to meet his hosts in the receiving line, but his gaze was still drawn straight to Paul and Lady Lucinda, who were dancing together in perfect accord.

He made his way down the stairs, stopping to chat with his acquaintances. He greeted the duke and duchess, and then saw the Russian ambassador beckoning to him.

"Lieutenant Colonel Delinsky? I have some news for you. Perhaps you might care to visit me tomorrow at around two o'clock?" The ambassador winced as the orchestra reached a crashing crescendo. "This is hardly the place to share anything."

Con bowed. "I agree, sir. I will meet you at two."

He turned away and headed toward the card room. Perhaps he could bury himself in there for a few hours and try not to worry about what the ambassador had to say to him.

"Lieutenant Colonel Delinsky, what a nice surprise!"

He found Lady Lucinda in front of him, and her evident delight in seeing him made him smile back at her. She looked beautiful in a gown of white satin, with red roses in her hair. He brought her gloved hand to his lips and kissed it. He hadn't been joking when he'd told Paul she was exactly the kind of woman he would have liked to marry.

"My lady. You look wonderful."

She blushed and kept her hand in his. "Thank you."

Even though he knew he should keep away from her, he found himself asking, "Would you care to dance?"

"I have saved the supper dance for you."

"That will be delightful." He bowed again, and she turned away with a smile. He tried to remember what Paul had said about her being Machiavellian and found it hard to believe.

After their dance and during supper, he found himself revising that opinion. To his consternation, she'd made no effort to include Paul in her invitation to supper and had spent the entire time gazing worshipfully into his eyes. If he hadn't known better, he would think she was looking for a lover.

She fanned herself and looked longingly toward the windows that led out to a balcony at the back of the house. "I wonder if I might prevail on you to take me outside for a breath of air? It is so hot in here."

"If that is what you wish, my lady, but I must warn you that it is quite cold out there." He rose and looked down at her. "May I fetch you a shawl?"

"If you ask one of the footmen to fetch it for you, they can bring it out to me."

"I'll do that, my lady." Con searched the room for an available footman and could see no one. He moved out into the main ballroom and immediately collided with Paul.

"Are you looking for someone, Delinsky?"

Con drew in the sight of Paul in his evening clothes and committed it to memory. "I was looking for a footman to fetch a shawl for your wife. She is rather hot, and I offered to accompany her out on to the balcony."

"I'll fetch it for you and meet you there."

Paul moved away, and Con turned back to collect Lady Lucinda. She tucked her hand into the crook of his arm and stepped out on to the balcony. A cold gust of wind immediately made her shiver.

"Are you sure you wish to be outside, my lady?" Con inquired. "I'm concerned that you might take a chill."

She looked up at him, and he forgot all about the cold and found himself staring into her beautiful eyes. His hand fisted in an effort not to cup her cheek and bring his mouth down to hers. She let out her breath and it condensed in the air between them.

"Lady Lucinda, are you by any chance trying to seduce me?"

She blinked slowly at him like a cat. "Why ever would you think that?" She put her hand on his shoulder and moved closer until they were face-to-face.

He wanted to step away, but his body was already tightening and responding to her nearness, to her scent, to *her*.

"We should go inside."

She sighed. "I suppose we should."

It seemed to take forever for her to release him and turn away. She walked along the balcony and opened another set of the doors. Con followed her in and almost crashed into a piece of furniture before he realized the room was in complete darkness.

"Oh, my goodness!" Lady Lucinda turned around and flung herself into his arms, almost toppling him over. "I hate the dark!"

For one glorious moment, he held her, his face pressed to the coils of her hair, his arm wrapped around her waist. The sound of someone clearing his throat from the still-open door brought him to his senses. He turned to find Paul illuminated against the moonlit sky, Lady Lucinda's shawl in his hands.

Con set Lady Lucinda back on her feet and immediately stepped away from her. "St. Clare, this is not what you think. I . . ." But Paul wasn't even looking at him, let alone listening.

Paul pushed past Con and lit a branch of candles, illuminating the room and his wife's extremely guilty expression.

"Shut the door, Con, will you, and give us some privacy?"

Lucky made a slight movement toward the outer door, and Paul held up his hand.

"Stay exactly where you are, my lady."

Lucky subsided into a chair, and Paul returned his attention to a stricken-looking Con.

"It's all right, Con. I'm not going to call you out. I know exactly where the blame for this episode lies. I told you my wife had a devious mind, didn't I?"

Con walked across to the fireplace and stirred the dying embers to life. "Are you suggesting that Lady Lucinda wanted you to find us together in these embarrassing circumstances?"

"She probably wanted you to be found together by someone."

"Ah, that's why she asked me to get a footman to fetch her shawl."

"Exactly. She probably thought you'd be mortified to be found with her in a private setting by one of the servants, and worried that they would tell me."

"But you offered to fetch the shawl yourself."

Paul swung around to glare at Lucky. "Which actually makes things a lot simpler."

She opened her eyes wide at him. "I have no idea what you are talking about. Lieutenant Colonel Delinsky has behaved like a perfect gentleman."

"Apart from when he thought about kissing you."

Con's startled gaze flew to his face. Paul studied them both for a long moment, aware that they'd surprised him, and that he hadn't expected them to look at each other like that, *ever*. But hadn't Lucky told him that she liked Con, and that it wasn't always about him?

"I didn't kiss her, Paul," Con said.

"I know, but you wanted to." He smiled. "It's all right, Con.

I thought Lucky intended to throw us together, but I obviously misunderstood her purpose."

Lucky stood up, her color high. "I wanted to make you jealous, you dolt!"

"Then you succeeded." He inclined his head an inch.

"You don't understand," she sighed. "I knew you would balk if I tried to force you and Constantine back together. I thought it would be better if I made you jealous enough to demand I leave him alone."

"And discovered in the planning that you were not as averse to flirting with Con as you might think."

"If I might be allowed to contribute to this discussion?" Con snapped.

Paul looked away from Lucky into Con's furious face. "Be my guest."

"I am not a toy to be tossed between you for your amusement, and I resent being treated as one!" Con glared at them both. "There are several perfectly acceptable solutions to your dilemma."

"There are?" At that moment, Paul wasn't sure if he wanted to hit Con or fuck him. "I'm sure you are going to enlighten us."

Con took up a commanding position on the hearth rug, his hands behind his back. He looked striking in his dress uniform, the blue of the coat bringing out the silver-gray of his eyes and the pure whiteness of his hair.

"Before I was married, I met an older couple, friends of my parents, who decided to take me up and introduce me to society. I was grateful for their interest, as I found them far better company than my parents or my peers."

"Fascinating." Paul leaned back against the desk. "But what exactly does this have to do with our 'dilemma'?"

Con ignored him and carried on speaking. "After a while, it became obvious that the lady was also interested in taking me to bed. I was intrigued by the possibility, but determined not to offend her husband, who had also befriended me."

"You were always an honorable man, Con," Paul murmured.

Con inclined his head a frosty inch. "Thank you for that, at least. Eventually the husband came to call on me and revealed that he would be more than happy for me to have his wife, as long as he was able to join in." He paused. "In truth, the idea excited me and, being young, I agreed. As we grew accustomed to each other in bed, I also realized that the husband desired me as well, and that I was willing to let him fuck me.

"I was quite content, until they told me they had to move to France. I tried to convince my parents to let me leave with them." He shrugged, the motion showing off his elegant, muscled frame. "Of course, I was a little too passionate for their liking, and they were horrified when I admitted to being in love with both members of the other couple. After my lovers left, my family married me off pretty damn quickly to quiet the rumors."

"And the point of your story is?" Paul asked.

Con's gaze narrowed. "Isn't it obvious? You don't need to fight over me. I'm quite willing to have you both. Or not, as the case may be." He bowed and headed for the door. "Perhaps when you have made up your minds, you will inform me of your decision. Good night."

As the door closed with a definite bang behind Con, Paul stared at Lucky. Her mouth was slightly open, and she looked as flabbergasted as he felt. She shot to her feet, her fingers smoothing down the satin of her dress.

"We should return to the ball."

Paul nodded. "Indeed we should."

Hours later, Lucky paced her bedchamber and thought back over the events of the ball and Constantine's surprising declaration. She tried to imagine a young version of him in bed with his married couple and blushed. She'd seen more than one couple copulating at the pleasure house and hadn't been shocked at all. Was it possible that Constantine wanted both her and Paul?

When he'd looked at her on the balcony, she'd wanted him to kiss her, had sensed he was close to doing it anyway. She also knew what held him back: his honorable nature and his relationship with Paul. She wrapped her arms around herself. And what had she been *thinking*? She'd only been married a few weeks, and she was already lusting after another man?

But her marriage to Paul was scarcely destined to be normal. She'd already accepted that and offered him his freedom. Was it destiny that she and Paul were attracted to the same man? She had to talk to Paul, had to know what he was thinking.

She picked up her candle and let herself in through the door that connected their chambers. The dressing room was empty so she went on through to Paul's bedchamber. He was sitting in a chair by the fire in just his shirt and trousers, staring into the flames, a glass of brandy in his hand.

He went to rise, and Lucky held out her hand. "Are you still angry with me?"

He sat back and looked up at her, his brown eyes full of shadows and wary caution. "Not really."

"But I behaved very badly."

"No worse than Con or I." He abruptly rose to his feet and started taking off his shirt. "Come to bed."

"Now?"

His head emerged from the shirt. "Why not?"

"Don't you want to talk about what happened?"

"Not really." He grimaced as he worked the buttons on his trousers and stepped out of them and his underclothes, leaving him naked and most definitely aroused.

He reached for Lucky and drew her against him, his mouth urgent on hers, his hands roaming her body. She kissed him back and touched him in return, glorying in the hard planes of his back and shoulders, the insistent press of his wet cock against her belly.

He groaned and thrust his hand into her hair, drawing her head back so that he could ravage her mouth more thoroughly. She barely noticed when he maneuvered her on to his bed and came down over her, her nightdress gone, his mouth covering her breast.

He wedged his hand between her legs and stroked her there until she opened herself to him. His fingers plunged inside her in a demanding rhythm while his thumb worked her bud.

"Are you wet for me, Lucky, or is this for Con?" he whispered.

"That's not fair." She moaned as he slid inside her and began thrusting. "I can't think, I can't defend myself when you are, ah . . ." She climaxed, and he kept up the fast rhythm, pushing her onward and upward to another wave of sensation.

He gathered her closer, one arm moving lower to tilt her hips and spread her even wider. "You want him, don't you, Lucky? You want him like this, just like I do." He shuddered in her embrace and came inside her in hot, pulsing waves that made her gasp his name.

After a long while he rolled off her, his hand still tangled in her hair, his thigh heavy against her hip. She stared up at the dark embroidered canopy over her bed and tried to rearrange her scattered thoughts.

"Paul?" she whispered.

He stirred beside her, but he didn't respond.

"Paul, how does it feel when a man like Constantine Delinsky takes you to bed?"

His hand tightened in her hair, and she felt him tense.

"Does it feel different from how it is when you bed me?"

He sighed. "Do you mean because I fuck him in a different hole?"

She felt her cheeks flush. "Yes."

Paul slid his hand down over her hip and around the curve of her buttock, his long fingers circling the pucker of her arse. She was already wet, and he gathered his seed on his fingertip and swirled it around her tight entrance.

"I can tell you, but I'd rather you experienced the difference yourself."

He eased the very tip of his finger inside her and gently circled it around. He'd entered her like that before, had pushed his whole finger deep while he fucked her, and she'd seemed to like it. He wanted to give her more now, more fingers and then his aching cock.

He moved away from her to find some oil to ease his passage, and she lay still, watching him, her eyes dark with arousal, her body displayed for his pleasure. And he did like looking at her. She was his in a way that no other woman would ever be. He thought of them together, the three of them, and his cock stiffened even more.

He returned to Lucky's side and knelt over her, spreading her legs wide and sliding a cushion under her buttocks. The mingled scent of their lovemaking rose from her skin, and he bent his head to kiss her now swollen clit. He licked her slowly and lavishly, tending to each fold of her skin, sliding his tongue deep inside her even as he worked his oiled finger deep in her arse.

She bucked against his questing tongue and he murmured his approval, sucking her clit into his mouth and making her come. He added a second finger, and took his time helping her grow accustomed to the sensation of being stretched and open to him in more than one way. Her fingers grazed his scalp, and he looked up at her.

"Do you like this, Lucky?"

"Yes." She bit down on her lip.

"Touch yourself while I fuck you, touch your breasts. Imag-

ine what it might feel like if there were two men tending to
your every need, two mouths, two cocks."

"Paul . . ."

"Touch yourself, Lucky."

She cupped her hands around her breasts, and he wanted to
come at the luscious sight. Instead, he bent his head and eased a
third finger inside her arse. He almost wished they were at the
pleasure house, and he could use a dildo to show her exactly the
difference between the two types of penetration. Maybe he
should do that next time, or maybe there was an even better solution.

He returned his attention to her sex, flicking her bud with
his tongue, working her arse, his thumb delving into her cunt
with every deep stroke. She started to shudder around him, and
he buried his face against her, sucking up every tremor, every
lush emission from her soaking wet cunt. His cock was dripping now and aching to be buried deep inside her.

He forced himself to crawl up her body, paused at her
breasts to add his tongue strokes to her fingers plucking at her
nipples, and then came down over her mouth, giving her a taste
of herself.

"I'm going to fuck your arse, Lucky."

"Like you fuck Constantine?" she whimpered and he bit
down on her lower lip.

"Just like that, Lucky."

He rolled her on to her front and positioned her over the
pile of pillows, her back arched, her beautiful, shapely arse exposed. He slicked oil over his cock and went inside her with his
finger to test her readiness.

"Please, Paul."

He slowly pressed the crown of his cock against the tight
ring of her arse and eased forward, rocking back and forth to
gain entrance, aware of how narrow the space was and how
much his cock loved that.

She made a low sound, and he kissed the back of her neck. His fingers played lightly with her clit and cunt, distracting her from what else he was doing. "It's all right, Lucky; relax and let me in. I won't hurt you."

Her breath hissed out, and he slid deeper, devoured by her body, his cock a throbbing, thrusting presence buried inside her tight sheath.

"Ah, God." Paul breathed out hard as he waited for Lucky to adjust to his penetration. "So tight, Lucky."

He stroked her clit and gently rocked his hips. "Con's bigger than me, thicker, wider. When he fucks me, I feel so full I can't think of anything except what he is doing to me. He'd feel big to you here, in your sex and in your mouth." He shuddered and started to move a bit faster, his fingers plunging inside her in counter-rhythm to the thrust of his shaft. "Oh, God. Lucky, can you imagine Con in your mouth, in my mouth, both of us inside you?"

She climaxed so suddenly that he came with her. The intensity of it left her gasping and sobbing his name. Paul remained on top of her, his heart beating so hard that his whole body was shaking with it.

When he moved away from her, he went to wash himself and brought a clean bowl of water and a cloth back to Lucky. For once she wasn't asleep; her gaze was fixed on him as he carefully wiped her clean. She was so sensitive that she flinched when he used the cloth too heavily, which made him hard again, which made him want to lick her clean instead and make her come for him until she was screaming his name and begging.

Aware that she still hadn't spoken, he sat back and studied her. "Did I offend you?"

"No."

He cupped her face. "I shouldn't have brought Constantine Delinsky into our bed."

"I started it."

"Sometimes a fantasy can make lovemaking more exciting," he said carefully. "It doesn't mean it has to become a reality."

Something changed in her expression and she struggled to sit up. "Are you still denying that you want Constantine in your bed?"

"I can hardly deny it, can I? But as I said, it doesn't mean that I have to act on it."

She raised her chin at him, and there was a gleam in her eyes that reminded him of the Duke of Wellington at his most belligerent.

"When we married we made a bargain."

"Indeed we did."

"You said you would take a lover after I found one."

He desperately searched his memory. "I believe I said *something* to that effect."

"Actually you *promised*." She smiled at him, and he had a sense of impending doom. "I have decided to take Constantine Delinsky as my lover, which means you can have him, too, with a clear conscience."

Paul stared at her and then started to laugh.

21

"Ah, Delinsky, a pleasure."

"Ambassador."

Con bowed to the Russian ambassador and took a seat in front of his desk. His head was pounding and his mouth dry. After the ball on the previous night, much to Gregor's annoyance, he'd drunk his way through a whole bottle of brandy and passed out on the floor. He'd woken up late, his dreams full of a naked Paul and Lady Lucinda entangled with him in bed.

". . . as I mentioned, Lieutenant Colonel, I have some information for you."

Con focused his attention on the smiling man in front of him. "I appreciate that, sir."

"You might not feel that way after you have heard what I have to say. It seems that there is more than one witness who saw your wife leaving Moscow with the French army."

"So it is highly likely she survived, then." Con frowned. "Have you received any news of her since then?"

"My contacts are still working on that. If we can find no fur-

244 / Kate Pearce

ther word of her, it might still be safe to assume that she died on the retreat. Many thousands did."

"I appreciate your efforts on my behalf, ambassador, but I hate to cause you so much extra work. Would it be easier if I took up the investigation myself at this point?"

"There is no need." The ambassador smiled. "In truth, I am quite enjoying myself."

"Then I will gladly leave it in your capable hands." Con rose. "I hope Countess Lieven is well?"

"Indeed she is. In fact, she has proved most useful in your little affair. Her acquaintance is legion."

"So I understand. Thank her for me, won't you?"

"You can thank her yourself. She told me to invite you to dinner on Friday night. She intends to gather a select group of people together who might be able to help you."

"I would be delighted." Con bowed. "Thank you, ambassador."

He exited the ambassador's office and headed down the wide staircase. There were several people milling around in the hallway below, mainly petitioners hoping to be allowed to speak to the ambassador or one of his staff. Con recognized several old army uniforms from units decimated by Napoléon. The people who inhabited those uniforms bore the look of survivors from hell. And it had been hell. Beneath his polished exterior he bore the same scars.

"*Vashe vysokoblagorodie.*"

Con stopped as one of the veterans grabbed hold of his sleeve. "*Da?*" he automatically answered in Russian.

"Have pity on an old soldier, sir. My English is not good. Help me explain my case to the ambassador."

"How can I help you?" Con drew the man to one side and listened patiently as he listed his grievances. Finally he nodded. "I'll do my best for you, Ivan Petrov. Wait here."

He strode back up the stairs, intercepted one of the ambassador's secretaries, and explained his errand.

The man sighed. "They all want our help, and we can't please them all."

"He is only asking for what is his by right. His pension for fighting for his Tsar and his country."

"And he might be lying, sir. He's just a peasant. They are simply too lazy to work for a living."

Con stared at the young secretary until the man had the grace to blush. "Did you fight in the damn war?"

"No, sir."

"Then you have no right to judge those who did." Con favored the man with his best commanding stare. "I suggest you attend to his claim, or I will be speaking to the ambassador."

"Bravo, Delinsky."

Con looked up into the face of one of his old army comrades. "Sergei Kalasov."

Sergei turned to the hapless secretary. "Do as Lieutenant Colonel Delinsky says, imbecile."

The man scuttled away, and Sergei held out his hand to Con. "It's been a long time, my friend."

"Indeed it has. Thank you for your help. It seems those who served Mother Russia are to be ignored or forgotten in these more peaceful times." Con returned the handshake. "Have you been in England for long?"

"I'm just visiting. I'm attached to the Russian embassy in Paris."

"Indeed? That must be interesting."

Sergei grimaced. "It is hard sometimes to forget the past, but needs must."

Con nodded. "Do you have an hour to spare for me? We could have dinner at my club."

"That would be delightful." Sergei followed Con down the

246 / Kate Pearce

stairs and out into the street. "I've been waiting to speak to the ambassador, but he's been busy all day."

Con hailed a hackney cab and they were soon deposited at the door of his club, which was populated mainly by former and current military men and was far less intimidating than White's or Brookes's.

When they were seated, Con turned back to Sergei. "When did you sell out?"

He grimaced. "As soon as I could. After our regiment was practically annihilated it seemed there was nothing left to fight for."

"I understand. I almost sold out myself," Con replied. "I was lucky enough to be seconded to one of the British regiments. After that, I had no time to question my commission; I was too busy."

"Killing Frenchmen."

"Yes." Con thanked the waiter, who brought them a bottle of brandy. In his present condition, he reckoned the cure to his headache might prove to be more brandy. At least it would dull the pain.

"You are situated in London, then?"

"Indeed. The regiment is overseas en route to India. I was asked to stay behind and liaise with the Duke of Wellington's staff."

"Lucky for you."

"I suppose so. But it is more likely that they simply do not need me anymore and have found a way to keep me busy."

Sergei laughed. "You can hardly wish for more fighting, my friend, can you?"

"Good God, no," Con said. "I hope I never have to go to war again."

"Amen." Sergei held out his glass and Con clinked his against it. "And how are your family, Delinsky?"

"My mother is still in Saint Petersburg. My cousin Michael continues to administer to what remains of my estates."

"Only Natasha accompanied you then?"

Con made himself meet Sergei's interested gaze. "Unfortunately not. My wife went missing in Moscow."

"During the French occupation?" Sergei groaned. "I beg your pardon. I didn't mean to raise such unhappy memories."

"There is no need to apologize. It is in the past."

"You have not remarried?"

"No." Con decided it was time to change the subject, although it was strange that no one from the embassy had already asked Sergei about Natasha. "Have you married?"

Sergei looked smug. "I recently married a beautiful Frenchwoman named Louise."

Con raised his glass. "Congratulations. I wish you many years of happiness together. Did she accompany you on this trip?"

"She did. She wanted to see London and have some riding habits made for her." He shrugged. "Apparently London tailors are the best in the fashionable world at this."

"So I've heard." Con smiled. It seemed that Sergei's wife already had her husband under her thumb. Louise also might be able to help Con. "Are you perhaps going to Countess Lieven's dinner party on Friday night?"

"I believe we are."

"Then I look forward to meeting your wife." Con looked up at the waiter who had come to stand by his chair. "I believe we can go into the dining room now. Perhaps you can tell me more about your charming wife while we eat."

Lucky stared at the letter in her hand and then at Milly. "Did the person who brought this say why it was returned?"

"No, my lady." Milly frowned. "Should I have asked?"

"It doesn't matter, Milly. It just seems rather odd."

Lucky studied the crossed-out address, trying to see whether the pen strokes resembled Jeremy's. Now she was even more worried that Paul had somehow found out about Jeremy and arranged for his murder. She placed a hand over her belly. Surely that was ridiculous? But Paul did have a deadly side that most people were completely unaware of.

Part of her wanted to forget about Jeremy and accept this convenient disappearance as the good thing it undoubtedly was for her peace of mind. Her conscience, however, still troubled her. She'd rather Jeremy was alive somewhere, fomenting mischief, than lying in an unmarked grave.

"My lady?"

Lucky smiled at Milly. "It's all right. Thank you for bringing me the letter. I must have written down the wrong direction."

"That's probably it, my lady. Good thing His Grace can frank the letters for you, so you don't have to pay to send it out again." Milly moved toward Lucky's wardrobe. "Are you dining at home tonight, my lady?"

"I believe I'm going out, but only to see Miss Ross, so I don't need to dress up."

"Right you are, then." Milly brought out a plain cambric gown in a yellow print. "Will this do?"

"It is perfect." Lucky stood so that Milly could help her undo the back of her dress. "Can you make sure to have the carriage ready for me in half an hour?"

After helping Lucky into the clean gown and pinning up her hair, Milly went off to arrange for the carriage. Lucky glanced at the clock and hurried to find a suitable bonnet and her gloves. It was almost six, and Paul would be home soon. She'd managed to avoid him all day. She had no intention of speaking to him until she'd thought about Constantine Delinsky's extraordinary proposal and her equally provocative offer to Paul.

She assumed Paul wouldn't be happy with her avoiding him,

but she needed to speak to someone who wasn't directly involved in the matter. Who better than Emily, who combined a shrewd common sense with a female insight into the pleasure house no one else in Lucky's world had.

She shivered as the carriage moved off and hastened to cover her knees with one of the thick fur rugs and rest her booted feet on a hot brick. It wasn't far to the Knowles town house, but the frigid air had a breath of snow in it and a stillness that warned of worse to come.

Emily greeted Lucky with a smile and immediately invited her up to her bedchamber to chat. She explained that she was having her dinner on a tray upstairs and that Lucky was welcome to join her. There was no sign of the other members of the Knowles household, either Emily's parents or her brother, Richard, which at least explained the dinner tray.

After a nice warming meal, Lucky tucked her feet up under her and sat beside the fire with Emily opposite.

"You seem a little perturbed, Lucky," Emily said. "Is there something wrong?"

"Too many things to count."

"Can I help you with any of them?"

Lucky gave Emily a grateful smile. "I'm not sure, but you are my only hope."

Emily frowned. "What has Paul done?"

"He hasn't done anything. Well, not much. In truth, he's the one who is trying to stop anything from happening by being too noble and self-sacrificing and I . . ."

Emily held up her hand. "I have no idea what you are talking about. Can you slow down?"

"I'm not sure how to explain it to you."

"From the beginning?"

Lucky hesitated, and Emily leaned forward to touch her knee.

"I promise I'll never speak a word of this to anyone unless you ask me to."

"I know that," Lucky replied. "It's just that things are rather complicated."

Emily sat back. "Let me guess. Paul has realized he still wants Constantine Delinsky."

"That is part of it, but . . ."

"That's quite enough!" Emily said. "I *knew* he would never keep his promises."

Lucky stared at her friend. "Emily, don't jump to conclusions. I *know* Paul wants Constantine; the thing is . . ." She looked down at her clenched hands. "I think I want him too."

Silence greeted her announcement. When she found the courage to look up, Emily was just staring at her, open-mouthed.

"Oh, dear."

"It's not quite as bad as you might think."

"Are you sure?"

"Yes, because Constantine offered to . . . to bed us both."

"Oh, my word." Emily rose to her feet. "Stay there a minute, Lucky. I want to see if anyone has returned home."

"What does that have to do with . . . ?" Lucky's question went unanswered as Emily ran out of the room. She sat back and tried to contain her impatience. When Emily reappeared she had Lucky's cloak in her hands.

"Helene isn't here, so she must be at the pleasure house. Let's go."

Lucky put on her cloak. "What are you talking about?"

Emily maneuvered her toward the door. "Helene is the only woman who might be equipped to help you with your problem."

Lucky allowed herself to be led down the stairs and into the waiting carriage. She couldn't disagree with Emily's assessment.

Madame Helene was indeed the only woman who might be able to offer her some helpful advice.

"Where exactly is Lady Lucinda?"

Paul looked around Lucky's neat bedchamber as if he might spot her hiding in the closet or something. She was definitely hiding from him—that he was sure of. He glanced speculatively at her black-haired maid. He'd known Milly for years. She was fond of Paul but devoted to her mistress, and probably not averse to lying for her.

Milly bobbed him a curtsy.

"She went out, sir."

"I can see that. Where exactly did she go?"

"To have dinner with Miss Ross at Knowles House, sir."

"Did she say when she would be back?"

"She didn't, sir."

"And did she leave any message for me?"

Milly looked uncomfortable. "I can't say she did, sir."

"Thank you." Paul took one more look around the deserted bedchamber and then went through to his own. Jordan was waiting to dress him for dinner, and Paul waved him away. The duke and duchess were attending a function at court. If Lucky wasn't here, there was no need for him to dress up in all his finery and sit at the table by himself.

Paul sat by the fire and contemplated his options. He could go after Lucky and demand that she speak to him, but that would accomplish nothing. He knew from past experience that she would talk to him when she was good and ready. He wasn't even sure what he wanted to say to her.

The idea of Con offering to share himself with both of them had both shocked Paul to the core and excited him beyond measure. To have access to the man and woman he most wanted seemed like a dream come true. He knew Con loved to bed women, but Lucky? Was she intent on offering herself up as a sacrifice for him? Sharing herself with another man probably went against everything she had been brought up to believe was proper.

Paul sipped at the hot toddy Jordan had left for him. And when it came down to it, Lucky was still a duke's daughter and had played the part successfully her whole life. But didn't he know her better? Hadn't he seen that spark of interest at the pleasure house for the forbidden, for the unknown?

He put his glass down on the table with a thump. If Lucky continued to run away from him, he would never find out her opinion on anything.

"Devil take it!" Paul muttered. Sitting by the fire didn't suit him at all. Perhaps it would be better if he took his worries to Ambrose at the pleasure house.

"Ah, Lady Lucinda! How are you?" Madame Helene exclaimed.

She was sitting in one of the offices of the pleasure house in a simple muslin day frock, a smear of ink on her sleeve and a pair of spectacles on her nose. There was a pile of account books on the desk and a candelabra shedding light on them at her elbow. She still looked about the same age as Lucky and Emily, and twice as beautiful.

Emily took Lucky's hand. "Helene, Lucky needs some advice."

"Are you all right, *ma petite?*" Helene frowned and waved her into the nearest chair. Her gaze fell to Lucky's waistline. "Are you unwell?"

"Not really, Madame. I just need your help on a rather complicated personal matter."

Although Lucky knew that Emily must have been dying of curiosity, she headed for the door. "I'm going to the kitchen. Come and find me when you have finished." She blew Lucky an airy kiss.

In the silence that followed Emily's departure, Helene drew up another chair close to Lucky's and sat down.

"Are you with child?"

"I'm still not sure."

Helene frowned. "You still haven't bled?"

"But that is not unusual for me." Lucky glanced down at her flat stomach. "I certainly don't feel as if I'm breeding."

Helene sighed. "Well, time will show the truth of that. What else is worrying you?"

Lucky stumbled through her tale. Helene nodded and didn't interrupt until Lucky ran out of words.

"Constantine Delinsky offered himself to both of you?"

"Yes," Lucky whispered. "Do you think he meant it?"

Helene sat back. "I'm sure he did. Although I know Constantine has feelings for Paul, he does tend to prefer women in his bed." She hesitated. "Would you want that?"

"To be in Constantine's bed?" Lucky bit down on her lip. "I think I would." She raised her gaze to Helene's. "Is that wrong of me?"

"I told you before you married Paul that you did not have to have a conventional marriage, only one that suited you both. The real question is, are you doing this for yourself, or simply because you want Paul to be happy?"

Lucky sighed. "I don't know. I never imagined I would have to make such a decision. I expected Paul to find himself a new lover eventually, and for me to turn a blind eye to it like all the other ladies of the *ton*."

"I don't believe your father has ever had a mistress."

"That's because he and Mother made a love match." Lucky swallowed hard. "But even they would never understand that their only daughter is considering becoming an adulteress less than two months after her wedding."

"I think they would understand better than you think, but I still don't recommend you ask their advice."

Lucky managed to smile. "They would be horrified. I'm glad to hear that Constantine Delinsky really does like women. Thank you for listening to me. I still haven't quite decided what I want to do at this point. I also need to talk to Paul."

"Yes you do, and I'm glad if I helped you in any way at all." Helene patted Lucky's hand. "Relationships can be so difficult, but you must follow your heart and be honest about what you want, regardless of how you might be judged. Do you want me to take you down to the kitchens? I think we'll find Emily there."

Paul reached the pleasure house and made his way through the back door into the kitchen. To his surprise, Ambrose was again sitting across from Emily Ross at the table. They appeared to be arguing about something, and neither of them noticed Paul discarding his outer garments in the doorway. Eventually he cleared his throat and Ambrose looked up.

"Lieutenant." Ambrose forced a smile.

"Ambrose, Miss Ross." Paul continued to divest himself of his gloves. It was none of his business if Emily and Ambrose wanted to fight, and he certainly wouldn't interfere. "It is damn cold out there tonight."

Emily rose with a sigh, his cheeks flushed. "I suppose *you* want to talk to Ambrose, don't you? I'll go and find Helene."

Paul watched her stomp out of the room and turned to Ambrose. "Why is Miss Ross so out of sorts? Is she coming down with a cold?"

"No, I believe she just hates not being involved in everybody's lives."

Paul raised his eyebrows. "Has she been lecturing you, my friend?"

"She . . . wants things from me that I am unable to give her."

"What sort of things?"

Ambrose shook his head. "I'm not ready to talk about that yet." He paused. "She has been complaining about you, though."

Paul sat down at the table. "What did *I* do?"

"She wouldn't tell me, but I gathered it has something to do with Lady Lucinda, and that you are to blame."

"*Obviously*. Why do women always have to confide things to each other?"

"Aren't you just about to confide in me?"

"Well, that's different." Paul settled more comfortably into his seat and put his elbows on the table. "I need help."

"What have you done?"

"I haven't done anything." He ignored the disbelief on Ambrose's face and kept talking. "Constantine Delinsky offered to bed me and my wife."

"*What?*"

"Exactly."

"Is he really that desperate to get you back?"

"No, I think it is a little more complicated than that." Paul rubbed his face. "He is rather taken with my wife."

"And how does she feel about him?"

"That, my friend, is the question."

Ambrose whistled softly. "She is here, you know."

"Who is?"

"Your wife. She and Emily came to find Madame Helene."

"That was rather astute of her."

"She isn't what I expected at all, Paul."

Paul smiled. "I know. Despite her age, she is remarkably intelligent and willing to go after what she desires in a straightforward manner reminiscent of her father."

"In truth, the perfect woman for you."

Paul's smile died and he held Ambrose's gaze. "Yes, she is. I don't want to lose her, Ambrose. I'm not sure if I want to risk everything to go after an impossible dream of having them both."

"If your wife is as intelligent as you say she is, at least do her the courtesy of sharing your worries with her."

"Of course I will. We promised to be honest with each other. She has always been one of my best friends."

Ambrose sat back. "Then go and find her and *talk* to her, not me."

Paul rose. "But I like talking to you." He hesitated. "And if I can help you with your other matter, please let me know."

Ambrose's mouth set in a stubborn, defeated line. "There is nothing more to say about that."

"I'm sure Miss Ross would disagree with you. Now where did you say my wife could be found?"

22

"Ah, there you are, Lucky. Just the woman I wished to see."

Paul waited to see whether his wife would turn and bolt, but although she looked a little apprehensive, she remained where she was by the door of Christian's office.

"Paul. Emily said you were here."

"And you didn't immediately try and escape me? At least that's progress."

She braced her hand against the door frame and met his gaze. "I wasn't running away. I just had to think."

He gestured into another empty room farther along the corridor. "And are you ready to talk to me now?"

She followed him into the room and waited while he lit some candles and stirred up the embers of the fire.

"Did you know that Constantine Delinsky was going to say that?"

Paul was still kneeling in front of the fire, but he turned to face her. "No, I didn't."

"I wondered whether you had planned it between you."

"No." He waited until she sat down and then sat opposite

her. "I can understand why you might think that, but it came as a shock to me too."

"Yet you knew Constantine was happy to bed women."

"In truth, he prefers women. I am the exception, not you."

She nodded as though he confirmed what she had already heard. "Do you think he means it?"

"I believe so. Con is one of the most straightforward men I have ever met." It occurred to him that Con reminded him of Lucky. Perhaps that was why he found them both so attractive. "The thing is, Lucky, I know how I feel about you and Con, and I know how Con feels about me. The pieces that are missing are yours and Con's to fill."

"Will you not think me shameful if I let another man touch me?"

He took her hand. "Lucky, how could I?"

She wouldn't look at him. "Most men prefer their wives to be chaste and obedient—at least until they have two or three sons to safeguard the succession."

"You know I'm not like that."

"But why not?"

"Because I've never fit in with society. I don't care what they think of me, and I don't believe I ever will."

"But you will be a *duke!*"

"I'm aware of that, but I've realized that it doesn't change who I am inside of me, who I want to be." He kissed her fingers. "I want you to do whatever you feel is right. If you want Con, have him. I'm hardly going to object."

She gazed at him then, the expression in her clear blue eyes a mixture of hope and dread. "You are far too good to me."

"Lucky, I am not. I'm simply trying to be honest with you. Would it help if we talked to Con together?"

"Now?"

"Why not? I'll send a note around to his lodgings and see if he wants to meet us here." He rose and held out his hand.

"We'll await his answer in the kitchen while we sample some of Madame Durand's famous cooking."

Con looked up at the façade of the pleasure house, studied the note Gregor had given him once more, and then stuffed it into his pocket. Despite having been the one to "throw the cat among the pigeons," as he believed the English phrase went, he was surprisingly on edge. The note had been signed by both of the St. Clares, so he assumed they were both present and awaiting him.

Once inside, he undid the buttons of his thick army overcoat and stamped his booted feet clean of the muddy slush from the street. A footman retrieved his hat and coat, and Con spent a moment warming his hands in front of the fire before the man returned.

"Lieutenant Colonel Delinsky, sir? Would you follow me?"

Con followed the footman out of the hall and down into the more private areas of the pleasure house. A pleasant aroma of baked apples and cinnamon reached him as the footman opened a door and stood back.

"Here you are, sir."

"Thank you."

Con entered what appeared to be a kitchen and found the St. Clares sitting at a large pine table. Paul, of course, was eating, and Lady Lucinda appeared to have just finished. Despite the delicious aromas there was no sign of anyone else in the cavernous space.

"Con, how kind of you to come out in such horrible weather," Paul called out to him. "Madame Durand made hot chocolate for everyone. Come and sit down."

"Thank you."

It wasn't quite the scene Con had imagined, but he was more than willing to get warm before he had to deal with anything too complicated. Life in the army had taught him and Paul to take care of their basic needs before their emotional ones. He took the seat beside Paul and nodded at Lady Lucinda, who was sipping from a bowl of hot chocolate. She acknowledged him with a shy smile. He allowed his gaze to linger on her face for far longer than was polite.

The drink was indeed delicious and contained a hint of cognac or something that warmed his very bones. Paul ate his way through another piece of the apple pie Con had declined. For a man of such slight build, Paul certainly ate well.

Eventually even Paul finished his repast, and the three of them faced each other over their hot chocolate. Con decided that as he had laid down the challenge, he might as well go on the offensive.

"I assume you want to talk to me about my offer."

Paul glanced at his wife and they both nodded. "Indeed we do."

"You may speak as frankly as you please, Paul. I think we are beyond the polite nothings of the conventional world."

"I should hope so," Paul answered. He shot another look at his wife. "Actually, I think you should talk to Lucky first. As I mentioned to her earlier, you and I know where we stand; she doesn't." He rose. "Perhaps you might care to explain yourself."

Con experienced a moment of pure panic. "Without you being present?"

Paul's smile was sweet. "I trust you both. I'll be in Christian Delornay's study if you need me."

They watched Paul leave and silence fell between them.

"Have I embarrassed you?" Con asked softly.

Lady Lucinda had the grace to blush. "A little. I didn't imagine getting myself into such a complicated situation quite so early in my marriage."

Con studied the deep lines engrained on the pine table and traced one with his forefinger. "If you feel coerced into this, you have a perfect right to make your feelings known. Neither of us wishes to hurt you."

"But if I agree, I will be giving you both what you want."

He raised his head to stare straight into her eyes. "Not at your expense. Never that." He took a careful breath. "I didn't expect to meet a woman like you again in my life. I certainly didn't expect you to be the wife of my lover."

Her smile was beautiful and, without thinking, he reached out and traced the curve of her lip. "I admired your courage from the first moment I met you. I appreciated you even more when I understood that you had married Paul knowing exactly who and what he was."

She shrugged. "But I've always loved him. It wasn't exactly difficult."

"Not many women would agree with you." He hesitated. "I keep wondering what would've happened if I'd made you tell me your name when we first met, whether I would've stood a chance with you."

She sighed. "And I have wondered the same thing."

He cupped her chin and stared down at her beautiful face. "Then you no longer doubt my sincerity in this offer? It isn't all about Paul."

"So it seems." She brought her hand up and placed it over his. "Will you think it shocking if I confess I have thought about you?"

"In what way?" His body came to life in an instant.

She blushed, and he could feel the heat through his skin.

"In all ways a woman can know a man. Isn't that shocking?"

He smiled. "Not to me. Are you willing to try then?"

"I suppose I am."

He leaned into her and kissed her soft mouth, felt her lips part, and took gentle possession. She tasted sweet and wholesome, and yet he still wanted her naked and writhing beneath him.

"Shall we go and find Paul?" She licked her lips, and he immediately wanted to kiss her again. "My lady, if you change your mind at any point, you can always go back. I believe I speak for Paul when I say that neither of us wants to do anything that might hurt you."

"I know that."

She rose, and he held out his hand and she took it willingly. He glanced down at her.

"You will have to show me where Paul is awaiting us. I'm not familiar with the private side of the pleasure house."

"I only know where he is because I met with Madame Helene here earlier today."

"Is this your first visit to the place, then?"

She looked up at him. "No, I've been here before with Paul."

"He brought you here?"

"How else was I to understand the kind of sex he enjoyed?"

Her blend of common sense and curiosity made him want to smile. He could imagine her trying just about anything. It wasn't surprising that she had refused to allow her unpleasant encounter in the gardens at the Mallorys' ball to either ruin her or define her.

"The man you were escaping when I found you at the ball. Has he caused you any further annoyance?"

"He tried to blackmail me into marrying him, if that is what you mean."

"Ah, which explains why Paul decided to marry you."

"I know." She sighed. "I shouldn't have allowed it."

"Why not? Paul did the right thing."

She smiled up at him. "And you would do the same, wouldn't you?"

He stopped walking and cupped her chin. "I wish I had."

She blushed and started walking again. "But you are already married."

"In name only."

They had reached an open door and Lady Lucinda went through it. Paul sat by the fire, his booted feet stretched out toward the grate, his expression thoughtful. He jumped up when he saw them.

"I assume it went well because you are still talking to each other. What was that about your wife, Con?"

Con relayed the latest information he'd received from the Russian ambassador and his hopes for a speedy conclusion to the long-drawn-out matter of his disappearing wife. Lady Lucinda perched on the arm of Paul's chair and regarded him intently.

"Have you discovered who has been sending you those letters warning you to leave things be?"

"No, I haven't discovered that yet, but I'm having dinner with the ambassador and some other Russians next week. Perhaps I'll have a clearer idea of who my enemies might be after that."

Paul frowned. "If someone felt it necessary to write to you, it would indicate there was a mystery to be solved."

"Or something to hide," Lady Lucinda added. "Be careful, Con."

He smiled at her anxious tone. It was strange to be with people who cared about what happened to him again. He'd become quite used to fending for himself. Paul had wrapped his arm around his wife's waist, and she was leaning back against him. Con wanted that, too, that physical closeness, that emotional contact.

He swallowed hard, walked across to the fireplace, and sank down on to his knees in front of the St. Clares. He rested his forehead on Paul's knee.

"Thank you."

He felt Paul's hand in his hair. "For what?"

"For agreeing to this."

Another hand joined Paul's, and he recognized Lucinda's lighter touch and shuddered.

"God, Con . . ." Paul whispered.

Con wasn't quite sure how it happened, but Paul and Lucinda were down on the floor with him, and he was kissing them and they were kissing him, and, even though they were all fully clothed, it was one of the most erotic and exciting moments of his life.

Paul's kiss was familiar, but Con took his time with Lucinda, learning what she liked, what she needed, what they both needed from him. His cock was hard, and so was Paul's, but neither of them made any effort to attend to them. It was all about the taste of Lucinda's sweet mouth, of Paul's, of Con's helpless response to them both.

He opened his eyes to find Lucinda sitting sideways in his lap and Paul clamped to his side, the hot pulse of Paul's shaft against his arm. Paul's fair hair was tousled, and there was an unmistakable gleam of lust in his brown eyes. Con imagined he looked the same. Lucinda was dazed with pleasure, her mouth swollen with their kisses; her skin flushed a soft rosy pink.

"This is not the best place for this," Paul murmured. "I'd rather a nice soft bed than a hard floor."

Con met his gaze. "I agree, but perhaps we shouldn't rush this?" He glanced pointedly at Lucinda.

Paul groaned and bent to kiss the top of his wife's head. "I've just remembered. I have an early appointment with your father and his secretary tomorrow morning."

Whether the appointment was real or a fabrication, the mention of the duke had a startling effect on Lucinda, who tried to scramble out of Con's embrace. He winced as her bottom rubbed against his hard cock, and then her knee narrowly missed incapacitating him as she finally broke free.

"Oh, my goodness, it is late, isn't it?" She patted ineffectually at her disordered hair, her gaze straying to Con's groin. "Perhaps I should go and make myself presentable. I'll wait for you in the kitchen, Paul."

She hurried out without saying good night to Con, who groaned and fell back on the floor, one hand cupping his aching balls. Paul made as if to follow Lucinda, and then paused at the doorway to look back at Con.

"Are you all right?"

Con couldn't help but rub his thumb along the ridge of his shaft. "I will be in a moment. You just run along and take care of your wife."

Paul leaned against the door. "Let me watch. Let me watch you come."

Con unbuttoned the placket of his breeches and shoved down his underthings. His cock sprang free, and he wrapped his fingers around it and pumped himself hard. It didn't take long for him to come all over his hand. When he finished, Paul was beside him again, licking him clean, taking the taste of Con into his mouth and on to his fingers.

Con tensed as Paul opened his own breeches and placed his wet fingers around his shaft. He could only watch as Paul climaxed, too, his expression somewhere between pain and pleasure. When he'd finished he brought his dripping fingers up to Con's mouth and Con sucked on them.

"I've missed you, Con, missed this. Have you?"

"What do you think?" Con whispered. "I'm already hard again just thinking about you."

"And my wife?"

"God, yes."

Paul's kiss was fierce and unexpected. "I'm going to tell her what we just did while I have her. She'll love it."

Paul stood and buttoned up his breeches, leaving Con on the floor. "Perhaps we should arrange a room here for another night? It will be safer. I'll speak to Ambrose on my way out and let you know when we can meet again. Good night, Con."

Paul blew him a kiss and was gone, leaving Con still lying there and already anticipating what would happen the next time they met. He licked his lips, tasted them all, and smiled for the first time in a very long while.

23

It seemed far easier to *imagine* being with two men than to actually be in the same room with them while they stripped off their coats and chatted about inconsequential things Lucky had no knowledge of. Not that watching the men strip was that much of a hardship. They were both beautiful in their own ways, Paul's elegant strength a striking contrast to Constantine's taller, more muscled frame. Both of them bore the scars of their war-like profession. Lucky had a strange desire to kiss every single one of them.

She studied the lush surroundings of the large bedchamber Paul had escorted her to in the pleasure house. The curtains were drawn against the bitter chill of the night, and the gray satin bedcovers had been pulled back. Paul had waited several days to see if she was going to change her mind about anything before proposing that Con join them at the pleasure house. She'd agreed, her dreams filled with salacious images of the two men, her body restless and suddenly unsatisfied.

But the reality was slightly different from her dreams. Paul had already stripped down to his shirt and breeches before he turned to her.

"Is something the matter, Lucky?"

Of course he would notice. She'd never been able to escape his scrutiny. Lucky folded her arms more tightly over her chest.

"Nothing at all, Paul."

"Do you not want to undress?"

She gave a nervous laugh. "Not really."

He took her hand and kissed it. "Are you regretting this?"

"A little."

Paul glanced across at Con, who was looking worried. "Lucky is going to watch for a while. Is that acceptable to you, Con?"

"Whatever she wants." Con came over, too, and took Lucky's other hand. "Perhaps she might like to sit on the bed so that she will have the best view possible."

They led her over to the large bed, and Paul lifted her up onto the mattress. She scooted backward until her shoulders touched the oak headboard and wrapped her arms around her raised knees.

"Are you sure you are comfortable, Lucky?" Paul asked.

"Completely."

"And you don't mind if Con and I start without you?" That made her smile, and Paul grinned back at her, which somehow helped. "If you change your mind and want to participate at any point, there is no need to ask, just go right ahead."

Lucky nodded and concentrated on her breathing as Paul and Con joined her on the bed. Paul cupped Con's cheek and leaned in to kiss him, and Lucky was enthralled by the sweetness of Con's shuddering response. It occurred to her that on her previous visit to the pleasure house she'd not seen Paul kiss anyone so deeply or so movingly.

It also underlined the difference between what Paul had

chosen to show her at the house and what he had concealed. This slow seduction was nothing like the showy pursuit of sexual pleasure she'd seen before. Deep inside her she started to feel warm and almost like crying.

Paul was removing Con's shirt now, his movements slow and deliberate, as if every inch of skin he revealed was precious and needed a moment to be appreciated and examined. Con was trembling, his gaze fixed on Paul's face, his hands clenched at his sides. Lucky wanted to lean forward and stroke the lines of tension from his jaw.

She unclasped her hands, and then froze as Paul helped Con remove his breeches, leaving him kneeling naked on the bed. Heat pulsed and throbbed between her legs as if she were the one about to fuck him. His cock was already stiff and wet at the crown and straining away from his flat stomach.

Lucky sighed and Paul turned to her, his expression gentle. "Would you like to touch him, Lucky? He is quite beautiful." He traced a finger down Con's almost hairless chest and then rested it on the very tip of his cock. "Con loves to be touched. I should imagine he would like to feel your hands on him very much."

Con gave a small nod as if speech was beyond him. Lucky found herself reaching out and touching his arm. He shivered, and his cock jerked and grew even wetter.

"You could just stroke him, Lucky, learn him, while I suck his cock," Paul murmured.

Without waiting for an answer, Paul rearranged his position on the bed until he was slightly to one side, allowing Lucky a fine view of both him and Con. He lowered his head and licked a long, slow line along the underside of Con's cock. Lucky shivered as Paul's tongue peeked out and lazily circled Con's crown, probing the wet slit.

She was wet, too. She could feel it between her legs, along with a restless ache that would only grow and torment her until she gained release. Perhaps she didn't want to remain quite so uninvolved as she'd thought. Since Jeremy had taken her innocence by force, she'd realized she had a horror of being passive, of being *taken*. But these men didn't want to hurt or control her; they wanted to share themselves with her. Paul moved again, and this time he sucked Con's shaft deep into his mouth, making Lucky and Con gasp. Con closed his eyes and brought his hand down to Paul's hair, his fingers clenching and releasing in time to Paul's sucking.

Recklessly, Lucky put her fingers on Con's shoulder and felt the fine tremors running through him. He turned his head, and his mouth brushed hers and she was lost. She kissed him in the rhythm of Paul's mouth, and he responded in kind, his tongue playing with hers in an enticing duel that simply made her want to press herself against his warm, naked flesh. He brought his hand to the nape of her neck to hold her still, but she had no notion of escaping him, no need to be anywhere than with him and Paul on the bed.

She jumped as she felt Paul's hand on her thigh, shoving up her skirts, his fingers heading straight for her wet, needy core. She moaned into Con's mouth as he continued to kiss her, wondered how Paul could concentrate on both of them at once when she was already drowning in sensations.

Con groaned and his muscular body went rigid, his hips slamming forward into Paul's mouth as he spent himself. Even as he recovered, Lucky found herself flat on her back, Paul over her, his hand still working between her legs. He pushed her knees wide apart and rucked up her petticoats to display her wet sex.

"Beautiful, Lucky," Paul breathed. "Help me, Con."

The two men had her out of her garments quicker than a lady's maid, and Paul settled over her breasts, while Con took his place lower, his mouth descending to suck and lick at her most tender flesh. Lucky could hardly breathe, let alone scream, as she climaxed. Paul took Con's place between her legs and thrust his cock inside her again and again.

After her second climax, he held himself still and framed her face with his hands.

"Do you mind if Con fucks me?"

"I told you I did not."

He roughly kissed her mouth. "I meant right now, while I'm still inside you."

"Will it hurt?"

"Me or you?"

"Either of us."

His smile was beautiful. "No, I think you'll enjoy it, and I certainly will."

"Then go ahead," she said politely, making Paul kiss her again. She sensed Con moving behind Paul, and the smell of almond oil drifted over her. Then Con's face appeared over Paul's shoulder and he smiled at her.

"Thank you, my lady."

Lucky gasped as Paul was pushed even deeper inside her and focused on hanging on to his shoulders. Con took over the driving rhythm, and Lucky tried to keep her eyes open against the pleasure so that she could watch both men as they fucked. It was a rewarding experience and only pushed her own pleasure higher until she came hard and felt Paul quiver and join her, followed by Con in a few seconds.

Her breath exploded out as both men collapsed over her, but they quickly disengaged themselves. Lucky lay flat on her back, unable to move as her senses slowly returned to her. Her clothes were strewn all over the bed and the floor, and the candles had almost burned down. So much for her sitting and watching. It had taken fewer than five minutes for her to forget her scruples and get involved.

Paul came up on one elbow and looked down at her. "Are you all right, Lucky?"

She felt her cheeks heat. *Now* she felt embarrassed, which made no sense at all. "I'm fine."

He kissed her forehead. "Stay there and I'll get you a wash-cloth."

She attempted to rise. "I can do that for myself."

"I want to do it for you. Stay there."

Paul got off the bed, and Con followed him over to the screens that concealed several jugs of warmish water, bowls, and soap. Paul took one of the cloths and wiped Con's face.

"Thank you, Con."

Con took the cloth from him. "For what?"

"For letting Lucky find herself."

"I'm glad she did."

Paul placed his palm flat on Con's chest and captured his nipple, making the other man's breath hitch. "I still want to bend you over the nearest couch and fuck you so hard and so deep that you're begging."

Con's pupils dilated until they were almost black. "Begging you to stop?"

"No." Paul kissed Con's taut nipple. "Never that."

"You know I'll let you fuck me like that in a heartbeat." Con's cock was already hard again and pressing insistently against Paul's hip.

"But you'll have to wait." Paul smiled. "My lady comes first in all of this. What I want, a poor second."

"Agreed," Con murmured. "Although I'll be thinking about you having me like that all night now."

"Anticipation is good for you, my friend. Now let me go and attend to my lady."

Paul left Con pondering his dreams and returned to Lucky's side. He dunked the washcloth in the soapy water and wrung it out before gently rubbing it between her thighs.

"I was just telling Con that I'd like to fuck him hard over the back of the couch."

Her gaze drifted down to his groin, where he was already half-erect.

"Right now?"

"No, I told him he'd have to wait.

"Why?"

He pressed the cloth against her clit, and she shivered. "Because it would be quite brutal for you to watch. Men aren't quite so careful with each other as they are with their ladies."

She licked her lips and squirmed against his hand. He kept rubbing her even though she was now quite clean.

"I wouldn't mind," she said carefully.

He fought a smile. He'd already begun to realize that beneath her calm exterior, his wife was obviously intrigued by the darker elements of making love. Who would've imagined that? He slid his hand over her buttocks and imagined how she might like being thoroughly spanked and then fucked. His cock lengthened, and he looked over toward Con, who was just emerging from behind the screens.

He whispered into Lucky's ear. "Shall I do it? Shall I fuck him hard? He wants to. He likes it when I make him beg."

She shivered beneath him, her nipples now hard against his chest and the scent of her arousal engulfing him.

"If that is what you wish."

He looked into her eyes. "No, it must be what you wish. Con can wait if you want him to pleasure you first."

"Yes, my lady." Con had come to stand beside the bed. "I am willing to do whatever you need."

Lucky looked at Con and then back to Paul. "I'd like to see you together."

Paul kissed her nose. "Then you shall."

He climbed off the bed and waited until Lucky sat up and wrapped a sheet around herself before turning to Con.

"Come here."

Paul loved the cool note of command in his lover's voice, the way Con studied his body, his cock, his mouth. He walked over to the chair Con indicated and waited until Con bent over, resting his face on his folded forearms and presenting his arse for Paul's inspection. Paul kicked his feet slightly wider apart and smoothed his hand over Con's taut buttocks.

Then there was silence and Paul wondered what Lucky was thinking. Did she like seeing him ready to fuck Con, or did it frighten her? Con shifted his weight, and Paul noticed that his cock pressed against the brocade of the chair. He used his finger to rim Con's arse, and Con groaned and arched his back.

"Can you see how eager he is, my lady?" Paul asked Lucky. "Normally I'd take my time using my fingers to play with his cock and widen him, but he also likes it when I take him hard with just my cock." His dry fingertip eased inside Con and Paul caught his breath.

"Is that what you want, Con? A good, rough fuck?"

"Yes."

"Yes, what?"

"Yes, please," Con managed as Paul pushed his finger deeper. His own shaft was so stiff it prodded Con's arse. Paul shivered as he released the first cold drops of oil on to his fingers and shaft. The welcome surge of slick wetness made his progress easier. When he replaced his finger with his oil-slicked cock, it was far easier for Con to take him deep. Even so, his breath hissed out, as Paul drove inside him and then retreated and did the same again and again, each thrust slamming his thick length deep and hard. Paul groaned in time to each thrust, his balls tight and eager to come.

He reached around and grabbed Con's cock, bringing it away from the chair and high up against his stomach.

"Don't come yet," Paul said. "Not until I give you leave. Take what I am giving you and ask for more."

"Yes, give me more, please . . ."

He altered his strokes, still slamming into Con but shorter

now and rougher. His hand gripped the base of Con's shaft so hard that he couldn't have come even if he'd wanted to. Paul looked down and watched himself thrust into him, the slap of his balls against Con's flesh, the hard bones of his hips, his cock . . .

"Ah, God, Con, it's too much, I can't . . ." Paul gasped and rewarded Con with a further tightening of his grip on his cock that would probably make him see stars.

Paul shoved deep and held still. "Come for me then, come for my wife."

Con obliged, his come shooting out over his belly and Paul's fingers in a thick, pumping stream. Paul was panting as though he'd been running for his life when he came, his cock so drained he doubted he would ever be able to fuck anything again.

When Con moved away to wash, it took all Paul's remaining strength to turn around and crawl onto the bed. He lay on his back and simply stared up at the ceiling. He blinked as Lucky's face loomed over him.

"Are you all right, Paul?"

"I'm . . ." He licked his lips and tasted blood.

"I didn't know that you could be so . . ."

"Masterful?" Paul smiled. "I am a man of many talents. But both Con and I can be gentle as well." He reached over and patted her knee. "You have no need to worry."

She straightened. "I wasn't worried. You said that you behaved differently when there was no woman involved. I asked to see what you did."

He found himself chuckling and she looked indignant. "Your acceptance of the oddity of my life continues to amaze me."

She looked adorably embarrassed. "I suspect I am quite depraved."

"And you haven't even had Con yet." She blushed a fiery

red, and he hastened to reassure her. "We don't all have to reciprocate equally. I was the selfish one tonight. I had both of you." He winked at Lucky and saw her fight a smile. "Don't tell me you are jealous."

"No, I'm still new at this, remember?"

"Indeed." Paul found himself yawning. He caught Con's eye and patted the bed. "Come here, my friend. After I've washed, perhaps we all deserve a nap."

Much later, Con woke up and found himself staring right into Lady Lucinda's eyes. Earlier, he'd taken his time washing himself with the lavender soap Madame Helene favored and the scent was still strong. Even his hair was damp, but he felt refreshed, his body humming with a bone-deep contentment that felt so right he wanted to stay in this room and on this bed forever.

"You are awake, my lady?"

"I am." She rolled on to her back and looked up at him, her face pale in the moonlight surrounded by a cloud of tangled dark hair.

"Did we frighten you earlier?" he whispered.

She regarded him seriously, her blue eyes fixed on his. "No, you were . . ." She swallowed hard. "Magnificent."

Beside her, Paul snorted, but he didn't seem fully awake.

"I would never use you like that," Con murmured.

"I know."

She touched his arm and his beleaguered body came back to life. He leaned closer until he could only see her lips and kissed her as sweetly as he could. She sighed and kissed him back, her generous mouth awakening his desire to please her, as he had pleased her husband. "You are beautiful, my lady. I am honored to be here with you."

She slid her hand into his hair and held him close. He wanted to bury his face between her breasts and stay there all night. He enjoyed making love with Paul immensely, but Lucinda was equally alluring in her own way. He slid his hand over her hip and cupped her mound. "Did I please you when I fucked Paul? Did you like him having both of us?"

She shivered against his murmured words, her body now turning toward him, her nipples two hard nubs against his chest. He slid his fingers lower. "Did I make you wet?"

She moaned something incomprehensible, and he started to move his fingers in and out of her in a slow, slick rhythm that promised sexual fulfillment. He guessed it was somehow easier in this half darkness for her to respond to him, to forget about guilt and society and everything else that insisted what they were doing was wrong.

He eased another finger inside her and used his thumb on her clit. She gripped his shoulder hard, her nails digging into his skin, and he dropped his head to nuzzle and play with her breasts. Her breathing shortened, and he increased his stroke, pushing her onward toward the pleasure that they both sought, and then pushing her over into it, and burying her cries in his mouth when she finally climaxed around his still thrusting fingers.

He looked forward to making love to her properly, but not tonight, not when they were all so new to this, especially Lucinda.

Her hand tightened in his hair. "Please, Con, please don't stop."

His cock responded to her plea and stiffened, but again he resisted the temptation, using his fingers on her while his trapped shaft rubbed against her hip. She wrenched her mouth away from his.

"Don't you want me after all? Was this all to get to Paul?"

He felt Paul stir close by and wondered how long his lover had been awake and listening. He cupped her chin. "Of course not. I'm just trying to be careful."

"Of what?"

"Of you." He gazed down at her puzzled face. "Paul might not want me inside you."

"Why not?"

Her confusion seemed quite genuine. Con couldn't help but glance over at Paul, who was watching them intently.

"Paul? Do you want to explain it to your wife?"

"I'm not sure what you want me to say, Con."

Con released his hold on Lucinda. "Most men would not want me spilling my seed inside their wife."

"Why not?" Paul asked, echoing Lucky.

Con raised his eyebrows. "Because of the succession, of course."

"I don't care about that." Paul shrugged. "Do you, Lucky?"

In a sudden flurry, Lady Lucinda grabbed the nearest sheet and wrapped it around her. She was biting down on her lip and looked as if she was about to cry.

"Whatever is wrong, my lady?" Con inquired.

"Nothing is wrong. I just want to go home. I'm tired and I can't sleep in an unfamiliar bed." She crawled off the bed and started looking for her clothes in the darkness.

Con shared a mystified glance with Paul, who raised his shoulders in a helpless gesture that signified utter confusion.

"It's all right, my lady." Con came after her. "I'll help you dress while Paul calls your carriage."

After one more look at her distraught face, Con realized it would be pointless trying to work out exactly what had upset Lucinda. He could only suppose that the enormity of what she'd done had suddenly overwhelmed her. It wasn't an uncommon reaction, but Con devoutly hoped she would change her mind again. If not, this might be the first and last night he spent with the St. Clares. Nothing would persuade him to continue if Lucinda wasn't happy.

He helped her on with her clothes, asking her nothing, expecting nothing more than that she turn around at his direction. Eventually she was dressed to his satisfaction. He looked around and saw that Paul had already gone to fetch the carriage.

"If I have erred in any way, my lady, please accept my apologies." He paused, but she didn't say anything, so he labored on. "I should not have assumed that you wanted me in that way."

"You didn't assume anything. That's because you are a good man. I'm the one who . . ." She stopped talking and pressed her lips together as if she wanted to cry.

"Do you want to tell me what's wrong?" he said gently. "Or is it something that is between you and Paul?"

She shook her head, her gaze full of anguish. "It's not you, or Paul, Constantine. It's me. It's all my fault."

Before he could ask her any more, Paul returned and, after a hurried good-bye to Con, took his wife out to their waiting carriage. Con could only hope that she might confide more readily in her husband. He shoved a hand through his hair and regarded the rumpled bed. The night had proven to be far more than he had bargained for. From the ecstasy of having them both to the concern about Lucinda, his emotions were as unstable as a stormy sea.

He was too tired to do anything now. With a soft curse, he crawled back on to the bed and went to sleep.

Lucky sat in the corner of the carriage and tried to pretend that Paul wasn't sitting right next to her. His concern for her was so palpable that she wanted to cry. Her body ached both from Paul's lovemaking and the different, unsatisfied pain of pushing Constantine away.

He'd thought everything was his fault, when it really was Lucky's. She'd ruined their evening because she'd suddenly realized what it would mean if she was indeed pregnant. Could she pass off Jeremy's child as Paul's heir? Worse, could she give

Paul such a child and worry forever afterward about his somehow recognizing the child as Jeremy's? She'd promised to be honest with him about everything, but this seemed far too complicated to confess. If she admitted she might be pregnant to him, she might have to admit it to herself.

Her mind flapped around like a canary trapped in a cage. From what Madame Helene had told her, if she was pregnant, she would have no way of knowing whether the child was Jeremy's or Paul's until it was born, and even then that could be difficult. So did she confess, or wait and see? Paul might not mind if she bore Constantine Delinsky's child—he was, after all, in love with Con—but he probably wouldn't be so sanguine if it was Jeremy's.

It was also still possible that she was simply late with her courses. . . .

"What's wrong, Lucky?" Paul asked.

She turned her face away from him and pretended she hadn't heard him speak.

24

"What a wonderful gathering, Delinsky, eh?" The Russian ambassador beamed at Con and opened his arms wide. The wine had flowed lavishly at dinner, and the guests had imbibed freely. Now the footmen were circling with prized Russian vodka, while Countess Lieven dispensed tea from her samovar.

"It has indeed been wonderful." Con spoke in French, the language of the aristocracy, as did most of the guests, although he could also hear some Russian. "I must compliment your chef."

"Thank you." The ambassador looked around the large room. "Now, may I suggest you seek out the representatives from our embassy in France? If anyone has any information on your wife, it will be them."

"I will, sir." Con bowed. "In fact, I already have an acquaintance who is stationed there."

"Well, good, good." The ambassador patted his shoulder. "Unofficial channels can sometimes be much more rewarding than official ones."

Con moved away and headed for Sergei, whom he'd spotted in the far corner of the room, hanging protectively over a petite blond woman who could only be his new wife.

"Good evening, my friend." Con bowed.

"Good evening, Delinsky." Sergei smiled and put his arm around the woman's shoulders in a very un-English way. "Lieutenant Colonel Delinsky. May I introduce you to my wife, Louise?"

Con took her hand and kissed it. "My pleasure, my lady. Felicitations on your recent marriage."

"Oh, thank you, sir," she responded after quickly glancing at her husband as if for reassurance. Con reckoned she could barely be out of the schoolroom and was charmed by her shy sweetness. Although she was closer in age to Lady Lucinda than to Con, she was nothing at all like Lucinda. Con couldn't imagine Lucinda ever being a simpering miss.

Sergei smiled down at his wife, obviously smitten, and Con found himself smiling too. "Would you care to study the ambassador's art collection, my lady?"

She nodded, and he offered her his arm. "How are you enjoying London so far? Is this your first visit?"

Con soon had her chatting to him like an old friend, her shyness forgotten and her pragmatic French sense of humor revealed. His years of serving with the Duke of Wellington's staff had made him an accomplished flirt, and he was happy to use his talents to amuse his friend's wife if it put her at ease. After procuring a glass of tea, he sat next to her on a convenient couch and Sergei joined them.

"I hear that you have been seeking information about your wife, Constantine?" Sergei asked.

"That is correct. There was some suspicion that she might have left Moscow in the train of the French army. I am wondering if she managed to find her way to France."

Sergei patted his wife's hand. "Louise might be able to help you with that. She grew up in diplomatic circles and knows everyone Russian in France."

Louise turned pink. "Not quite everyone, Sergei, but I do have a wide acquaintance." She turned to Con. "What did your wife look like?"

"In truth, she was rather like you, my lady. Her hair was blond, and she had blue eyes. Her name was Natasha."

"How old would she be now?"

"About three-and-thirty."

"Do you have a picture of her?"

Con thought hard. "I think I still have the miniature that was painted for our wedding."

"Perhaps you could lend it to me. I can show it to the people I know who either fought in the war in Russia or were involved in the diplomatic efforts afterward in France."

"That would be most kind of you, my lady," Con murmured.

"It would be a pleasure. Such a terrible thing to have happened, Lieutenant Colonel."

Con raised her hand to his lips. "Thank you for your help. You are an angel."

"Now, now, Con," Sergei laughingly admonished. "The lady is already taken."

Con stood and smiled down at his friend. "Have no fear. Your wife has eyes for no one but you, Sergei."

He walked over to the sideboard to fill up his vodka glass. Three hours in the ambassador's house, and he was becoming as sentimental and flowery as any Russian.

"Constantine Delinsky?"

He looked up into a face he hadn't expected ever to see again and went still. "Count Andrei Fedorov?"

His hand was grasped in a hearty grip. "My boy, how good it is to see you. Anna and I often wondered what had become of you during the war."

"I'm hardly a boy any longer, sir," Con replied. "Are you living in England now?"

"No, we're still in France. I retired last year from the diplomatic service, and we have a house in the south of France."

"And your wife is well?"

The count's brown eyes darkened. "She is rather frail. But she will be delighted to hear that I have found you again."

Con couldn't quite believe he was standing in a London drawing room talking to the man who had been his first male lover. And they were being so civilized. It was truly amazing how time changed things.

His mouth quirked up at the corner. "Should I belatedly apologize for my appalling behavior?"

Andrei laughed. "Hardly. You were a young and passionate man. Anna and I were flattered that you tried to risk everything to run away to France with us."

Con shrugged. "I was indeed passionate and believed my life would be over if I couldn't leave with you both."

"But I heard that you married."

"After my attempt to escape to France, my family insisted I wed rather quickly. They thought it would force me to settle down. Unfortunately the war intervened and my life has been fairly chaotic ever since."

When Andrei moved closer, Con inhaled his familiar spicy scent and was momentarily thrust back into the past when he'd been foolish enough to believe he could have anything he wanted.

"Actually, Constantine, I came over to England specifically to see you."

Con tensed. "For what purpose?"

"I also heard that your wife was missing, presumed dead."

"That is correct."

Andrei hesitated and looked around the crowded room. "Perhaps I might visit you in a more private setting."

"Can you at least tell me if Natasha is alive?"

"I can't tell you anything until I speak to Anna. I promised her that I would seek you out and then report back to her as to what manner of man you had become. Her health is uncertain, and she rarely leaves the house."

"I am sorry to hear that she is unwell, but she must know that I am a man of honor." Con drew himself up to his full height.

Andrei patted his arm. "It is all right, my friend. I will tell her that you are as worthy as we both assumed you would be."

"All I want, Andrei, is an end to this uncertainty. I don't wish to cause any unnecessary scandal for Natasha or her family."

"I shall tell Anna that. I'm sure she will want to see you for herself."

Con wanted to argue, but he knew Andrei well enough to know that he would get no further. And now, at least, he had two new avenues to explore, whereas before he'd had none.

"Thank you, Andrei." He handed the older man one of his cards. "Please come and visit me whenever it is convenient for you. I'm looking forward to hearing what you have to say."

Andrei nodded, and Con realized he had no inclination to return to the artificial gaiety of the party. He made his excuses to the Lievens and headed out into the night. It had started to snow again, and the streets were unnaturally quiet and muffled. In his agitation, he ignored the offer of a hackney cab and struck out on his own.

Eventually he found himself standing outside Haymore House. Would the St. Clares still want to hear about his wife, or were they done with him? Damnation, he needed to share the tale with someone who cared. God, he hoped they still cared. . . . After a quick prayer, he walked up the stairs to the front door and knocked.

* * *

Lucky put down her book and stared at the empty chair opposite her. Paul had attempted to keep her company until she'd acted like such a shrew that even his good humor had evaporated and he'd stomped off to his study.

Of course he'd sat down with an ulterior motive. He wanted to know what ailed her, and what she had meant by running away from him and Con in the middle of their night of passion. Lucky got out her handkerchief and loudly blew her nose. She still had no idea how to explain how she'd felt or how she wanted Paul to react. And that was the most frightening thing of all.

Her gaze shifted to the window and the flurries of snow that brushed against the glass. Jeremy still hadn't replied to her letters. If she did carry his child, should he be told? Or what if he was already dead, and Paul had murdered the father of his wife's child? She shuddered. Her life was beginning to resemble one of those horrible Greek tragedies her father liked to read.

She assumed that Paul wouldn't want her to go anywhere near Jeremy. But it was also highly likely Paul had warned Jeremy away from her. Lucky had no doubt that Paul could kill a man if necessary. He'd fought in a long, bloody war, and it had changed and hardened him in ways even Lucky didn't care to investigate.

If Jeremy was indeed alive, what if he later found out that Lucky had given birth to his child? Knowing his nature, he'd probably try to blackmail her again, and then Paul would call him out, and everything she'd tried to avoid would come to pass anyway. She blew her nose again and fought the urge to cry.

She found herself standing up. She refused to allow her dread of a scandal to rule her. Her father always said that facing one's fears was far better than trying to outrun them. He'd hate to see her skulking in her bedchamber like a coward.

She rang the bell for Milly and put on her stoutest pair of

boots. Her gaze fell on her writing desk, and she crossed the room to sit down and find a clean sheet of paper. She wasn't quite stupid enough to leave the house without telling her husband where she was going. The trick would be in when he received the information, and how late. If all went according to plan, she would be on her way back to Haymore House before he even realized she was gone.

Milly came in, and Lucky looked up from penning her note. "Milly, I need my warmest coat and hat."

"Are you going out in this weather? I thought you'd decided to stay put," Milly asked.

"I just need to set my mind to rest about something," Lucky said reassuringly, but Milly didn't look convinced. "I should be back within the hour. You won't even miss me."

She finished writing her note to Paul, and Milly helped her into her fur-lined coat and matching hat. When Milly finished fussing over her, and issuing dire warnings as to the likelihood of Lucky catching a chill, Lucky held out the note.

"If the weather worsens, and I do not return within half an hour, will you give this to my husband? It contains the address I am going to, so that he can come and collect me in the carriage."

"You are walking, my lady?" Milly squawked.

"I'm not going far. It seems pointless to use the carriage unless I have to." Lucky patted Milly's shoulder. "Just do as I ask you, and all will be well."

Milly shrugged and took the note. "I'll be watching that clock like a hawk, my lady, so you'd better be quick or I'll send his lordship after you."

Lucky gave her suspicious maid one more airy smile and headed for the door. "Thank you, Milly." She escaped through the door and made her way down the back stairs to the kitchens. The front doorbell jangled and made her jump, but at least it drew the butler into the hall and away from her. At this point, she had no desire to bump into either her husband or her parents. Once she'd established whether Jeremy was dead or alive she would at least know how to proceed.

Paul drank another glass of brandy and pushed the accounting books away from him. He'd had no idea that the Duke of Ashmolton owned so many properties or so much land. The thought of being the one in charge of administrating it all one day made him break out in a cold sweat. Despite his expectations, he'd chosen not to interest himself in the running of the Ashmolton estates, and now he was regretting it deeply.

He shoved his hand into his hair and groaned. What if he ruined everything like that idiot Tilney-Long and left his family destitute? Lucky would never forgive him.

And thinking of Lucky, he was still no nearer to understanding why she had run out on him and Con. He'd tried to get to the bottom of it, but she had been remarkably evasive. So evasive, in fact, that they'd ended up snapping at each other like an old married couple and achieved nothing.

In his soul he was certain that she'd enjoyed every minute of their dual sexual attention. But something had upset her, and he didn't like his Lucky to be upset. He thought of her sitting alone in her bedchamber and immediately felt guilty. He was older and more experienced than she in all ways, and yet he'd been the one to storm off in a huff. He stacked the books neatly on the desk and finished his brandy. She deserved better from him. He'd go back up there and try again.

When he entered Lucky's room there was no sign of her, and he glanced over at the bed. Had she retired in a sulk? That wouldn't be like her. When she was worried about something, she was rather like a dog with a meaty bone who wanted to extract every tiny scrap and morsel of flesh before letting it go.

Milly came out of the servants' door, squeaked, and clutched her hands to her bosom. "My lord, you scared me!"

"Where is Lady Lucinda?"

Milly's gaze flicked to the clock on the mantelpiece. "I'm not sure, sir."

"Well, she isn't here. So where is she?" Paul demanded.

Milly cast another agonized glance at the clock. "Can I answer you later? I promised my lady . . ."

Paul walked up to her and glared down into her stricken eyes. "Tell me now, or you will no longer work for this family."

Milly's mouth fell open. "How can you say that, sir? You wouldn't . . ."

"I damn well would, if you don't tell me where your mistress has gone."

Milly sighed and held up a folded piece of paper. "She told me to give you this if she hadn't returned in half an hour, but she's barely been gone ten minutes."

Paul opened the note and felt as if his blood had frozen. He took a deep breath and looked at Milly. "She didn't take the carriage?"

"No, sir, she said it was only a few minutes to walk, and that you would fetch her in the carriage if the weather worsened."

Paul tucked the letter into his pocket. "If she returns, tell her that I have gone in search of her. Ask her to meet me in the library at her earliest convenience."

"Yes, sir," whispered Milly.

Paul turned to the door. "And Milly? Thank you. If Lady Lucinda is angry with you, you may tell her I threatened you with dismissal. She will be so annoyed at me for saying that, she'll forget your transgression."

"Thank you, sir." Milly's face crumpled with relief. "Thank you."

Paul almost ran down the stairs, his mind working on several issues at once. He didn't even want to think about what he was going to say to Lucky when he found her. First, he needed to arm himself, and then decide whether it would be better to take a carriage or call a hackney cab.

"Paul? What's wrong?"

He'd almost run into the tall frame of Constantine Delinsky, who was just taking off his heavy winter coat and handing it to the butler. Paul spared him a quick glance before hurrying past him to his study.

"Put your coat back on, Con. I need you."

He opened the door to his study and found his army pistol and sword, which he always kept in excellent condition. Con appeared at the doorway, his expression mystified but alert. Paul unlocked his store box, took out the bag of gold coins, and stuffed it into his pocket.

"Do you have your pistol, Con?"

"No, I don't, only my sword stick. I was at a dinner party. Paul, what's going on? You look as if you are about to flee to the continent."

Paul checked his pistol and buckled on his sword. "Not quite yet. We'll see how things go. Did you drive yourself here?"

"No, I walked."

Paul grimaced. "I wish I was involved with less hardy spirits. I can't decide whether it will be quicker to walk or to drive."

"It's cold out there, but not unbearably so," Con said. "It depends where we are going."

"Pulsom Street."

"That's not far at all."

Paul nodded and headed back out into the hall where the butler was already awaiting him with his coat and hat.

"Thank you, Parsons."

He stepped out into the wintry night, Con behind him, and set off at a brisk pace across the square.

"Can you tell me exactly whom we are visiting on Pulsom Street?" Con asked.

"Mr. Jeremy Roland."

"I'm not sure if I am acquainted with him."

"He's the bastard who raped Lucinda."

"I thought you had already dealt with him."

Paul actually found himself grinding his teeth. "Apparently not well enough, as my wife left me a note informing me that she'd gone to visit him."

"I wonder why she did that?"

Paul stopped walking and turned to face Con. "Because she is a fool?"

"She is hardly that. There must be a reason."

Con's levelheadedness only served to ignite Paul's temper. "Maybe after her experience with us, she realized she wants him back, or this is one of her ridiculous schemes to sacrifice herself for my bloody benefit."

Con put his hand on Paul's shoulder. "I understand that you are upset, my friend, but I'm still convinced Lady Lucinda must have gone there for another reason. Perhaps he is black-mailing her."

"Stop being so damned *reasonable,* Con. At the moment all I want to do is get my hands on her, put her over my knee, and spank her until she cries and begs me to stop."

"And I'm sure you will be able to do that very shortly. What number are we looking for?"

"Thirty-two." Paul scanned the front doors as they walked past. "Here it is."

Lucky knocked on the plain, brown-painted door and waited anxiously for someone to answer. No one came, and she knocked again, harder. Eventually the door opened a crack to reveal a slovenly woman in a bloodstained apron that smelled of the slaughterhouse.

Lucky tried to smile and not to breathe in at the same time. "Good evening, ma'am. Is Mr. Roland at home?"

"Not to the likes of you, he ain't."

"I beg your pardon?"

The woman peered closely at Lucky. "He's got no money to pay for game girls. He's barely paying my rent since those thugs did him over."

Despite the biting cold Lucky felt her cheeks heat. "I'm not a game girl. I'm part of his family. His parents asked me to call on him when I visited London."

"What's your name, then?"

Lucky desperately reviewed the scant personal details Jeremy had given her about his family. "I'm his cousin, Mrs. Maude Kimble. Ask him if he'll see me."

The door was shut in her face. She was left shivering on the doorstep and stamping her cold feet until the woman returned.

"All right, you can go up. Second room on the left is where he's at. Maybe you could take him back with you to the countryside. He needs something to sweeten his temper. I'm getting back to my meat pies."

Lucky offered the woman a sixpence, which was accepted without thanks, and made her way across the grimy, dimly lit hall to the uncarpeted staircase beyond. The house smelled of damp, unswept chimneys and overcooked food. Somewhere a baby was crying and a woman was singing a lullaby to it.

Lucky followed the woman's directions and went up the uneven stairs, doubt clouding her every step. Did she even need to see Jeremy? She'd already established that he was alive; wasn't that enough? But she had to make sure he never bothered her or Paul again.

She knocked on the door and heard a feeble reply. Easing open the door, she went inside and prepared herself to meet her unpleasant and unwanted suitor.

"I wondered if it might be you, my lady."

Lucky stared transfixed as Jeremy's familiar voice came out of an almost unrecognizable face. His features were so swollen and misshapen that she could barely see his eyes. His nose was obviously broken, too, and from the way he reclined with his foot up in front of the fire those weren't even the most serious of his injuries.

Lucky brought her gloved hand to her mouth, and Jeremy laughed.

"Do you see what your honorable husband did to me? He is a vicious bastard. I can only hope you'll put him in a rage soon, and he'll do this to you."

"Paul didn't do this."

"Who else would? You shouldn't have blabbed to him. Once he found out that you'd lied to him about our relationship, he had to obliterate me to maintain the fiction that you married him for love."

Lucky leaned back against the wall, needing the support. "That isn't true."

Jeremy sat forward and gripped his cane, his eyes full of hate. "You have no idea what a monster you married, have you? He only stopped short of killing me because my uncle is a viscount."

"He wouldn't . . ."

"Then why are you here? Have you decided you love me after all? Or has he finally frightened you into running away? I could tell you some tales about his conduct in the war that would make you vomit."

"I came here because my last letter was returned to me unanswered. I was concerned for your health."

Jeremy spat toward the fire. "Concerned for your future, you mean. You didn't care one bit about me. You set that bastard on to me hoping he'd kill me." He fixed her with a malevolent glare. "When I regain my strength, I'm going to take this whole matter to my uncle and destroy the Ashmolton family reputation once and for all."

"No!" Lucky whispered. "You can't do that."

"I can do whatever I want. You are no better than any whore who offers herself to the men down by the docks. Why do you deserve any consideration from me?"

Lucky stared at him as he struggled to his feet. Below them, there was a commotion in the hallway and the sound of shouting.

"I will not let you destroy my family."

He laughed. "You've already destroyed it. Wait until the *ton* hears about your visiting me in my rooms."

The now-familiar voices rose, and she heard footsteps on the stairs. How foolish had she been to come here? Jeremy had no intention of being reasonable.

She couldn't let Paul near him again. Paul would kill him if he heard the vitriol pouring from his mouth. "I'll pay you to keep quiet, I'll do anything!"

"You will damned well not!" Behind her, the door was flung fully open. Paul's furious voice made her want to curl up and hide. Instead she walked toward him and blocked his path.

"Leave him alone, Paul." She saw the shock in his brown eyes as her words registered. He reached out a peremptory hand to set her aside but she evaded his grasp. "Haven't you done enough to destroy my family's reputation? Why did you do this to him?"

His mouth thinned, but at least he turned his anger on to her. "Get out of my way, wife."

"I'll not let you kill him, Paul."

"I don't believe I asked for your opinion, my lady."

She shoved at his chest. "He can't defend himself!"

"So?"

She'd never seen Paul in such an icy rage. It was like watching a frightening stranger.

"So you can't kill him." She glimpsed Constantine behind Paul. "Constantine, *tell* him."

"Lady Lucinda does have a point, St. Clare. Perhaps when Mr. Roland is recovered you can meet him on the dueling ground."

Paul turned his head to look at Constantine, and Lucky held her breath. "You won't act for me now, then?"

"Paul," Con said softly. "I understand how you feel, but this is not the right time. Scum like this will find their own just reward."

Paul let out his breath and lowered his pistol. "It seems I am overruled, Mr. Roland. But rest assured, I will return to finish this conversation when you are fully recovered."

"So that you can beat me again?" Jeremy sneered. "And you chose him, Lucinda, instead of me. You *chose* this madman who attacked me and left me for dead. You wanted me dead!"

Lucky shook her head. "I didn't know, I . . ." But she had hoped, she had *prayed* that Jeremy would somehow be stopped. Was she just as guilty as Paul?

"I didn't come looking for your wife, St. Clare. She came crawling back to me, remember that." Jeremy started to laugh. Lucky pushed blindly past Paul and headed for the stairs. This was all her fault.

All of it.

At the top of the stairs, Paul grabbed her elbow.

"Lucky . . ."

She wrenched out of his grasp. "Let me go!" Her foot slipped on the uneven planking and she fell backward, arms flailing, with nothing to break her fall. Her breath hissed out and she felt each painful jolt of her descent. She was almost grateful when her head hit the floor at the bottom of the stairs and she stopped moving.

She looked back up the stairs to see Paul's horrified face and started to cry. She rolled awkwardly on to her front and crawled toward the newel post to pull herself upright. Pain punched her in the stomach, and she bent over with a gasp.

"Lucky, are you all right?"

She couldn't see, couldn't hear, all her focus was on the gripping agony within her. Her last thought, as she crumpled to the floor again, was of a red-black tide of hurt crashing over her and drowning her forever.

25

Paul paced his study, nursing the glass of brandy Con had given him and replenished regularly without being asked. Con sat by the fire, his face in shadow, his intent to stay with Paul and share his pain all too evident.

Paul stopped walking. "You should go home, Con."

"I don't think so."

"I don't need to be . . . coddled."

"I'm not coddling you. I'm waiting to hear how your wife is. Don't I at least deserve that?"

Something in Con's voice made Paul stare at him more closely. "I'm sorry, Con. It must have been a shock for you as well."

Con just nodded, his mouth set in a grim line. "I feel somewhat responsible."

"You do?"

"Of course. What if Lady Lucinda turned to her seducer because my introduction into your bed secretly horrified her? What if Mr. Roland was right?"

"I don't think that's it, Con," Paul said gently. "I think you were right in the first place. Didn't you hear her offering to pay him off? But why?"

He sat down opposite Con and rubbed a hand over his unshaven chin. "I thought we had settled everything earlier this month."

"By leaving the bastard barely alive and even more filled with hatred for you?" Con asked.

Paul winced. "I should have known that Seamus would be too thorough."

"Better to have killed him," Con mused.

Paul looked down at his hands and remembered them covered in Lucky's blood. "I don't know anymore, Con. I swore I'd never kill another soul after the war, but at this moment, I wish him dead."

The door to the study opened, and Paul got to his feet.

"Dr. Jones wishes to see you, sir," Parsons said. "And I have sent your message off to the duke and duchess and impressed upon the footman the urgency of the matter."

"Thank you, Parsons." Paul nodded and then turned to the doctor. "How is my wife?"

Dr. Jones bowed. "Her ladyship is sleeping now. She has a large bump on her head, and she lost some blood. She will need to regain her strength." He coughed. "Was her ladyship in the family way, sir?"

"I'm not sure," Paul managed. "She didn't say anything directly to me."

"Well, it's possible she didn't even know herself yet."

Paul felt as if he were staring down into the gaping jaws of a mine shaft. "She was breeding?"

"As I said, sir, I'm not sure. But she certainly isn't now. The fall appears to have done away with any possibility of that. But I wouldn't worry too much, sir. Your wife is young and healthy, and I'm sure she'll give you an heir for the dukedom in good time."

"I don't care about the damned dukedom. . . ." Paul said fiercely. "I care about my damned *wife*."

Suddenly Con came up beside him and gripped his upper arm. "Thank you, Dr. Jones. As you can see, Lieutenant St. Clare needs time to absorb this news. I assume you will be calling again tomorrow?"

"Indeed I will." The doctor picked up his bag. "Unless you wish me to wait until the duke and duchess return?"

"No, I thank you," Paul managed. "I'll give them the news myself. They will be relieved to hear that Lady Lucinda is not in any danger."

"As you wish, sir. Good night. I will be back in the morning."

"Good night, Dr. Jones," Con replied. "Let me escort you out."

Paul waited until their voices faded and then sat down and put his head in his hands. His throat seemed to have closed up and his eyes stung. He couldn't remember the last time he'd cried, but he suspected he was fairly damn close to disgracing himself now.

He heard the door close, and then Con was kneeling in front of him, one hand on his knee.

"Paul?"

"If she was pregnant with his child, that might explain why she was offering him money."

Con sighed. "That is one explanation, yes."

"Surely it's the only one? It also explains why she was so eager to marry me as quickly as possible." He raised his head and stared into Con's sympathetic gray eyes. "I'm not a complete fool. I wondered if that was the case at the time. I even convinced myself that if she was already with child, I would accept it."

"That was very good of you."

"But why didn't she *tell* me? And why in God's name did she feel it necessary to visit that man?"

"Perhaps she didn't quite know, as the doctor said. Perhaps she just suspected . . ."

"So she went to him to do what?" Paul stood up. "To *ask* him if he made her pregnant? To beg him to take the child?" He smashed one fist into the other. "Sometimes Lucky's insistence upon sorting things out for herself goes too far. What in God's name was she hoping to achieve?"

Con rose too. "I think you'll have to ask your lady for the answers to those questions." He hesitated. "And perhaps you might ask her in a less accusatory manner."

"I'm so angry with her, Con. She could have died, she . . ." Paul sank down on to the nearest chair. He felt Con caress his hair and the weight of his hand on the nape of his neck.

"You are angry because you love her. Remember that. She is young and she loves you very much." Con sighed. "I think I will take your earlier advice and leave you be. You are right. This really is none of my business. I have brought nothing of worth into this relationship, only sadness." He kissed the top of Paul's head. "I'm sorry, my friend. I'll leave you in peace. Give Lady Lucinda my best."

Paul put his hand over Con's. "Thank you for staying with me tonight. Your help was invaluable."

Con's smile was sweet and tinged with regret. "Let me know how Lady Lucinda goes on and if she wishes to see me again. I suspect she won't, but a man can hope, can't he?"

Paul watched as Con left the room. He had a horrible feeling that he might never see him again. His breath shuddered out. Perhaps he wasn't meant to love people. All he seemed to do was hurt them. Perhaps Gabriel had been correct to enjoy him physically and not want him in any other way. Was he fundamentally weak? Had his years of not taking anything seriously, and of avoiding responsibility, been a true measure of his abilities after all?

Even Lucky thought she needed to shield and protect him. She'd put herself in danger trying to find out what had happened to the man who might have fathered her child. Guilt churned in Paul's gut. Was that the kind of man he wanted to be? One who hid from his responsibilities? Surely he owed Lucky and the Haymore family more than that?

After a long while he heard the duke and duchess arrive in the hallway and went out to greet them.

The next morning, Paul waited until after the duke and duchess and the doctor had visited with his wife before he went to see her himself. She was in bed, her face discolored from the fall, and her skin as pale as the linen bedsheets. He nodded at Milly to leave and brought a chair up to the side of the bed.

"How are you feeling, my lady?"

She looked down at her tightly clenched hands. "I'm . . . I'm so sorry, Paul, I was so stupid, I should not have gone there. . . ."

He reached out and covered her restless fingers with his own. "It's all right. You don't have to explain anything."

"But I want to, you must think I—"

He forced a smile. "I think you did what you believed was necessary. My only regret is that you didn't feel you could trust me enough to help you."

"It wasn't that." She swallowed hard. "I was trying to fix everything myself."

"I know. But that doesn't matter anymore, does it? All you have to do is concentrate on getting better." He rose to his feet. "I'll come and see you tomorrow, my dear, if that is acceptable?"

He smiled and turned for the door. He'd realized after a long night of thinking that there was no point in berating her. The fault lay with him. She'd done what she had to do and confronted her foe, thinking him either too weak to do it for her or incapable of understanding her needs. In a strange way he almost admired her for exposing him so competently, for showing him how foolish he'd been to enter into a marriage with his best friend and think to go on in the same way.

"Paul, won't you even talk to me anymore?"

Her voice was wobbling, but he couldn't turn around and face her quite yet. He wasn't used to concealing how he felt from her, and she'd know he was struggling.

"Of course I'll come back and talk to you, my lady. But your mother said I mustn't disturb you for too long, and I would hate to incur her wrath."

He reached the door, opened it, and fled.

Lucky stared after Paul and only realized she was weeping when two fat tears splashed down on to her tightly held bed covers, darkening the silk. He hadn't wanted to hear her excuses. He'd been courteous and distant, and so not like her Paul that she'd lost her nerve and let him walk away without settling anything.

But what was there to settle? She'd been foolish, and he'd obviously decided he'd had enough of her antics. She deserved his lack of interest. He was probably regretting ever marrying her. Another more horrible thought caught her. What exactly had the doctor told him about her accident? Her mother didn't seem to know anything apart from the fact that she had fallen and bruised her face and ribs.

She had to assume the doctor had been more forthcoming with Paul. She brought her knees up to her chest and hugged them, ignoring the dragging ache in her belly and the worse anguish in her heart. It was so unfair that when she needed to be strong she felt so decidedly weak and feminine and . . . *drat it,* weepy.

"Are you all right, Lucinda?"

She looked up and saw her mother through a blur of tears.

The next moment she was enfolded in her mother's arms. She rested her face against her shoulder and cried to her heart's content.

"It's all right, my love. There'll be another chance. I lost several babies early. You might take after me."

Lucky raised her head to stare at her mother. "What do you mean?"

"Did you think I wouldn't bully it out of that poor doctor?" The duchess's face softened. "You were carrying a child, weren't you? I'm so sorry, love. It was very early days. Were you even sure? You hadn't mentioned it to me. Was Paul upset? I'm sure he won't hold it against you. He . . ."

"He knows?"

"I assume he must. The doctor would have told him first." The duchess frowned. "Why? Has he not mentioned the matter to you?"

Even as she shook her head, Lucky realized that Paul hadn't said a word about her being pregnant or not. "He only came in for a few minutes to assure himself that I was feeling better. We didn't really have time to talk."

She hoped that was true; although she had a sneaking suspicion that Paul would never bring the matter up again. He'd probably assumed that if there had been a child it wasn't his and reacted accordingly. And it was her fault. She'd promised to be honest. She'd lied not only to Paul but to herself by choosing to ignore the possibility of being pregnant and worrying more about Jeremy than about her own husband and marriage.

She realized her mother was speaking again.

"Do you want me to have a talk with Paul, Lucinda, and see if I can gauge his feelings about this matter?"

"No, thank you, Mama. I'd much rather talk to him myself."

Her mother kissed her on the brow and got off the bed.

"That is very wise. It's possible that he is too distressed to think about the proper way to go about things, although he will have to learn the skill when he is the duke. You'll handle him beautifully, Lucinda. You are, after all, very good friends."

Lucky pressed her lips together and nodded as tears threatened again. The duchess blew her a kiss.

"This sadness is quite normal for a few days, my dear; after all you have lost the beginnings of a child. But try not to let it overwhelm you. You are young and healthy and, more important, a Haymore."

26

Con rubbed at his eyes and tried to concentrate on the newspaper Gregor had brought with his late breakfast. A frantic missive from the Duke of Wellington's secretary about some Russian general's imminent arrival had been delivered at dawn, and he'd spent several hours replying to it. He needed to sleep, but he'd also received a note from Andrei suggesting he and Anna come round for tea.

Gregor was quietly thrilled by the announcement that his master was having tea with two other Russians and had spent the morning polishing his samovar and grumbling about the lack of availability of Russian delicacies in the middle of London.

"A letter just arrived for you, sir."

Con took the sealed letter from Gregor and inspected the handwriting, which was unknown to him. He broke the seal and spread out the single sheet. It was from Sergei's wife, Louise. Apparently, as soon as she saw the miniature of Natasha Con had sent around, she realized she'd seen a woman who was very like Natasha both at the French embassy and in society. Louise believed she was married to a high-ranking French army officer who had survived the fall of Napoléon and risen to new heights in the current regime. She would find out the woman's exact surname and send it to Con.

Con raised his eyebrows. So it seemed Natasha had reinvented herself completely. Had she assumed he was dead and not cared enough to check? He supposed that in the confusion of war it was possible she would have done anything to survive. He couldn't even blame her for that. He and Paul understood that desire better than anyone.

Not that Paul cared whether Con survived anymore. . . .

In the past two weeks, Con had heard nothing from Paul or Lady Lucinda, but that didn't surprise him. He had no idea how Paul intended to deal with his concerns about Lucinda. He could only hope that his erstwhile lover would regain his normal sweetness of temper and treat his wife with the care she deserved. If Paul didn't, Con might even break a lifelong aversion to interfering and set his friend straight.

A knock on the door had Gregor scurrying to answer it and Con startling awake. He stood and pasted on a welcoming expression as Gregor ushered in Andrei and his wife. Anna took off her cloak, and Con couldn't help smiling. Her face was far thinner than he remembered, but her bright blue eyes were just the same.

"Constantine, my dear." She held out her hands.

He took them and kissed her on both cheeks before drawing her into his arms. She felt quite insubstantial; her lush curves had disappeared, leaving her as frail and light-boned as a bird.

He cupped her cheek. "Anna, you are as beautiful as ever."

"And you are still charming." She laughed up at him. "I'm not surprised you ended up in our bed."

"I was very grateful for the experience." Con led her to a chair by the fire and waited while Gregor fussed around with tea and tiny cakes. "Do you intend to stay in London for long?"

Anna exchanged a glance with Andrei. "Not really. I hate being away from home. Traveling is very fatiguing."

"Indeed," Con answered. "It was kind of you to put yourself to the trouble of seeking me out."

"There was nothing else we could do. When Andrei told me that there were inquiries afoot as to what had happened to your wife, I said we had to speak up."

Con put down his cup and sat forward. "You have seen Natasha?"

Andrei took up the tale. "As you might imagine, we were trapped in France during the worst months of the French campaigns, trying to keep an eye of Napoléon and yet avoid being shot as spies." He grimaced. "It was a difficult time, especially after the disastrous Russian front. Soldiers began to trickle back, speaking of the mass destruction of the mighty French army, and the mood grew very ugly against any Russians situated in Paris."

"That must have been difficult for you," Con said, trying not to betray his impatience. "I did hear a rumor that my wife left Moscow with the French army. Is it possible that she managed to reach Paris?"

Andrei nodded. "We were introduced to Natasha at a small gathering after a church service. She seemed to be alone, so we tried to befriend her. It wasn't until much later that someone whispered that she was the mistress of a high-ranking French officer. Obviously we were concerned that her motives for seeking out her Russian compatriots might not be as pure as we had imagined."

"You thought she might be a spy."

"Indeed. When Anna eventually confronted her, Natasha insisted she was nothing of the sort, that she simply missed her homeland and regretted running away from her family. She said she had sought out Anna and me because she knew we had once meant something to her husband—you."

"And did you believe her?"

Anna sighed. "She seemed genuinely upset that we would think her a spy. And to be truthful, she didn't seem to be quite clever enough to carry off such a deception."

Con smiled. "It's all right. She was very sweet but not particularly clever."

"It occurred to us that it was possible she was of use to the French. She liked to gossip, and she might have inadvertently provided private information about the Russians she mingled with to her lover and his household without realizing it."

"And what happened after you confronted her?"

"She didn't come back to church and she stopped visiting us." Anna bit her lip. "She did write to tell me that she was moving to Toulouse with her lover, and that was the last we heard from her."

"That was almost fourteen years ago?"

"Yes." Anna glanced at Andrei, who nodded encouragingly. "However, we recently moved out of Paris and into a larger country house in the south of France."

"Andrei said that you had moved. Did you not want to return to Russia?"

Anna shivered. "I don't think I'd survive my first winter back there. I need the warmer climate so that I can breathe. We have made some nice friends who don't seem to mind that we are Russian. I am very happy there."

"I'm glad." Con noted Andrei's stricken expression and wondered how long Anna would get to enjoy her southern retreat.

"What Anna is trying to say is that we were told there was another Russian woman living near us," Andrei said.

"Don't tell me it was Natasha."

"That would be too much of a coincidence, but this woman,

Madame LeNy, an ex-spy of some sort, became a friend of ours. I think she has connections with every Russian who has ever dared step into France. When I heard you were looking for Natasha, I immediately contacted her, and she promised to find out what she could."

"But you haven't heard back from her yet, I assume?" Con rubbed his forehead. "Every time I think I am getting closer to finding out what happened to Natasha, the trail runs cold."

"At least you know she survived," Andrei said encouragingly.

"I suppose that is something, although in truth it makes things more complicated."

"Do you wish to marry again?" Anna asked, her expression lightening.

"Alas, the woman I love is already married."

"That wasn't a problem for us, Constantine."

Con sighed. "And I thought it wasn't a problem for me."

"The husband objects?"

"Not quite. I believe he loves us both, but he seems determined to push us away and become respectable. Not that I blame him."

"Ah, the English are so unromantic. We will soon know what happened to Natasha, Constantine, and mayhap you will gain your happiness too." Andrei patted his knee. "I expect to hear from Madame LeNy any day now. She is remarkably quick."

Con managed to smile. "Thank you both for coming all this way to help me. I appreciate it more than I can say."

Anna rose and kissed his cheek. "It is our pleasure, Constantine. If we hadn't been involved in your life, you wouldn't have been married off so young, so we feel responsible for both you and Natasha."

Con saw them out and told Gregor to take the rest of the afternoon off. All he wanted to do was sleep and think about the peculiar way his life was turning out. His wife remained maddeningly elusive, and his commitment to Lady Lucinda and Paul seemed to have disappeared. He'd sent flowers to Lucinda but heard nothing in return. Was he cursed never to find love without pain?

A rustling sound at the front door drew his attention, and he got to his feet. Had Gregor forgotten his key or was someone trying to break in? He opened the door and found a flaxen-haired boy trying to stuff something under the door. The boy tried to run, but Con was stronger if not quicker and caught hold of his arm.

"Let me go!"

Con tightened his grip and pushed the boy up against the brick wall while he opened the note one-handed and quickly read it.

"Who are you?" He stared at the boy, noting the delicate features and the pale gray of his eyes. "Why are you leaving me these notes?" He winced as the boy kicked him hard in the shin, and he readjusted his grip.

"I don't know what you are talking about! I wasn't doing anything."

Con frowned and studied the boy more closely. His accent held more than a hint of French and nothing of the gutter. He was also remarkably clean for a street urchin.

He spoke in French. "What do you want from me, boy?"

The boy stopped struggling and glared at him. "Leave her alone. Can't you read?"

"But—" Con wasn't allowed to finish his sentence as the boy sank his teeth into Con's wrist.

"Damnation!" Instinctively Con loosened his grip as blood started to well from the puncture wounds. Before he could recover, the boy slipped out from his grasp and ran away, disappearing into the winter gloom like a shadow.

* * *

Lucky paused at the bottom of the grand staircase and waited for Paul to acknowledge her. He seemed too intent on the arrangement of his scarf to notice her, so she cleared her throat. He instantly looked up and the pleasant smile she had begun to dread illuminated his features.

"My lady, I didn't realize you were coming downstairs this evening."

"My mother thought it was time for me to be up and about again. It has been two weeks."

His gaze slid over her. "You do not have to do what your mother tells you anymore. If you want to stay in bed, stay in bed."

She gripped the handrail of the stairs. "But I do feel better. And I was hoping to see you." She hesitated. "Are you not staying for dinner?"

He glanced down at his coat. "Actually, I was just going out."

"Oh," Lucky whispered. "Are you going to see Constantine?"

He finally met her gaze. "No. I haven't seen him since your accident."

"Why not?"

He looked away. "Your mother said he sent you some flowers."

"He did. It was very kind of him."

"And have you thanked him yet?"

Lucky felt her cheeks redden. "Not yet."

He inclined his head an inch. "Then you understand why I haven't contacted him either. There hardly seems any point."

"Then where are you going tonight?"

"To meet with your father at his club. He has some acquaintances he wishes to introduce me to. There is a parliamentary seat becoming vacant that I might be suitable for."

"*You?*"

He raised his eyebrows. "Yes. Do you think me incapable of understanding politics?"

"No, I just didn't think you were interested in becoming part of the establishment."

His smile was a ghost of its former self. "I am part of the establishment. God willing, I'm destined to be a duke. I assumed you would be pleased that I finally intend to grow up and take my place in society."

Lucky struggled with another desire to cry. "But I liked you just the way you were."

"A weak man that you could rule and manipulate?"

"No! Never that." She let out her breath. "Paul, what's happened? Why won't you talk to me anymore?"

He bowed and glanced at the clock on the mantelpiece. "I'm sorry, my dear. I have to go and meet your father. Perhaps I'll have the pleasure of your company at dinner tomorrow night." He hesitated. "Please don't come down to eat just for your mother's sake. You still look rather tired, and I'd hate to see you wear yourself out. I want you well and happy."

He nodded and walked out of the front door, leaving Lucky stranded in the hall. His distant kindness and consideration was crushing her. She glanced over at the hallway that led to the dining room and turned back up the stairs. There was no point trying to charm or communicate with an empty room.

As she ascended the stairs, her conscience niggled her about Constantine. Paul had obviously abandoned him, but why? What did Paul think he had to prove to them both? She still didn't understand, and he was giving her no opportunity to talk to him.

She halted at the top of the stairs. She hated this new sense of uncertainty in her life. She was caught between her fear of Paul thinking she was meddling in his affairs again and her usual desire to fix things. If she talked to Constantine, would Paul consider that another betrayal? But she couldn't stand this indecision. She had to do something or she'd end up confronting Paul over the ducal dining table and revealing far more than she'd like to her horrified parents.

She found herself smiling as she pictured the scene and a faint spark of hope lit up inside her. If anyone needed to act in a more mature manner, it was her and not Paul. She would not allow herself to give up. If she did, all the pain and suffering she had endured would mean nothing, and that was unacceptable. She had to make Paul see that he was loved for himself and *that* was worth risking everything for.

Milly glanced up and smiled as Lucky hurried into the room. "Did you enjoy your dinner, my lady? You look much better."

"I haven't eaten yet, Milly. Can you get me something on a tray?" Lucky sat down at her writing desk. "And then can you have this note delivered to Lieutenant Colonel Delinsky?"

Con presented himself at Haymore House promptly at two and was admitted to Lady Lucinda's presence by the butler.

"Good afternoon, my lady."

Lady Lucinda held out her hand to him. "Lieutenant Colonel. It is so good of you to call."

He bent and kissed her hand, noticing that she was still a little pale but very composed. She wore a pretty long-sleeved lilac gown that made her eyes look very blue. His feelings couldn't be denied. He wanted to stare into those beautiful eyes forever, wanted to wake up to them, to see them smiling at him every day.

The butler retired, and Lady Lucinda's gracious smile vanished. "Constantine, I am so sorry."

"About what?" He took the seat closest to her and held her hand.

"About dragging you into my appalling blunders."

He kept hold of her hand. "Are you sure you want to talk about that?"

"Oh, for goodness' sake. Please let me talk about it! Paul won't even let me apologize to him. He keeps telling me that everything is all right and that I'm not to worry."

"Perhaps he doesn't know what to say to you."

"He knows what he wants to say. But he's convinced himself that everything is his fault, and that he needs to change into a different man so that I will be able to depend on him absolutely and not get into scrapes."

"That doesn't sound like Paul," Con said cautiously.

"Exactly," she sighed. "But I know him, Constantine. I've had a lot of time to think this through. He's convinced himself he doesn't need either of us."

"I guessed he didn't need me," Con said wryly, "but I can't imagine him thinking he can do without you."

"He can't do without either of us." Lucinda's mouth set into a stubborn line. "If we don't get him back, he'll turn into some boring Member of Parliament and a political mouthpiece for my father and his cronies."

Con was quietly amused by her vehemence but tried not to show it. "And how will you stop that from happening if he refuses to talk to you and ignores me?"

Lucinda squeezed his hand. "I'll need your help for that. We'll take him somewhere where he can't get away from us and *make* him listen."

The butler entered the room, and Con hastily dropped Lady Lucinda's hand.

"My lady, I apologize for interrupting you, but there is a letter for Lieutenant Colonel Delinsky that was described as extremely urgent."

"Thank you." Con took the letter and looked at Lucinda. "Do you mind if I read it?"

"Please go ahead." She gestured at a nearby desk. "There is paper and ink if you wish to reply."

Con used his knife to break the seal and studied the writing on the covering sheet. "It is from an old friend of mine. He apologizes for not bringing the note personally, but he has had to return to France because of his wife's ill health."

Con grimaced at that bad news and hurried to open the letter. It was written partly in French and partly in Russian. As he began to read, Con had to sit down and squint at the tiny writing.

> *Apologies, my old friend, but Anna is unwell and I must take her back to France with all speed. I enclose a letter from Madame LeNy. Apparently your wife is here in London with her "husband" and children. He is working at the French embassy.*
> *Yours, Andrei.*

Con sat back as the pieces began to form a pattern in his head. "She has children."

"Who does?"

"My wife." Con looked up at Lucinda. "Apparently my wife is married, currently living in London, and has children by another man. I caught a young boy leaving one of the anonymous notes under my door last week. I wonder if that was her son warning me off?"

He shot to his feet and began to pace. "When she knew I was looking for her, why didn't she seek me out herself instead of sending her child? What did she think I would do?"

"Force her to come back to you?"

"Why would I wish to do that when I've found you and Paul? That's the last thing I want."

Lucinda regarded him seriously. "You still want us?"

He came down on one knee in front of her and took both of her hands in his. "I think I could love you both."

"Oh, good," she sighed, "because I think I could love you too."

Con stared into her eyes and couldn't look away. "Are you really feeling well, Lucinda?"

"Yes, remarkably well, considering everything." She disengaged her hands. "What do you plan to do about your wife?"

It seemed she really didn't want to talk about anything after all, but he was content with that. He'd learned that grief was a contrary beast that manifested itself in its own particular time and way. He just hoped either he or Paul would be able to help her through it when it finally broke through her reserve.

"I still don't know her last name, or where she is residing, or why she hasn't faced me herself." He frowned. "I also cannot fathom why I haven't met her at any social functions if she is based in London."

"Perhaps she moved here quite recently."

"That's possible. Louise didn't mention how long Natasha had been here."

Con rose and began to pace, his hands behind his back. "I just want to talk to her. Is that too much to ask?"

"I think that is perfectly reasonable, Constantine," Lucky said firmly. "Perhaps something happened to her in Moscow, and she has no recollection of her previous life with you and truly believes she is a different person."

"Then why would she send notes trying to dissuade me from investigating the past?"

"That's a good point. Maybe she didn't know that her son was writing the notes."

Con shook his head. "It still makes no sense. I need to speak to her."

"And hopefully you'll soon be able to do so." Lucinda

stood too. "Will you let me know what happens? I would like to help you."

He smiled at her. "Thank you. I'd be honored to share my woes with you—as long as Paul doesn't object."

Her smile disappeared. "I'll have to discuss it with him. If he ever lets me near him again."

Con bowed low and kissed Lucinda's hand. "I understand. And now I must leave you in peace. I have a meeting with the Duke of Wellington's secretary at four." He hesitated. "Don't despair, my lady. I'm sure everything will work out as you desire."

"I hope so, Constantine," she said softly. "I really do."

Lucky remained in her sitting room curled up in front of the fire, her feet tucked up under her, and read a racy novel Emily had recommended to her. It held her attention so well that she jumped when Paul appeared before her with a branch of candles in his hand.

"Are you all right, my dear?"

She blinked at him and let the book fall to the floor. He looked tired, the faint lines around his brown eyes more prominent, and his smile was perfunctory. "I'm quite well, sir." If he refused to call her Lucky anymore, she'd be damned if she called him Paul.

He set the candles on the mantelpiece and sat opposite her. "You didn't come down for dinner."

"I didn't realize the time."

He slowly exhaled. "I thought you might be avoiding me."

"Avoiding you? You are the one who disappears every time I try to have a conversation with you."

He shifted in his chair, his gaze fixed on his clasped hands. "I hear that Constantine Delinsky visited you today."

"Yes, he did." Lucky deliberately kept her answers short. If he wanted to know about Constantine, he would have to ask properly. "Is that why you finally decided to talk to me?"

"Did you invite him, or did he take it upon himself to visit you?"

Anger grew in her chest. She was tired of his prevarication, and if he was at least willing to speak to her, she would make the most of it. "Does it matter?"

"It matters to me."

"I suppose you think he came crawling around begging for news of you. Well, he didn't. He came to inquire as to my health and well-being. We didn't even mention you."

"As I said, Con has always preferred women, and he is very fond of you."

"In truth, he loves me."

Paul's gaze flew to her face as if he was surprised at her combative tone. "That is hardly surprising."

"He is certainly more considerate about asking how I feel than you are."

Paul swallowed hard. "He is more considerate about everything. I should have asked you how you did as soon as I sat down."

"You should have asked after I fell down the stairs!"

Paul winced. "I know. But I didn't know what to say."

"Because you assumed the worst?"

"I didn't want you to berate yourself for what happened."

"You *assumed* that I was carrying another man's child and hadn't thought to mention it to you."

He looked at her steadily. "Yes."

"And you didn't want to ask me about that."

He shrugged. "No. What was the point of causing you more pain? If you had carried that man's child to full term, I would have accepted it as mine and loved it because it came from you."

Lucky drew in a painful breath at his simple words. "But we

don't even know if that is true, Paul. It's a possibility, but there are others. The child might have been yours, or there might have been no child at all. I've never had regular monthly cycles, and I might just have been late. I just don't know."

"Lucky . . ."

She swallowed hard. "I almost wish I hadn't recovered so quickly. It feels wrong somehow."

"In what way?"

Her eyes filled with tears. "If I had been pregnant, how could I not mourn forever over a loss caused by my own stupidity?"

"You weren't stupid, Lucky. You did what you thought was necessary to protect yourself. I understand that." Paul sat back, his placating smile firmly in place. "Please don't upset yourself."

Lucky blew her nose and glared at him. "I didn't go and see Jeremy to protect *myself*. I went to protect you and my family."

"Do you think that makes me feel any better? A man should be able to protect his own family. I failed to do that. The fault is mine."

"No!" Lucky realized she was almost shouting. "We are married and we should protect each other. I don't want to turn into one of those women who rely on their husbands for everything! Can't you see that?"

"And I don't want you to." He paused and met her gaze. "But you promised to be honest with me, and you weren't. How do you explain that?"

"Because I didn't know for certain if I was pregnant or not. I asked Madame Helene's advice, but even she said—"

"Wait," Paul interrupted her. "You discussed this with Madame Helene and not with me?"

Lucky realized she was twisting her hands together on her lap. "Madame is a very knowledgeable woman."

"Indeed she is."

"I had to talk to someone."

Paul sighed. "You could have talked to me."

"And then what? You would've regretted marrying me even more!"

"I don't regret marrying you."

Lucky closed her mouth and stared at him.

"I don't regret it at all." He rose from his chair.

"But what about Constantine? You are in love with him, not me," Lucky whispered.

His smile was sweet. "Lucky, I love you both, but I am married to you." He hesitated, his hand on the back of the chair. "If you want him more than you want me, I'll let you go. I'll never hold you in a marriage that is abhorrent to you."

"It's not a question of letting me go. I'm not here against my will. I love you, Paul. I've always loved you." She raised her chin. It was time to take the gamble of her life. "If you can give Constantine up, so can I."

Paul frowned. "That's not necessary."

Lucky rose, too, and faced him, her anger gone, replaced by a quiet, burning certainty. "It doesn't work like that, Paul. Either we both love him, or we don't."

His expression faltered, and she saw the regret in his eyes. "Then we don't love him."

Lucky picked up her book from the floor and wrapped her shawl around her shoulders. She walked past Paul, her head held high, and only looked back at him when she reached the door.

"I don't believe *that* for a second!"

By the time Paul gathered his wits and chased after Lucky, she was already at the bottom of the stairs and heading toward the dining room. He caught her by the elbow and steered her into one of the empty salons.

"What in damnation is that supposed to mean?"

She raised her chin to look at him, her blue eyes clear. "I think you know."

"If I knew, I wouldn't be asking you to explain yourself, would I?" he snapped.

"You are trying to become the man you think I want you to be."

"And what's wrong with that? You're the one who is always reminding me that I'm going to be a duke!"

She sighed. "I wish I hadn't. Forcing myself to behave like a Haymore has led me into all kinds of stupid decisions."

"Like marrying me rather than facing your parents with the truth."

"No." She touched his cheek. "That was actually one of my better choices."

He turned his head until his mouth brushed her fingertips and breathed in her particular scent.

"And your point is?"

"I don't want you to be a copy of my father," she said earnestly. "I want you to be yourself."

He swallowed hard. "I don't think I know who I am anymore."

It was so quiet that he could hear her soft breathing and the faint beat of her heart.

"*I* know you."

He wanted to bury his face between her breasts and weep. "I thought I'd destroyed your love for me. I'm so sorry, Lucky, sorry for everything."

"I could never stop loving you." She hesitated. "More to the point, do you think you could love me?"

He framed her face in his hands. "I do love you. I always have."

She frowned. "Is that all you have to say to me?"

"What else is there? Madame Helene was right. If we chose

to love each other *and* Con, and it makes us happy, what does it have to do with anyone else?"

Her eyes shone with tears, but she kissed his nose. "Now come and eat your supper, and let me tell you what Constantine had to say about his errant wife. I think he might need our help."

27

Con stared up at the façade of the discreet dwelling on Plaistow Street and considered his approach. If he used his real name, would Natasha let him through the door? Somehow he doubted it. The last thing he wanted was to cause a scene and bring them both to the attention of the *ton*.

He lifted the knocker and rapped sharply on the door. It took but a moment for a butler to reply. Con mustered his most earnest smile and increased the thickness of his Russian accent.

"Good morning. Is your mistress at home?"

"Good morning, sir. Might I ask who is wanting to call at such an early hour?"

"My name in Count Andrei Federov. I am an old friend of the family visiting briefly from France. Ask Madame if she will see me on a matter of urgency regarding my wife."

The butler stepped back to allow Con into the hall. "I will go and inquire if Madame is receiving visitors."

Con resigned himself to a long wait. Even if it was Natasha, she might not remember the Federovs or care enough to see them again. He could only hope her natural curiosity would overcome her scruples. The house, even though furnished in the most elegant style, was clearly rented, which he hoped indicated that his wife and her family weren't intending to remain permanently in England.

The butler came down the stairs and bowed to Con. "Madame will receive you now, Count Andrei."

"Thank you," Con said.

He ascended the stairs behind the butler, careful to conceal as much of himself as he could before Natasha got her first good look at him. If he could just get rid of the butler and into the same room, he would conclude his business with her regardless of her desires.

"Count Andrei Federov, Madame."

Con stepped forward and took Natasha's hand. Her mouth opened, and Con murmured, "Don't scream, Natasha. Let your butler leave so that we can talk in peace."

Her blue eyes fixed on his face and she paled. He felt her trembling and helped her sit down again. When the door closed behind the butler, Con took a seat opposite his wife and studied her carefully. He hadn't seen her for fourteen years, and yet she hardly looked much older. She still had that helpless air of fragility that had both enchanted and exasperated him as a youth.

"Constantine, how did you find me? Why did you find me?" Natasha whispered, her hand pressed to her throat. "What do you want?"

Con stared at her. "What do you think I want?"

Her lips trembled. "To ruin me?"

"Why would I want to do that?"

She looked away from him, and he tried to think of a more conciliatory approach. "I didn't intend to find you. I simply wanted to end our marriage by declaring you dead."

She shuddered. "That was hardly kind."

"I thought you *were* dead. It wasn't about kindness or the lack of it. I simply wanted to end the uncertainty."

"And instead, you have stirred up all this trouble for me."

Belatedly Con remembered something else about Natasha. Everything had always revolved around her needs. "Natasha, you are hardly blameless in this. You chose to leave Moscow with our enemies and come to France. You chose to marry another man without first finding out if I was living or dead."

"Of course I didn't try and find out about you! It would have caused the same horrible scandal you are trying to create now!"

"But your marriage is invalid because I am still alive."

Natasha hunched her shoulders at him. "I married Claude in a civil ceremony in France. It is not the same. And I had very good reasons for leaving Moscow with him! Did you know that people were eating their horses and dogs?"

"I feared that would happen. That's why I wrote and pleaded with you to leave the city before the French arrived."

"There is no point in arguing about it now, Constantine. I had to leave, and Claude was willing to take me." Her blue eyes filled with tears. "If you hadn't been so selfish and come home instead, I wouldn't have been left with no other choice."

Con bit back his retort. There was no point in reminding her that his military duties had prevented him from rushing to her side or explaining his anguish at abandoning her. She would only ever see her own part in any crisis.

"As you said, there is no point in rehashing the past. The question is, what do we intend to do now?"

"What do you mean?" She stopped dabbing at her eyes with her lace handkerchief and fixed him with a suspicious stare.

"As you said, I have inadvertently stirred up the Russian community and have perhaps compromised your identity. Does your husband know about me?"

"Of course not. I told him you were dead."

Con winced at that but persevered. "Who else apart from Andrei and Anna Federov know your true identity?"

"No one. Once I realized I had been foolish to seek their help, I kept away from the Russians in France."

"So it is possible that we could quietly arrange for a divorce by applying to a Russian Orthodox bishop or even the Tsar. It would take time, but I'm sure another year or so won't make much of a difference to us."

"There is no need to be sarcastic, Constantine. This is entirely your fault anyway." Natasha sniffed.

Con ignored the provocation and carried on speaking. "If you don't intend to tell your husband the truth, I assume your French civil union will stand if neither of us protests it."

He rose to his feet. "Shall we leave it at that, then? I'll tell everyone that your death has been confirmed, and eventually people will forget I even asked the question."

"You make it seem so simple."

"It is simple. I just wish you had sought me out so that I didn't have to resort to discovering you by stealth."

She swallowed hard. "I didn't think you would be so reasonable, Constantine. You had a very quick temper when we were married."

"So you just hoped I'd be killed during the war, leaving you free to do whatever you wanted?"

She stiffened. "That is none of your concern. I did what I had to do. I was frightened and alone and . . ."

Con held up his hand. "I know, Natasha, and I don't blame you for accepting help when it was offered to you." And to his surprise, he realized that he really didn't. All his anguish and guilt over her supposed death had disappeared with his discovery that she was alive. "You were very young and in an intolerable situation."

She looked at him then. "That is very sweet of you."

He wondered if she would finally apologize, but knew it

was unlikely and that it didn't matter anymore. He tried to picture Lucinda behaving like Natasha. She would have found a different way to survive, and would never have abandoned him or Paul so easily in the first place.

"Do you intend to stay in England, Natasha?"

"With you here?" She sighed as though he were being deliberately difficult. "I don't want to be forever avoiding you at all the best functions. That would be tiresome." She shrugged. "I *suppose* I will have to persuade Claude to return to France. It will not be too difficult. He still hates the English."

Despite everything, Con found himself wanting to smile. Only Natasha could trivialize fourteen years of suffering and uncertainty into something that only affected her social standing and convenience.

"I will endeavor to ignore you in the meantime, then." He bowed. "It might help if you didn't send your children around to my lodgings with threatening notes."

Her smile died. "Whatever do you mean?"

"Your eldest son," Con explained patiently. "I caught him trying to deliver one of the notes you wrote me, but he escaped."

Two red spots of color highlighted Natasha's cheeks. "You must be mistaken. Why would I seek you out? I want nothing to do with you!"

"Perhaps you might have a word with your son, then, and explain that," Con said gently.

"My eldest son is only eight. I doubt he is the boy you claim to have seen!"

Con inclined his head. Natasha had never been a very successful liar, but he was disinclined to get into an argument with her now. "I'll keep you informed through the Russian ambassador as to my efforts for our legal divorce, Madame, and bid you good day. Thank you for seeing me."

Con went down the stairs, where a solitary footman lingered by the door. For the first time in many years he felt at peace within himself. While he waited for his hat and coat, he glanced back up at the landing where he heard the chatter of young voices. He doubted Natasha would want her children to see him, so he backed farther into the shadows below the staircase.

As the children stomped down the stairs, they argued happily in French about a number of seemingly unconnected subjects all at the same time, with no one actually answering anyone. Con found himself smiling as he listened. He missed that cheerful sense of family more than he wanted to admit, but he'd left all that behind in Russia, and he certainly didn't want to return there.

"Count Andrei?"

He turned to find the footman looking uncertainly around the hall over the heads of the children, who, of course, all turned to look at him too. There was nothing he could do to avoid their attention, so he smiled and took the proffered garments with a murmured word of thanks in Russian. He tried to avoid looking directly at the children and their governess as he passed, only noticing that there were two girls and a boy and that the boy appeared to be the youngest.

At the bottom of the steps he looked back and caught the pale gray gaze of the eldest girl, who was glaring at him in a most un-child-like way. Con couldn't tear his eyes away, and eventually the nursery party swept past him with their governess and headed toward the park.

"Oh, God," Con murmured as a thousand possibilities rushed through his head. He hurried back up the steps and pushed past the startled butler. He pounded up the stairs and headed for the room where he'd last seen Natasha.

She wasn't there, and he turned around wildly.

"Natasha! Damn well come back here and face me!"

There was no reply, and he strode back toward the landing,

only to find his way barred by the butler and several other burly members of the household.

"Madame wishes you to leave now, sir," the butler said loudly. "If you do not, she will call the watch."

Con stared at the butler for a long moment before he could remember how to speak in English. "Tell your mistress that she cannot hide from me forever. I will be back, and I will demand some answers!"

He pushed past the butler, went down the stairs, and back into the street. His gaze strayed in the direction the governess had taken, but he had no grounds for his suspicions and no intention of confronting a child. He realized he was shaking and that he had no idea what to do next.

He needed someone to listen to him, but who in God's name would want to do that? His gift of keeping people at a distance meant he had few true friends and many acquaintances. He wanted the St. Clares, but even though Lucinda had offered to help him, she was at odds with Paul, and he wouldn't make things worse for either of them. He was truly alone.

He spotted a hackney cab and climbed in, giving the driver his address. If he had no one to talk to, and no one who cared, he might as well go home and get drunk.

"There is a person here who wishes to see you or Lady Lucinda, sir," Parsons announced.

Glad of the interruption, Paul looked up from the accounts book. "What kind of 'person,' Parsons?"

"A Russian, sir."

"Do you mean Lieutenant Colonel Delinsky?"

Parsons looked pained. "Of course not, sir. The lieutenant colonel is a *gentleman*."

"And this person is not?"

"He claims to be Lieutenant Colonel Delinsky's servant."

Paul put down his pen. "Then why didn't you say so? Send him in immediately."

Parsons returned with a short, swarthy-faced Russian whom Paul had no difficulty in recognizing from his visits to Con's lodgings.

"Gregor, it is a pleasure to see you again. How may I help you?"

After a grudging nod at Parsons, Gregor took off his hat and faced Paul. "My master is sick."

"Has he seen a physician?"

Gregor sniffed. "He is drinking. It is not good for his soul."

"Did he ask you to come and see me?"

"No, he did not. He has too much pride."

"But you think I should come anyway."

Gregor thumbed the brim of his hat. "He needs you, sir. Something terrible has happened if he starts to drink."

Paul scribbled a note to Lucky and then stood up. "I'll come with you."

He didn't bother to call for a carriage or his horse, he just hailed a hackney cab and placed a reluctant Gregor inside it with him. The servant insisted he could walk. Paul thought it more likely that he didn't want Con to know he'd been interfering in his affairs. He did agree to wait until Gregor slipped back inside Con's apartment before he announced his arrival at the door.

Paul waited for a few minutes in the freezing cold, and then banged on the door. Gregor opened it, and Paul played his part, pretending that he'd just called on the off chance of seeing Con.

Gregor ushered Paul into the living room and immediately disappeared again. The fire was blessedly warm. Con sat in front of it in his shirt and breeches, one hand gripping a bottle of what Paul guessed was vodka.

"Are you all right, Con?" Paul asked quietly.

"What do you want, Lieutenant?"

Con slowly turned toward him, and Paul went still. He'd never seen Con drunk before. He now understood why Gregor was worried. There was no trace of Con's usual good humor and calm nature in his eyes. Just a terrible cold rage as deep as the worst excesses of a Russian winter.

Paul took the seat opposite Con and continued to study his friend. "What's wrong?"

"Can't a man enjoy a drink without everyone worrying about him?"

"Some men, yes, but you're not known as a drinker, Con."

Con took another long swallow from the nearly empty bottle. "There's a reason for that. I don't like the man I've become."

"Then why are you doing it?"

Con shrugged. "Because I don't particularly like myself anyway at the moment."

"What happened?"

"I found my wife."

"And . . ."

"She is happily married to another man, the Frenchman who *saved* her in Moscow."

"I can understand why that might have upset you."

"It didn't. I have no feeling for her at all. I thought she was dead."

"Then what's wrong?" Paul opened his hands wide. "Did you harm her in any way?"

"Of course I didn't." Con fixed him with a deathly glare. "Mind you, if I'd managed to get a hold of her the second time, I'm not sure what I would've done to shake the truth out of her."

"Does she not wish to acknowledge you?"

"Damnation, Paul, I don't want her to! I want to forget she ever existed. I want to be free of her selfish, inconsiderate lies, but how can I when I don't know the truth?"

Paul crouched down in front of Con and took the bottle out of his hand. "Let me help you. Come home with me, and we'll sort this out, I promise you."

Con looked down at him. "Why would you help me? You have everything I've ever wanted, you *were* everything I ever wanted, and you threw me away."

Paul swallowed hard. "I thought I could, but I can't. I need you, Con. I need you and Lucky more than anything. Will you please come back with me?"

He went still as Con leaned down and locked one hand around the back of his neck, drawing him upward until his mouth ground against Con's. He sighed and let Con inside, accepting both the strong bite of the vodka and the darker tones of Con's anger. Paul moaned as Con fumbled with the placket of Paul's breeches and wrapped one hand around his semi-erect cock. God, it felt good to be fondled so roughly, to want it but fear it at the same time.

Breathing hard, Paul wrenched away from Con and ripped open the other man's breeches. Despite his drinking, Con was already hard, and Paul bent his head to take him between his lips, sucking and licking until Con started to fuck his mouth, shoving his thick length down Paul's willing throat. Paul took all of him, letting Con have control, ignoring the ache in his own shaft in his eagerness to give Con exactly what he needed.

"Paul, oh, God, I want, I need . . ."

Con pulled away, and Paul found himself being half carried, half dragged toward Con's bed. Con pushed him facedown on to the mattress and climbed on top of him, pulling down Paul's breeches to the knees. A moment later Paul felt the welcome slickness of oil, and then Con was thrusting deep inside his arse in a steady driving rhythm that made him want to groan with every punishing stroke.

He set his teeth and endured each pounding thrust until his

whole body awakened and the friction turned to pleasure and such exquisite need that he never wanted it to stop. He wanted Con there fucking him until he screamed. He reached around to touch his own dripping cock, but Con caught his wrists and drew them over his head, stretching him out farther, making him unable to avoid each deep, penetrating thrust.

"I want to come, Con, let me come."

Paul sighed as Con wrapped one of his hands around the base of his straining shaft, but his relief was short-lived as Con's grip tightened.

"Not yet," Con growled as he continued to fuck Paul's arse, their slick skin now sliding against each other, bodies straining, and heartbeats as loud as their breathing. His strokes shortened and became more shallow but no less intense. Paul closed his eyes and allowed the red-black tide of lust to consume him, and then felt Con freeze over him and the hot rush of his peak, both of their climaxes pouring out.

Paul stayed under Con until his breathing evened out and then waited for his friend to move. After a moment, he realized that Con's face was buried against his shoulder and that he was weeping.

Lucky peered out of the window into the rainstorm, Paul's note clutched in her hand. Should she go to Constantine's lodgings or not? She had a horror of repeating the same mistake she had made with Jeremy. According to Parsons, Paul had left over an hour ago, and he had not returned.

A knock at the door had her turning to see Milly entering the room.

"There's another note come for you from Lieutenant St. Clare, my lady."

"Thank you." Lucky read the terse sentences and looked up at Milly. "I have to go out. I'll need my stout boots and warmest coat, and please call me a hackney cab."

"Again, my lady? You have a perfectly fine coachman sitting there doing nothing. Why not use him?"

Lucky didn't answer. Neither Milly nor the coachman needed to know that their mistress's next destination was a notorious house of pleasure.

When she arrived at Madame Helene's, she did as she had been instructed and went through the back of the house to the kitchens, where Ambrose awaited her.

He bowed. "My lady. Your husband and Lieutenant Colonel Delinsky are in one of the private bedchambers at the rear of the house. I'll take you up there."

"Thank you, Ambrose." Lucky glanced up at him as he held open the door for her. "Is everything all right?"

"Your husband is fine, though the lieutenant colonel is a trifle foxed. But we have been endeavoring to restore him to his usual self."

Lucky frowned at that and allowed herself to be guided up the back stairs and into a far quieter area of the house. Ambrose knocked on one of the doors and then opened it and ushered Lucky inside.

Paul stood and came across to her. His smile was so welcoming it made her feel warm. There was also a purpose to his voice that had been missing recently. "Lucky, I'm so glad you are here." He led her across to where Con was sitting by the fire; his head back against the chair, his complexion even paler than usual. "Con's in trouble, Lucky, and he needs us."

Lucky sat on the footstool and put her hand on Con's knee. "How can we help you?"

He looked down at her. "Neither of you need to do anything. I was just a little drunk, and Paul mistook—"

Lucky squeezed his knee hard. "Con, don't be silly. It is obvious that something is wrong. We want to help you." She glanced up at Paul, who nodded. "We love you."

"Perhaps Con no longer thinks he needs us because his wife is alive," Paul said.

"You found her?" Lucky asked.

"I did. She has remarried and is living mainly in France." Con's voice strengthened. "And she is *not* the reason why I do not wish to involve you in my dilemma."

"Is it because you don't wish to break your marriage vows?" Lucky said. "Paul and I seem quite capable of doing that with you, but only with you."

"It's not that either." He sighed, and Lucky hated the sound of defeat in his voice. "I'm not sure if I am a good enough person to be involved in any kind of relationship anymore with anyone."

"That is ridiculous," Lucky said firmly. "Tell me exactly what happened with your wife."

A small smile trembled on Con's beautiful mouth, and he looked at Paul. "Your wife is very determined, isn't she?"

Paul shrugged. "Indeed she is. It is one of her most admirable qualities. You should just tell her what she wants to know."

"All right, then. Everything went surprisingly well when I met Natasha. She was just as keen as I am to avoid a scandal, and for us to settle the matter of our official divorce in private through the advocacy of the Russian ambassador."

"Did you realize you wanted her back?" Lucky asked.

"Not at all. She was exactly the same, rather self-centered and concerned only for her social position."

"Oh," Lucky said. She couldn't help but feel a measure of relief at his words.

"She cannot compare with you, my lady," Con added, and Lucky fought a blush.

"Then what went wrong?" Paul asked as he took a seat on the arm of Con's chair.

Con sat forward, and Lucky noticed the faint abrasions of

another man's stubble on his neck. She looked back at Paul and noticed his slightly swollen mouth. She didn't begrudge them their bed sport. She only wished she had been able to join in and comfort Con herself.

"After we had concluded our business, I mentioned to Natasha that I'd caught her son delivering her notes to me. She denied it, saying that her son was too young. I knew she was lying, but I didn't wish to destroy the accord we had built up, so I decided to leave." He took in a deep breath. "While I was in the hall, her children descended with their governess, and I realized that she was correct. Her son *was* too young to have been out on the streets by himself."

"Did she hire someone, then?"

"I'm not sure." He swallowed hard. "The eldest of her children, a girl, stared at me very deliberately when she passed by. It took me far too long to realize that she had been the boy I'd caught. It took me even longer to realize she had my eyes. . . ."

"What do you mean?" Lucky whispered.

"What if she is *my* child? What if Natasha left with the Frenchman because she knew she was carrying my child and took the only way out she could think of?" Con covered his head with his hands. "And if that is true, what kind of a man, a *father*, does that make me?"

Lucky struggled to gather her thoughts. "What did Natasha say?"

He grimaced. "She refused to talk to me and threatened to have me thrown out on the street."

"So you still do not know . . ." Lucky rose to her feet and Paul followed suit. "Do you have your wife's address?"

Con looked startled. "Whatever for?"

"If she will not talk to you, perhaps she will agree to speak to me instead."

"For what purpose?"

"To find out the truth," Lucky said. "Isn't that what you want?"

"And what if it is true?" Con whispered. "What should I do then? I doubt Natasha has mentioned anything about me to her children." He rubbed his eyes. "What right do I have to walk into that child's life and destroy everything she thought she knew of herself?"

"He has a point, Lucky," Paul murmured.

Lucky wheeled around to face Paul. "But doesn't Con also have a right to know the truth? Whether he chooses to act on the matter is a secondary issue. And surely the child has a right to know who her true parents are?"

"Lucky . . ." Paul held her gaze, the sympathy in his eyes almost oversetting her.

"You think I'm saying this because of what happened to me, don't you? Well, you might be right." She swallowed down a sob. "I wanted to be honest with all of you, that's why I . . ." She stopped and covered her mouth with her hand.

Paul came over and wrapped her in his arms. "It's all right, I understand now, I really do. You wanted to stop this kind of uncertainty in later life for any child of ours."

She rested her forehead on his shoulder, glad that he finally seemed to accept what she had done and why. After she regained her composure she looked over at Constantine.

"I'm sorry, I should not have spoken so harshly to you. You must do what you please."

He nodded and then fixed her with his calm silver gaze. "I trust you, my lady. I'd like you to go and see Natasha for me and find out whatever you can about the matter."

She moved out of Paul's embrace and went to Constantine, cupping his face in her hands. "Thank you, Constantine. Thank you for your trust."

28

"Your wife is rather self-centered, Constantine, and very reluctant to disclose anything about her past. She was, however, happy to receive me and then lecture me on the shortcomings of English society as compared with the French." Lucinda took the seat Con offered her and sat down, her expression defeated.

Con had returned home early that morning, and the St. Clares had come to tell him about Lucinda's afternoon meeting with Natasha.

"It's all right, my lady," Con answered her with a smile. "I didn't expect her to tell you anything important at a first meeting."

Lucinda sat forward and took off her gloves. "But I did get to meet the children before I was firmly but politely encouraged to leave."

"You met them?"

Lucinda held his gaze. "The eldest girl looks very like you, Constantine, although her hair is slightly darker."

Con swallowed and touched his head. "My hair turned this color when I was about twenty, as did my mother's."

"Natasha is also blond."

"I know, but you thought the girl looked like me?"

"I did." Lucinda glanced at Paul, who was also listening intently. "I managed to speak to her for a moment when her mother was ordering the tea. Her name is Anastasia. I asked her when she hoped to come out, and she said she was only just fourteen so it would be *years*."

"She is fourteen? Then she could be my child."

"I didn't press her further. She seemed like an intelligent, pleasant young lady, Con."

Con stared down at his hands. "I'm still undecided about what to do about this. If she is my child, I suppose I could force Natasha to give her up to me."

"Or force Natasha to resume her marriage with you, and then you could bring your daughter up together," Paul said.

Con stared at Paul. "Do you think that is what I want when I have finally found happiness with you both?"

Paul took Lucinda's hand. "But we would understand, if you wanted your child more than you wanted us."

"Why can't I have you as well?"

"You know the law, Con. If Natasha and her husband decided to dispute your claim to the child, would she try and blacken your name to preserve her own? You have been very discreet, but there are people who might suggest you are morally unfit to bring up a child. Even though you would probably win your case, do you want to subject your daughter to that?" Paul sighed. "God knows, Con, Lucky and I don't want to lose you again, but we will not be the cause of your downfall and disgrace."

Despite what Paul was saying, Con found himself smiling at both of the St. Clares. "You do this because you love me, don't you?"

"Of course."

He swallowed hard. "I don't deserve that."

Lucinda took one of his hands and Paul the other. "We are all unworthy of love sometimes, but luckily we have each other to remind us that love comes in many forms and that we are all ultimately forgivable."

Con squeezed both of their hands. "Thank you. I've been so alone. . . ." He found he couldn't continue, but it didn't seem to matter, as he knew that, somehow, they understood him better than he understood himself. Paul kissed his cheek and Lucky stood on tiptoe to kiss him as well, and for a moment he was enfolded in their love and more content than he had ever been in his life.

"We'll do whatever you want, Constantine," Lucky whispered. "Whatever makes you happy."

He solemnly kissed them both and stood back to observe their faces. "Thank you. I need to talk to Natasha first. Then I'll be in a better position to decide what to do."

Paul nodded and headed for the door. "Let us know what happens." He paused to help Lucky with her coat. "Just in case it all works out well, you should know that Lucky and I are looking at a property this afternoon in the street behind this one." He glanced down at his wife. "We have decided that we need our own home, and this seems like an excellent neighborhood."

Con saw them out and then returned to his seat by the fire. It was imperative that he see Natasha again, but he had no idea how he would get into her house now that it was barred to him. If Natasha had nothing to hide, why had she fled from him?

A knock on the outer door roused him from his thoughts, and he waited for Gregor to answer it. The knock came again, and Con decided to do the honors himself. When he opened the door, he found the blond-haired boy who had delivered the notes standing there. He decided to take a gamble.

"Anastasia?"

She scowled at him. "Why did you come to our house?"

Con stared at her for a long moment before opening the door wide and inviting her inside. Despite his shock, he was determined to remain as calm as he could and not frighten the child away again. He took his customary seat by the fire and waited to see if the "boy" would join him.

"Did your mother send you?"

"Of course not."

"Did she ever send you?"

"No, I did this by myself."

Con indicated the chair opposite his, and Anastasia sat down on the edge of it, her eyes downcast, her mouth a sulky and resentful line.

"You sought me out by yourself? For what purpose?"

"I told you. I wanted you to leave my mother alone."

"Did your mother explain why I was seeking her in the first place?"

"Not directly. I overheard her talking to her maid one day about you. She wished you were dead."

"Ah. And did you then ask her about me?"

Her gaze met his and then slid away again. "She grew very angry with me and forbade me to mention your name again."

"But you chose not to take her advice."

"I wanted to know the truth."

"So what did you do?"

She shrugged. "I asked her maid. She likes to gossip, and I am her favorite."

"And what did she tell you?"

"That you claimed to have been married to my mother."

Con met her gaze. "I *am* married to your mother. I have the marriage documents to prove it."

"That can't be right." Anastasia frowned. "She can't be married to two people at once, can she?"

"No," Con said gently.

"Then why can't you just go away and leave us in peace? None of us want you. We love our father."

Con let that hurt sink in and not show. "In truth, I have no intention of distressing you or your mother. I want to formally dissolve our union. Then we will be free to live our separate lives."

Anastasia shifted in her seat. "I know that too. I listened at the door when you came to visit."

"You are certainly resourceful, my dear." Con wanted to smile. "But if you know that your mother and I have agreed to legally separate with as little fuss and attention as possible, why did you come to see me?"

He held his breath as the silence grew longer and she stared down at the floorboards.

"What else is bothering you, Anastasia?"

She looked up right into his eyes and it was like looking into his reflection. "I don't look like them."

"I beg your pardon?"

"The rest of my family. I don't look like them, but when I saw you, when I saw your face . . ." She shivered. "I began to wonder."

"To wonder what?"

"If your claim to be married to my mother was actually true. I want someone to tell me the truth, and I thought you might do it."

Con let out his breath. "I was married to your mother in eighteen hundred and eleven when I was eighteen and she was seventeen. We spent very little time together because I was already with my regiment fighting against Napoléon. In the summer of eighteen twelve, I left her at our family home in Moscow, and that was the last time I saw her. I believed she was killed during the French occupation of Moscow."

"Why didn't you know for certain?"

"Because by the time I was able to get back to Moscow it

was a smoking ruin, and there were thousands of missing or deceased people. It was like looking for a needle in a haystack."

"When did you find out she might have survived?"

"Quite recently, when I attempted to formally declare her dead through the Russian embassy. Does that answer your questions?"

"Oh." Anastasia frowned down at her clasped hands. "I was born in eighteen thirteen."

"Indeed," Con said. He wanted to ask for the exact date, but he didn't want to push her.

"In France."

"Yes."

She glared at Con. "In March."

Con rapidly did the calculation and stayed silent, his heart hammering against his ribs.

"Is that why my mother is currently packing up our household again and driving my father mad with her hysterics?"

"You are returning to France?"

She watched him carefully. "Will you try and prevent it?"

He wanted to, God, he wanted to keep this unknown child here and learn all there was to know about her, to find out what made her happy and sad and . . .

"No, I will not try and prevent you leaving."

"Even if it turns out that you might be my father?"

He made her look at him. "Do you want me to keep you here?"

She bit her lip and tears filled her silver eyes. "I don't want anything to change. I want my family, I want my brother and sister, and I want to go home."

Con smiled and reached out for her hand. "Then you will have those things. Let me escort you home and reassure your mother that I will never attempt to disrupt your life."

Anastasia stood and kept hold of his hand. "Thank you."

He rose and looked down at her. "There's nothing to thank

me for. All I ask is if you ever need me for anything, anything at all, you will find me. I'll do anything in my power to make you happy."

She smiled at him for the first time, and he led her toward the door, his heart breaking, even as he knew he was doing the right thing for her, if not for himself.

"Now, let me take you home."

"And you just let her go?" Lucky asked.

She sat on his bed with Con's head in her lap; Paul stretched out on his other side.

"What else could I do? The poor child was terrified that I was going to destroy her entire existence." He sighed. "I did tell her and Natasha that if they ever needed anything from me, they just had to ask."

"You were polite to the end." Lucky smoothed his white hair. "Even though she is probably your child, and you have the right to take her away from her mother?"

He groaned. "Damn it, don't remind me. It was one of the hardest things I've ever had to do in my life."

"And one of the bravest," Lucky added.

Con turned his head slightly so that he could look up at her. "I'm not that brave. I just knew I had friends who would endeavor to love me enough to heal the wounds."

"Friends?" Paul asked, stretching out his hand to Lucky.

"Lovers, then," Con replied. "If that is what we have decided."

Paul smiled and Lucky brought his hand to her lips. "I certainly hope so, seeing as Paul has just purchased the lease on the house next door."

Some of the anxiety on Con's face disappeared. "Truly?"

"I know it won't make up for the loss of your child, Con," *or of mine,* she silently added, "but at least we can help each other heal and move forward into a better, more loving future."

"Amen to that," Con murmured and kissed her stomach.

If she was fortunate, she'd give both him and Paul more children to replace the lost ones, children they could love without reserve and watch grow up together. Despite what society might say, she was in the privileged position of having the love of two wonderful, honorable men. She'd matured enough to realize that she didn't want to lose either of them and be damned to what society might think of her.

"We are indeed lucky," Paul agreed.

Lucky winced while Con actually chuckled.

"Lucky indeed. Now when are you both moving in next door?"

Please turn the page
for an exciting sneak peek of
Kate Pearce's next sizzling installment
in her House of Pleasure series

SIMPLY SCANDALOUS

Coming in January 2013!

1

London 1827

"Surely you are exaggerating, Emily." Richard Ross studied his sister's indignant expression. "Paul St. Clare is heir to a dukedom."

Emily raised her chin. "Lucky is my best friend. Do you think she would lie to me?"

Richard put his half-empty bowl of hot chocolate down on the kitchen table. It was early in the morning, and most of the staff at the pleasure house had already gone home. If one discounted Madame Dubois, the cook, and Ambrose, he and Emily had the kitchen almost to themselves.

"But think of the scandal!"

Emily sniffed. "The higher the rank of the individuals involved, the less of a scandal there seems to be. Think of the Duke of Devonshire. His domestic arrangements were highly unorthodox. It is *because* Paul is heir to a duke that the *ton* will look the other way and pretend that he and Lucky have a perfectly respectable marriage." Emily put her elbows on the table and rested her chin on her hands. "In truth, their marriage is respectable. It's not as if Constantine Delinsky has moved in with them."

"He maintains lodgings on the same street, but he practically lives in their house. Everyone knows that he shares Paul St. Clare's bed. Doesn't your friend Lucky object?"

Emily grinned at him. "Are you shocked, brother of mine? I never thought you were so stuffy. What if I told you it was far more complicated than that?"

"What do you mean?"

"Constantine shares Lucky's bed too."

Richard just stopped himself from gaping like a fool. "He beds them both?"

"They all bed each other."

Richard shook his head. "I would never have thought it of Lady Lucinda. She seemed like such a nice, quiet, well-behaved young lady."

"Unlike me, you mean."

"You are sitting in the kitchen of a notorious pleasure house at three o'clock in the morning," Richard pointed out. "That hardly helps your reputation."

Beside Richard, Ambrose cleared his throat. "Miss Ross is not allowed upstairs, Mr. Ross. Madame Helene was very insistent about that."

"More's the pity," Emily groused. "I'm practically on the shelf. Why shouldn't I have some fun?"

"Because our revered father wishes you to marry well and be happy. You know that."

Emily glanced at Ambrose, who kept his gaze fixed steadily on Richard. "And what if I refuse to marry well, and marry where my heart is?"

"That is something you will have to take up with our father." Emily's face fell, and Richard felt compelled to continue. "But as his own second marriage was scarcely an orthodox one, perhaps he will be more willing to listen to you than most parents."

"I doubt it. He thinks I need the stabilizing influence of a wealthy, titled man. What he doesn't understand is that most of those men view me with great suspicion because of *his* decidedly odd marriage to Helene."

"Would you like me to mention it to him?" Richard asked.

Emily smiled. "I don't want to add to the friction between you two. I've already told him, but he chooses not to believe me." She sighed. "Eventually he'll have to face the facts. I'm three and twenty. All I can hope is that I'm not too old to marry before he listens to me."

Richard reached across and took her hand. "I'm sorry, Em."

"It's not your fault. And I truly am happy that after his disastrous relationship with our mother, Father has Helene in his life."

"You don't know that."

She raised her candid gaze to his face. "That he is happy?"

"Our mother was scarcely any happier than our father was, and she blamed him for that."

"You weren't there. You were away at school and then at university. Despite what Mother told you, she brought most of her unhappiness on herself."

Richard carefully released Emily's hand. "We'll never agree about that, will we? Perhaps we should talk about something else. Isn't it time you were going home?"

Ambrose got to his feet. "I'll call for your carriage and find your maid, Miss Ross."

Emily shot Ambrose a glare. "I asked you to call me Emily."

"And I've explained several times why that would be inappropriate."

Richard stared entranced as his sister and the manager of the pleasure house continued to glower at each other. Has he missed something very obvious? Was his sister in love with the dark-skinned ex-slave and pickpocket Christian Delornay had saved from the streets?

Ambrose bowed. "I'll fetch your maid."

Emily turned away, but not before Richard had seen the hurt in her eyes. He waited until Ambrose had most uncharacteristically slammed the kitchen door before turning to his sister.

"Is Ambrose the reason why you spend so much time here? I thought you were just avoiding your social obligations."

"What on earth does it have to do with you?"

Well used to the ways of his stubborn sibling, Richard didn't take offense at her combative tone.

"I'm your brother and I care about your happiness." He hesitated. "Have you told anyone how you feel?"

She hunched her shoulder at him. "If you mean have I told Ambrose, I have. He told me to stop behaving like a spoiled little girl and find a proper husband."

"*Ambrose* did?"

"That's what he meant, although he put it in a far more conciliatory way."

"Perhaps he had a point," Richard said quietly.

"Because he's too *different*? Because his skin is too *dark*?"

"Emily . . ."

"You are as bad as he is. I don't care about those things, so why should anyone else?"

"You are still very young and—"

Emily spun around to face him. "I am three and twenty and old enough to know what I want!"

"And what about what Ambrose wants? Is he to have no say in this?"

Emily opened her mouth to reply and then closed it again as Ambrose reentered the room with her maid.

"I'll see you to your carriage, Miss Ross," Ambrose murmured, his face a smiling mask that mirrored Emily's.

"Thank you, Ambrose. Good night, Richard."

Emily hurried out before Richard could even attempt to kiss her good-bye. He sat back down with a soft oath and stared at the kitchen door. He didn't like being at odds with Emily, but he wasn't sure how to make amends without offending her further. If she asked for his help to intercede with their father, or even with Ambrose, he would do so willingly, but he was past the age when he thought to force his opinions on anyone. He'd wait to be asked and, in the meantime, keep his own counsel.

Ambrose came back into the kitchen rather slowly, his expression distracted. He directed his gaze at Richard with a visible effort.

"Is there anything else I can help you with, Mr. Ross?"

"You can start by calling me Richard."

Ambrose half smiled. "And risk the wrath of your sister? If you don't mind, I'll continue to call you Mr. Ross. She would never forgive me if I made an exception for you and not for her."

"My sister is a very determined woman."

"I know that, sir. But she is still young."

"For God's sake, don't tell her that," Richard shuddered.

Ambrose sighed. "It's too late. I already have." He picked up Emily's empty cup and took it over to the sink. "Are you staying the night, Mr. Ross?"

Aware that Ambrose had deliberately changed the subject, Richard rose to his feet. "I'll just take a stroll through the pleasure house and then I'll probably turn in."

"Excellent, sir. I did ask one of the maids to ready your bedroom on the off chance that you would be staying."

"You are a marvel, Ambrose. Thank you."

"I am certainly a first-class servant."

Richard paused at the door. Was there a hint of bitterness in Ambrose's words? "You are far more than that. Christian sees you as more of a brother than I am."

Ambrose's smile was sweet. "I doubt that. Blood after all *is* thicker than water."

Richard wasn't so sure, but he didn't feel up to discussing the interesting family dynamics of the Delornay-Ross clan at this point in the evening. He nodded a farewell to Ambrose and started up the stairs to the main levels of the pleasure house.

There weren't many guests in the larger of the salons, and those were mostly naked and writhing in a tangle of bodies on the pile of silk cushions. Richard recognized a Member of Parliament, an archbishop, and a prominent social hostess energetically fucking each other while the woman's husband watched and commented from the nearest couch.

He managed to avoid gazing directly at any of them, and made his way to the buffet table, where he poured himself a glass of excellent red wine. There was no sign of his half brother Christian Delornay or his delicious wife, Elizabeth, but Richard knew they would be somewhere on the premises making sure everything was running smoothly. Christian was eager to prove he could manage the pleasure house his mother had founded as well if not better than she had.

Richard sipped at his wine and sighed. At least Christian *had* a purpose. All Richard was supposed to do was wait for his father to die so that he could assume his title. It seemed a ridiculous waste of his life. Sometimes he dreaded the thought of assuming the enormous responsibilities that went with it. He almost wished he were back in France avoiding Napoléon's soldiers and saving forgotten souls. Life seemed sweeter when all he had were his wits and strength to protect him. . . .

None of his family had any idea what he'd been doing in France. His father thought he'd stayed there to avoid coming home. In the beginning, that had played a part in his decision, but the real thrill had been the dangerous and deadly work he performed for the government. And that couldn't be spoken of in polite society. So his family continued to think he was a boring, brainless, *ungrateful* drone.

He drained his glass and refilled it, his attention caught by an influx of new people at the door. A young man of medium height dressed in the latest fashion was laughing up at one of his companions. Something about the joy on the man's face reminded Richard of a woman he'd once known—a woman he'd foolishly loved to distraction. . . .

He stiffened as the little group came toward him, aware that they were all speaking French and that he knew at least two of them from his previous activities on the continent.

"Ah, Mr. Ross. Good evening to you."

Richard bowed in response to the cheerful greeting of the tall, blond-haired peer. "Good evening, Lord Keyes, gentleman."

"Not taking advantage of the facilities, eh, Ross?" Lord Keyes nudged his arm, and Richard almost tipped red wine everywhere. "No lovely ladies to tempt you tonight, or do you like to watch, eh, eh?"

Richard smiled politely and stepped away from Lord Keyes. He'd already noticed that despite his outward display of drunkenness, Lord Keyes's blue gaze was as watchful and sharp as ever. Only a fool would underestimate him. Many had.

"Actually, I was just considering retiring."

"You're spent, then, are you?"

"Indeed. Have you just arrived, my lord?"

"Aye, we've been to the theater." Lord Keyes put an arm around the shoulders of the slight, dark-haired man. "I was just introducing my young friend here to the pleasures of London."

The man stuck out his hand. "I'm Jack Lennox, Mr. Ross. It is a pleasure to meet you."

As he shook the proffered hand, Richard found himself studying the perfection of Jack Lennox's features. He looked as if he had stepped out of a painting or a young lady's dreams.

His likeness to the deceased Violet LeNy was quite extraordinary.

"Is it your first trip to London, sir?" Richard asked.

"No, Mr. Ross, I was born here, but I must confess I haven't been back since well before the war."

Richard smiled. "You will perhaps forgive me for remarking that your command of French is that of a native."

"I'm aware that makes my claim to be English sound rather suspicious, especially since the recent conflict." Mr. Lennox's grin was meant to be disarming, but Richard wasn't quite swayed. The mere fact that Keyes had deliberately introduced Lennox to him meant something was afoot. "Perhaps the more I speak English, the more convincing I will become."

"I'm sure of it, sir. Are you planning on making your home here in England?"

"I would like to, but, naturally, there are various plans that need to be put in place before I can achieve my aim." Mr. Lennox shrugged. "I heard that you spent many years in France yourself, Mr. Ross."

"I suppose Lord Keyes told you that."

"Among others. It seems we have several acquaintances in common."

"Indeed." Richard studied Mr. Lennox. "Is that why you instigated this conversation?"

"*Instigated,* Mr. Ross?" Lennox raised his eyebrows. "You make my motives sound rather suspect. Perhaps I merely wished to exchange pleasantries with a man who speaks French as well as I do."

"You came in with Lord Keyes and Sir Adam Fisher, who both speak excellent French. Are they not up to your high standards?"

"No, I fear they are not."

Richard met the other man's vivid blue eyes. "What do you want, Mr. Lennox?"

"To talk to you."

"We are talking." Richard glanced over his companion's shoulder and saw that the other men had moved on to other more salacious pursuits involving the hasty removal of their clothes. "Do you not wish to join your friends?"

"Only if you wish to come with me."

"I thought you wanted to talk."

"We're in a pleasure house. I assume you can talk and fornicate at the same time?"

"Not and make any sense."

Jack Lennox laughed out loud. "You are a man after my own heart, Mr. Ross. Perhaps we might just share a glass of wine together before we adjourn for the night?"

Richard studied the other man's amused expression. Despite the openness of his manner, there was something dangerous lurking at the back of Mr. Lennox's eyes, something ruthless that demanded to be recognized. Richard had met his own kind too many times before to be fooled. For the first time in a long while, he felt a lick of excitement curl through his gut.

"Of course, Mr. Lennox. Would you like to join me at the far end of the salon, where I hope we shall remain relatively undisturbed?"

He led the way past the piles of writing bodies to the quieter end of the salon, where several chairs were grouped around small tables. He took a chair that allowed him to see the rest of the room, and waited to see which seat Jack Lennox would pick. Lennox sat directly opposite him, half-blocking Richard's view, a brave move that Richard could only admire.

"Now, Mr. Lennox. What can I do for you?" Richard signaled for one of the waiters and asked for some brandy to be brought to them.

"It is a delicate matter, Mr. Ross. One I am not quite sure how to approach."

"Are you under the impression that I can somehow help advance your career? If that is so, you are quite mistaken. Lord Keyes is the man for that kind of thing. He already holds an important position in the government and is connected with all the best families."

"Lord Keyes has already offered to help me, Mr. Ross." Jack Lennox thanked the waiter for the brandy and then turned his intent gaze back to Richard. "The matter I wish to speak to you about is a more personal one."

"Yet you hardly know me, sir."

"Which presents me with some difficulties, I know. But this request is not entirely on my behalf." Jack Lennox hesitated. "I am charged to deliver a message to Madame Helene Delornay. I understood from Lord Keyes that you have some connection with her."

"I might have." Richard sipped his brandy and wondered exactly what Keyes had told Lennox. "But since you are in her house of pleasure, why not simply ask to meet Madame herself?"

"I understood that she no longer runs this establishment."

"She still looks in occasionally. Why did you not speak to her son, Christian? He is in charge now."

"Because I am not sure if the message I bring will be welcome to Madame Helene." Lennox's smile was roguishly charming. "I hoped you might act as a—how do you say it?—a go-between."

"That is certainly the correct phrase, but I'm not sure if I like the idea at all. Why should I offer myself up for such a potentially hazardous duty?"

Jack Lennox sat forward, one hand clenched on his knee, and lowered his voice.

"My grandmother knew Madame Helene when she was a young woman. I believe they shared some terrible experiences during the revolution. I'm unsure if Madame Helene would wish to revive those memories. I hoped you might intercede with her, or her son, on my behalf."

Richard studied the other man. He'd always considered himself an excellent judge of character. There was a sincerity behind Lennox's words that couldn't be denied. Instinct also told Richard there was far more to the story. Did he want to become involved, or did he wish Jack Lennox and his grandmother to the devil?

"Why didn't your grandmother just write a letter to Madame?"

"Because she is reluctant to commit anything to paper. She is extremely suspicious. After surviving the twists and turns of a revolution, I can understand her fears, although it makes my task more complicated."

"I can see that." Richard let his gaze linger on Jack Lennox's perfect face. If the man did stay in London and was accepted by the *ton*, the ladies were going to swoon over him in droves. "Is there somewhere I can reach you when I have made my decision?"

Disappointment flashed in Jack Lennox's eyes, but he quickly masked it. "Of course. I'm staying at thirty-three Curzon Street. Do you know it?"

"The Harcourt family house?"

"My grandmother knew the previous viscount before the revolution. They remained friends until he died. The Harcourt family are in the country, so I am not disturbing anyone too greatly."

"Then I will contact you there." Richard rose and held out his hand. "It was a pleasure to meet you, Mr. Lennox. Do you intend to stay and sample the delights of the pleasure house before you retire? I think Lord Keyes and his party are still rather occupied."

Jack shook his hand and then glanced around at the orgy

going on behind them. "I heard there was more on offer here than that. Is it true?"

Richard smiled. "Indeed. What do you prefer? Madame boasts she caters to every sexual taste known to man or woman."

"Or both?" Jack held his gaze. "I am not averse to sharing my bed with either sex."

Richard gently disengaged his hand from Jack's grip. "Then take yourself up the stairs to the second level, and ask Marie-Claude to help you discover what you desire."

"You will not come with me? Perhaps we could find a willing woman to share."

"Alas, I am rather tired, but thank you for the offer. Good night, Mr. Lennox."

"Good night, Mr. Ross."

For a moment Richard wondered what it would be like to share a bed with a man who reminded him so strongly of Violet. Would he feel desire for him? Richard squashed that thought and turned toward the door. It wasn't the first time he'd been propositioned by a man at the pleasure house, but it was certainly the first time he'd stopped to think about it.

Perhaps his association with the Delornay family was starting to erode his morals. Richard smiled as he unlocked the door that led into the servants' stairwell and headed toward the private quarters at the rear of the house. Not that his morals had been particularly strong to start with. Surviving in a war-damaged country had taught him that right and wrong were more fluid concepts than he had ever imagined.

A fire had been lit in his bedchamber, and his bed was warm from the hot bricks Ambrose had directed to be placed at the foot. Richard sighed as he took off his black coat and started on the buttons of his waistcoat. In the morning he would talk to Lord Keyes, and then, depending on the result of that interview, he might approach Christian with Jack Lennox's request.

Richard pictured the young man and found himself smiling.

Such arrogance and *such* determination in a beautiful exterior package. Had Lennox gone home, or had he succumbed to the lure of the pleasure house and found himself another man to play with? Richard stripped off his underthings and lay in bed, his hand automatically cupping his cock and balls. His last thought as he drifted off to sleep was a startling image of Lennox, Violet and himself naked and writhing on the silken covers of his bed. . . .